Her life could not h...

Anne Marie was dress... in a ... cloth with a white ruf... at her neck, her only adornment a silver cross on a green ribbon.

Gazing into her clear eyes, Kit felt an odd sensation in his stomach and caught his breath. Damn it! She was lovely. Not exquisitely dressed, painted and adorned like the beauties of Elizabeth's court, but with a quiet, graceful beauty that moved him deeply. He was aware once more of dismay at the nature of his task, which was in truth to spy on her.

Author Note

It has been a delight and a privilege to work on this Elizabethan series with Paula Marshall, an author I respect and admire. The Elizabethan age was a time when light began to penetrate the darkness of ignorance and suspicion, but it was also a time of danger and intrigue.

Each book is an individual love story but with a continuing undercurrent of mystery linking them. Through the eyes of young lovers, we have tried to portray the pageantry and ceremony of the four seasons of Elizabeth I's reign, from the spring of her joyous coronation through the summer of her life to a glorious autumn and finally to the chill of winter. We hope that you, the reader, will enjoy these stories as much as we enjoyed writing them.

These are the novels which make up **The Elizabethan Season:**

Spring	–	MAID OF HONOUR
Summer	–	LADY IN WAITING
Autumn	–	THE ADVENTURER'S WIFE
Winter	–	THE BLACK SHEEP'S BRIDE

Love to you all,

Anne Herries

The Elizabethan Season

THE ADVENTURER'S WIFE

Anne Herries

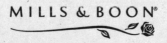

*First published in Great Britain 2004 by
Harlequin Mills & Boon Limited,
Eton House, 18-24 Paradise Road,
Richmond, Surrey TW9 1SR*

© Harlequin Books S.A. 2004

Special thanks and acknowledgement are given to Anne Herries for her contribution to The Elizabethan Season series.

ISBN 0 263 84087 5

148-0504

*Printed and bound in Spain
by Litografia Rosés S.A., Barcelona*

Anne Herries lives in Cambridge but spends part of the winter in Spain, where she and her husband stay in a pretty resort nestled amid the hills that run from Malaga to Gibraltar. Gazing over a sparkling blue ocean, watching the sunbeams dance like silver confetti on the restless waves, Anne loves to dream up her stories of laughter, tears and romantic lovers.

Other novels by
Anne Herries

THE ABDUCTED BRIDE
CAPTIVE OF THE HAREM
THE SHEIKH
A DAMNABLE ROGUE

and in the Regency series
The Steepwood Scandal

LORD RAVENSDEN'S MARRIAGE
COUNTERFEIT EARL

and in
The Elizabethan Season

LADY IN WAITING

Chapter One

October 1586

'You may rely on me,' said Sir Nicholas Grantly to the man with whom he was sharing a flask of good French wine in his parlour. 'Should Lady Hamilton find herself in need of assistance while you are in the north I shall be pleased to help in any way I may.'

Sir Christopher Hamilton was some fifteen years younger than his neighbour, a tall man, powerfully built, with the look of an adventurer about him from his years at sea in the fleet of ships commanded by the great Sir Francis Drake. His skin had a slightly bronzed appearance, his mouth, harsh in repose, could be merry when he smiled, yet it was his eyes that sometimes gave him away as a man of strong passions, for they could be as stormy as the Atlantic Sea. At the moment, however, they were soft and smiling.

'I knew I might rely on you, sir. You and Lady Grantly have been good friends to my mother these past years, and I believe I may speak plainly?'

'Of course. Something troubles you, Kit?'

'As you know, I have spent the past five years sailing in Drake's fleet, and we have dealt the Spanish a bloody nose or two; a dangerous business but one that has brought both wealth and honours. The knighthood Her Majesty was pleased to bestow on me for services rendered, and the introduction to Sir Francis Walsingham, which you yourself effected...' He paused, as if not quite sure how to proceed for the moment.

Nick nodded, understanding instantly. Having worked secretly for Walsingham in the past, he was instinctively alert as he guessed much that his friend might not say. 'Tell me only as much as you feel right, Kit. I am aware that sometimes it is unwise to speak too openly of these things.'

Kit nodded, his eyes darkening in thought. 'While my father lived I did not need to concern myself overly with the estate, but his death has left my mother in some part vulnerable. Neither Edward nor Jack are old enough to help her much, and indeed are sad scamps more likely to cause her worry than ease it. I think my late father's steward an honest fellow and I trust him, but I am uneasy...'

'You need say no more. I shall ride over from time to time to see all is well. How long do you expect to be away?'

'I am not certain.'

Kit hesitated, unsure of how much he ought properly to confide in his friend and neighbour. He trusted Sir Nicholas as much as any man he knew, but Sir

Francis had insisted that their interview remain a secret.

'For it seems that I find a new plot against Her Majesty at every turn,' Walsingham had told him. 'And I believe that the girl's father may in some way be involved in a devious plan to rescue Mary of Scots and set her upon the English throne even now. With the discovery of the Babington conspiracy I have proved that Mary did indeed put her seal of approval on that devilish plot; she has been tried and found guilty of treason, and yet the Queen will not sign the death warrant, plead as I might for her to make an end to it.'

Kit had realised he was being asked to spy upon the girl who lived with his mother's kinsmen as their ward. She had been sent to them as a child of a few years as a surety for her father's good behaviour, and Kit knew that Beth Makepeace had come to love her as a daughter. For himself, he had seen the girl only once on a long ago visit to Drodney with his parents, and could hardly remember her—and yet it went against the grain to be asked to spy on someone who was almost family.

'You are to visit Mistress Makepeace at the castle of Drodney, I believe?' Nick asked, as Kit remained silent, apparently lost in thought.

'My mother thought the northern air might do me good.'

'But your wound has healed?'

'Aye, I am better, though the fever left me feeling low for a time. A change of air perhaps…'

Kit left the sentence unfinished, not liking to hide his true purpose from a man he respected. It was true that Lady Sarah Hamilton had suggested that a visit to her kinswoman might help her son recover his former zest for life, which had been dimmed both by the sad loss of his father and the wound taken in an encounter with a Spanish treasure ship. However, the real reason for his journey was very different.

'It will not seem strange that you visit your kinswoman,' Walsingham had told him in their private interview. 'I am concerned that the girl is given more freedom than she should properly have, for she is hostage to her father's good behaviour.'

'Is that fair to the girl?' Kit had asked, his brows lifting. 'If the father is the danger, surely it would be better to imprison him?'

'Lord Angus Fraser is an important man among the Scottish nobility,' Walsingham replied. 'He is a Catholic and supported Mary after Darnley was murdered and she married that dangerous fool Bothwell. Had she not been so reckless she might even now be still upon Scotland's throne. If I could I would arrest Fraser, but it is beyond my power for the moment. He gave his bond that he would remain at his home in Scotland, but I know for certain that he has travelled to Spain at least twice in the past few years, and I suspect that he may have had a hand in the Babington plot, but was clever enough to keep his name out of it.'

'But surely with Mary safely imprisoned there is nothing that he or any other can do?'

'If Mary were dead…' Walsingham shook his head sorrowfully. 'But Her Majesty will not put her hand to the warrant and until the traitor is dead, we shall always have those who would use her for their own ends.'

'You speak of Spain, I think?'

'Aye, King Philip of Spain has always had an eye for England's throne,' Walsingham replied. 'He would make Catholics of us all and bring back the stench of burning to England's fair land.'

'Not if Drake's band of sea captains have their way,' Kit said grimly. His time at sea had brought him into contact with men who had suffered at the hands of the Spanish Inquisition and what he had learned from them had made him staunchly Protestant. He made up his mind to do as Walsingham asked. It was for the sake of England and of all right-thinking men. 'But if you believe the girl represents a danger I will do what I can to help you in this matter.'

'The girl is no danger in herself, but I think the father may try to get her away before whatever plot he is concerned in comes to fruition, and I would not have him succeed.'

'I shall keep a watchful eye and send you word if I see anything that troubles me,' Kit had promised, and on that note they had parted, Kit to return briefly to his home to advise his mother of his intention to travel north to the castle of Drodney, which guarded the borders between England and Scotland, and to ask Sir Nicholas to keep a friendly eye on the estate.

'Should you ever need help yourself for whatever reason, you may come to me,' Sir Nicholas said, because Kit had been silent for some minutes and was clearly still bothered by something. 'You may trust me in an emergency—on your own part or that of the State, for I have been in Walsingham's confidence in the past. Had I not had private reasons for retiring from public life, I might still be one of his couriers.'

He might have said spies, for Walsingham was the great spymaster, and it was mainly due to his vigilance that so many attempts against the Queen's Majesty had been foiled these past years.

'Yes, I had suspected that might have been the case,' Kit said. 'I think there are many who have served in like cause. For the moment you will forgive me if I say nothing, but should the need arise I shall come to you, Nick.'

'I shall be happy to serve if I can,' Nick replied and smiled. 'And now you must stay to dine with us. Catherine would be happy to see you, I know, and young Lisa is over her fever at last. My boys are sad scamps, much like your brothers, Kit, but they would be thrilled to hear about your adventures. Young Harry has told me he intends to be like Drake when he is a man grown, and I believe he may, for he loves the sea. John is very different and I suspect that he may have a leaning to the intellectual…'

In good humour with each other, the two men went into the parlour where Lady Catherine Grantly sat with her needlework. Seeing the way she smiled at her husband, Kit thought that he had seldom seen

such love in a woman's eyes, and he found himself
envying his friend. If he could discover such a woman
then he might be content at last to give up his adventuring and settle down. But a woman of Catherine
Grantly's equal was not often met with, and Kit's own
experience with women had not been a happy one.
The woman he had offered for at nineteen had
spurned him in favour of an older, richer man, and
by so doing had set Kit's feet on the path to wealth
and honour, for if he had married he would never
have gone to sea.

His mouth curved in a wry smile as he recalled the
spirited beauty he had loved as a youth. Madeline was
married now to Lord Carmichael, a man much older
than herself, and he believed that she took lovers to
alleviate her boredom. She had hinted that she would
not be averse to having Kit in her bed, and had his
time not been promised to Walsingham he might well
have taken her at her word!

His eyes sparkled with amusement at the memory.
Madeline's chagrin at being turned down had wiped
away any bitterness he might still have harboured
over her rejection, for she had not been able to hide
her disappointment.

The young Christopher Hamilton had been quiet
and awkward, a very different man from the one who
had returned rich, powerful and influential after his
years at sea. Yes, had he been a vengeful man he
might have taken pleasure from being the one to say
no this time. As it was, he merely felt a fleeting regret
for a pleasure that might have been.

His mind was occupied with the things he had discussed with Walsingham and wondering what he might find at Drodney Castle. What kind of a girl was Anne Marie Fraser, and would he discover that she was involved in some kind of secret plot against the Queen?

'Do you think Anne Marie is happy?' Beth Makepeace asked of her husband as they sat over the fire enjoying a cup of mulled ale at the end of their busy day. 'She has been very quiet of late.'

'Anne Marie is a good, dutiful girl,' he replied. 'She has never been a trouble to you, Beth. The Lord knows she has been a blessing to us these past years, for we have been sent no children of our own, and the girl is like a daughter.'

'But she is not our daughter,' Beth said, looking anxious as she warmed her hands before the fire. 'You know I love her as my own, Thomas, but when Sir Francis Walsingham sent someone to interview her last year she was reminded that she is merely a hostage for her father's good behaviour. I believe that hurt her deeply, more than we might guess.'

'Aye, I have noticed something in her manner since then.'

'Do you think they will ever allow her to marry?'

He was thoughtful for a moment before he answered, and then spoke with a heavy seriousness that frightened his anxious wife. 'It has been my fear that they will give her in marriage to a man she does not know and cannot love. I thought that might have been

Walsingham's purpose in sending for a report on her life here.'

'Surely not?' Beth looked at him in alarm. 'The Queen is not so cruel. Pray tell me it is not so, husband. I should refuse to allow it!'

'You could do nothing if the order came from London,' Thomas Makepeace said, and leaned forward to hold his hands to the fire. They were gnarled with rheumatism and chapped from the cold, a testimony to the hardness of life at the castle. 'Anne Marie is our ward, not our daughter, much as we love her, and we must obey our orders.'

Outside the partially opened door of their private chamber, Anne Marie Fraser listened to their conversation. She was very still, her lovely face pale, her serious eyes reflecting both fear and anger. Over the years she had learned to hide her passions behind a demure manner, though sometimes her eyes gave her away. She had known since childhood that she was a prisoner here. As kindly as she had been treated, the fact remained that she was not free to come and go as she pleased, or to live anywhere else.

She had been a very small girl when the men came to take her from her home and her nurse, who had wept bitterly at the parting. Anne Marie could not remember her mother, Lady Margaret Fraser, who had died soon after she was born, but she remembered Morag, who had nursed her from a babe, and of course her father.

Lord Angus Fraser was a big, heavily built man, black of hair and beard, with fierce grey eyes and a loud voice that had frightened her as a child. She was not afraid of him now, for she had seen him three times in the past five years; twice he had visited her in the presence of her guardians and once he had come to her when she was walking alone on the hillsides that surrounded the castle. There was a spot where she liked to stand and gaze out at the sea, which foamed and thrashed about the rocks below. She was allowed to walk on the cliffs alone, for there was no path down to the cove below; the face of the steep cliff was too dangerous for her even to attempt escaping by that route.

Anne Marie had thought of escape a few times since her father's last visit. He had told her that she must always remember she was a Catholic and a prisoner of the English.

'Your mother was French and I am a Scot,' Angus Fraser had growled. 'Do not allow these English dogs to indoctrinate you with their faith, daughter. They are heretics and would burn had I my way. One day Mary will take her rightful place on the thrones of England and Scotland, and I shall be at her right hand. Then you shall be restored to honour as the wife of a Catholic gentleman of rank.' His eyes were very fierce as he laid a hand upon her arm. 'Do not let them marry you to a heretic, Anne Marie. Far better that you should die than accept such dishonour.'

She had promised that she would never marry other than as he directed and he had kissed her briefly on the cheek before taking his leave.

'One day soon I shall come for you, Daughter,' he

had promised. 'My plans are not yet complete, but you must be ready to leave when I say. And the time will be soon now.'

Anne Marie had watched him walk away with mixed feelings. She had always known that she was not Beth Makepeace's daughter, but there was a part of her that wished she were. Beth had been kind and loving and Anne Marie had gradually come to love her. As she grew older and began to question, Beth had not prevented her from using the Bible and cross which had been her mother's. In private she was permitted to worship in her own way, though outwardly, she'd had to appear to accept the Protestant faith.

In Elizabeth's England there were many who did much the same. Queen Elizabeth had begun her reign with a show of tolerance towards the Catholics, but as the years passed and there were too many attempts against her throne, that tolerance had waned. There were fines for those who neglected to attend church on a Sunday, and other more severe penalties for those thought to have committed a traitorous act. Indeed there were many disadvantages to being a Catholic in England, for the chance of honour and high office was not often met with.

Anne's wandering thoughts were recalled as Beth Makepeace began to talk of her kinsman.

'It is many years since we saw Christopher, husband.'

'Aye, he will have changed, I dare say. He will be a man now.'

'And knighted by Her Majesty…'

Anne Marie turned away, walking slowly up the worn stone steps to her own chamber at the top of the tower. The castle was old and had stood here for centuries, guarding the borders between Scotland and England, dealing with raiding parties of lawless Highlanders who came stealing cattle from the English villages about, and giving warning of any likely attack. In winter it was bitterly cold, the water she used for drinking sometimes freezing in the ewer overnight. There were no fireplaces in the bedchambers, and they slept beneath piles of coverlets and furs. However, Anne Marie was used to the discomfort, and though her hands sometimes became chapped with the cold in the worst of the winter, this was only late October, and the snow had not yet fallen.

It was wrong of her to listen to her kind guardians talking privately, she knew, but it was the only way she could learn of what went on in the wider world outside the castle. She had recently heard Beth speaking of the arrest of Mary of Scots, but she was not certain what that meant, as one of the servants had come along the passage and she'd had to move on.

Surely Mary, once Queen of Scotland but deposed after she married Bothwell, the man most people suspected of murdering her husband, the Earl of Darnley, had been a prisoner for many long years? She had fled to England after the Scottish lords had defeated her in battle, seeking sanctuary from England's Queen and begging her *sister* to help her. For they were both women in a world that was too often at the mercy of men and sisters beneath the skin. At first moved by her plea and refusing to hand her over to her enemies, Elizabeth had wanted to help her regain her throne. However, her advisers cautioned against it and Mary had been kept under close house arrest, not quite a prisoner and yet not quite free.

Anne Marie had often thought of the poor woman who had been so full of life and gaiety when she first came to Scotland as a young widow of the French King. How sadly her life had turned out. In a short space of time she had gone from being fêted and spoiled in France, to a lonely prisoner. Her first mistake had been to marry the Earl of Darnley, a coarse brute of a man who had behaved ill towards her by her murdering her secretary, Rizzio, and her second mistake had been to marry the man who had caused her downfall. Her third perhaps was to throw herself on the mercy of the Queen of England.

But what had happened recently that had caused Mary to be taken to the castle of Fotheringay? Anne Marie had tried asking Beth, but her guardian had refused to be drawn on the subject.

Entering her chamber, which was furnished with a truckle bed, a table, a chair and an oaken coffer for her clothes, Anne Marie went over to the niche in the thick stone wall that held her prayer book and the wooden cross she used for her devotions. She bowed her head and prayed for peace of mind and for Mary of Scots, but asked nothing more for herself.

In truth, Anne Marie did not know what she wanted of life. At almost twenty years of age, sixteen of which had been spent as a hostage at Drodney, she was a beautiful woman. Her hair was a very dark brown, long and straight, her eyes wide and clear, the irises a bright blue. Her complexion had a freshness that came from her habit of taking long walks no matter how inclement the weather, and though she was not much above a man's shoulder in height, she was perfectly formed.

Had she not been held hostage these many years, Anne Marie would have been married long since. At nearly twenty she would be considered quite old for marriage, and it was unlikely that she would ever find love or happiness. Even if a match was arranged for her, it would most probably be to someone she neither knew nor liked.

The prospect was not particularly pleasing and Anne Marie thought she might prefer to remain as she was now. Her father's promise to take her away had faded from her mind. It was many months since she had seen him and she thought that he had probably forgotten her. Besides, she knew that he did not love her—not as Beth Makepeace loved her. He was merely concerned that his enemies should not continue to use her against him.

Her prayers finished, Anne Marie walked over to the arrow slit that served as her window in the tower. As she gazed out at the night a shooting star suddenly flashed across the sky.

'I wish,' she said. 'Oh, I wish that something wonderful would happen. I wish that I was free…that I could fall in love…'

In another moment she was laughing at herself. She had made three wishes and only one would be granted if the old superstition were true. But of course it was merely nonsense. Nothing was likely to happen. She would stay here, forgotten, until she died.

The morning had dawned fine and bright. As Anne Marie left the castle for her walk, the sun was shining and there was a mild feel to the day. She smiled at the guard who stood sentry at the East Gate. He bowed his head in acknowledgement, allowing her to pass through without challenge. She could walk only as far as the cliff edge, for there was no way down to the sea below.

Sometimes Anne Marie was allowed to visit the village at the bottom of the hill at the west side of the castle, but only when accompanied by Beth and one of the men at arms. Sometimes she and Beth would gather herbs and wild flowers on the way, and on rare occasions Thomas Makepeace would ride with her and a groom in the hills and valleys about Drodney.

'You must be allowed your exercise, my dear,' he told her kindly. 'I like to see the bloom in your cheeks and the air will do you good.' But he was a busy man and she did not ride as often as she would have liked.

Her chief pleasure was in walking, reading and of late sketching. She had brought with her that morning a pensel and a tiny leather-bound journal with sheets of plain vellum that Beth had bought her as a birthday gift. Anne Marie used them sparingly, for both the pensel and the journal had been sent specially from London and were expensive.

Sitting on a cushion made of her cloak, Anne Marie stared out at the sea. It was that morning a curious dark blue topped with greyish white foam and she longed for a palette of colours so that she could capture the true essence of that angry water.

'What are you doing?'

Absorbed in her contemplation of the view, Anne Marie had not been aware of the man's approach. For a moment her heart raced with fear, but then it stilled as something stirred in her memory and she knew him. He had visited the castle but once before when she was a child of some ten years, but his image had stayed in her mind because he had put her up on his pony and taken her riding outside the walls of Drodney. She believed he might have received a scolding for taking her without permission, but he had left the next morning and she had never known.

'I was thinking that I should like to paint the sea,' she replied. 'To sketch it in pensel would not do that colour justice.'

'No, you are very right,' Kit said, and sat down beside her on a piece of rock, gazing out as she did to the sea and endless sky. 'It is a magnificent view, though somewhat daunting at times. Do you often come here, Mistress Fraser?'

'I was not sure you would remember me.' Her eyes widened as she looked at him; they were as cool and clear as the autumn sky but a much deeper blue that reminded him of other skies. 'I come most days. I am allowed to walk here alone, you see.'

'And you are not allowed to walk to the village?'

'Not alone,' she replied, her tone more wistful than she knew. 'When Master Makepeace can spare the time he takes me riding, but that is not often. Sometimes Beth comes with me to the village. Once a month there is a market. It is possible to buy silks and ribbons from the pedlars, but Beth sends to London for most of our needs.' She handed him the tiny journal. 'This was a gift for my birthday last year.'

Kit took the book and looked at the pages. There were exquisite drawings of the castle, the cliffs, the sea and various people, including Beth and Thomas Makepeace. Some were in pen and ink, smudged slightly to give them shading, others in pensel. He examined the pensel curiously, for though they had been produced in England for some years now, he had never handled one before. It was not more than a finger's length above its flat silver holder and he guessed that it had been much used.

'Have you no paints, mistress?'

'I am fortunate to have this,' Anne Marie replied. 'Until Beth bought it for me I had only a slate. She says that she will buy me some colours at Christmas, but she has very little money of her own and I fear paints are too expensive.'

Kit frowned as he returned the book to her, his eyes moving over her intently. He felt the injustice of her treatment, for there was surely no need to deprive her of such simple pleasures! Indeed, it was a sin to do so, for her life could not have been easy here.

She was dressed in a plain gown of black cloth with a white ruff at her neck, her only adornment a silver cross on a green ribbon. Her hair was covered with a neat black cap at the crown, but streamed down her back in heavy tresses.

Gazing into her clear eyes, he felt an odd sensation in his stomach and caught his breath. Damn it! She was lovely. Not exquisitely dressed, painted and adorned like the beauties of Elizabeth's court, but with a quiet, graceful beauty that moved him deeply. He was aware once more of dismay at the nature of his task, which was in truth to spy on her.

'I should go back,' she said, as if something in his look had disturbed her, and he offered his hand to help her rise. After the merest hesitation she took it and he bent to retrieve her cloak, shaking it before placing it about her shoulders. Gazing down at her he was aware of an urgent desire to kiss her, and had to berate himself mentally. She was no tavern wench to be tumbled in the hay! She smiled, a faint flush in her cheeks, as she said, 'I thank you, Sir Christopher. I was turning a little cold.'

'Will you not call me Kit as you did when we were children?'

'It might be frowned upon,' she said, her gaze clear and honest. 'How long do you stay with us, sir?'

'Oh, for a few weeks or so,' he said vaguely, made uncomfortable by those candid eyes. He had not expected to be so attracted to her, and it pricked at his conscience to know that he was here under a false flag. 'My mother thought the northern air might do me good, and it is many years since any of us visited Mistress Makepeace, though I believe my mother writes quite often.'

'Have you been ill, sir?' Anne Marie glanced up at him and he felt the pull of those eyes once more. His stomach churned and he understood that what he felt was desire—the desire to possess her, to touch that soft white skin and kiss those full, sweet lips.

'I was wounded in a battle with a Spanish ship,' he explained, fighting the fierce passion she had unwittingly aroused in him. What was wrong with him? He was like a green youth, the sap rising as if he had no control. 'She was a merchant ship and loaded down with silver from the New World. Her crew put up a fierce resistance when we boarded her, and that was when I was wounded.'

'Are you a pirate, Sir Christopher?'

'I am what is called a privateer,' he replied with an odd smile. 'I sail under Drake's command and with the blessing of Her Majesty Queen Elizabeth. Our mission is to harry the Spanish and take what we can of the wealth they have stolen from the New World. In the first half of this century the Spanish were the most powerful nation on earth, but their ships are clumsy compared to ours. At sea we have the advantage of them, though they are fierce and oft-times cruel on land. If we did not do what we can to relieve them of some of their wealth they would become too powerful and represent a danger to England.'

'I have read in a pamphlet that they sometimes slaughter innocent natives of the New World. Someone told me that that was lies, set about by those who hate them. Tell me, sir—what is your opinion?'

Kit felt his throat tighten with desire as he gazed into her eyes. He swallowed hard and averted his gaze as he replied, 'Let me assure you that what you read was true. Whoever told you that the pamphlet lied was misinformed. I have heard and seen things that I would not repeat in a lady's hearing, but which I found shocking.'

Anne Marie nodded, accepting his word. Her father had told her she was being fed lies by Beth but she had not quite believed him. She knew that he had friends in Spain, and suspected it might be from there that he was expecting help in his plan to rescue Mary of Scots.

Perhaps this man would tell her the truth? He seemed open and outgoing and she thirsted for news of the outside world.

'Have you heard of the arrest of Mary of Scots?'

Kit's nape prickled as she spoke. How could she have heard this? It was known only to a few and of very recent occurrence.

'That she has been sent to Fotheringay? I know it to be true, mistress. But how do you know of this?'

'I heard Beth speak of it to her husband but was not sure what was meant.'

'Few know of this, Mistress Fraser. Your guardians should be more careful in their talk.'

'It was but a chance remark I heard in passing.' He

nodded but frowned, and she drew a deep breath. 'I would know why she has been sent there,' Anne Marie said. 'What has she done that she is so condemned? Until recently I believe she was given as much or more privilege than I.'

'And she betrayed that privilege,' Kit said sternly, remembering belatedly why he had come. 'She plotted with the traitor Babington to murder Elizabeth and take the throne of England by force. She is a vain, foolish creature and will no doubt forfeit her life for this latest treachery.'

Anne Marie's hand flew to her throat. Her eyes widened in fear as she saw his harsh expression.

'Surely she cannot have done anything so wicked?'

'I assure you it is proven by Walsingham. If the Queen was not a woman of conscience and compassion Mary would have been executed long before this for other crimes. As yet Elizabeth has stayed her hand, but I think it must come at the last.'

'God have mercy!' Anne Marie said and crossed herself. 'You may call it justice, sir, and perhaps it is—but I feel for Mary's plight. You have been accustomed to freedom and cannot know what it is like to be kept a prisoner for so many years. If Mary of Scots truly did what is said of her it was because it was her only hope of freedom.'

Kit's gaze narrowed as it centred on her face. 'Are you so unhappy, Mistress Fraser?'

A warm blush suffused her cheeks.

'I—I have been lucky in my guardians, sir. Mistress Makepeace has always been kind and loving towards me. I would not have you think me ungrateful.'

'But you long for freedom?' Kit looked at her profile as she was silent. Her expression gave no hint of her feelings and he guessed that she had learned to keep them in check, but a tiny nerve flicking in her throat told him all. 'I should not have asked such a question,' he said softly. 'Forgive me if you can.'

Anne Marie turned her eyes on him. There was a hint of accusation in their depths.

'There is nothing to forgive. It was but an idle question. The answer is that I have learned to long for nothing. I expect only what I am given, that way I am not disappointed.'

She gave the appearance of calm, a modest, emotionless creature without passion. Why did he not quite believe in this face she showed to the world?

Surely such beauty could not belong to a woman of so little passion? Kit was convinced that the picture she presented of modesty and compliance was not the true one.

They had reached the castle gate and passed beneath the old stone arch. Seeing Sir Christopher, the sentry saluted and stood to attention.

'Are you a person of importance these days?' Anne Marie asked, a hint of mischief in her eyes.

Kit laughed deep in his throat. She was not so emotionless that she had no sense of humour!

'Oh, I think not,' he murmured. 'The poor fellow must have confused me with someone else.'

Anne Marie stared at him in silence for a moment,

and then her laughter rang out. It was clear and joyous, like the sound of tinkling bells, and so surprising that it shocked the man at her side. His stomach clenched and he was captivated by the charm of the woman thus revealed. How delightful she might be if she were not so restricted by her life at the castle.

Once again he felt an urgent desire to take her in his arms and wondered at himself. Why should this woman have such a marked effect on him? It was not often that he met a wench that made him burn as she did, and within such a short time of meeting her. Had he run mad, or was it simply too long since he had taken a woman to bed?

'Why do you stare at me so?'

Her laughter had stilled and there was apprehension in those wondrous eyes, as if she thought she had done something wrong and might be reprimanded for it.

'Your laughter pleased me,' Kit said, realising that he had been staring at her for several minutes. He was a damned fool and must control this urge. 'Forgive me if I offended, mistress. I meant not to be rude.'

'You were not rude, sir. I wondered if I had offended you?'

'I do not believe that is possible.' He smiled down at her. Beside him she was diminutive—the fairy sprite of many a poem! He knew a mad temptation to sweep her up on his horse and ride away with her. 'You are sweet company, Mistress Fraser. Would that

I had words to tell you, but I am a common sea captain and do not have the gift of a silver tongue.'

'Oh, I think you rather an uncommon man,' Anne Marie replied, a little smile about her lips. 'I am fond of poetry but I have no talent for it either.'

'You have other talents,' Kit murmured. 'Not least your skill at drawing likenesses. Will you take mine, Mistress Fraser? I believe my mother would like to have it by her when I am away.'

'Are you often away?'

'I have been for some years past. I am not certain of the future. My father died a month before I returned from my last voyage. My mother was managing but ill, and I fear it may be too much for her. I am reluctant to leave her again too soon, though for the moment she is well enough and has kind friends about her.'

'I am sorry for your father's death.'

'As I was. When we parted he was in the best of health. It was a sudden chill. He was six and forty and seemed young for his age. I expected him to live for many years more.'

'My mother died when she was but twenty,' Anne Marie said, feeling the sting of tears. 'I never knew her, though she survived my birth by some months. She took a fever and was dead within hours.'

'That was a tragedy for you and your father. I believe your father did not remarry?'

'No, he has never done so. I think he…'

Anne Marie was silent all at once, lost in thought. She was not sure why Lord Fraser had not taken a second wife. He had always been a staunch supporter of Mary, but why remain unwed? Unless he had hoped…but surely not? He could not hope to take his place as Mary's consort when she became Queen?

It was a foolish idea and one that Anne Marie dismissed at once. There were other more important men who must have similar aspirations. If Lord Fraser was prepared to risk all on such a slender hope he was a reckless fool. No, no, she decided. His purpose was nobler. He wished to restore the Catholic faith to the people, and to see Mary in her rightful place.

'What do you think, mistress?' he asked, as she remained silent too long.

Anne Marie was recalled to the present. Sir Christopher was looking at her curiously, as if he hoped to read her thoughts. She blushed and shook her head.

'Why nothing, sir. Nothing that would interest you.' Nor that she dared repeat to anyone. She hesitated as they entered the castle together. 'I think I must leave you now, sir. Mistress Makepeace will be waiting for me. It is my habit to report to her on my return. She likes me to help her in her stillroom. To be mistress of a castle is a big responsibility. There is no physician for leagues, and if anyone in the castle is ill the task of caring for that person falls to Beth, and sometimes in the village too. She hath some skill for it, and I help her where I can, for she has much to do.'

The castle was in fact like a small walled town, with its own blacksmith, carpenter, mason, farrier, bakery and a cookhouse for the men, besides many other small tradesmen who worked within the castle walls but lived in the village below.

'Go then,' Kit said and then laid his hand upon her arm, as she would have turned away. 'Do you walk every morning?'

'Most mornings if it is fine,' she agreed and lowered her gaze.

'Perhaps you would like to ride with me tomorrow?'

'We should need permission from my guardian.'

'I have not forgot,' he said with a rueful laugh. 'I shall speak to Thomas and see if he will permit the pleasure—a pleasure as much for me as you, mistress.'

'If permission is granted I should very much like to ride with you, sir.'

Anne Marie turned away, a smile on her lips. If only she could go riding with him! It would be such a joy. Yet she must not, dare not hope for too much. It would be a bitter disappointment if Sir Christopher's request should be denied.

Chapter Two

To Anne Marie's delight, her guardian was pleased to grant permission for her to go riding on the morrow with his wife's kinsman. Both Thomas and Beth Makepeace were much taken with their visitor and assured him that the girl could go out in his company as much as it pleased him to indulge her.

'She is a good, dutiful girl and will give you no trouble, Sir Christopher,' Thomas Makepeace confided to him. 'Had I the time I would take her more often myself.'

'I have given my word that you shall be safely returned to the castle at night,' Kit told her. 'And that provided, I have permission to take you where I will. Which means that we might visit the fair when it comes to Norham next month.'

'Do you mean it? Will you still be here?' Anne Marie looked at him in disbelief. She could hardly believe what she was hearing. She had never been further than the village of Drodney, and though Norham Castle was but a few leagues inland from them, she had heard it was a much larger castle and that the village was a stopover for men driving their cattle to the markets in Durham. Besides, she was excited at the prospect of being taken to a fair for the first time in her life. 'Oh, will you truly take me, sir?'

'I always mean what I say,' Kit promised her, a smile on his lips as he saw the excitement she could not hide. 'But you must promise not to try to run away from me, for it would reflect badly on the Makepeaces if you should disappear while allowed some privilege.'

'I promise I shall not run away from you, sir.' She gave her word at once, fearing to have her pleasure snatched away at the last moment. 'I do give you my word that I shall not attempt to escape while in your care.'

'Then we are agreed. We shall ride every day, and as a special treat I shall take you to the fair.'

To ride in the hills with him was such pleasure to her that Anne Marie would have asked for nothing more. However, the promise of a visit to a fair was tantalising, for though she had never been to such an event in her life, she had heard from others that there were strange and wondrous things to be seen. Yet still she did her best to suppress her excitement lest he should change his mind.

Her life had been so quiet, so set in its routine, that she had seldom thought beyond the boundaries of her small world, and the taste of freedom now revealed to her had roused longings that she had kept at bay these many years. And it was all because of the man who had come so unexpectedly into her life, awakening her, causing her to…

He was faithful in his pledge to ride with her each morning, and Anne Marie began to look eagerly for his tall figure in the courtyard. He had dismissed the need for a groom to escort them, helping her to mount and dismount himself.

'You ride well, Mistress Fraser,' he told her as they returned from an enjoyable gallop one morning a week after their first meeting. 'I thought you might be inexperienced but you hold yourself well. Indeed, you deserve a better mount than the horse you ride.'

'I am well content with Beth's old mare,' Anne Marie said, giving the horse a pat as Kit came to lift her down. The touch of his hands about her waist set her heart fluttering but she hid her feelings as always. It would not do to let him guess how much it pleased her to be with him, for she knew that she was expected to be modest and dutiful as befitted a girl in her position. If sometimes she felt the urge to run and shout and sing for sheer joy at the freedom he had given her, she suppressed it. 'I am fortunate to be able to ride at all, sir.'

'You are the daughter of a noble lord of Scotland,' Kit said, finding himself suddenly angry on her behalf. It was wrong that she should have been kept here a prisoner for all these years, a hostage for her father's good behaviour. 'A decent horse should be provided for your use. Your father should see to these things.'

Anne Marie smiled and shook her head. 'My father bears an old title, it is true, but he has little money, sir. Our home had no more comfort than this castle. I cannot recall much about it myself but I am assured it is true. Beth is paid nothing for my keep and her husband has only his pension as warden of the castle, which in truth is little enough. Sometimes I believe he finds it hard enough to pay the men who serve him.'

'Can this be?' Kit was surprised. It was known that the Queen herself was forever short of money, which was why she was always graciously pleased to accept a gift of treasure stolen from the Spanish to fill her coffers. However, he thought it foolhardy to keep the master of a strategic fortress short of coin to pay his men. Although an uneasy truce held between Scotland and England for the moment, there was always the threat of raiding parties. 'Then I shall speak to Thomas. Perhaps something may be achieved between us.'

Anne Marie looked up at him. 'I pray you will not ask too much of my kind guardians, sir. Beth has fed and clothed me at her own expense these many years. I would not ask more of her.'

'The expense shall not fall on them,' Kit promised.

He was determined that some changes should come about to provide more comfort for the girl. She had made a deep impression on him. It had shocked Kit to discover how little she had and he was aware of an urgent concern that her life should improve, not only while he was staying at the castle but after he had returned to his home.

The matter of a suitable mount was easy enough to

put in train, and when he returned to London he would arrange for various paints and canvases to be sent for her use. He might also settle a small pension on her for her clothes and personal items, though he would need to discuss that with Beth Makepeace for the sake of the girl's pride. He was not sure what more he could do for Anne Marie. Unless some kind of pardon could be granted her?

Perhaps he would speak to Walsingham when he next saw him. He had observed nothing so far that would lead him to suspect that either Anne Marie or her father were involved in any plots against the Queen, but it was early days yet, and he would need to keep a watchful eye for the remainder of his stay.

Anne Marie had begun to relax her guard a little in his company, and to laugh more often when he teased her. Yet he did not flatter himself that she trusted him enough to confide in him. If indeed there was anything to confide.

Kit was not sure what Walsingham expected of him. All he could do was observe and follow his instincts, and for the moment he was inclined to believe Anne Marie innocent of any complicity.

It was much colder the morning that Kit sent word he had some business elsewhere and could not ride with her that day. Anne Marie was disappointed, for these past two weeks she had enjoyed getting to know Sir Christopher and she had begun to like him, perhaps more than she ought. It was foolish to come to rely on him when he would leave Drodney in a few weeks. But how could she help it when he was always so considerate of her, so kind and thoughtful?

He had told her much about himself and his home, describing the escapades of his younger brothers and making her laugh at his stories. He also told her about his adventures on board his ship, and these sometimes made her tremble, though she believed he did not always tell her the whole truth, but made the life sound more exciting and less dangerous than it really was.

She had started to look for his tall figure as he walked about the courtyards of the castle, and her heart lifted insensibly every time she saw him coming towards her. How handsome he was, and so distinguished. It was little wonder that the guards respected him, saluting and standing to attention when he approached.

All the craftsmen about the castle were her friends, from the cobbler who mended the heels of her shoes to the baker who often had a small basket of cakes and buns for her. Although they all knew she was a prisoner, she was thought of as the Makepeaces' daughter and well liked.

Having spent most of the morning talking to the men and women who were the lifeblood of the small, self-contained community, Anne Marie decided to take a walk as far as the cliff edge. It was a while since she had walked alone, and she enjoyed the crisp air, wrapped in her cloak against the cold, her head down as she let her thoughts wander. She had missed Sir Christopher's company this morning, and she would miss him even more when he returned to his home in Devon. Indeed, she did not know how she would bear it when he was no longer with them.

'Where have you been, Daughter? I have looked for you here these past three days. I had begun to wonder if you were ill.'

Anne Marie was startled by the voice she had not expected to hear. Where had Lord Fraser come from, and why had she not noticed his approach?

'You surprised me, sir. I was not expecting you. Does my guardian know you are here?'

'No, and he must not,' Angus Fraser said frowning at her. 'I charge you to keep all that I say to you secret, Daughter. Give me your word that you will do so.'

'Yes, of course, Father—but how did you come here if not from the castle?'

'That is a secret known only to Frampton and myself.'

'Who is he, Father?' she asked puzzled, for she had not heard the name before. 'Is Master Frampton a friend of yours?'

'You do not need to know, nor should I have spoken his name,' her father said and glanced over his shoulder as if he was afraid of being overheard, which was foolish, for there was no one to be seen. 'He is merely someone who made it possible for me to come here to you like this. When the time is right, he will help you to escape from the castle and join me. It is my intention that you shall go to France for your own safety.'

'For my safety?' Anne Marie stared at him, a shiver

running down her spine. Something odd in his manner frightened her and made her wary. 'I do not understand. Am I in some danger?'

'If what we plan comes to pass it may be that your life would be forfeit,' Lord Fraser replied, his thin, ruthless face set hard. 'It is the reason you have been kept hostage these many years, and has been a great hindrance to my plans, for I would not have you die so cruelly, my daughter. But it shall not happen. I have other plans for you, Anne Marie, and I would not have my enemies take a harsh revenge on you for what I do.'

'I am sure that neither Beth nor Thomas Makepeace would harm me, Father.'

'They would do as they were ordered, especially if…' He frowned at her again. 'What we plan is dangerous and if it should fail you might be used against me. For the sake of honour I could not remain at large if your life was the price of my freedom.' He shook his head. 'Believe me, Daughter, it is better that you should leave here before anything happens that might bring you to grief.'

'Is this something to do with the fact that Mary of Scots has been taken to the castle of Fotheringay?'

'So you know of this? I suppose you heard it from Mistress Makepeace. She always had a loose tongue.'

'You wrong Beth, Father. She is a good, honest woman. She seemed to shocked to learn of the arrest and asked her husband why it should be.'

The look on Lord Fraser's face was so fierce and

so angry at mention of his Queen's arrest that Anne
Marie was momentarily afraid he meant to strike her.

'That devil Walsingham tricked her and falsified
her hand,' Lord Fraser declared, his fists balling at his
sides as if in frustration. 'It was not enough that they
had kept her a prisoner these many years.
Walsingham is determined that she shall die, but we
are equally determined that she shall live and take her
rightful place on the thrones of both England and
Scotland. Frampton says that Walsingham has
thwarted him in the past, but with my help he is certain of success this time.'

'Is what you plan not very dangerous for you,
Father?'

'There is danger if our plans are discovered,' he
replied. 'But we are not such fools as Babington. We
put nothing on paper, and we do not brag of our plans.
Frampton has but now returned from Spain, where he
has been living for some years. He has made influential friends there and we have been promised help
if we can achieve Mary's escape from the castle.'

'But surely that is impossible, Father?'

Anne Marie stared at him anxiously. If it had not
been possible to get Mary free of her captors before
she was taken to Fotheringay Castle how could they
possibly free her now?

'With Frampton's help we should be able to smug-
gle a small force of men into the castle and bring
Mary out. She will be taken to a ship and thereafter
to a place of safety until the invasion of England has

been completed, and the bastard Elizabeth disposed of once and for all.'

Anne Marie was chilled by such talk. It was treason even to speak of the Queen so disrespectfully, and her father would surely lose his head if his plans went awry. She knew that he had always hoped that a way might be found to restore Mary to the throne, but had thought it more a dream than an actual belief. He had changed somehow, and she felt that someone else was influencing him, pushing him into action rather than his merely talking of his hopes and dreams—perhaps this man he called Frampton?

'How can Master Frampton help you to enter Fotheringay, Father?'

Lord Fraser looked uneasily over his shoulder, then crossed himself. She sensed then that he was afraid of the man he called Frampton, though apparently prepared to trust him in this matter.

'In truth I know not, Daughter, but he hath some strange power. I know not how he does it, but the guards at Drodney were in some kind of trance as I passed through the gates, for they saw me not.'

'How can this be?' Anne Marie asked. She too made the sign of the cross over her breast, for the coldness had spread throughout her body and she was aware of fear such as she had never felt before. There was some mischief afoot here! 'Is he in league with the Devil?'

'You must ask no more questions, Daughter. I have said more than I ought on this, for our plans depend on secrecy. That devil Walsingham seems to have spies everywhere.'

Anne Marie knew a sudden, urgent anxiety for her father. 'If I were you, Father, I should not put too much faith in Master Frampton. You might do better to sever all connection with him.'

Lord Fraser glared at her. 'I have not asked for your advice, Daughter, nor shall I. You know nothing of these things and I waste my time speaking of them to you. Your duty is to obey me. Be ready, for the hour of your deliverance is at hand.'

'Yes, Father.'

'I shall leave you now.'

Anne Marie nodded, watching as he strode off in the direction of the castle. Tears stung her eyes. She knew that she could not expect love from this man, Lord Fraser, her father, but she was hurt by his harshness. She had spoken merely out of concern for him, because his words had frightened her. How could her father have passed unseen through the castle gates? What kind of power did this man Frampton have over the guards—and her father?

It was clearly unnatural and she found the idea repugnant. Anne Marie knew that there were poor souls who suffered terrible ills because they were possessed by devils. She had heard the evils of hell and damnation for those who consorted with demons preached of from the pulpit in the castle chapel many times, and feared the Devil's power. It was believed that evil spirits walked the earth at night, and because of it many shuttered their windows after dark and would not venture out lest some evil befall them.

Touching the silver cross at her throat, Anne Marie whispered a prayer, asking God for his forgiveness and protection for her father, who was surely risking his immortal soul as well as his life.

She was frowning, anxious for her father and uneasy about her future, when she suddenly saw Sir Christopher standing outside the castle gate. A shiver of apprehension went through her. Had he seen her talking with her father?

'Mistress Fraser,' Kit said as he came up to her. His eyes went over her with concern and she knew that her hands were trembling. 'You look pale. Methinks you have spent too long gazing at the sea this morning and turned cold.'

'The wind is bitter this morning, sir.'

Somehow she could not bring herself to meet his eyes. She had been told it was her duty to go with her father, but suppose he tried to take her when she was in Sir Christopher's charge? She had given her word that she would not run away from him. Besides, she was not at all sure that she liked the idea of leaving all that was familiar to her. She would never see Beth again, and that made her feel unhappy. Her life here had been hard at times, but she had become accustomed to it and she had no idea of what her father planned for her. The future seemed uncertain and frightening, and she felt very alone.

'Is something wrong, Anne Marie?'

Kit looked at her, eyes narrowing intently.

Something was bothering her. Was it because he had cancelled their appointment to go riding this morning—or for some other reason? When he was approaching the castle he had seen two men riding away in the opposite direction, yet when he had mentioned this to the guard on duty the man had seemed puzzled, denying that anyone had passed by.

Clearly the man was lying. Had he been bribed to let someone in—someone who perhaps wished to speak with Mistress Fraser?

The riders had been well muffled against the wind and he had not caught sight of their faces, but from Anne Marie's behaviour he sensed that something had happened that morning. She looked nervous and unhappy, even frightened.

'If you were ever troubled by something I would be happy to listen,' Kit said gently, his gaze centred on her pale face. Her start of fright confirmed his suspicions. She was very nervous about something that had happened here today. 'You may trust me, Anne Marie. I would do all in my power to help you.'

'There is nothing you can do, sir,' she said. She longed to confide in him but knew that she must not, for if she did her father's life might be forfeit. 'If you would excuse me, Beth will be waiting for me. I should go to her.'

'Stay a moment,' Kit said, laying a hand on her arm, as she would have passed him. 'I do not wish to pry into something that does not concern me—but I am your friend.'

'Are you?' Her clear eyes gazed up at him, and he

felt his stomach spasm with desire. In that instant Kit
knew that he was falling in love with her. He had felt
something from the moment of their meeting, but until now he had not acknowledged what it meant. He
was aware of a need to hold her and touch her, and
to protect her from harm. 'I—I am bothered about
something, sir, but, forgive me, I cannot speak of it
just yet.'

'Then I shall not press you,' he said. 'And now, I
have a surprise for you.'

'A surprise for me?' She stared at him in wonder.
'What can you mean?'

'I shall show you why I was unable to ride with
you this morning,' Kit said. 'Come to the stable and
meet your new mare. I bought her specially for you
and I hope you will be pleased with her.'

'You have bought me a new horse?' Anne Marie
could only continue to stare at him as she struggled
to take in what he was saying. No one had ever done
such a thing for her! 'But…why did you do that?'

'Because it is fitting that you should be properly
mounted,' Kit said. 'You have been neglected for too
long, Anne Marie—and I intend that your life shall
change for the better.'

'Change? I do not understand. How can my life
change?'

Her heart was beating so strongly that she felt
breathless. Her father had warned her that her hour
of deliverance was near, and now Sir Christopher was
telling her almost the same thing, though she did not
think he meant her to run away.

'For a start I have the means to see that your circumstances here are improved, but there might be more I can do. I promise nothing for the moment, Anne Marie—but when I leave here you shall not be forgotten.'

Only the last few words made any impression on her, and her spirits sank. 'Are you leaving soon?'

'Not for another week or so, but I cannot stay much beyond that,' Kit told her, and saw the disappointment in her eyes. It seemed that she would miss him, or would it be her new-found freedom she missed? 'I do promise that I shall do all I can for you.'

She saw that he was not to be pressed further, and indeed she was so confused that she knew not what to think. She might even have left Drodney before he did! Her heart beat rapidly, partly from fear and also from some other emotion she could not name, but which gave her pain. She was not at all sure she wanted to go away with Lord Fraser. But what else could she do if he demanded it? He was her father and he had the right to command her as he would.

They had been walking as they talked, and now as they approached the stables she saw that one of the young grooms was leading a pretty white mare about the yard, and gave a cry of delight.

'Oh, but she is lovely,' she said, gazing at the mare in a daze of happiness. 'Did you truly buy her for my use, sir?'

'She is yours,' Kit told her, smiling as he saw the pleasure his gift had given her. 'I am assured that she is a good-natured beast but spirited withal. I think she is just right for you, Anne Marie.'

'I love her,' she cried and went to pat the mare's soft nose. 'By what name is she called?'

'She has no pet name,' Kit said. 'You may call her as you wish.'

'Then I shall name her Starlight,' Anne Marie said recalling the shooting star she had seen passing across the sky the night before Sir Christopher's arrival. She had wished for something wonderful to happen, for freedom and to fall in love, and, glancing shyly at the man who had given her such a delightful gift, she realised that in a way all three had begun to come true. 'You are very kind to me, sir. I do not know how I can ever repay you.'

'I ask for no payment. It is little enough. I would do much more for you if it were possible, Mistress Fraser.'

Her heart jerked and she looked at the mare, giving all her attention to the prancing creature as she tried to cover her confusion. For years nothing had happened to her, and now too much was happening all at once. Her emotions were churning inside her and she was in turmoil as she tried to sort out what she truly felt.

Was it foolish of her to feel so drawn towards Sir Christopher? His smile made her heart beat faster, and her limbs seemed as if they would melt every time he touched her. What was happening to her? What were these strange new emotions he had roused in her? She had no experience to help her and knew only that she felt happier when he was with her.

Her thoughts whirled as she tried to think sensibly. Were these feelings those a woman might feel for the man she married?

But what foolishness was this? She knew nothing of love and even if she were attracted to Sir Christopher it could surely come to naught. She was by instinct and birth a Catholic, despite having been brought up to give lip service to the Protestant faith. She had vowed that she would never marry other than in the true faith. Besides, such a marriage was not likely to be favoured—was it? Her father would never allow it; he had his own plans for her and they did not include marriage to an English Protestant.

Oh, it was all so bewildering! Anne Marie did not know what to think. Would she marry Sir Christopher if he asked her? She was not sure of her own feelings towards him, except that it made her happy to be with him. Perhaps that was merely because with him she was free to leave the castle?

Her duty was surely to Lord Fraser? He was her father and he had the right to demand her loyalty. Yet he was telling her she must leave Beth Makepeace without a word, and her heart cried out against it. Beth was the only mother she had ever known.

Anne Marie's conscience was troubling her sorely as she was encouraged to ride her mare around the castle yard. Looking about her at the smiling faces of the men and women who worked within the compound, she realised that this was her home. She had found kindness here and these people were not to blame that she was a prisoner—and yet they would be blamed if she escaped.

Sitting on a stool and looking out through the slit that was her only view from the tower, Anne Marie tried to come to terms with her feelings. She could not doubt that Sir Christopher had stirred something deep within her, making her aware of longings and needs she had suppressed for too long.

To return to the life she had known would be the cruellest fate of all, and she had already begun to dread the day of his departure. How would she live when he was not there to take her riding and fill her heart with laughter?

Oh, but she would not let herself think of a future so bleak and empty that it filled her with a hungry ache. He had promised he would take her to the fair before he left, and she would think only of that.

Anne Marie had never seen so many people. The fair had come to Norham and Sir Christopher had brought her as he had promised. She smiled at him as he helped her down, giving the reins of their horses to the groom who had accompanied them.

'It is so exciting,' she said, looking about her. 'Oh, what is that man doing, Sir Christopher?' She clutched at his arm in her excitement, not wanting to miss a moment of this special day.

'That is the sword swallower,' Kit told her. 'I expect he eats fire as well. Yes, see—his assistant is handing him a flaming torch. He will swallow that in a moment.'

'Is that not very dangerous?' Anne Marie was amazed and stood watching the fire-eater in fascination. She had never seen anything of the kind before, though once a troupe of travelling tumblers and fools had come to the castle to entertain them at Christmastide. 'Will he not hurt himself?'

'I dare say it is a trick,' Kit said, amused by her innocent pleasure. 'There are many such conjurors at fairs, I believe. Some call themselves magicians, but I think most of them are tricksters, though some of the things they do seem to be magic for one cannot tell how the trick is done—and they are vastly entertaining.'

'Do you believe in magic?' Anne Marie asked, looking at him intently. 'These tricks the conjurers perform—do you think it is possible to make someone invisible?'

'I do not know.' Kit frowned as he saw the shadows in her face. There was something about her then that alerted him. She had been subdued of late and he was certain that something—or someone—troubled her. 'They say there are many things that cannot be explained in Heaven and Earth, and I dare say it is true, but I am not sure that I believe in magic powers. Every magician I have ever seen worked by sleight of hand.'

'But there are those poor souls possessed by demons…'

'So it is said,' Kit agreed. 'Though I have wondered if some other explanation for their malady might be found if we had but the power to discover it through study and medicine.'

'Do you deny the Devil, sir?' She gazed at him earnestly, and he could see that she was troubled.

'I deny his works,' Kit said. 'But just as there is a power for good that we call God, so there must be a power for evil—and the Devil is as good a name as any.' Kit's gaze narrowed as he saw her anxious look. 'But why let such things trouble you, mistress? We are here to enjoy ourselves. Come, let me buy you some trinkets from the pedlars. I think that we may find something to amuse you here.'

'Oh yes, there is so much to see,' she agreed, making an effort to dismiss the shadow that had come so suddenly upon her. She would not think of things that frightened her today.

Anne Marie smiled shyly as she took the arm Kit offered, and they began to thread their way through the milling crowds that had gathered for the fair. Country folk had come from miles around to buy and enjoy themselves, and there were all kinds of amusements to be found. Stalls selling everything imaginable, from curious carved ivories brought from far-off lands, wooden dolls and carvings of animals, ribbons and laces, costly materials piled high, hot pies and sweetmeats, to tools for working on the land and pretty trinkets of all kinds.

Anne Marie forgot her cares as she clung to Kit's arm, finding his presence comforting as they were crushed by the press of excited folk. They ate hot meat pies, apples covered in crisp toffee and other sweetmeats, and Anne Marie chose several small trinkets for herself.

'They are but baubles,' Kit told her, because she protested that he had already spent too much on her when he told her to choose some material for a new gown. 'I have but started as yet, Anne Marie. Do you like this blue silk? I think it would become you—or do you prefer the green?'

She was bewildered by the choice and could not make up her mind, and in the end Kit bought both and had them delivered to the inn by the merchant.

'We shall dine there before we go back to Drodney,' he told her. 'Meanwhile all our packages may wait there for us that we may enjoy greater freedom.'

Games of all kinds were going on about them: wrestling in a booth, shooting arrows into a barrel, games of chance, bowling for the prize of a sucking pig and many others. It was as they were passing a tent selling ale that Anne Marie felt someone was watching her and she turned her head to look, feeling cold as she saw the man's eyes on her.

She did not know him, but there was an oddness about the way he looked at her that made her feel uncomfortable. He was a man well into his middle years, slightly stooped and dressed in shabby black velvet, not remarkable in any way—except that there was something chilling about his eyes. She felt almost mesmerised as she looked at him, as if he was somehow pulling her towards him, exerting his will over her, and her hand trembled on Kit's arm.

'What is it?' Kit looked down at her, seeing her pale face and the way she stared fixedly at something. Glancing in the direction of her gaze, he saw the man and, sensing something odd in the stranger's manner, frowned. It was almost as if the fellow had some kind of hold over her. 'Do you know him, Anne Marie?'

Kit's voice seemed to break the spell, and she looked up at him, feeling suddenly able to breathe more easily.

'No, I have never seen him before,' she said. 'It was just…the way he stared at me: it frightened me. I did not like him.'

'Nor I,' Kit said. The man had turned and disappeared into the crowd or Kit might have gone after him and asked his business. Yet he did not wonder why the fellow had been staring at her, for she was lovely enough to turn the head of any man. He took her arm protectively. 'Come, mistress, we shall go to the inn and bespeak our meal, for we must soon think of returning.'

'Yes…' Anne Marie shivered. She was not sure why she had felt so disturbed by the brief exchange of looks, except that she had sensed some malice in the man with the strange eyes. 'Yes, we must not be late or Beth will worry.'

'I have arranged the use of a private bedchamber for your comfort at the inn,' Kit said, smiling at her as they made their way through the crowds that were as thick as ever about the stalls. 'You may need to refresh yourself before we dine.'

She thanked him from his thoughtfulness, and parted from him soon after the innkeeper showed them to a parlour, where a fire burned merrily in the huge open grate. From somewhere there was the smell of roasting meat as it turned upon a spit, and the warm, frothy odour of beer straight from the barrel was in the air.

The innkeeper's wife took Anne Marie up to the bedchamber, keeping guard at the door while she made use of the comforts provided within. Feeling very much more comfortable, she went out into the passage after a few minutes, thanking the woman who had made sure she had the privacy for which Sir Christopher had paid. With the village packed with strangers, the inn was full to bursting, and only those who had made prior arrangements were able to avail themselves of a little privacy.

The innkeeper's wife went off to offer her services to another lady, and Anne Marie made her way downstairs to the little parlour where she was expecting to meet Sir Christopher. There was a welcome fire but to her surprise Sir Christopher was not there, and she hesitated on the threshold, wondering what she ought to do, until the innkeeper told her that he had gone on a private errand and would join her shortly.

She sat down at the table near the window and glanced out as the innkeeper poured a glass of hot spiced ale for her. Her heart caught with fright and she shrank back, as she saw the man who had been staring at her earlier standing in the yard talking to someone else. They were in earnest conversation and did not notice her, so that she was able to watch for some seconds before they parted. What troubled Anne Marie so sorely was that the second man was her father.

What was Lord Fraser doing here? Had he seen her? Would he try to approach her? Yet he had seemed concerned with business of his own. The man in dusty black, who had been staring at her so oddly earlier, had clearly been angry, and her father had seemed to argue. Could they have been arguing over her?

'Do not look so anxious,' Kit's voice behind her startled her. 'I have been finding out a little about that fellow who stared at you. It seems that he has been staying here at this inn for a few days. His name is Frampton, but our host knows nothing more about him.' That was not quite true, but he had no intention of telling her the rest for the moment.

'Frampton?' Anne Marie's eyes widened in alarm and her heart drummed. 'Are you certain?'

'Aye, Bevis Frampton. A poor creature apparently, who seems to suffer from a permanent cough. I do not think you need trouble yourself further about him, Mistress Fraser.'

'No…' Yet Frampton was the man her father was expecting to help him get a small raiding party into Fotheringay Castle. If it was the same man—but of course it must be or they would not be here together!

'It was just his eyes; they seemed to mesmerise me so that I could not look away, and it frightened me.'

'Yes, I felt something myself,' Kit agreed. 'I have read accounts of Merlin and magicians of ancient times, particularly in lands to the east where these things are practised more than here. And I believe that these men may have had such an art long ago—the art to control another's mind by the power of one's will, and through their skill seemed to perform miracles, even to the extent of bringing the dead to life. I believe there is a Latin word for it, *hypnoticus,* which I think means to put to sleep or something of the kind—though I do not profess to understand the art.'

'To put to sleep? Yes, it was as if my eyelids grew heavy, as if I could have slept and yet I was not tired…' Anne Marie looked at him a little fearfully. 'Could such a power cause others not to notice what was going on around them?'

Kit's eyes narrowed as he looked at her, sensing that she was afraid, and that something played upon her mind. She had asked him earlier that morning if he believed that the conjurors could make someone invisible. Clearly something was bothering her. Could she have been frightened by some strange happening?

'Will you not tell me what worries you so, Anne Marie?' he asked softly. 'I think you have been sorely troubled for some days now. There are dark shadows beneath your eyes and I sense that you have not slept well of late.'

'I admit that I am troubled in my mind,' she said.

'I cannot tell you for I have given my word to some-one—but I believe my father is in some danger.'

'Lord Fraser? You have seen him?' Kit was alert but held his excitement in check for fear of frightening her. 'He told you something that disturbs you?'

'I must not say more,' Anne Marie faltered. She longed to confide in him, for her mind had been sorely taxed these past days, but even to say so much was a betrayal of her father's trust. 'But I fear that he may risk not only his life but his immortal soul.'

'Mayhap I could do something to help him, if you were to trust me? Why not tell me what it is that plays so on your mind?'

'I cannot,' she said, her eyes misty with tears. 'I gave my word, Kit. I swear that I would tell you if I could, but I cannot. I owe a duty to my father...'

'Then I shall ask no more,' he said and reached across the table to touch her hand. 'But if you should need a friend, you may speak to me. Believe me, my only wish is to serve you.' In the moment that he spoke it was the truth, though in another his conscience smote him as he realised he had deceived her. He had set out to win her friendship under base pretences and felt guilt because of it. But he had not expected to find himself so drawn to her. She had aroused his protective instincts and he felt the need to defend her as he would a helpless kitten.

Of the other feelings she aroused in him Kit thought little. A true man must always be roused to desire by a woman as fair as she. Yet in a corner of his mind a little voice told him that it might just be more.

'I wish that I could tell you all,' she said in a whisper. 'You do not know how much I wish that it were possible.'

Kit smiled and pressed her hand, but did not ask for more details. It was enough to warn him that Walsingham was right, and that some plot was afoot. He had a name that would help him, and he would see what more he could learn of what had frightened Anne Marie so much that she had been unable to sleep of late.

'Come, eat your meal,' he said. 'This is a day of pleasure. Consider well, mistress, and come to me before I leave for London in the morning if you would confide in me.'

'You are going away so soon?'

She felt a crushing pain inside her, her eyes reflecting her emotions more truly than she knew, her hands trembling as she felt the sweep of desolation.

'I have business I must attend,' Kit said. 'But I shall return as soon as I can make the journey. I hope that I may have news for you on my return.'

'What kind of news?' She looked at him, feeling an insensible surge of hope as she saw the way he smiled at her. Surely that look in his eyes must mean he cared a little for her? 'Pray tell me what you mean, sir.'

'I must consult with others first,' Kit replied and reached across to touch her cheek with the tips of his fingers. She was so lovely yet so pale. 'But if what I hope comes to pass we shall spend many another pleasant day together in the future, Anne Marie.'

She cast her eyes down, her cheeks suffused with colour as her heart seemed to thump against her ribs. What was he saying to her? She was so naïve, so innocent of the ways of men. Surely he could not be saying what he seemed to promise with his eyes?

Oh, it was all so very confusing and troubling. Anne Marie did not know what to think or feel. She was not sure that she was in love with him, for she did not truly know the meaning of the word. But her heart told her that there could be no greater happiness for her than to be this man's wife. He was so kind and generous and she would be free from the loneliness of her confinement if she married him—but he had said nothing that promised marriage. She was a fool to let herself hope!

Besides, there was the matter of her promise to her father that she would not let them wed her to a Protestant—and the plans Lord Fraser had made for her. If he had his way she was to be spirited from the castle and taken…where?

She did not know, but she thought it might be to France or Spain. She had no illusions about what would happen to her then. She would be married to a man her father had chosen, a marriage of convenience that would give Lord Fraser some advantage. Her own opinions and hopes would count for nothing. Something deep inside her protested that she did not wish for such a marriage, and yet she knew it to be her duty.

Oh, what was she to do? She wished with all her heart that she could confide everything to Kit but knew that she must not. Lord Fraser was a self-confessed traitor and she knew Kit to be loyal to his Queen.

If he guessed that Lord Fraser plotted to bring a foreign invasion force to England's shores, he would be bound by his conscience to do all he could to stop it—and she would be responsible for her father's downfall and likely death.

'It would have caused too much fuss to take her from the fair,' Lord Fraser muttered, feeling chilled as he looked into the cold eyes of the man he had come to meet in secret. 'If it can be achieved I would like Anne Marie's disappearance to be a mystery—that way there is less chance of discovery.'

'Why not leave the girl where she is?' Frampton asked. 'She is of little value to the cause. We should act now, swiftly before we are suspected. You waste too much time over an insignificant girl.'

'She is my daughter and her worth to me is greater than you may think. I must consider what may happen if our plan does not succeed...' Lord Fraser broke off as the other man's eyes narrowed to menacing slits. 'I do not suggest that it will not, merely that I need to think of the future for myself and my daughter.'

'It is as well for you that I find you necessary to my plans,' Frampton muttered, and Lord Fraser shivered as he looked into those compelling eyes, then quickly away. Sometimes he thought Frampton could look into his very soul and it scared him, it scared him more than he dared admit even to himself. 'Very well, you may leave the girl to me. We have wasted enough time on this matter. Now tell me, are the others with us…'

Anne Marie spent a restless night. She was haunted by the man with the strange eyes, and had a nagging fear that he had some evil power over her father. She felt instinctively that Lord Fraser's plans were doomed to failure and almost wished that she had confided her fears to Sir Christopher.

Yet how could she have done so? To have spoken of that which she had promised to keep secret might have condemned her father to a traitor's death in the Tower of London. Kit had told her she might trust him, but she had not dared and now it was too late. He had left the castle at first light and she was very much afraid that she would never see him again.

Perhaps it was best that she had not spoken. Sir Christopher had been kind to her. He had seemed almost to promise a future that might hold much happiness, but it would be foolish to hope for too much. His visit had brought her a kind of freedom, but it was over and she expected that her life would be much as it had been before he came.

In that however, she was mistaken. When she went down to the great hall that morning she was met by Thomas Makepeace, who told her that she was to ride every day in future.

'You will be accompanied by two grooms when I

cannot spare the time to ride with you,' he said. 'Sir Christopher was concerned that you should have the chance of beneficial exercise and if I may have your word that you will not try to give the grooms the slip I shall allow it.'

'You are kind, sir. I give my word that I shall do only my duty.'

Anne Marie was conscious of guilt as her guardian accepted her word. She knew that she had not given the promise he had asked of her, for the choice was not entirely hers. If Lord Fraser demanded she go with him, she could only obey. It was her duty as a daughter.

In her heart she hoped that her father would forget her, that he would leave her to her quiet life at the castle, but her common sense told her that he would not. She was needed to serve some purpose or he would not have troubled himself to come for her, and she sensed that the time was near when Lord Fraser would come to fetch her.

Chapter Three

'I believe there is a plot to rescue Mary of Scots,' Kit told Walsingham at their meeting. They spoke deep within the bowels of the old palace of Whitehall, where their words could not be overheard. It was cold, damp and dark, the flaring torches bringing only a flickering light to the gloom of the undercroft. Here beneath ancient stone arches much went on that would not bear the light of day, and many a poor wretch had breathed his last prayer before being taken to the Tower. 'Fraser is involved and half a dozen others, mostly northern Catholics, from what I could gather.'

'How can they hope to succeed with so few?' Walsingham asked and frowned. 'It would take a hundred men or more to storm the castle, and Mary is always watched.'

'I was able to discover only scraps of information, sir, for they keep their business secret as best they can. I have a few names but little more.' Kit hesitated. 'You may curse me for a fool and think my wits have gone awandering, Sir Francis, but I believe there is some idea of using the black arts to spirit Mary of Scots away from beneath the noses of her guards.'

Walsingham swore softly. 'I have known it these many years! There is an enemy I have sensed but never seen with whom I have crossed swords many times. This is his work again. I had thought when John Dee fled to Poland that the threat from that source was at an end, and indeed there has been nothing to make me think otherwise for some years now.'

Kit wrinkled his brow in thought. 'Do you speak of Her Majesty's astrologer? I have heard of Doctor John Dee, a man of some learning and skill in the art of reading charts that tell of the future. Did he not forecast that Queen Mary of England would die and Elizabeth come to the throne shortly before it happened?'

'Aye, so I understand. And had a hand in Mary of England's death mayhap. There are those who accused him of it, and had I my way he would have been dealt with long since. The man was a danger to Her Majesty, though she would not have it so. I had him watched at his home at Mortlake, for 'tis certain he dabbled in the black arts there, but before I could gather enough evidence to arrest him he fled abroad where he has been ever since, though of late I believe he has fallen on hard times. The Pope has condemned him for dabbling in the black arts, and I think he goes in fear of his life—though others court him in the hope that he may yet discover the secret of the Philosopher's Stone.'

'You think Dee may be behind this scheme?'

'I know not for sure, but I have for years been aware of the existence of a master plotter, seeing his hand in a dozen attempts to cause unrest in the country; it seemed for a long time that no irritant was too small, no plan too large for this man. Though I know him not, I have seen him in my dreams, for his hatred haunts me. He is a man of shadows, a man of darkness as someone once named him, a man consumed with hatred for Elizabeth. I was convinced it was none other than Dee, but he is still abroad, though he has hopes of returning to this country, I believe.'

Kit was silent for a moment, remembering a girl's unspoken fear, then, 'Have you heard of a man by the name of Frampton—Bevis Frampton?'

'Frampton?' Walsingham's eyes narrowed. 'I have heard the name before. Why do you ask?'

'I believe he is deeply involved with Lord Fraser. I saw him watching Fraser's daughter when we visited a fair at Norham. There was something odd about him—a strange, chilling look in his eyes that frightened Anne Marie. Indeed, I found it disturbing. It was something that Mistress Fraser said then that set me on the path to discovery. Since leaving Drodney I have discovered that Fraser has been seen several times at Norham meeting openly with the other men, and in secret with Frampton. It seems that Frampton acts through Lord Fraser but has no contact that I could discover with any other of the plotters.'

Walsingham nodded; it was much the pattern he had seen used again and again over the years, the man of shadows never becoming too deeply involved but staying always in the background, controlling others.

'You took Mistress Fraser to the fair?'

'Aye, I did,' Kit answered boldly, though he knew it might anger the other man. 'She is innocent, sir, though I think Fraser might seek to use her through marriage if he could. Mary's escape is but a part of the plot, for they need foreign intervention to invade England and put her in Elizabeth's place. It is in my mind to make it impossible for Fraser to use his daughter for an alliance with some foreign noble.'

'How do you intend to deal with the girl? Her Majesty would not have Mistress Fraser murdered if she is innocent as you say.'

'It was my intention to marry her. She would then be of no further use to Fraser.'

'I see your visit went other than I intended,' Walsingham said with a wry smile. 'But since you bring me valuable information I shall not accuse you of playing me false.'

'I hope rather that you will plead my cause with Her Majesty, since the girl is under her protection.'

'You are bold, sir, and you ask much—but married to you the girl presents no threat. It was in my mind to arrange something of the sort for her. As well wed to you, Sir Christopher, as another. I shall speak to the Queen—but now, tell me all you know of these plotters. Has Fraser returned to Scotland?'

'Nay, I think not.' Kit frowned. 'I have no proof of this but I believe it is in his mind to spirit his daughter away before the attack on Fotheringay, lest she should be used against him in some way.'

'Then you should waste no time in returning to Drodney. Bring the girl back to London and in the meantime I shall do what I can to root out this nest of traitors.'

'And you will speak to Her Majesty on my behalf?'

'Patience, Sir Christopher. Bring the girl to me and I shall decide her fate. In the meantime, there is more important work. I want Fraser and the rest of the conspirators in the Tower where they belong.'

'And Frampton?'

'Yes, I believe it might pay to give Master Frampton a little taste of Her Majesty's hospitality…' The look in Walsingham's eyes chilled Kit and he knew that he would be an enemy to be feared. ''Tis a visit that may be long overdue.'

'He was at Norham when I left, and I have set someone to watching him. If anything happens he will send me word.'

'You may do one more thing for me if you will,' Walsingham said with a nod of his head. 'You may deliver a message for me to someone at Cambridge. He is studying at Benet College and has been in some trouble for his absence—on business for me. I have promised a letter for his tutors that will excuse him.'

'Of course. It will take but a day or so,' Kit acquiesced even though his patience was sorely tried by this request to take a message to another of Walsingham's band of *useful* friends. Only God knew how many spies he employed! 'May I know the name of the gentleman?'

'He bears your own in part,' Walsingham said. 'Christopher Marlowe, a scholar of some merit, who I believe will one day be a great playwright. I have seen something of his work, though none is yet published, and I have faith that we shall see him come to fame.'

'I believe Christopher is a common enough name and often shortened to Kit as in my own case, but it may prove amusing to meet this gentleman. If you will give me the letter I shall see it is delivered, sir.'

'Thank you, Sir Christopher. You may safely leave the fate of Master Frampton and Lord Fraser to me now, but I should advise you to make all speed to Drodney once you have completed my errand—for it would not please the Queen if Mistress Fraser were to disappear…'

It was now ten days since Kit had left for London, and the hard frosts that November brought to this part of England had curtailed Anne Marie's riding expeditions for the moment. For two days it had been too bitter to venture out with the horses, the ground icy and dangerous, but that morning there was a pale sun that had begun to thaw the icicles from the castle walls.

Although the earth was still too hard to risk her precious mare, Anne Marie decided that a brisk walk would clear her head. She had been dreaming these past nights, strange, unpleasant dreams that troubled her when she woke. She could remember very little but knew that they had frightened her, and she sometimes felt listless.

A walk would take away the dull headache that plagued her. Or perhaps it was her heart that ached the most, she thought as she went down to the great hall. She knew it was foolish to think so often of Sir Christopher, but she could not help herself. She missed his smile and the touch of his hand. Were her feelings what the poets described as love? How could she know when she had no one to tell her these things? She only knew that his going had left an aching void in her life.

Oh, she was so foolish! She must forget him.

Beth was speaking to one of the servants in the hall, but at Anne Marie's approach she turned to greet her with a smile on her face.

'Are you going for a walk? It is very cold, Anne Marie. You must be sure to wrap up well, for I would not have you take a chill, my love.'

Her kindness brought a lump to the girl's throat, and on impulse she went to kiss Beth on her plump, soft cheek.

'You are always so thoughtful of me.'

'You know that you are dear to me,' Beth said, giving her an anxious look. Anne Marie had shadows beneath her eyes, and she was too pale. 'You seem tired, my love. I hope you are not ill?'

'It was merely a bad dream that kept me from my rest last night,' she replied. 'I have a little headache and I think I shall feel better for some air.'

'Go then,' Beth said and smiled. She had a few minutes earlier received some news that she believed would please the girl, but it would keep until she returned from her walk. 'We shall work together on your new dress this afternoon, Anne Marie.'

Anne Marie smiled and thanked her, and then, pulling the hood of her cloak over her head, she walked on and out of the door, which led directly to the East Gate.

The wind tore at her cloak and she shivered, feeling its bite. It was so fierce that she almost turned back, but she knew that such bitter cold might mean a fall of snow before long and then she might not be able to get out for some days. When the worst of the winter set in they sometimes became marooned in the castle for days at a time. A heavy fall of snow could make the roads impassable in these hills.

The thought of the long, lonely months ahead weighed heavily on Anne Marie. Would she ever see Kit again? She had begun to think of him as Kit of late, though she knew it was foolish to think of him at all.

He had seemed to like her a little. She believed that he had meant to be kind, and she would never forget his generosity in buying her her own horse, but she believed that once he was back at home he would have other matters on his mind. He would forget her within a month. Why should he remember? He was free to come and go as he wished, and he must know many women—ladies who were more sophisticated and cleverer than she.

Anne Marie could not hope to hold his interest. She knew nothing of life outside the castle, her education stretching only as far as the books that had been provided for her use by Beth Makepeace, and what her guardian had managed to teach her.

She had a little Latin and a little French, some skill at the harp and at needlework. Her life had revolved about the castle, her time given to helping Beth in her stillroom and on occasion nursing the sick. A man of Sir Christopher's stature would want much more from the woman he married. She had been foolish to think of it!

As the sea boiled and thrashed about the rocks below, Anne Marie stood gazing blindly into the distance. Her loneliness at that moment was such that she toyed with the idea of throwing herself into the angry water, letting it drag her down, down to its murky depths.

'You would be a fool to waste your life, Mistress Fraser.'

Startled, she swung round to find herself staring into the strange, compelling eyes of the man she had seen briefly at Norham fair. How was this possible? Was there some secret way from the cove below after all? Or was there something more sinister here?

A trickle of icy fear ran down her spine, and she glanced about her, aware of the isolation of their situation and the danger she was in. Her mouth felt dry, and her breath caught in her throat as she looked at him.

'Who are you, sir? How came you here?'

'You must not ask questions,' he said, his eyes cold, dead and fearful. 'I have come to fetch you. You are to come with me now. Your father awaits you below in the cove. A boat will put into shore tonight and you will be taken out to a ship that rides at anchor in the lee of the cliffs, out of sight of the castle.'

'No!' Anne Marie felt a shaft of fear. This man was evil, she sensed it instinctively, and she resisted him with all her strength, though she felt the power of him, and those eyes compelling her, bending her to his will. 'No, sir. I do not know you. I shall not come with you. You cannot compel me.'

'Foolish girl!' His eyes seemed to glitter with a strange light, the pupils almost silver as he held her gaze and she could not turn away. What was happening to her? She felt herself drawn into his net against her will. Her limbs were useless, for they would not obey her. 'You waste precious time. You shall come with me; I command it. Your father will not move as I direct unless you are safely on your way to France, to the wedding that he has arranged for you that will bring him wealth and influence.'

'No...' Anne Marie tried to break away from the mesmerising gaze of those terrifying eyes. She did not want to go with this man; he frightened her. There was a peculiar smell about him, the smell of sulphur, and it choked her, making it difficult for her to breathe. 'I want to stay here...' The thought was in her mind that Kit might come for her. 'No, I shall not...'

'You will do as I command you. Look into my eyes

and know that you have no will but mine. You are but clay in my hands, and I may do as I will with you. You have nothing to fear if you obey me, but all if you defy me.'

Anne Marie found herself unable to move or speak. His eyes dominated her, preventing her from running away. Her mind was not yet subdued and she tried to fight him, but he was too powerful and her tongue seemed glued to the roof of her mouth, her lips frozen as she tried to speak and mumbled unintelligible sounds.

She was aware of the stench of evil and knew that some terrible force was issuing through the man who compelled her with his eyes. He was the tool of some dread demon and she was helpless against his power. There was nothing she could do as he moved towards her, his eyes holding hers.

'Please…' The thought formed in her mind though she could not speak it. 'Oh, Kit, please come to me. Please save me…'

'You would defy me still?'

He read her mind! Anne Marie gave a little cry as the man raised his hand, moving it across the front of her eyes as if pulling down a curtain, and then she was falling, falling into the blackness of a bottomless pit. She would know nothing more until she wakened to find herself on board a ship bound for France, nor would she remember anything that had taken place here on this lonely clifftop.

'Thank God you have come!' Beth cried as her kinsman strode into the room where she was pacing agitatedly about the floor. 'She has gone, and I fear for her life.'

'Gone?' Kit stared at her in dismay. Leaving his ship in port a little further down the coast, he had ridden throughout the afternoon to get here sooner than his letter had promised, anxious to see Anne Marie once more and tell her of his plans for their future together. 'How can she have gone? She did not break her promise to Thomas that she would not give the grooms the slip?'

'The cold has been too hard for her to ride these past three days,' Beth said, wringing her hands in her anxiety. 'This morning she said she was going to walk as far as the cliffs, as she used to do every day until you bought her the mare. She looked pale and tired, and she kissed me before she left and thanked me for my kindness...' Beth gave a little sob of despair. 'When she did not come back by dinnertime I sent the men to search for her. They found nothing but this...' She held out Anne Marie's silver cross and the green ribbon she had used to display it about her neck. 'It was found right at the edge of the cliff...'

'You cannot think that she...' Kit was aware of a grinding fear in his stomach. 'She would not throw herself down?'

'I cannot think it,' Beth said. 'She has been quiet and pale of late but I thought it was because she...because she missed you, Kit.'

'She knew I would return soon. I told her I would come when I could. I have been longer than I intended because I had to make a detour before I joined my ship at Greenwich. Knowing that the roads might be impassable if the weather worsened, I had previously ordered my ship brought from Devon. When we anchored I saw that it was beginning to snow and I rode through the worst of it on my way here. Anne Marie would surely not choose to run away in such weather?'

Beth wrung her hands in distress. 'Your letter giving word of your intention to visit us again reached me minutes before she went out. If only I had told her! I blame myself for the neglect.'

'Nay, I do not think this mischief is of Anne Marie's making. She would surely not have left her cross behind, for it was precious to her—besides, the ribbon has been torn. I suspect foul play here.'

'That is what Thomas said,' Beth agreed. 'He is out searching with his men as we speak. They have gone down to the village, for the only way into the cove is through the village itself.'

'She could not have found a path down the cliff face?'

'It is much too steep and there are no caves. Had there been any way of escape, Thomas could not have allowed her solitary walks. We were charged to keep her safe as our ward, and I fear it will go hard for Thomas if he is accused of negligence.'

'But how could she have disappeared if no one saw her leave?' Had there been bribery here or something perhaps even more sinister? Kit frowned as he recalled Anne Marie asking if a magician might somehow blind others to what was going on about them. He had known then that she was afraid of something—or someone. 'You are certain there is no way down from the clifftop? And the only way down to the village is through the West Gate?'

'If a cave exists none hereabouts know of it.' Beth's eyes filled with tears. 'She must have been so unhappy to cast herself to a watery grave.'

Kit shook his head. He could not, would not believe that Anne Marie would do such a thing. Her courage and determination to make the best of her life here at the castle had aroused his admiration. Why should she suddenly take her own life?

'Something troubled…' He broke off as he heard footsteps behind him and turned to see Thomas Makepeace stride into the room. 'What news?'

'A small boat was seen to put into the cove just before dusk,' Thomas said. 'We were just too late. It is my belief that they have taken her out to a ship.'

'On a night like this?' Beth shuddered. 'It has been snowing for the past hour and the wind is rising now that it has stopped. They will not dare to put to sea in such weather surely?'

'A ship was seen sheltering just down the coast from here earlier in the day,' Thomas went on as if his wife had not spoken. 'A fisherman went out but found the sea too rough for his business and happened to see the ship riding out the weather in a cove that is not visible from here—tucked just around the curve of the cliff. He said that he has seen the ship in these waters before, and knows her to be the *Belle*

Rosemarie; the master is an Englishman but trades regularly with France. He thinks him a decent man but not above some smuggling if the chance of profit arose. His ship is stout but I doubt that she will put to sea this night. She will lay up until morning and hope for a lull in the storm.'

'Then if I leave now I may return to my own ship and with luck cut her off before she can reach the coast of France.'

'You have your own ship within reach?' Thomas looked at him with dawning hope. 'If you could bring her back to us, Kit.'

'She shall not return here,' Kit said and looked stern. 'Her future lies elsewhere. I have been ordered to take her to London.'

'Mercy on us!' Beth cried. 'She could be imprisoned in the Tower for trying to escape from us. They might torture her...anything! My poor, poor child. She is doomed to an unhappy fate.'

'Not if I have my way,' Kit said and turned. 'I must go. There is no time to waste if I am to have a chance of preventing the *Belle Rosemarie* from reaching France.'

'We must pray that I am right and her master will not put out this night.'

'He cannot know that his vessel has been seen,' Kit said. 'No man of sense would put out on such a night. If he has sheltered in that cove before he must think himself safe from detection. If luck is with us, I may intercept her yet.'

'But you must eat something before you leave,'

Beth said. 'The snow has ceased but it is a raw, bitter night.'

'I thank you for your concern,' Kit replied, a grim look about his mouth. 'But I may eat when I have Anne Marie safe.'

So saying he strode from the room, leaving Beth to stare at her husband in distress.

'We shall speak later, wife,' Thomas said gruffly as he saw the despair in her eyes. 'I must make sure that Kit has a stout horse to see him on his way— and a flask of good brandewine to keep the cold from his bones.'

Beth nodded, but said nothing as he followed Kit from the room, her heart aching for the girl she loved so dearly. Where was Anne Marie? Was she safe? Had she gone of her own free will or had she been forced?

If her husband and Kit were right, the cross had been torn from around her neck. It would take some force to tear the ribbon like that—who could have done such a thing? And why had it been done? Surely there was no reason to deprive Anne Marie of her most treasured possession?

Beth took the cross and put it into a little coffer. She would keep it safe for the girl she loved as a daughter, and perhaps one day she would be able to give it back to her.

'I pray you God to keep her safe,' she whispered. 'Protect her from evil and bring her back to those who love her.'

* * *

Anne Marie choked as someone put a small cup of water to her lips, and opened her eyes. For a moment she stared blankly at the man holding the cup, then she saw his anxious face and blinked.

'Where am I?' she asked. 'How came I here, Father?'

'You were brought here at my request, Daughter. Do you not remember?'

'I remember a little. I was standing at the edge of the cliff and then...' She stared at him in bewilderment. 'I do not know. I was there and now I am here. How can this be?'

The expression in his eyes was very odd, as if he knew something that filled him with fear or horror. 'I was told you had fainted. You have been out of your senses for some time, daughter. I had begun to think that some harm had befallen you.'

'I think I am quite well,' Anne Marie said as she sat up. She pressed a hand to her forehead. 'But my head aches...and I am very thirsty.'

'Drink some of this water,' Lord Fraser pressed her. 'Then I must leave you for the moment. You are quite safe, Daughter. Captain Wilcox is a good, honest man, and you will be met when you reach France. I shall join you in a few weeks.'

'Are you not to come with me?' Anne Marie stared at him. It was all so confusing. She wished that she might remember how she had come here but her mind seemed blank concerning this. 'Why are you sending me to France, Father?'

'You will be safe there,' her father said. 'You will

not remember, Anne Marie, but your mother was a Frenchwoman and from an influential family. I am sending you to your cousins and a marriage will be arranged for you soon.'

'I am to marry someone I do not know?'

She stared at him, a chill creeping over her. No! She could not marry some stranger when—when her heart was given to another. For surely that was what had happened to her? She did love Sir Christopher. Yet she would never see him again. He had gone away and in all likelihood forgotten her. Besides, her duty was to her father. Oh, what choice had she? She was here and she would be forced to obey.

'Your cousin Pierre Dupont is a handsome fellow and wealthy,' Lord Fraser replied. 'He has asked for this alliance and has promised to aid me in my cause if I send you to him. His last wife died in childbed and he needs a good, obedient girl to be a mother to his son.'

'How old is he?'

'His age has nothing to the point,' her father replied sternly. 'You are my daughter and you will obey me in this.'

Anne Marie lowered her eyes and sighed. Her head did ache so much and it seemed that she had no choice but to do as her father ordered her. Besides, it had been foolish to dream of another or of the freedom to please herself. She was a pawn, a thing to be moved at another's direction. One side or the other had used her all her life and it seemed she was to be bartered once again.

'Yes, Father. I shall obey you. I must rest now.' Her will to resist had gone for the moment. All she wanted was to sleep. She was so very tired.

'*He* said it would be so once you came to your senses.' Anne Marie felt the touch of her father's hand upon her brow. 'I must leave you, Daughter. I am needed here for the time being, but as soon as the way is clear I shall come to you. Fear not, Anne Marie, there will be honours in plenty for the future. You shall be fêted and made much of when I am chosen to sit beside Mary on the thrones of England and Scotland.'

Lord Fraser's voice seemed to come from a long, long way away as Anne Marie drifted into sleep. She was having a dream. None of this was real. She would wake up in her tower room at the castle and all would be as it always had been.

The storm was raging about the ship, which was tossed upon the waves like so much matchwood, its mast brought down by gusting wind that had hit them some two hours after they had left the shelter of the English cove.

'You should stay below,' Captain Wilcox had told Anne Marie when she had tried to go on deck earlier. 'My men have too much to do trying to save the ship to look after you, Mistress Fraser.'

'Are we going to sink?' She looked at him fearfully. 'I heard a fearful crashing sound…'

'The main mast came down,' he replied, 'but we are not holed. I should have stayed longer in port but

I was told it was urgent to get you to France. Now all we can do is to ride it out and wait for the storm to abate. When it is calmer we can rig up some kind of a sail and limp home.'

Anne Marie nodded, and went back below. She was feeling a little queasy, the tossing motion of the ship making her want to vomit. A few minutes after she was back in her cabin she was sick, not once but several times. Feeling too ill to think of anything but the danger of their situation, she crawled back on to the bunk bed provided and hugged herself as she felt the pain in her stomach.

She had eaten nothing for hours, and had retched the last time on an empty stomach. This was beyond her worst nightmare, and she almost felt it would be a relief if the ship went down. At least if she drowned she would not feel so very ill.

Oh, why had her father sent her on this ship? She wished that she might be back with Beth at the castle and tears filled her eyes as she thought of her friend. Beth would be so worried about her—and Thomas might be dismissed from his post as warden of Drodney because she had escaped. Where would they live then? She hated to think of her friends in trouble because of her.

Why had she run away? It hadn't been in her mind when she went out for her walk. Had she been ordered to leave—or persuaded? She wished that she might remember but she could not. She remembered feeling very unhappy and then…nothing.

Oh, would this wretched storm never be over?

Anne Marie closed her eyes and prayed for release. Her hand reached out for the cross she always wore and discovered it was missing. What had happened to it?

She would never have left it behind if she had intended to escape. A picture flashed into her mind and she seemed to feel it being torn from her in rage and fear—but was the picture real or merely her imagination?

Why should someone tear a cross from about her neck? Her father would never have done it. What kind of a man would want to rob her of her mother's cross? It was silver but of no great value.

It puzzled her and she wished again that she could remember how she came here. She had been standing at the top of the cliffs and then...only darkness.

There was no way down to the sea from the clifftop, at least none that she knew. So she must have been taken somehow: but by whom and how?

It was so strange that she should have no memory of what had happened to her. A shiver ran through her and she felt an icy chill at the nape of her neck. She had a sense of some evil having been near her, and she crossed herself, whispering a prayer for God's forgiveness and protection.

'If I have sinned show me Thy mercy,' she whispered and wished for the comfort of her mother's cross. 'Show me what I must do, for I am lost and have no help but Thee.'

A feeling of peace came over her as she prayed, and closing her eyes once more she slept.

* * *

The storm had abated. Anne Marie could feel the difference when she woke. She was no longer sick to her stomach and her headache had cleared. She found some water in an ewer. It was warm and brackish but it eased her thirst a little. As she was wondering what to do next someone knocked at the cabin door.

'May I come in, Mistress Fraser?'

'Yes, captain.' Anne Marie put a hand to her hair. It felt tangled and untidy and she was aware that she needed to wash.

'I have brought you food and ale,' Captain Wilcox told her as he entered. 'We have no warm water for you to wash but if you can make do with cold I shall have a bucket brought to you.'

'Thank you, that is kind. May I come up on deck later?'

'In an hour or so perhaps,' he replied. 'At the moment the men are clearing the deck. Once we have rigged up some kind of sail we shall be able to get under way again.'

'How soon shall we be in France?'

'Not until after nightfall,' he replied. 'But do not fear, mistress. I shall see you safely to an inn where you may wait for your cousins.'

'Thank you…' she began and then stopped as she heard voices shouting above them. 'What is that?'

Suddenly there was a terrific roar and she looked at him in fright. 'What is happening?'

'Someone has just put a shot across our bows,' Captain Wilcox replied with a frown. 'Stay here, Mistress Fraser. I shall go up and see what is happening. I do not think it can be pirates in these waters, but mayhap an unfriendly ship…'

Anne Marie watched as he left the cabin, feeling her knees go weak. She had thought herself safe after the storm but now she wondered what could happen next. Who had fired on them—and why? Could it possibly be something to do with her? Surely not! She was not important enough for anyone to come after her.

There was a little water left in the ewer. Anne Marie wetted a corner of her gown and used it to wipe over her face and hands. It didn't make her feel much better, but there was nothing more she could do for the moment. She looked at the bread and meat the captain had brought her but pushed it away, her appetite gone as she wondered what was going on above her head. Did someone imagine Lord Fraser was on board? Had his plans to rescue Mary of Scots been discovered? Would they both find themselves in the Tower before nightfall?

Christopher gave the order to put a shot across the bows of the *Belle Rosemarie* as a warning. He had been chasing it for some time, gradually gaining on the slower vessel with a grim determination, and he meant to brook no defiance from its captain. If they did not yield he would board and fight his way to Anne Marie!

Yet the vessel was a merchantman and unarmed, and already he could see the panic spreading among the crew as they feared for their lives. Kit's ship was a fighting craft and his men well used to taking their prize. He saw that there would be no resistance and his grim expression softened a little. He had no particular quarrel with the captain—providing no harm had come to the girl. Yet if he should find her father or the man who had abducted her…Kit's mouth drew into an angry line. They should feel the full force of retribution in the Tower!

'What do you mean by this, sir?' The captain blustered as Kit swung aboard, his tall powerful figure domineering the other man. 'You have violated international law and your Queen shall hear a protest from my ambassador.'

'Think yourself lucky if you do not swing from the yardarm before another hour has passed,' Kit said so savagely that the captain turned pale. 'Tell me at once—the girl you abducted…'

'I abducted no one,' the captain said indignantly. 'Her father paid me to take her to France and you have no right…' He was silenced as Kit moved towards him and he was seized by his jerkin and held dangling, his feet swinging above the deck. 'She is below and unharmed, sir. I swear it.'

'Pray that she is of the same opinion,' Kit said and dropped him so that he fell to his knees. 'Pray for your life, sirrah, for if I find otherwise you are dead.'

Hearing the tread of heavy feet outside her cabin, Anne Marie steeled herself, fearing the worst. She turned as the door opened, her head raised proudly as she waited for whoever it was to enter.

'Mistress Fraser...'

Anne Marie stared in astonishment, her heart racing wildly, so wildly that she could scarcely breathe let alone answer him for some seconds. He was here! For a moment her whole being seemed to flood with happiness, but then she saw the expression on his face and her feeling of happiness died.

'Sir Christopher! What are you doing here?' she managed when she could find the breath to speak.

He was glaring at her, a look of displeasure in his dark eyes.

'I came to rescue you,' he said. 'But it seems you came here willingly—or so Captain Wilcox tells me.'

'Willingly?' Her heart was jerking with fright now as she saw that he was angry. Yes, of course he was angry, for he thought her faithless and uncaring. 'I—I do not know. I think my father commanded me and I obeyed.'

'Do you always obey your father?'

Anne Marie found that she could breathe again. 'Is it not the duty of a daughter to obey her father?'

Kit knew that she had him there, for it was the duty of a daughter to obey her father's wishes, but it made him angry that she had run away from him, when she must have known that he was coming back for her. If she had any feeling for him she would surely not have done so!

'It depends whether or not what her father commands is treason.'

Anne Marie's hand flew to her throat. He sounded as if he was threatening her, as if he believed she deserved to be punished. Pride came to her rescue as she lifted her head to meet his furious gaze.

'You may think it treason, sir,' she said, appearing calmer than she felt. 'But for my father it is duty—to his Queen. Mary of Scots has been a prisoner too long. It is time she was freed.'

'Have a care what you say, mistress,' Kit warned, his mouth harsh and his eyes cold. 'If anyone else should hear such treason you would be sent to the Tower and I could do nothing to save you.'

'You should have let me go to France,' Anne Marie said, and wondered at herself. She did not want to go to France to be married to her cousin—but she did not like it when Sir Christopher looked at her this way. She had done nothing wrong! 'It would have been better for all concerned.'

'That is a matter of opinion,' Kit replied, plainly angry. 'I have been ordered to take you to London. It is for others to decide what is best for you, Mistress Fraser. Your father's treachery has been discovered, and no doubt he will join you in the Tower ere long.'

'My father...' Anne Marie's hand crept to her throat once more. She knew what must be Lord Fraser's fate if he were captured. 'I pray that you are wrong, sir.'

'You condemn yourself, Mistress Fraser.'

She had not meant that she wanted her father's plans to succeed, merely that Lord Fraser should not be taken, but she could see that he believed the worst.

'I meant only...' she faltered as she saw his expression, her head going up proudly once more. She would not grovel, even to him.

'You must come with me now,' Kit said. 'Have you nothing with you? No clothes—no possessions?'

'Nothing,' she replied and felt the sting of tears behind her eyes. But she would not give way to them, for tears were weakness and she had learned to hide them. 'Where are you taking me?'

'To London,' he said, his face hard, expressionless. 'It is as I am ordered...and I must obey my orders.'

He was saying that he would obey his orders as she had obeyed her father. She looked at his stern features and her heart sank. She had thought she knew Sir Christopher and believed she loved him, and also that he cared something for her, but this man was a stranger. She did not know him, and she was a little afraid of him. He would take her to London, and there...she shut out the thoughts of what might happen to her.

She would not think about that yet.

Chapter Four

The cabin she had been brought to after the transfer from the *Belle Rosemarie* to the *Golden Fleece* was larger and more comfortable than the one she had been in previously, and must obviously belong to its captain, Anne Marie thought. The ship set sail almost immediately, and she had been left alone with her thoughts, which, considering that she expected to find herself in the Tower before many days had passed, were less than pleasant.

However, she had been alone only a few minutes when someone knocked at the door and then a young cabin boy entered. He was bearing a tray with a cup of wine, a small ewer of water and a plate of sweet biscuits, also some dried figs and other fruits.

'Captain says he begs your pardon for the poor fare, mistress, but a meal shall be prepared later, and he will join you here for supper.'

Anne Marie ran the tip of her tongue over her lips. She was hungry, for she had not eaten for many hours now, but she felt dirty and her most pressing need was for a wash.

'Thank you,' she said as he deposited the tray upon what was clearly the captain's desk, for there were instruments used for navigation and some charts lying there. 'What is your name please?'

'Ned, Mistress Fraser.'

'Well, Ned, do you think it would it be possible for me to have some more water so that I may wash?'

'Cook is heating some water now, Mistress. Captain's hipbath is behind here…' He crossed the floor of the cabin to pull aside a curtain, which revealed a small wooden tub. He pulled it out into the room, then turned to grin at her. 'Captain says you'll find all you need in that chest by the window, mistress. Two of us will bring water to fill this, and empty it when you've done. You can lock the door for privacy, mistress.'

Anne Marie smiled and thanked him. His cheerful, friendly manner had lifted her spirits and she sat down to eat and drink, finding the wine good and the fruit both sweet and succulent. By the time she had finished her meal, the cabin boy had returned with another man. Again they knocked before entering and spoke to her respectfully as they prepared the bath for her comfort.

'Captain sends his respects and asks that he may dine with you in two hours,' the older man said. 'He begs that you will make free of anything you find in his cabin.'

'Yes, Ned told me,' she said. 'I thank your captain for his consideration. May I know his name please?'

'Why, 'tis Sir Christopher Hamilton,' the sailor replied. 'You are on board his ship, Mistress Fraser.'

'Oh, I did not realise it was Sir Christopher's own ship,' she said, her heart racing. 'I—I see, thank you.'

After the sailors had left, Anne Marie went to lock the door of the cabin, then opened the sea chest that had been pointed out to her. To her surprise she discovered that there were not only all the things she would need for bathing inside, but also several items of female clothing. Taking them out one by one, she found an overskirt of soft green silk, matching bodice and petticoats and even silken hose.

Had Sir Christopher meant her to make use of these things? They were clearly expensive and more stylish than any gown she had ever worn, and Anne Marie laid them reverently on the bed, stroking the fine material with her fingertips.

Both Ned and the older man had told her she was to use anything she found in the cabin, and Anne Marie decided that she would take them at their word. She carried the soap, brush and towel over to the hip-bath, and then slipped out of her clothes.

The water felt so good! It was warm but not too hot, and she sighed as she felt the luxury of it fold over her. When she had asked for water to wash she had not expected such luxury as this. Even at the castle a bath had been something special, and allowed her only once a month. Often in the winter she had been forced to make her ablutions in water that was barely above freezing.

Anne Marie used the little brush to scrub at her skin, enjoying the scent of the soft soap that had been provided for her comfort; it was highly perfumed, and she suspected that it had been purchased with a woman in mind. Perhaps she was not the first woman to be a guest in Sir Christopher's cabin? It seemed likely, for she did not imagine he would use soap like this for himself.

Yes, there must have been others. Why else would there be a gown in his sea chest?

The thought was not pleasing and she put it from her mind. She knew so little of men and the world outside the castle, but she believed that her father had taken mistresses in the past, for she had heard Beth say as much to Thomas. Perhaps it was the way of men; she had no one to guide her, for her guardian had never spoken to her of these things.

A little frown creased Anne Marie's forehead as she wondered exactly what Sir Christopher had in mind for her. She was not sure how long it would take for the ship to reach London, but she doubted it would be before nightfall. He had sent word that he intended to share his supper with her—did he intend also that he should share a bed with her? Was that why the cabin boy had been grinning at her? Did the crew believe that their captain intended to bed her?

Although ignorant of so many things, Anne Marie was not unaware of the intimate relationship between men and women. She had seen birth and death in the cottages of Drodney village, and also lovers walking hand in hand, gazing into each other's eyes. She had also seen the mating of horses in the castle courtyard, the ram put to the ewes, and so had some idea of the cycle of life. Beth had scolded many a serving wench for allowing one of the men at arms to bed her, and a child had often been the aftermath of that disgrace.

Would Sir Christopher take such cruel advantage of her? Anne Marie wondered. Her instincts cried out against it. He was a gentleman and he had shown her nothing but kindness…at least he had been kind to her until that confrontation on the *Belle Rosemarie*.

Anne Marie bit her lip. He had been very angry with her then, but indeed it was not her fault. She had not wanted to run away from him…now where had that thought come from?

She tried to remember what had happened on that windswept clifftop and failed. It was as if there was only darkness in her mind concerning that time, but she was somehow certain that she had not wanted to run away. She did not know what had happened, and yet she was sure that it had been against her will to leave.

Lost in her thoughts, Anne Marie became aware that the water was turning cold. She climbed out and dried herself, wrapping the generous cloth about her. She had washed her hair and she sat down on the bed, rubbing at it for some time to dry it as best she could, then dressed in the pretty silk gown. She had found a comb and was beginning to pull the tangles from her hair when someone knocked at the door, and she went to answer it, expecting it to be the cabin boy come to carry away the water.

Opening it, she gave a little gasp as she saw it was Sir Christopher himself, her cheeks flushing as she stepped back to admit him.

'I see the gown fits you,' Kit said looking at her thoughtfully. 'Perhaps a slightly darker shade of green might have been better—but it will do for the moment, I dare say.'

'It was very kind of you to say that I might borrow it...'

'It was bought for you,' he replied and frowned. 'But I came too soon. You are not ready.'

'I think I stayed overlong in the bath. It was such luxury,' Anne Marie said, 'and one I did not think to meet with on a ship, sir.'

'When we have been at sea for months the only water it sees is salt,' Kit replied with a wry smile. 'Which is a necessity for health, Mistress Fraser, else we should all stink worse than a dead rat, but most of us prefer to be clean—even if it means a dip in the ocean. I've thrown many a cabin boy in fully clothed rather than put up with his stink another day.'

Ignoring this sally, Anne Marie raised her clear eyes to his. 'If the gown was intended for me, you always meant to bring me on board this ship—was it always your intention to take me to London?'

'It had been in my mind to remove you from the castle of Drodney for some time,' Kit replied, eyes narrowed. 'Why do you ask?'

'Why did you come to the castle, sir?' Anne Marie

looked at him suspiciously. 'You said that my father's treachery was discovered—did you play some part in that?'

'I cannot lie to you,' he said. 'It was my duty to expose Lord Fraser's treachery and I but did my duty.'

'You used me!' Anne Marie's eyes suddenly flashed with temper as she realised that she must somehow have helped to give her father away. 'You pretended to care about me, to feel something towards me—and all the time you were trying to trap me. Everything you said to me was a lie! You gained my confidence in order that I might betray my father— and I did. I was a fool to trust you.'

'That is not true,' Kit said though he knew that her accusations were justified in part. 'I asked you to trust me, Anne Marie. Had you done so I might have been able to save Lord Fraser from his own foolishness. I might have spoken to him, persuaded him that his plans were doomed to failure and that he should forget them.'

'He would never listen to you. He would hate you as an enemy as—as I do!' Her head was up, a hard glitter in her eyes. 'I shall not forgive you for what you have done, sir.'

'Do not be so foolish, Anne Marie…' Kit advanced towards her. 'All is not lost if you will but listen to me…'

'Why should I listen to anything you say?'

She flew at him in sudden rage, beating at his chest

with her fists, and all the time knowing it was useless but driven beyond bearing by his cruel betrayal.

'You care nothing for me! You will see me cast into the…'

'Be quiet, you little fool,' Kit muttered, then he caught her wrists, holding them as he pulled her hard against him. He was breathing fast as he gazed down into her face, and then he gave a little moan, and catching her to him he lowered his head to kiss her. His mouth was hungry, demanding, as it devoured hers, sending shivers winging down her spine. At first she fought him, struggling against him like a bird in a net with no hope of winning free, but then she felt her will melting and she quietened, leaning her head against his shoulder as he released her mouth at last.

'That is better,' he said, a little smile on his face as he let her go. 'I always suspected that meek face was a disguise, and now I see that I was right. You have a temper, Anne Marie.' There was satisfaction in his face and she saw that her loss of control had pleased him.

'You think you may do with me as you will,' she accused him angrily. 'I dare say you imagine I shall fall willingly into your arms. But I warn you that I shall fight you if you seek to seduce me, sir. I may be naïve but I am not a fool.'

Kit stared at her, then threw back his head and laughed. Did the wench imagine that he had plied her with comforts merely to tumble her? He could not deny that he was tempted, for in that gown with her hair still damp and hanging down her back in a scented mass she presented a delicious prospect for any red-blooded man.

'But I am so much stronger than you,' he pointed out, driven by some devil to tease her. 'What is to stop me throwing you on that bed and taking my fill of you?'

'You—you devil!' Anne Marie cried. 'Oh, I was a fool ever to trust you. I hate you. Do you hear me, sir? I hate you!'

'Your lips belie your words, mistress,' Kit said knowing that he truly deserved the name she called him, for if he were fair to her he would put her mind at ease and tell her what he intended. 'But perhaps I may offer something that would change your mind?'

'Nothing would change my mind. I would rather die than submit to such—such wickedness.'

'Come, Anne Marie.' Kit's eyes danced with mischief. 'I cannot believe that you would rather find yourself a prisoner in the Tower than my mistress.'

'I am not to be so easily bought. I am innocent of any complicity in my father's treason, and shall soon be freed when the Queen hears my story.'

'And what is your story?'

'That I...' She stared at him for a moment, then shook her head. 'I do not know...' she whispered as the fight suddenly drained out of her. 'I do not know how I came to be on that ship, sir. I swear it was not of my choosing.'

'But you must remember, surely?' Kit's eyes narrowed, losing their teasing sparkle as he saw the way her whole body drooped. 'Were you taken against your will? Did someone render you unconscious in the struggle?'

'I cannot remember,' Anne Marie confessed. He saw a hint of tears in her lovely eyes and realised that she was sorely distressed by her inability to remember. 'I was alone on the cliffs thinking…and then I woke to find my father giving me a cup of water. He said that I had been out of my senses for some hours and he was worried about me. From what he said I do not think he was present when…I was taken.'

'Your father was not on board the *Belle Rosemarie* when you left port?'

'No, for he said he had work to do and would join me in France when he could. I do not know where he went or what he planned, for he revealed nothing to me. I believe there was some plan to rescue Mary of Scots, but I was told nothing of it.'

Kit nodded, his eyes narrowed as he looked at her intently. 'Captain Wilcox said you were to be married to your cousin. He swears that he did not know you had been smuggled from the castle, and that he was told only that you were Lord Fraser's daughter travelling to her wedding in France.'

'My father told me he had arranged it, but—it was the first I knew of the match, though I suspected it was in his mind.' Her eyes were dark with unconscious appeal for understanding as she gazed up at him. 'I—I did not wish for it, Kit. Truly, you must believe me. I would not have left Beth without a word, for I know she must be worried.'

'She knows that I have come after you, and word

shall be sent to her as soon as it is possible. Once we are at home I shall see that a message is sent to her.'

'At home?' Anne Marie was puzzled. 'I do not understand you, sir. I thought I was to be taken to the Tower?'

'My orders were to take you to London. I said nothing of the Tower—*that* was your thought, Anne Marie.'

'You did say it,' she cried eyes flashing. 'Do not lie to me. You were angry and threatened me.'

'If I did then it was said in a moment of temper and I did not mean it,' he apologised. 'I had been anxious for your safety and spoke too hastily. For that much I ask you to forgive me.'

'How am I to believe anything you say after the way you deceived me when you came to the castle?'

'It was not my wish to deceive you, but I have my duty to the State. But I swear that I do not lie to you now. My intention is to take you to my home where you will be safe.'

She was silent for a moment, measuring him. 'Is your home in London? I thought…' Her breath caught in her throat as she saw something in his eyes.

'My home is in Devon. I am taking you there, to my mother. I shall leave you with her while I ride to London and speak to…someone concerning you.' His gaze narrowed. 'It is my belief that you were taken against your will, Anne Marie, for your cross was found at the edge of the cliff. It looked as if it had been torn away, for the ribbon was broken and shredded. Beth has it now and will keep it safe for you until it can be returned.'

'My cross?' Her hand went to her throat as if she missed it. 'Yes, I knew it had gone and I am certain I was wearing it when…I think it was taken from me.'

'Do you begin to remember?'

'No. I remember only that I was very frightened before the darkness came.'

'It is very strange,' Kit said, feeling vaguely uneasy. There was some mystery here, some hint of the unnatural that chilled him and made him think of Walsingham's words. Had this *Man of Darkness* Walsingham seemed to fear had some hand in this affair? 'But perhaps it was caused by a fall or a blow to the head. I have heard of such things before. Is your head sore?'

'No. I had a headache when I woke, but the bath took it away. I feel very much better now.'

'And you have forgotten to be angry with me,' Kit said. He smiled at her. 'I do not wish us to be enemies, Anne Marie, and I apologise if I have hurt you. This matter of your father…' he paused, considering how best to tackle the subject without offending her.

'Has he been arrested?'

'That is something I may be able to discover when I go to London,' he replied. 'I can promise nothing, Anne Marie. Lord Fraser has plotted against Her Majesty and his life is forfeit—but I would plead for him to be made a prisoner instead. I cannot promise that my plea will be listened to but I shall try.'

'You are generous, sir—and I was wrong to fly at

you the way I did.' She hung her head, clasping her hands in front of her as she strove for calm.

'Do not apologise, and do not pretend to be so meek,' Kit replied, his mouth twisting wryly. 'I know you now, mistress, and I prefer the termagant to the saint.'

'You mock me!' His taunts stung her and her head went up proudly, making Kit laugh at her reaction.

'Indeed, I do—and I fear we shall have some merry fights over it, mistress, ere we are done. Now I shall leave you while you complete your toilette and my men clear away the bath—and then I shall return to dine with you. If you will permit?'

'You know very well that you will do exactly as you please!'

Kit inclined his head. 'I see that you understand me,' he murmured wickedly. 'Do not hide your hair, Anne Marie. It looks well as it is. I shall return very soon.'

With that he turned and left her to stare after him. He was a man of contradictions, at one moment kind and gentle as he teased, the next stern and uncompromising. Indeed, she did not know how to take him.

What was in his mind concerning her? He had told her he was taking her to his home—did that mean that he had every intention of making her his mistress as he had threatened?

Her heart was beating madly and she was not sure how she felt about that, though for one moment in his arms she would have counted the world well lost for love.

* * *

Anne Marie spent a restless night tossing in Kit's bed, which he did not share with her. He had after all not taken supper with her, for the ship had run into a bank of fog as it glided like a ghost down the coast of England, and she was left to eat alone. Her mind was restless, her thoughts worrying at her as a dog with a rat in a hole.

Several times she went to the porthole to look out, but it was impossible to see anything, and the stillness that hung over the ship seemed to cut out all sound, as if they were hidden in a blanket. The motion of the ship was gentle but she was aware of the water lapping the sides of the vessel, giving it a rocking motion.

It was of course a relief to know that she would not be sent immediately to the Tower, though if the Queen was angry when she learned of the plot against her, it might be that Anne Marie would eventually be sent to join her father. He would of course be confined in the Tower if he was arrested.

She prayed that he had not been caught, because she was a dutiful girl and though she had never known him well enough to love him, she wished him safe.

Would she ever see Beth again? With the future so uncertain Anne Marie felt that it was perhaps unlikely, but perhaps Kit would allow her to write to her former guardian. She would ask him when they reached their destination.

Her thoughts turned to Kit's home and the mother he had spoken of. Anne Marie had never been to the south of England, nor had she lived in a small country house such as she imagined the Hamiltons' home to be. What would it be like? Was she to be a prisoner there as she had been at the castle?

The inclement weather conditions continued for some days, which meant that the *Golden Fleece* could only limp to her home port in Devon, and during all that time, Anne Marie saw Kit only briefly.

She was allowed to go up on deck for some air for short periods, but there was little to see because of the dense fog, though once she caught sight of a light from a ship they passed and heard the men calling to each other as if in warning. It was an eerie feeling, and Anne Marie went on deck only when the cabin began to feel as if it were closing in on her. Would this journey never be over? And why was Kit ignoring her?

She spent endless hours sitting alone, her thoughts far from happy as she pondered the future, and then at last she heard his footsteps and the knock that heralded Kit's arrival. She drew a deep breath as she called out that he might enter, her hands curling at her sides as she waited for him to speak.

'You will forgive me for the neglect,' he said, his eyes moving over her face, noting the signs of tiredness caused by yet another restless night. 'I fear the journey tires you, Anne Marie. I had thought it easier for you than days of hard riding, but I had not reckoned with this damned fog!'

'Indeed, I have been very comfortable, sir,' she answered, as formal as he. He had become almost distant towards her, and it was as if that kiss had never happened. Perhaps he was already regretting his decision to disobey his orders and take her back to Devon rather than to London. 'It is not your hospitality that keeps me sleepless.'

'You are worrying about your father?'

Anne Marie dropped her gaze as she replied, 'He was foolish to become involved in a plot that could surely never have succeeded—but I would not have him lose his head for it.'

Kit swore beneath his breath as he saw her pale face. He would not have caused her this pain for the world, but Fraser was a traitor and his duty had been to England and Queen Elizabeth.

'If there is aught I can do it shall be done, Anne Marie.'

She acknowledged his words with a faint smile, but she knew that he would be able to do little for Lord Fraser if he were caught. Besides, her sleeplessness had not been caused merely by fear for her father.

'You are considerate, sir.'

'Try not to worry too much for the future,' he said gently. 'I am but a rough brute of a sea captain and I do not have the manners of a gentleman of the court, but when I set my mind to something I do it.'

Now what did he mean by that? His smile and gentle tone had reassured her in part, for he seemed to be saying that he would have a care for her future—but in what way? Had he taken her response when he kissed her for acquiescence in his plans to make her his mistress—and how did she feel about it if he had?

'You frighten me, sir. I do not understand you.'

'There is nothing to fear. I give you my word.' He frowned. 'You must grow weary here in the cabin. Why do you not come on deck more?'

'I did not wish to be in the way when your crew are so concerned for the ship.'

'You will not be in the way,' he said and smiled at her. 'Come with me now and I will show you how we steer the ship.'

She hesitated for a moment, then shook her head. 'I prefer to stay here for the moment, sir.'

Kit's brow furrowed and she could see that her answer had displeased him. Almost at once she wished she had given him a different response, but stubbornness held her back. He might profess to be concerned for her, but nothing could change the fact that he had lied to her—he had set out to trap her father!

She remained silent and he went away, leaving her to the solitude of her thoughts once more. If only she had some material she could use for her drawing, or an embroidery frame and some silks!

Getting up, Anne Marie went to the porthole and looked out. She thought the fog might be lifting, for she could see something in the distance. It looked like the shoreline but she could not be sure, for in another moment it had disappeared into the fog once more. She sighed as she went to sit down again.

Would this journey never end? And what would happen to her when it finally did?

* * *

'I fear you have had a wretched journey, my dear,' said Lady Sarah Hamilton as she drew Anne Marie into a warm embrace. 'What my son was thinking of to force you to travel in such weather I do not know— but men are always so thoughtless.'

The fog had at last cleared, and once on land the sun had appeared from behind the clouds, making the last part of their journey pleasant enough. A gentle horse had been provided for Anne Marie and she had ridden beside Kit through countryside that delighted her. Despite the austerity of winter, the landscape had a gentle prettiness that was missing from the Border country, and she thought that it would be delightful in spring. If she was still here to see it by then!

But she must not think of the future! She had decided that she would take each day as it came, and for the moment there was nothing to disturb or upset her. Lady Sarah was a pretty, plump woman with soft brown eyes that smiled most of the time. There were occasions when her eyes and face were shadowed with sorrow, but that was because she was still in mourning for her beloved husband. Her nature was clearly to be cheerful and kind, and it was obvious that she was trying to gather the threads of her shattered life and look to the future.

'It was so thoughtful of Kit to bring you to me,' his mother exclaimed, as she drew the girl into her small parlour. It was a warm, comfortable room that would be sunny for most of the year, the walls panelled in soft light oak, and the floor made of the same material and brushed with sweet herbs that gave it a faint perfume. 'For I am sorely in need of a companion, and it will be a delight to me to have you in my home, Anne Marie.'

'You are kind, Lady Hamilton,' Anne Marie replied with a little blush. What had Kit told his mother concerning her? She seemed to be welcoming her as a guest rather than a prisoner. 'This is such a lovely house—and so warm. At the castle it is always cold.'

'Yes, I imagine it must have been,' Lady Hamilton frowned slightly. 'I always think that Beth and her husband would do better to retire to a home of their own. I dare say Thomas might do a dozen things that would bring him as much revenue, and it would be more comfortable for Beth.' She smiled encouragingly at Anne Marie. 'I have had a fire lit in your bedchamber these past three days, my dear. As soon as I heard Kit was bringing you here; I know you must have been so uncomfortable on that wretched ship.'

'Oh, it was not wretched,' Anne Marie said. 'It was far more comfortable than the *Belle Rosemarie*.'

'You have been on another ship?'

'Briefly,' Kit answered for her. 'Do not plague Anne Marie with questions, Mother. I will tell you everything later. I dare say your guest would like to rest for a while before we dine.'

Lady Hamilton frowned at her son, but said no more on the subject as she led the way up a wide wooden staircase, showing Anne Marie into a pretty chamber on the first floor.

'This is for me?' Anne Marie looked about her with delight. 'But it is lovely. Am I really to sleep here?'

The bed was a half-tester, with a brocaded silk canopy hanging above the head. There were matching covers and curtains at the windows, which looked out to a beautiful view of gentle rolling downs, trees and a small stream meandering into the distance. Also in the room were various chests, stools, and a table by the window with a chair that had two arms and cushions to the back, and something that intrigued her.

'Pray what is that box with the sloping lid, ma'am?'

'Why, open it and see,' Lady Hamilton said with a smile. 'Kit had it sent down from London for you, I believe.'

Opening the lid, Anne Marie looked inside and caught her breath as she saw that it was divided into sections. In the top section there were various brushes and a pensel, and beneath in the deeper well lay a selection of materials used for making colours.

'It is a painting box,' Anne Marie exclaimed. 'I see now why the lid slopes to that little ridge—I can rest my paper against it when I am working.'

'Yes, I thought that was what it must be,' Lady Hamilton said. 'Beth told me that you draw a little, my dear. You must show me something one day.'

'My book was left behind...' Anne Marie drew a shaky breath. 'But this is so much better. I have always wished for some colours to bring my pictures to life.'

'I think that your life in the castle has not been

always happy,' Lady Hamilton said. 'I do not know the whole of your story, my dear, for Kit has not yet told me—and I shall not pry. But I want you to know that you are welcome here for as long as you wish to stay. And I hope that will be a long time, for I have often wished for a daughter to keep me company. I have wished that my son might take a wife, but he does not seem to think of marriage.'

Anne Marie felt the sting of tears, but blinked them away. Her hostess's kindness overwhelmed her, and she thought that she would like to stay here in this beautiful, warm house for ever. Yet she dare not hope for too much, for the summons to London might come at any time and then she might find herself Her Majesty's guest in the Tower! She had not forgotten Lord Fraser's warning, for he had told her that her life might be forfeit if he broke his bond not to con-spire against Queen Elizabeth.

'You are so generous, ma'am,' she said. 'But I think that you should know that my father is a traitor and may be arrested at any moment—and it was his intention to send me to France.'

'I had guessed most of it,' Lady Hamilton said. 'For Beth Makepeace writes often to me, and she told me that your father was headstrong and that she feared he might one day attempt something of the sort. Her concern was for you—for what punishment might fall on you if your father was too reckless.'

'If—if Sir Christopher had not rescued me I should probably be in France now. Lord Fraser was sending me to my mother's family…'

'And would that have pleased you?' Sarah Hamilton's soft brown eyes rested on her face with gentle inquiry.

'I do not know…no, it would not,' Anne Marie said with a surge of frankness. 'I think I would rather be here than anywhere else in the world.'

Sarah Hamilton laughed, her intuition telling her much that neither her son nor this girl was likely to confess just yet.

'Then I am glad that Kit did what he did, though it was an impetuous act and we must wait to see what comes of it.'

'You think that he may have brought trouble upon himself?' Anne Marie looked at her anxiously. 'His orders were to take me to London…'

'My son has some influence at court. Sir Francis Drake thinks highly of him, and there are others who may help him if they choose. We must hope that he succeeds in winning a pardon for you, though I must tell you now that I believe there is no hope for your father once he is taken.'

'I understand that,' Anne Marie said, clasping her hands before her. 'You will forgive me if I say that I hope it will not happen?'

'Lord Fraser is a traitor,' Sarah Hamilton replied. 'If he were to come here we could not hide him, Anne Marie. It would be our duty to report him to the magistrates. My late husband was a magistrate himself, and he was very strict in his adherence to the law. If I learned that your father had attempted to see you, my duty would be clear.'

'Then we must hope that he does not,' Anne Marie replied. She understood that her kind hostess was telling her to keep any such meeting secret, and she knew that she could not expect more. It seemed that she was a guest and not a prisoner in this house, but she must not abuse their trust. 'I will promise you, ma'am, that I shall do nothing to bring dishonour to your family—or to endanger you in any way.'

'Thank you...' Sarah broke off as a youth poked his head round the door. 'What do you want, Edward?'

'I came to see where you were, ma'am,' he replied, looking curiously at Anne Marie. 'Is it true that your father is a traitor, Mistress Fraser?'

'Edward!' Sarah cried. 'How dare you address Mistress Fraser in that way? I am ashamed of you—for listening to things that are private and do not concern you, and for having so little concern for our guest's feelings.'

'I am sorry, Mother.'

'And so I should think!'

Seeing the way he hung his head, Anne Marie smiled forgivingly.

'Please do not scold him, ma'am. He spoke thoughtlessly and did not mean to upset me.'

'I will not have my son show such a shocking lack of manners,' Sarah Hamilton said. 'You will apologise, Edward.'

'Yes, ma'am.' Edward Hamilton looked rather sulkily at Anne Marie. 'I apologise if I have offended you, mistress.'

'I thank you for your apology,' Anne Marie said. 'And I am not offended.'

'What did you come for, Edward?' his mother asked, clearly still annoyed with him.

'Jack has let the boar in with the sows again,' he replied. 'I told him not to but he would do it, even though you told him he should have a beating if he did it again.'

'Could you not have stopped him?' Sarah Hamilton gave a sigh of exasperation. 'He is two years younger than you and should follow your lead.'

'He only told me after he had done it.'

'Then I suppose I must give him the thrashing he deserves,' Sarah said. 'But it ill behoves you to tell tales, Edward. Go and find your brother and tell him I shall see him in his chamber immediately.' She turned to Anne Marie as her son went off. 'They are high-spirited and need a man's hand to keep them in check. When my husband was alive they paid attention to him, but I fear they do much as they please these days.'

'It was very bad of Jack to let the boar in with the sows,' Anne Marie said. 'But Edward was merely curious and I wish you will not be cross with him for my sake.'

'Then I shall not,' Sarah Hamilton laughed softly. 'They are a sore trial to me at times, my dear, but I love them dearly.' Sadness flooded her face. 'My dear husband was taken from me so suddenly and I fear that I let things go for a time, but I must make an effort to manage better, for the sake of my sons and

the estate. When Kit goes away to sea once more...'
She shook her head, her smile fading. 'But I run on
and I must go and find my son and administer the
beating that will hurt me more than it does him.'

Anne Marie merely smiled as her harassed hostess
hurried away. Lady Hamilton had too much to do and
her lively sons were not of much help to her. She
decided that she would try to help in any way that
she could—while she was here. She tried not to think
of what might happen to her in the future. For the
moment she had been brought to this lovely house,
and she must make the most of it.

She was certainly being made comfortable for her
stay, however long or short its duration. She began to
walk about the room, running her fingers lightly over
the various items provided for her use. The chair with
the arms and padded back was the most comfortable
thing she had ever tried. And the house was so warm.
She could not believe her good fortune. She had
scarce known that it was possible to live in such luxury, for she had lived so long with the bleakness of
Drodney Castle.

Oh, how good it was to be free, if only for a little
time!

She opened the box of colours and took out the
brushes, examining them more carefully. There was
one with a very fine tip of hair and others with more
stubby, thicker heads.

'I trust they are what you need, mistress?'

Kit's voice from the doorway made her start, and

she turned to him almost guiltily, as though he might suddenly take back his gift.

'They are wonderful, sir,' she said and gave him a shy smile. 'I cannot thank you enough.'

'I have ordered more materials for you,' he replied but made no attempt to move further into the room. 'You will have watercolours and oils, and vellum to work on.'

'I do not know what to say…' Anne Marie was conscious of tightness in her throat. 'You are so good to me, and I am grateful.'

Kit scowled at her, his expression becoming harsh.

'I do not ask for gratitude, Mistress Fraser.'

Anne Marie was silent. What did he want of her? The question trembled on her tongue but she did not dare to ask it.

'I wanted to make sure that you understood you are free to walk and ride as you please,' Kit went on, as she did not speak. 'I ask only that you respect my mother's trust and do not seek to run away while I am gone to London.'

'I have given you my word, sir. I shall not leave willingly.'

'It might be safer if you do not leave the estate unaccompanied,' Kit said with a little frown. 'I believe that your presence here will not be known for some time. It is my hope that I shall return long before any attempt could be made to kidnap or coerce you into leaving—but until then you will take care to keep within sight of the house or my servants unless accompanied by others.'

'So I am still a prisoner.'

'Damn it!' Kit said angrily. 'Do not look at me that way. I am concerned for your safety, Anne Marie. Pray do me the honour of believing that I hate the need to curb your freedom as much as you do.'

'I do not blame you,' Anne Marie said, the tears very near. 'When must you leave for London?'

'In the morning,' he replied his gaze narrowed and intent on her face. 'Walk in the grounds as often as you like and go riding with my mother and the grooms—but take care for your sake and my own. I would not have harm come to you, and I think you were in some danger when you were taken before.'

So he had believed her! Anne Marie was silent, unable to answer him. His eyes dwelt on her face for a few minutes more, then he turned and strode away, leaving her to stare after him and wonder.

Did he care for her a little? If she could only be certain of it, she thought she could accept anything, but she dare not trust her instincts. At one moment he was kind and gentle, at the next he was angry and demanding, a harsh stranger who threatened her.

What was she to believe?

Chapter Five

'I thought Beth Makepeace kept a good stillroom,' Anne Marie said one morning when they were making an account of the preserves, cures and ointments stacked on the storeroom shelves, 'but you have so much more here.'

'I am quite proud of my stores,' Sarah Hamilton agreed with a little smile of satisfaction. 'But we are fortunate with our weather in this part of Devon. Our orchards are almost always productive. We grow three kinds of apples, pears, and apricots and peaches on a south-facing wall. There are besides some large dark plums, damsons, mulberries, sloes, quinces, walnuts, almonds and filberts. And in my walled garden I have a strawberry patch as well as many excellent herbs and of course we grow all our own vegetables.'

'You have a well-stocked orchard indeed, and I know that among your herbs you have mint, rosemary, lavender, comfrey and sage, but there are many more dried herbs stored here that I have never used. I should like to learn more about them.'

'Many are for the tisanes I make to cure headache and fever, but others are for flavouring and some for ointment. I shall show you when I have occasion to use them and in that way you will learn.'

'I learned much from Beth,' Anne Marie said and gave a little sigh.

'Do you miss her?'

'Yes, sometimes. She was very kind to me.'

Sarah nodded, her keen eyes noting the signs of tiredness in the girl's face. She had clearly not been sleeping as well as she might, and she wondered at the cause.

'I do not know what Kit is about all this time. If he does not soon come home he will not be here at Christmas. I have decided that we shall celebrate for the sake of the children, and I have asked my neighbours to share our dinner that day.'

'Do you mean Sir Nicholas and Lady Grantly?'

Anne Marie had met their closest neighbours and thought them pleasant, generous friends. She was pleased that they were to come to the house at Christmas, for she suspected that it would be very different from any she had known at Drodney and was looking forward to the day. Already they had had children at the door singing carols, and Lady Hamilton had invited them in for hot pies and a drink from the wassail bowl, in which were mixed warm ale, roasted apples, a little sugar and nutmeg.

'Yes. Sir Nicholas has given me excellent advice these past few months and I wish to repay his kindness. My husband always put his faith in wool, for the golden fleece of our sheep has been the mainstay of our income. However, Sir Nicholas tells me that I should have the long meadow ploughed and sow grain in its stead.'

The Hamiltons were like many wealthy country gentry these days. Because the price of everything from sugar to needles, silver and other luxuries had soared they needed more coin. It cost as much as sixteen shillings to straw the floors of a house of this size and household soap was fourpence a pound!

'It must cost a great deal to run a house like this one,' Anne Marie suggested.

Sarah nodded. 'Indeed it does, my dear. Some of our neighbours have been reduced to taking land back from their copyholders when the elder of the family dies and the entitlement is due for renewal. It is a cruel practice for a whole family may be turned out of their home to starve. However, because Kit has amassed a great deal of money from his ventures our own copyholders are safe, and we may all sleep soundly in our beds.'

Anne Marie had seen the happy, smiling faces of the people who held their land from the Hamiltons, and she had felt a sense of peace as she watched their children at work or play. They had pink, healthy faces and did not seem to suffer from as many of the terrible ailments she had seen in children of the north of England, while visiting the sick with Beth. The men bowed their heads respectfully to her when she passed by, and whenever she went visiting with Lady Hamilton the children clustered round excitedly.

It was Sarah Hamilton's habit to give them small gifts of the violet confects she made herself: these were made by dropping the violets into thick syrup, which then crystallised. At the same time the women were thrilled to receive an ointment for their hands, or sometimes an orange or a lemon—bought at the vast expense of seven for fourpence—or perhaps, if their need was great, a side of bacon.

'Is Sir Christopher very wealthy?'

Sarah laughed softly. 'I dare say my son has more money than is good for him, but he has been generous to the boys and to me.'

'Edward and Jack were not best pleased with his latest gift to them.'

'Oh, but Mr Mountjoy was meant as a gift to me.' Sarah's eyes sparkled with the same sense of wicked amusement as was sometimes to be seen in Kit's eyes. 'He has brought some order to this house at last.'

Anne Marie gave a little gurgle of laughter. Master Mountjoy was a young man of some six and twenty summers. He was apparently of an amiable temper and a stout arm, and the boys had learned to respect him the hard way.

'Sir Christopher has told me not to spare the rod,' he had informed the ladies when invited to take supper with them one evening. 'I am not given to brutality but if they are to learn manners and respect as well as a little Latin, I must exert my authority.'

'You must do as you think fit,' Lady Hamilton had replied. 'But do not beat them so hard that they become ill or crippled, Master Mountjoy.'

'You may rest assured that I am a tolerant man, my lady, and shall temper justice with punishment.'

And so it had turned out. Both Anne Marie and Sarah found the tutor a pleasant companion. He could discourse on any topic they chose, from politics to what went on at court and poetry. He knew what plays had been performed recently at London's oldest theatre, which was simply called The Theatre, and he could quote from Thomas Wyatt, John Skelton and Master Hawes. He knew whole passages from Sir Philip Sidney's work by heart and talked well of many other poets and poems, some of which were anonymous and unknown to Anne Marie.

'He is indeed a welcome addition to my household,' Sarah said. 'Since he arrived I have had some leisure for my tapestry—but that is also due in part to you, Anne Marie. You have been such a help to me, my dear.'

'I have done but little—and it is a pleasure to me,' Anne Marie replied with a blush. 'I love living here, ma'am. I have never been happier.'

If that were the case, why were her eyes so often filled with shadows? Sarah believed she knew, but was wise enough to keep her own counsel. Kit would make all plain when he returned. But where was he? What was keeping him so long in London?

Had she but known, it was this same question that was robbing Anne Marie of her rest at night.

He had promised he would not be gone long, but it was now more than six weeks since he departed for London. Had something happened to him? He might have been set upon and robbed by rogues who had left him for dead by the side of the road. Or had he been thrown into the Tower for disobeying his orders concerning her?

Oh, where was he? Anne Marie was tormented by her fears, torn with uncertainty. Sometimes she believed that he had simply gone back to sea and that she would never see him again.

Kit followed the lady who had been sent to conduct him to Her Majesty's private chambers. For weeks he had been forced to wait idly until the summons came, and his patience was nearly at an end. Had Walsingham not warned him that to disobey again would result in a sojourn in the Tower, he might already have been on his way home.

His enforced stay in London had resulted in some good. He had visited the merchants of Cheapside and many importers of fine goods, buying quantities of silver, pewter and exotic spices. He had also purchased two carved cupboards for the parlour, a new down mattress, hangings and quilts, and a magnificent silvergilt salt cellar to grace the expensive table, which was made of Dutch walnut and had magnificent bulbous legs.

Beside the additions to the furniture, he had bought many small items that would please a lady. Most of which he intended as wedding gifts for Anne Marie.

All he needed was Her Majesty's gracious permission.

In a few minutes he would learn whether his request had been granted. Ushered into the Queen's chamber, Kit made her an elegant leg.

'Your Grace. I thank you for seeing me.'

Elizabeth's eyes flashed imperiously. 'You are an insolent puppy, Sir Christopher. You disobeyed your orders and have harboured the daughter of a traitor. Tell me why I should not instantly have you cast into the Tower?'

'I can think of none, ma'am. I must simply throw myself on your mercy, which I know to be bounteous and just.'

Elizabeth gave a harsh laugh. She had lost much of the charm that youth had once given her, her teeth blackened, and her pitted skin hidden beneath thick white paint. Her hair, which some said had grown thin and lifeless, was hidden beneath a wig of red curls. Yet such was her aura and her fame that men still called her beautiful and courted her for the favours she bestowed on them.

'You are bold, sir, and I am minded to teach you a lesson.'

'It shall be as Your Grace wishes—but should the invasion come I should not be able to join Drake and all those who have vowed to defend you and your realm to the death.'

'You speak plainly, sir. I like that and I know well that I may have need of you in the months ahead.' There was a hint of temper in her eyes. 'That foolish woman Mary of Scots hath been caught in a trap and now my people call for her death. They would have me cut off her head, but in doing so I bring the wrath of every Catholic in this land and abroad upon us. If she dies, I believe Spain will come against us.'

'It is indeed a sore trial to you, ma'am,' Kit said, understanding her dilemma. 'You are a woman of compassion and have spared her these many years when others bayed for her head, but Sir Francis Walsingham is right concerning this. While she lives there will always be someone who believes there is a way to place her on the throne in your stead.'

'Do you imagine I am not aware of the choice I face, sir?' Elizabeth gave a sigh of exasperation. 'Why must these burdens fall upon my shoulders? All my life I have lost those I most care for. I have sacrificed much for the crown I wear and sometimes I believe that there is a dark force waged against me, that at every turn I am thwarted and cursed. Am I never to find peace or happiness?'

Kit was silent for a moment. He knew that he was being shown a rare glimpse of the private woman. For more than six and twenty years Elizabeth had ruled alone, guided by her ministers but without a man at her side. There had been many to court and flatter her, and perhaps once she had come close to finding love. The strange, unsolved death of Amy Robsart, wife to Robert Dudley, now the great Earl of Leicester who was presently away fighting in the Netherlands against the French, had put an end to any likelihood of their marriage. Had Elizabeth followed the prompting of her heart, there would have been such scandal and fury that her throne might have fallen.

There was from time to time still talk of the Queen's marriage to a suitable candidate, but, since the departure of the Duke of Alençon after the breakdown of those negotiations, no longer in a serious way. Elizabeth was more than fifty, and since the hope of an heir had long been despaired of, there was no gain to be made from marriage. Now all those who strove to keep England safe from the Catholic threat were concerned to protect the Queen and preserve her life for as long as possible.

She was Gloriana, loved and adored by her people. Her reign had begun in turmoil and uncertainty, but she had carved for herself a place in history and in the hearts of her people. It seemed that England was a charmed land while Elizabeth reigned, and its people prospered. There were few who would not lift their drinking cups in a toast to her health these days, except of course for those who clung stubbornly to the Catholic faith.

'Your happiness comes from serving your people, Majesty.'

Elizabeth stared at Kit as he broke the silence at last, and for a second he saw regret and pain in her eyes, then she bowed her head to acknowledge the truth of his words. When she looked at him again the mask was back in place. She was Gloriana once more, the great queen of England, revered and adored, a virgin and an example to her people.

'You do well to remind me of my duty, sir—and I shall remind you of yours. You will bring Mistress Fraser to court, but only when she is your wife. It is enough that I have the problem of that foolish woman to contend with. Once Mistress Fraser becomes Lady Hamilton I trust you to make her behave, sir, and shall hold you accountable.'

'Anne Marie was taken against her will, ma'am. Lord Fraser had hoped to use her to his advantage. She is innocent of any crime, ma'am. Besides, she can have no value to her father once she is my wife.'

'Then return to your home and marry the troublesome wench,' Elizabeth snapped. 'I shall receive her only when she is safely wedded.'

With an angry gesture of her hand, Elizabeth dismissed him. Walsingham had persuaded her that it was best for all concerned, but talk of marriage made her angry. She hated it when her ladies married and would often forbid a match if it displeased her.

Kit believed that he understood the anger that lay behind her sudden change of mood. Elizabeth was possibly too old to have a child or experience the happiness of being truly loved for herself, but still too young to be content to live alone.

There was of course always a new courtier to flatter and make courtly love to her, but she was too intelligent to be taken in by false protestations of desire. She might enjoy the company of young and handsome men, but she was no fool, and must be aware that their eyes strayed to the lovely young women at her court. Her current favourite was said to be Robert, Earl of Essex. Recently returned from the Netherlands, where he had shown courage and skill at Zutphen, he had found great favour with the Queen.

Kit was smiling as he left Hampton Court. He knew that he owed his own happiness mainly to Walsingham's persuasive tongue, and also the gift of silver he had sent Her Majesty.

It was, he felt, a small price to pay for Anne Marie's freedom. As his wife she would be safe from any further attempt to spirit her away—and the danger he sensed she might be in from such an attempt.

What had happened on that windswept clifftop? It was a mystery he feared might never be solved, and it made him uneasy for the girl he wanted above all others as his wife.

He was very much in love, had been so almost from the first moment of seeing Anne Marie on that lonely cliff, her face wearing that pensive look as she stared out to sea. At first he had not wanted to admit it to himself, but he had known. Before it happened to him Kit would not have credited that it was possible to love at first sight, for he had ever been a cynic in such matters, but he knew without a shadow of a doubt that it had happened to him. He loved her and could scarcely wait to be home again and to make her his own.

'What do you suppose is in all these trunks?' Sarah Hamilton asked as the servants carried them through the hall on their way to her son's private apartments. 'Kit has told me in his letter where the furniture is to be placed, but he asks that the trunks are not opened until his return. It is all rather mysterious, do you not think so?'

Anne Marie's heart began to race like the wind. She tried to conceal her excitement and failed.

'Did—did Sir Christopher say when he expected to return?'

'The letter was written more than ten days ago,' Sarah replied. 'The wagons have been all that time on the road, for they kept together in a convoy to guard against attack by robbers, and were forced to wait when one of them suffered some damage to a wheel. Kit says only that he has been delayed and will return when he can.'

Anne Marie nodded, her disappointment sharp. With the arrival of so many wagons she had thought Kit would follow almost at once.

'Then we must not expect him for Christmas.'

'It seems not,' Sarah said. It was but two days away now, and a frenzy of preparation and baking had kept them busy from morning till dusk. 'We shall go ahead with our plans for celebration even if Kit is not here, Anne Marie. Lord, there is so much to do! I am so busy that I scarcely know where to turn. Would you be kind enough to take a basket of gifts for Nurse Alice for me?'

'Yes, of course. I should be glad to.'

Anne Marie agreed willingly. The old woman lived in a cottage on the estate. She had been nurse to Kit's father and grandfather, and had reached the considerable age of eighty years. She had gained the reputation of being a wise woman, much revered by everyone. It was Sarah's habit to take her food once a week and Anne Marie had accompanied her on several occasions. She knew the way well and would be back long before dark.

It was cold out but the sky had a curious brightness, the air crisp and fresh as she began her walk. A song thrush was trilling somewhere in a thorn bush and she could hear the lowing of cattle in one of the barns on the home farm.

There were only a few cows to provide milk, cream and butter for the house. In spring and summer they had their own supply of fresh meat from the pigs and sheep, some of which was salted down in barrels to provide for the winter. Only a few breeding animals were kept over winter, because sufficient fodder could not always be provided for large flocks.

Anne Marie was gradually learning from her kind hostess about the management of a country estate, which fell mostly on the lady of the manor. Lady Hamilton had so many responsibilities, for the welfare of her people was chiefly her concern as well as the ordering of a large house. Anne Marie had discovered that life in the country could be hazardous, especially for the poor people who had only what they could raise on their tiny strips of land or their back gardens.

It was much easier for the Hamiltons, of course, because they did not rely only on the land. However, Sarah was trying to manage the land more efficiently and she was greatly helped in this by some excellent books on the subject loaned her by Sir Nicholas.

Lost in her thoughts, many of which concerned the master of this great estate, Anne Marie did not see the young man approaching until he hailed her.

'Mistress Fraser,' Master Mountjoy said as he sprinted to catch her up. 'It is a pleasant afternoon for the time of year, is it not?'

'Very pleasant, sir. At Drodney we often had snow and ice by this time, but Lady Hamilton assures me that the month of December is sometimes very pleasant here, and it is usually only after Christmas that we get the snow lying thickly on the ground.'

'So I understand,' the tutor replied. 'I have not often been in this part of the country before, having lived mostly in the midlands.' He smiled at her. 'Where are you going, Mistress Fraser? May I walk with you for a while?'

'Yes, of course, if you wish.' She smiled at him. He often walked with her if he was free of his duties. 'I am going to take this basket of gifts to Nurse Alice, because Lady Hamilton is too busy.'

'She must find you a big help to her. I know that Sir Christopher was concerned because she was finding it difficult to manage after the sad loss of her husband.'

'Yes, indeed. I believe she was deeply shocked and grieved. Any woman must feel so left without their husband,' Anne Marie agreed. 'Where are your pupils this afternoon, sir?'

'Sir Nicholas invited them to go on an expedition with him. His younger children are much the same age as Edward and Jack. I believe they were going to a fair. I offered to accompany the party and help keep them in order, but Sir Nicholas said that he would manage and that I was to consider myself free for an hour or two.'

'That was kind of him. The children will enjoy the visit I am sure. I went to a fair some weeks ago, and found it fascinating.'

'If I had known you would like to go I could have taken you, Mistress Fraser.'

'Oh no,' Anne Marie said quickly, and blushed as she saw warmth in the young man's eyes. 'I am not sure that Sir Christopher would permit such a thing. He has asked that I stay within the bounds of his estate until he returns.'

Master Mountjoy nodded, his eyes thoughtful as they rested on her lovely face. He had been told a part of her story, and though he had made no mention of it, his duties included keeping an eye to her safety by reporting any unusual or strange happening to his employer.

'I am concerned lest there is an attempt made to kidnap her,' Sir Christopher had told him. 'I believe she is safe enough for the moment, but should you have reason to doubt you will write to me at once.'

'Then it is as well that I did not suggest it,' Master Mountjoy said easily. 'However, Sir Nicholas has a small menagerie of wild creatures and he has invited the boys to see them one day. Perhaps you might be tempted to accompany us, Mistress Fraser?'

'Wild creatures?' Anne Marie looked at him with interest. 'What kind of creatures, sir?'

'I believe there are some bears, which he rescued from a cruel master and which have bred into a family. Also badgers that have been found wounded and brought to safety to heal. I have been informed there are several owls that have had their wings broken, hawks that have suffered similarly and various other creatures.'

'It sounds most interesting,' Anne Marie replied. 'Yes, I should like to be a member of your party, sir.'

'I intend to make it a lesson for the boys,' he said looking thoughtful. 'It will do them no harm to learn compassion for their fellow creatures as well as more about the various species that inhabit our earth.'

'Perhaps then they will not be so quick to let the geese out into the woods or put the boar in with the sows,' Anne Marie said, laughing as she recalled the incident that had happened on her arrival.

'I believe I have cured that,' Master Mountjoy said. 'I find the best thing is to keep them busy, and I am trying to find new ways of doing that. When they return from the fair, they little know that I shall expect an essay of not less than one thousand words about what they saw there.'

'I see you are a hard taskmaster,' Anne Marie said with a smile. 'Do not forget that it is almost Christmas, sir.'

'It will be Christmas soon, but I see no reason why that should occasion slacking in their lessons. They will not of course work on Christ's birthday, but we shall continue as always both before and after the feast.'

Anne Marie felt a little sorry for the boys, who until the arrival of their tutor had been allowed to run free as they pleased. They could not be permitted to continue in that way, of course, but she knew how it felt to be a prisoner and understood that they might resent what had happened to them.

Master Mountjoy continued to walk with her to Nurse Alice's cottage. He waited outside while she went in and made inquiries after the old lady's well-being.

'I'm well enough, thank you, mistress,' Nurse Alice replied. 'I suffer from the agues this time of year but at my age I am lucky to be alive. Not many get past their middle years, let alone to mine.' She grinned toothlessly at Anne Marie. 'Make the most of your youth, Mistress Fraser. You're a pretty thing. 'Tis a crying shame that you are not wed. You should ask Sir Christopher to arrange it when he gets back from London. Why not that tutor? I've seen the way he looks at you, and methinks he would have you fast enough.' She gave a cackle of laughter. 'Grab him while the sap is still rising, that's my advice to you. Youth flees too soon, girl. Take your pleasures while you're young.'

Anne Marie shook her head, her cheeks on fire as she saw the saucy gleam in the old woman's eyes. She was a little embarrassed as she went back outside, and relieved that Master Mountjoy had not entered the cottage with her.

Since she had been several minutes talking to Nurse Alice, she had thought that the tutor might have given up his self-imposed vigil and gone on his way. However, despite the cold, which had turned bitter now that the sky had begun to darken, he was still there.

'You should not have waited, sir,' Anne Marie exclaimed as she saw him stamping his feet on the ground to warm himself. 'I could have walked back alone.'

'The night closes in fast,' he replied. 'I would not have you walk so far alone, Mistress Fraser. Besides, we shall soon warm up once we begin to walk.'

'Then let us walk fast,' Anne Marie said and laughed 'For it is cold enough to snow!'

'I think you may be right,' he replied, glancing up at the sky. 'I believe we may have snow before morning.'

'That will please the boys, for they were wishing for snow yesterday.'

It was as they approached the house that they saw a flurry of activity. It was clear that someone had arrived, and the grooms were leading away two horses.

'It would seem that you have visitors,' Master Mountjoy said. 'Did Lady Hamilton speak of a visitor?'

'No, she said...' Anne Marie's voice died away as a man came out of the house and started to walk towards them. 'I think it is Sir Christopher come home.'

Her heart was racing and she could scarcely breathe as she saw Kit's imposing figure. How tall he was, and so much broader in the shoulder than the young man by her side!

'Master Mountjoy.' Kit inclined his head towards the tutor, a slight frown creasing his brow. 'Mistress Fraser—where have you been? The hour grows late and it will snow ere long.'

Anne Marie sensed the disapproval in his tone, and her face paled as she realised that he was annoyed with her.

'I was merely delivering some gifts to Nurse Alice, as Lady Hamilton asked.'

'And I see Master Mountjoy accompanied you, which is as well, as dusk falls fast these winter afternoons. You must both be frozen, for it has turned bitter. Go in to my mother at once, Anne Marie, and warm yourself by the fire. Master Mountjoy, I would have a report of my brothers from you at your convenience.'

'Willingly, sir. Whenever you please.'

Master Mountjoy was all compliance, and yet Anne Marie sensed a faint hostility between the two men. She thought it odd, since Master Mountjoy was such a help to Lady Hamilton and had had a beneficial effect on the boys.

However, her main concern was for the way Kit had greeted her. Why was he angry with her? What had she done to displease him? She had not once strayed from the estate, and most of her walks had been taken either with Lady Hamilton on some mercy errand or with the tutor and his charges. She had gone riding only twice, and that accompanied by the boys and a groom.

Walking swiftly to the back parlour, where she

knew that a cup of warm, spiced ale and some honey cakes would be offered her, she did her best to hide her hurt.

She had longed for Kit's return so desperately, and now it seemed that he was angry with her. Or perhaps his stern expression meant that she was to be sent to the Tower after all?

Anne Marie changed into her best gown, the one she had found on board the *Golden Fleece*, before going down to supper that night. She wore the dress that she had made herself at Drodney for working in the mornings, and Lady Hamilton had found her two of her own cast-offs to alter for afternoons, but she kept Kit's gift to her for the evenings.

She brushed her hair hard to make it shine and left it hanging loose from beneath her modest cap of lace. She had no ornament to hang about her neck, but the gown was stylish enough to wear without more embellishment and she had always liked it.

When she went down to the dining parlour, where the new table had been placed in splendour with three chairs and several stools set about it, it was to discover Kit running his hand over the smooth wood.

He looked up at her approach, his features relaxing their stern expression after a moment. 'I was examining the table for any damage it might have sustained on the journey here.'

'I think it has not, sir,' she replied. 'I polished it myself with beeswax just after it arrived, and I think you may put your mind at rest. Lady Hamilton was most particular when they were carrying the table in, for she said it must have cost a great deal.'

'The cost is not important,' Kit replied. 'I merely wanted it to be perfect.' He did not add that he had bought it for her, as he had almost everything he had sent back from London, to give her pleasure in her new home.

He was disappointed that she did not seem more pleased to see him. She had been constantly in his thoughts all the time he was away, but it seemed she had managed well enough without him.

'Lady Hamilton was enchanted with the table and the cupboards. You must have been busy in London, sir.'

'I was damnably idle!' Kit replied with a scowl. 'Her Majesty kept me waiting day after day for an audience, and I dared not leave without speaking to her or I might have found myself being taken back by force.'

'I see…'

'Do you?' Again his eyes held a hard, cold expression as he looked at her. 'I rather doubt that you do, Anne Marie—but all shall be made plain to you before long.'

'W-what do you mean?' Her heart caught with fright. 'Am I to be taken to the Tower? Has my father been arrested?'

'I have no news of your father,' Kit replied. 'Walsingham was furious that both Fraser and Bevis Frampton slipped through the net he threw around them. How it was done is a mystery, for all the others were caught like rats, and have been imprisoned—but the two we most wanted have by some mysterious trick escaped.'

Anne Marie's heart hammered against her ribs as she saw the expression in his eyes. Did he imagine that she had somehow warned her father?

'I—I cannot pretend to be sorry that my father escaped arrest, but as for the other man, I did not like the way he stared at me that day. I blame him for my father's involvement in the plot to rescue Mary of Scots. I think that without his influence my father would have done nothing but talk and dream. It was Master Frampton who conceived this monstrous plan and I can only pray that Lord Fraser is safe in France or Spain.'

'Fortunately, I am the only one to hear such treasonable words,' Kit said, a glint of anger in his eyes. 'I warn you that you must say nothing of the sort when we go to London next month.'

'To London...' Anne Marie's hand crept to her throat. 'So I am to be imprisoned again.'

'I have not said so,' Kit growled. He wondered why he did not tell her the truth at once, but he had been angry and jealous when he'd witnessed her walking towards the house with Master Mountjoy. The rapport between them had been so obvious that he had been almost too angry to speak to her. 'I shall tell you of your future when I am ready, Anne Marie.'

'Please do not...' She had been about to ask him not to be angry with her, but she was interrupted by the arrival of another man, someone who was a stranger to her.

'This is Sir Robert Herriot,' Kit told her, his features relaxing into a smile of welcome. 'Sir Robert's home is in Cornwall and we journeyed here together. He is to stay with us overnight and then continue in the morning to his home if the weather be fit.'

'I am pleased to make your acquaintance, sir.' Anne Marie made him a respectful curtsey. 'We must hope that it does not snow too hard, for I believe it has just started.'

'I think you are right,' Kit said, glancing towards the window. 'If your journey is impossible you must stay for Christmas with us, Sir Robert. I am sure my mother would be glad to have you as a guest. In this house company is always welcome.'

'Indeed you are right, my son,' Lady Hamilton said coming into the room at that moment. 'But I dare say you have a wife and family waiting for you, sir?'

'A family but no wife,' he replied, a flicker of sadness in his eyes. 'My sweet Annis died giving birth to our son, who followed her to the grave a day later.'

'Oh, I am so sorry,' Anne Marie exclaimed, drawing a look from Kit that made her wonder what she had done wrong now. Surely he could not criticise her for feeling as she ought. 'It must be terrible to lose someone you love in that way. And to lose a child, too—it was so sad for you, sir.'

'I thank you for your kindness and understanding, Mistress Fraser,' Sir Robert said. 'I know you, you see, because Sir Christopher has spoken of you many times during our journey.' He smiled at her regretfully. 'I only wish that I might stay for your wedding, but my mother has been ill and I believe I must continue my journey as soon as possible.'

Anne Marie's startled eyes flew to Kit's face. Marriage? Her marriage—to Sir Christopher? How could this be? Sir Robert's casual remark was the first she had heard of marriage, and from Kit's expression he had clearly not meant her to know it yet.

She looked at Kit's face, hoping to glean something from his expression, but his thoughts were hidden from her. She felt as if she lay on a bed of thorns, tormented by her frustration and bewilderment over this sudden announcement that had come like a bolt from the sky.

'I think we shall talk later, Anne Marie,' Kit warned as he saw the shock in her face. She was clearly distressed, and he cursed Sir Robert for his careless words. Anne Marie would surely accuse him of deceiving her again. Yet he was hampered by the need for discretion and politeness and could say little in front of a guest. 'I believe my mother came to tell us that supper is about to be served?'

'Yes, indeed it is and there is a fine carp I would not have over-cooked,' Sarah Hamilton said, as if sensing the tension between them. 'Come along, Sir Robert. Pray take my arm and tell me about yourself and your home…'

Anne Marie gazed up at Kit as the others went to take their places around the table. Her eyes flashed with the anger she was trying to control.

'Of what shall we speak, sir?' she asked in a low voice, her lips bloodless, face pale with shock. 'I do not recall that you have asked me to be your wife—or made any mention of such an intention, though it seems you were pleased to tell Sir Robert. It would have been courteous to at least warn me of your thoughts, sir.'

'It was Her Majesty's order,' Kit replied wondering at the devil that prompted him. 'I intended to tell you later. Neither of us has any choice, Anne Marie. I am commanded to take you to court, but not until you are my wife.' She was angry with him anyway, 'twas as well to be condemned for an oxen as a lamb! She would likely argue against their wedding, so let her think it merely an order from the Queen and not the wish of his heart for now. He bowed to her, a wicked, mocking smile upon his mouth. 'Shall we take our places before the dinner spoils?'

Chapter Six

Anne Marie found it difficult to swallow a morsel of the baked carp, and it was impossible to eat the spiced pork swimming in rich gravy. She did manage a few mouthfuls of junket at the end of the long meal, but by that time her sense of shock had hardened to anger.

How dare Sir Christopher treat her in such a fashion? To tell his friend that they were to be married without consulting her first! Even if the order had come from the Queen, he might at least have discussed it with her. His behaviour was unpardonable! It was as if her opinion, her feelings, counted for nothing.

Besides, it was impossible. Why should the Queen wish for a marriage between Sir Christopher and Anne Marie? Was it a form of punishment for him because he had disobeyed his orders to take her to London? Was that why he was so angry, because he did not truly wish to marry her? She thought that perhaps he was resentful because he had been given no choice; that might explain his shameful treatment of her, but it did not excuse it.

The thoughts chased endlessly through her mind, distressing her and destroying her appetite, and she was none the wiser by the end of their meal.

It was Sarah's habit to retire to her private parlour after supper, where Anne Marie sometimes joined her for a few minutes before going to her own chamber. They had kept early hours while Sir Christopher was away, for in the dark evenings it was difficult to work or sew even by the light of the best wax candles. That evening, however, they moved into the larger parlour, where Lady Hamilton played on the harp for the pleasure of the gentlemen, and Anne Marie sang a sweet madrigal with Master Mountjoy. The ladies then left the gentlemen to their brandewine, going each to their own chamber.

Anne Marie sat for some time brushing her hair and gazing out of her window, from which she could see so much more than she had been able to from her tower in the castle. There was a bright moon, which highlighted the glistening snow that had continued to fall throughout the evening and was now lying in deep drifts where the land fell away to a hollow. She doubted that Sir Robert would be able to continue his journey in the morning, which meant they would have a house full of company over the Christmastide feast.

Sir Robert was a pleasant guest and had entertained her with court gossip during the meal. Anne Marie had smiled at his stories, which were amusing, though her mind was elsewhere. She was very angry at the way she was being given in marriage without a by your leave.

How could she marry Sir Christopher? He was a Protestant and her own preference was—what? If she was honest Anne Marie was not certain. She had attended service at the castle with Beth, and kept the rituals of her mother's faith in private. But what did *she* truly believe?

She believed in God, and her mother's cross had given her comfort. As for the rest, perhaps it did not matter so very much. In Elizabeth's England there were many that followed one faith in public and another in private. It was safer so.

Anne Marie sighed as she got up and walked slowly towards her bed, her mind in turmoil and knowing that she would find it difficult to sleep.

Perhaps she would have been content to marry Sir Christopher if he had cared for her, for she knew in her heart that she was deeply attracted to him. However, his manner had hurt her, making her throw up a shield to protect herself. He had made it clear that he was merely obeying his orders, and that had stung her pride. Especially as she had begun to realise how much he had come to mean to her.

How could she marry him knowing that he did not truly want her? It would be too painful, too shaming! Anne Marie acknowledged to herself that all other considerations were as nothing to her beside that fact. Sir Christopher had been ordered to marry her!

What could she do? Desperate thoughts of running

away filled her mind, but she knew they were impossible. She had nowhere to go and no one to help her, and she did not believe she could survive the reality of a harsh world alone.

Oh, why had Sir Christopher not let her go to France? She did not believe she would have been happy as her cousin's wife, but she could not have been more miserable than she was now.

She would not consent to this marriage! Surely they could not compel her if she were steadfast in her denial. She would say that it was against her faith and resist all pressure.

It was surely better to endure the Queen's anger than the humiliation of knowing she was an unwanted wife.

Kit looked out at the drifts of snow and realised that it would not be possible for Sir Robert to leave in the morning. He cursed himself for a fool. Why on earth had he brought the man here?

It was not as if they were close friends. They had met at court, and then again by chance on the road, and decided to travel together for greater safety. There were too many beggars and vagrants to make travelling alone safe these days. Though each man had a groom with him, neither was used to a large escort and they found the company pleasant enough.

Yet Kit would have preferred the solitude of a journey alone to what had happened that evening. He could not blame Sir Robert, for he *had* mentioned his coming marriage in passing. The fault lay in his own behaviour.

He ought to have spoken to Anne Marie immediately after he arrived. Indeed, he should properly have consulted her before he made his request to the Queen. He had thought only of protecting her and of his own wishes, and now it seemed that she did not wish for a marriage with him.

How could he have been so mistaken in her feelings? Recalling the time they had spent together at Drodney, Kit was almost certain that she had felt something towards him then.

Pacing the floor of his bedchamber in agitation, he began to understand that he was himself to blame for the change. He had been angry with her for running away from him, and he had been angry with her for finding Master Mountjoy pleasant company. Watching her sing that madrigal with the tutor had racked him with jealousy—jealousy he suspected was unfounded but which pricked all the same.

He tried to think calmly, to put aside his anger and consider this from Anne Marie's point of view. There was reason to believe she had not gone willingly from Drodney, and her friendship with the tutor was in all probability quite innocent. That had not stopped him resenting it.

It was his damnable temper! A wry smile touched Kit's mouth as he acknowledged his fault. Anne Marie did not know that he loved her, for he had not spoken of his feelings. He would have to spend the next few weeks courting her. Surely when she realised how he felt she would see that marriage with him was for her good?

Indeed, there was little choice for her. If she behaved foolishly again she might find herself a prisoner once more.

It was Christmas Day and the snow had turned to a crisp frost underfoot. The Hamilton family walked together to the church that morning, and were met there by Sir Nicholas Grantly, his lady and their children. After taking part in the special service of celebration and thanksgiving, they walked back to Hamilton House together.

They made a merry party despite the inclement weather, and were greeted with cups of hot mulled wine on their return. The wine warmed them, making everyone talkative and relaxed as they exchanged gifts and gossip.

'Lady Hamilton tells me that Sir Christopher has bought many fine treasures home with him, Mistress Fraser. I would almost think it his intention to marry.'

Lady Catherine Grantly smiled at her, and Anne Marie sensed that she was expecting an announcement that day. She blushed and made no answer. A day had passed since Kit's homecoming and he had not spoken again of their marriage. It was quite impossible for her to know what to think!

'I do not know what is in Sir Christopher's mind, ma'am,' she replied after a moment's thought. 'He has not discussed his plans for the future with me.'

'No?' Lady Grantly's eyebrows rose. She was a

beautiful woman some years younger than her husband, and it was clear that he adored her. 'Then I shall not tease you. I shall say only that I have always found Sir Christopher honest and generous. A woman might do much worse in a husband.'

Anne Marie gave her a nervous smile. She did not know how else to answer her, for her situation was an odd one. Until Kit chose to speak to her further on the subject she could have no voice on the matter. For the moment he was being polite, kind but slightly reserved, and she had responded in like manner.

His Christmas gift to her had been a little book of poetry bound in leather and a silver hand mirror. She had thanked him, giving in return a pair of kerchiefs that she had made and embroidered herself in fine linen purchased from a travelling pedlar with money given her by Lady Hamilton.

'You must have a little coin to indulge yourself now and then,' Sarah had told her kindly when the pedlar called to offer his wares at the house. 'I do not know why Kit did not think of it himself, my dear.'

Anne Marie thought privately that perhaps he had wanted to make sure that she could not run away from him. However, through the kindness of her hostess she had managed to buy or make gifts for all the family.

For Sarah she had painted an exquisite miniature of Kit. In oil on canvas, it was a true likeness and caused his mother to exclaim in delight when she saw it first.

'Oh, but this is beautiful, my dear,' she said and

passed it to her son. 'She has captured you exactly, Kit—that proud lift to your head and the smile are very like. Indeed, I vow she hath made you more handsome than you are.'

Kit studied the portrait carefully before handing it back to his mother.

'Were you a man you might rival Master Holbein or Nicholas Hilliard and become a court painter, Anne Marie. As it is I fear you must confine your talent to painting family and friends.'

Anne Marie blushed at his compliment, which was endorsed by Sir Nicholas and his wife as they too studied her work.

'I think you flatter me, sir. It was done with good intent, for I wished to repay Lady Hamilton's kindness to me, but I doubt that I have such skill as you would impart to me.'

'You have more than repaid anything I have done for you, my dear,' Sarah said. 'I shall always treasure this.'

'Perhaps you would care to paint my children?' said Lady Grantly into the silence that followed. 'I do not hesitate to commission a woman, though there may be prejudice elsewhere.'

'I should be happy to do so,' Anne Marie assured her with a shy smile. 'I wish for no payment, ma'am. When Master Mountjoy brings Edward and Jack to visit your menagerie I shall show you a drawing and if you care for it I can paint their likeness in oils.'

'You must accept some payment,' Lady Grantly

said. 'I shall have my dressmaker fashion a gown for you and honour shall be served.'

'You should accept, my dear,' Sarah said. 'Else you will offend.'

Anne Marie could only blush and thank the generous mother.

'But you must first approve the work or I shall not be satisfied.'

'Do not be too modest,' Kit said. 'You have shown your talent and cannot deny it. I know that you have done other work of equal quality that many an artist would be proud to claim.'

Anne Marie made no answer and Sir Nicholas turned the subject. She was allowed to sit quietly, watching as the children played with their gifts and quarrelled good-naturedly among themselves. It was a pleasant, happy scene, and she found herself envying the rapport between Lady Catherine and her husband. If only it could be that way with Kit and her! Oh, to be loved and spoiled as Catherine Grantly was! Such happiness was not granted to all wives.

'You look pensive,' a voice said close to her ear and she turned her head to see Master Mountjoy watching her with the same interest that she had given to the children. 'Shall I take these troublesome children off to the schoolroom?'

'Oh, no,' Anne Marie cried. 'You must not do any such thing, sir. I was just thinking how pleasant it was to see them so happy. You must know that I was brought up alone and never had brothers or sisters to play with.'

'Would you like children of your own?'

Anne Marie felt her cheeks warm as she saw the expression in the tutor's eyes. He was becoming too attentive to her and it made her uncomfortable.

She did not answer him but looked instead at Kit. He was staring at her, and his eyes held an angry light that made her want to jump up and run away. What had she done to displease him now?

She was relieved when the housekeeper came to tell Lady Hamilton that dinner was ready and they all moved into the dining-room for the feast that had been prepared for them. It was not usual for the boys to eat with the family, but on this day it had been decided that all the children would sit with their nurse at one end of the long table Kit had bought in London, and the adults would sit at the other. In this way there was less likelihood of upsets and yet for this special day they would all feast together.

And what a feast! There was a succession of rich dishes, beginning with stuffed trout in a light wine sauce; capons, a side of beef and a succulent goose with chestnut stuffing and roasted onions followed this. Removed with these dishes were some spiced cabbage, a dish of buttered turnips and sweet plums, and then came the junkets, pickled strawberries, sweet creams, cakes, quince tarts, custards and pies. All these were followed by walnuts, filberts, almonds, crystallised fruits and marchpane comfits, the table becoming littered with shells as everyone ate their fill.

Anne Marie enjoyed the meal, though she was conscious of Kit's eyes on her for much of the time. She had been seated between Sir Nicholas and Sir Robert Herriot, and they kept her well entertained, plying her with all the delicacies that were brought to table until she groaned and said that she could not eat another thing.

'I think it is time for some exercise,' Master Mountjoy declared when it was decided to repair to the large parlour once more. 'I shall take these young devils out of your way for a while.'

So saying, he gathered all the younger members of the party up and took them out with him.

'You have discovered a treasure in that young man,' Lady Grantly remarked to Kit as he offered her his arm. 'I like him much better than the tutor Sir Nicholas engaged for our children. Master Trent means well, but he is too old to control them as your man does.'

'Yes, I believe he does his job well,' Kit replied, holding back the words that came to mind. The man was too familiar with Anne Marie! He frowned, deciding that he would have to speak to Mountjoy and make the position clear, which meant he must first speak to Anne Marie.

He had waited until after Christmas, because he had not wanted to spoil this special day that they had all been preparing for for so long, but now he realised that it could not be further delayed.

Once settled in the parlour, the assembled company entertained each other. Lady Grantly played the virginals for them, and Sir Nicholas joined her to sing

an Italian madrigal for two persons. Sir Robert read
to them from a book of poems.

'And wilt thou leave me thus,
That hath given thee my heart
Never for to depart
Neither for pain nor smart:
And wilt thou leave me thus?
Say nay! Say nay!'

Anne Marie clapped as enthusiastically as everyone
else as he came to the end of Sir Thomas Wyatt's
lovely poem, which was a lover's appeal to his unkind
mistress. She was startled by a light touch on her
shoulder and looked up at Kit in surprise.

'Will you sing with me?'

'But we have practised nothing, sir,' she said. 'Will
you not sing alone this time? I have been busy taking
various likenesses while you were all performing and
I thought that would be my contribution to the enter-
tainment.'

'You sang with Master Mountjoy.' Kit frowned at
her.

'Because we had done so before to please Lady
Hamilton,' Anne Marie said and wondered at the flash
of anger in his eyes. 'I should like to sing with you,
sir, but not in public for the first time.'

'Very well,' Kit said. 'Show me what you have
done.'

She handed him the little book she had found
among the items he had given her for her work, and

he began to glance through the pages. His frown lifted as he saw the pictures of his brothers caught in their play, and of his mother smiling benevolently at the company.

'These are wonderful,' he exclaimed. 'So full of life and mischief—just like those sad scamps!'

Lady Grantly asked to see the book and it was passed round from hand to hand for examination until Anne Marie was blushing from the praise heaped on her.

After this the men went off to Sir Christopher's library to look for a pamphlet published by an anonymous poet, which he had brought home with him, and the ladies were left together for an hour or so. Sir Nicholas then returned and said that his carriage had arrived to take them home and that they must leave before it became too dark.

There was a flurry of leavetaking, and then the house was suddenly quiet. Anne Marie had remained in the parlour while Sir Christopher and his mother saw their guests off, and she was about to retire to her own chamber when he came in.

'I am glad to find you alone at last,' he said in such a tone that she felt she had committed some crime. 'I think it is time we talked, Anne Marie.'

'If you wish.' She sat down on the oak settle with a hard back, her body straight and stiff as she faced him.

'Do not look as if you are about to go to the stake!' Kit exclaimed in exasperation at her manner. 'You were not thus with Sir Robert earlier—or Mountjoy.'

Anne Marie raised her head to look at him, her eyes clear and accusing. 'They were not angry with me, sir.'

'I am not angry with you!' Kit swore and then checked himself as she gave him a startled look. 'No, really I am not, Anne Marie. I have been frustrated... hurt by your indifference to me when you showed kindness to others.'

'That is not so,' she denied, blinking hard so that she should not cry. 'I have merely been polite. It is not my fault if Master Mountjoy...' She faltered and stopped short. 'What have I done that has made you angry? When you came to Drodney I thought we might be friends. Why have you turned against me?'

'It is not I who has changed. You accused me of betraying you when we were on board my ship,' Kit reminded her tight-lipped. 'I but did my duty, Anne Marie. I would have spared your father if there had been some way, but it was not possible.'

'Has he been taken?'

'No, I think not—but it is bound to happen one day. You must be prepared for it.'

'I know,' she said and bowed her head. 'It is his own fault that he is hunted.'

'We must not talk of things that upset you,' Kit said. 'I want to discuss our marriage.'

'Do you imagine that it will not distress me to speak of that?' Anne Marie asked, her face pale and proud. 'I do not understand why Her Majesty has decided that we must marry, sir—but you must see her and tell her that it is impossible.'

'Why is it impossible for you to think of marrying me?'

'You must know that I am a Catholic, sir.'

'These things can be arranged,' Kit said. 'For my mother's sake and our neighbours, we shall be married in the village church—but I shall not force you to follow a faith against your own, Anne Marie. You know that you must appear to accept the Protestant faith, as you did today. That would be so even if we were not married, as well you know.'

'My faith is not the only barrier to our marriage, sir.'

'Pray tell me what objections you have and I shall see what can be done to amend them.'

'There is the question of my duty to my father. He has forbidden such a match, and I must obey him.'

'Your father is a traitor and you are a ward of Queen Elizabeth,' Kit said, a flash of temper in his eyes. He was angered by her seeming indifference to all that he was offering. He would swear that it had not always been so. What ailed the girl, or was she merely wilful? 'You owe him no duty. All this is nonsense, Anne Marie, and can gain you nothing. It is by the Queen's own order that we are to marry, and neither you nor I can change that now.'

Anne Marie jumped to her feet, stung by his reminder that he was being forced into this marriage as much as she. No doubt it was the reason he had been glaring at her ever since he came home!

'I shall not marry you, sir. I do not care what they

do to me—I shall be imprisoned or tortured but I shall not be your wife.'

How could she speak to him that way? He had surely done nothing to deserve such scorn from her. His pride stung, Kit moved to prevent her as she would have left the room, catching her arm and swinging her round to face him.

'What foolishness is this?' he demanded, his mouth tight with anger. 'What have I done to you to make you dislike me so? I swear it was not thus a month ago.'

'I liked you well enough then, but I did not know you,' Anne Marie cried, her expression defiant. Her eyes were bright like jewels, reflecting a temper she had hidden too well for too long. 'You cannot force me to wed you, sir.'

'Do not tempt me to show you what I can make you do, mistress,' Kit warned. 'Else you may not like what you discover. You are a foolish girl and must learn that you cannot always have your way.'

'I have never had my way,' Anne Marie cried. 'All my life I have been told what I must do and what I may not, even though Beth did her best to shield me from the harshness of my life as her husband's ward. Oh, why did you not let me go to France? Why did you take me from that ship and bring me here?'

The anger faded from Kit's face as he saw real distress in hers, and he let go of her arm, uncertain and unwilling to add to her pain.

'I do not wish to make you my prisoner but merely my wife. I am sorry that you dislike the idea so much,' he said softly. 'I shall do what I may to change your mind before the wedding—but I have already spoken to the parson and it is set for the third week of January. You shall be my wife, Anne Marie, and I shall do all in my power to make your life as comfortable as possible. In time I hope you may learn to be content if not happy, but if not...'

His voice died away, leaving her feeling close to tears. Her defiance had died with his anger, and she could not bear the way he looked at her. She backed away from him, shaking her head, fighting the tears that threatened to overcome her.

'I shall not marry you,' she whispered. 'You cannot compel me.'

With that, she turned and fled from the room, running past Lady Hamilton and Sir Robert as they stood together in the hall without so much as a word as she rushed up the stairs to her own chamber.

There she locked the door behind her and flung herself down on the bed to weep. Oh, what was she to do? It seemed that nothing she could say would change his mind. He was determined to obey his orders this time, and if he did it would break her heart.

'What is the matter, my dear?' Sarah asked her when they were alone the following day. During the night the snow had melted and then hardened to ice, and Sir Robert had taken his leave at first light, saying that he must return to his home and would risk the roads rather than delay his journey further. 'You were upset last evening, and you are very quiet—are you unwell?'

'No, I am not ill, ma'am. Perhaps a little tired.'

'I think you do not always sleep as well as you should.'

'No, not always. I hope Sir Robert will have a safe journey onwards.'

'Yes, indeed, we must hope so. It is terrible weather for travelling, but he did not like to stay longer. We shall miss him, for he was good company.'

'Yes…'

'It is not because he has left that you are sad?'

'What?' Anne Marie was startled, then smiled and shook her head. 'Oh, no, ma'am. I liked him well enough but I do not mind that he has gone.'

'Then it is my foolish son who has upset you,' Sarah said, her eyes seeing the swiftly hidden look of pain in the girl's eyes. 'It was unkind of him not to discuss the wedding in private with you—to have it sprung on you like that was shocking. I have told him that he was wrong and should apologise to you.'

'I was shocked,' Anne Marie admitted hardly daring to look at her. 'But I have told Sir Christopher that he must ask the Queen to change her mind.'

Sarah laughed and laid down her needlework, reaching forward to pat the girl's hand. 'One does not ask Queen Elizabeth to change her mind,' she said. 'It would be foolish and could only result in disgrace for Kit and for this family.'

'Oh…' Anne Marie stared at her. 'You mean that if I refused to marry him it would reflect badly on you?'

'It could ruin us,' Sarah said. 'There might be arrest and fines—all manner of things might happen. You must understand that Kit took a great risk bringing you here, Anne Marie. He was ordered to take you to London, but after what had happened he feared that you might be arrested and sent to the Tower. He did not want you to be so harshly treated, for he believes that you have not been given the life you deserve in the past.'

'Beth and Thomas Makepeace were good to me,' Anne Marie said, reluctant to be persuaded and yet feeling the power of Sarah's argument. 'It was just that I was never free to come and go as I pleased.'

'They did what they could for you,' Sarah agreed. 'Beth is a good woman and she loves you, but she could not give you the freedom you deserved. Surely it would not be a hardship to you to live here with us, my dear? I thought you happy enough with us these past weeks?'

'I have been happy with you. You have been kind and I enjoy being a part of your family.'

'Then what is it that worries you about this marriage?' Sarah smiled gently. 'If it is marriage itself that frightens you, you need not fear it, Anne Marie. My own dear husband was a kind and considerate lover, and I believe Kit will be the same. There is naught to fear from what happens in the marriage bed, my dear. Indeed, some women find great pleasure in being a wife. I did myself, and I believe it is the same for Lady Grantly.'

Anne Marie's cheeks were on fire, her eyes downcast. 'I cannot wed him, ma'am. I am so sorry for bringing trouble on you, but I cannot marry Sir Christopher.'

'I fear that you have little choice. My son's mind is set on this and indeed it is by order of the Queen. Give yourself a little time to think, Anne Marie. Would you really prefer to be a prisoner again?'

Anne Marie hung her head. It was all so difficult. She felt guilty when she realised that her defiance might bring the Queen's wrath down on this family, who had been so good to her—but how could she marry a man who did not love her?

'There are marriages of convenience where there is no love at all between the husband and wife,' Sarah was saying. 'I have heard of child brides being deserted after the ceremony and never seeing their husbands again. In these cases the man has married for property and finds his amusement in town. But I do not say that will be the case with you. Nor is it so with Lady Grantly, as I'm sure you must have seen for yourself when they stayed with us. Besides, I am sure Kit is very fond of you.'

She did not want him to be fond! And she knew well that not all marriages were happy and not all husbands faithful. Her own father had purported to love her mother, but she knew that there had been other women in his life, even when his wife still lived. She had been too young to know it at the time, but her habit of listening to her guardians talking privately had revealed many things to her—things that perhaps it would be better if she had never heard.

Anne Marie was conscious of an ache in her breast. She knew that she was fighting a losing battle, because every fibre of her being was telling her that it would give her pleasure to lie in Kit's arms. Yet he did not love her, and she would lose all pride if she let him see that she loved him so desperately.

There, she had admitted it to herself at last. The pain she had felt, the struggle going on inside her had all been because she denied the fact. She loved him and had done so for a long time.

'May I have a little space to think, ma'am?' she asked, her voice no more than a whisper. 'Then I shall give you my decision.'

'You must give your answer to Kit,' Sarah told her. 'But think long and hard before you deny him, my dear. Should you be obstinate he could do no more to help you, and you would be taken from our care and given to another custodian. I do not imagine you would be sent back to Drodney, and I fear you might find your life hard to bear. It might even be that the Queen would compel you to marry another man of her choosing, and to refuse again might seal your fate.'

Anne Marie inclined her head but said no more as she got up and left the room, making her way to her own chamber. She was in such turmoil, and her heart felt as if it were breaking. She must think carefully before she gave her answer.

'I understand that you wish to speak to me alone?' Kit faced her across the small parlour where she had asked for him to come to her. It was cold, for the fire had not yet been lit, and she was trembling, though whether from cold or another source she could not tell. 'My mother says that you have something to say to me?'

'I believe that if I were to refuse to obey the order from Her Majesty it would cause trouble for you and your family,' Anne Marie said, her face pale. She lifted her head, looking directly into his eyes. 'I do not wish to be the cause of distress to Lady Hamilton and the children—and if you are of the same mind, I have decided to accept the marriage on one condition.'

Kit's face showed no sign of his relief. Anne Marie had scarcely moved out of her chamber for three days, eating and drinking hardly anything, and he had begun to believe that she would go into a decline. Indeed, he had begun to think that he would have to return to court and beg for the Queen's mercy, when her request had at last been brought to him. He did not imagine that Elizabeth would have been pleased to hear that the marriage was not to go ahead, and he dared not think what might have been the consequences for Anne Marie.

'I am glad to hear that you have come to your senses, mistress,' he replied, looking and sounding more severe than he intended because of his sombre thoughts. 'May I know the nature of your condition?'

Anne Marie took a deep breath, then clasped her hands in front of her. 'The Queen has commanded that we two be joined in marriage—but she hath not commanded me to your bed. I realise that you have the strength and the power to compel me, but I shall never willingly consent to be your wife in truth or bear your children.'

Kit could not believe what he was hearing. Not come to his bed? Not bear his children—it was too cruel, beyond bearing! How could she make such a condition?

'Damn you!' he cried his temper bursting forth. 'That is ridiculous. I never heard such a thing and shall not agree to it.'

'It is no more than happens in many an arranged marriage,' Anne Marie said. Her face was very pale and she could not look at him. 'Some brides never see their husband after their wedding day. Their husbands prefer to live at court and leave them in the country to take care of the estate.'

'I am not one of those husbands.' Kit crossed the room in long strides, catching her about the wrist and pulling her close to him. She was startled and glanced up, her eyes widening. He was breathing hard as he looked down at her, nostrils flaring with his passion. 'Once you are my wife you *shall* be mine.'

He bent his head, his mouth seeking hers in a hungry, angry kiss that shocked her because it aroused an answering need in her, and though her mind resisted, her body welcomed him, melding with his as if it had always been a part of him. Oh, she wanted to be like this always, to let herself drift on the warm tide of desire he had stirred into being, and yet she knew that in the end it could only bring unhappiness. He did not love her, wanted merely to bend her to his will, to force her to obey that cruel order from the Queen.

His eyes were filled with angry triumph as he pulled away at last and gazed down at her. His mouth was loose with desire, his face working with the passion he sought to hold in check as he reached out to stroke her cheek and the white arch of her throat.

'You speak with two tongues, Anne Marie,' he said softly as his hand lingered at the nape of her neck, stroking the sensitive skin. 'Methinks you pretend too much that you do not truly feel. It is a habit forced on you by circumstance, but one you should curb. Be honest and admit that you are as caught by this as I...'

Kit was speaking of the feeling between them, but she thought he meant the Queen's order and was stung by the reminder that he was marrying her only because he had no choice. But he was a man and men took these things lightly. He would marry her and then desert her for another. Lady Sarah had told her it was often so.

She wrenched away from him, turning her back as she fought to recover her composure. What was she to do? She knew that he would bend her to his will, she would become his willing lapdog and lose all pride of self.

'I do not want to wed you,' she said with her back still turned towards him as the tears threatened. 'I do not love you and I shall fight you to the last.'

'So be it, my love,' Kit said and lifted the hair at the back of her neck. She felt his lips against the sensitive skin there and shivered as her body quivered with pleasure. 'You may fight me all you wish, but you shall be my wife, Anne Marie—and not only in name.'

She made no answer, nor would she turn to look at him, and in another moment she knew that he had left the room. She sank down upon a hard settle, feeling weak and drained. Her resistance had been for nothing. He had always meant to have her, and have her he would, no matter how much she protested.

She was honest enough to admit in her heart that a part of her rejoiced that the struggle was at an end and she would be his wife. Yet still her mind resisted.

He would have her, but she would never let him see that he had all of her. He might take her body, for her flesh was too weak to deny him, and once married he would have the right to make her his own, by force if he so wished—but he would not have her willingly. She would not confess her love.

She would hold out in this at least, for in that way she might salvage at least some of her pride.

Her decision made, Anne Marie lifted her head, her eyes bright with pride. She had wept enough and would weep no more. The die was cast and there was no path back for her. Indeed, she had never truly had a choice from the moment that Kit had come after her and taken her as a captive from the *Belle Rosemarie*.

Just why he had come after her she could not be certain. She supposed it must have been because he had been ordered to it—and yet he had disobeyed his orders when he brought her home.

Chapter Seven

The snow had come again, melted once more, and then the weather had turned even colder. The ground was now frozen hard, which might make it easier for the guests who were travelling to their wedding, Anne Marie thought as she looked out that morning. Had the thaw set in the roads would have turned to mud and been almost impassable.

Most of their guests lived within a short distance of the Hamilton estate, but some were travelling from other counties and would stay on for a day or two before attempting the return journey.

Anne Marie and Kit were to spend two nights at home before leaving for London. But she did not dare to think beyond the ceremony and the wedding feast, which would follow. For nearly three weeks she had tried to keep as much distance as she decently could between herself and Kit.

Surprisingly, he had not tried to impose his company on her, though he had taken her riding when the weather permitted. Since a groom always accompanied them she had not felt in any danger of another confrontation. Indeed, he had been everything that a gentleman should be: kind, considerate, good-mannered, pleasant company.

He had insisted on joining the party to visit Sir Nicholas's menagerie, and had seemed to enjoy the expedition as much as the children. Seeing him relaxed and smiling with his brothers made Anne Marie let down her guard for a while and it had been an enjoyable day.

Master Mountjoy had proved to be very informative about the animals they saw, and since his manner towards her had become more formal than it had been just before Christmas, Anne Marie was able to feel comfortable in his company.

The menagerie was cared for by a simple fellow called Ben, who had rescued many of the animals, bringing them back from the woods where he had found them wounded and caring for them. However, the bears had been bought from their cruel masters.

'We had one that gave birth to cubs,' Lady Grantly explained to her visitors. 'And then we saw another at a fair that we just had to rescue and I fear our little family has grown. I only wish that we might set them free, but I fear it is impossible. They could not fend for themselves, you see, and would soon die or be trapped, so we keep them in captivity for their own good.'

Anne Marie felt sympathy for the bears, whose plight she thought much like her own. She had been told she must marry for her own good, as well as that of the Hamilton family, and she could not help but resent her situation, for she was no freer than the bears. She had now accepted that there was no other way open to her, but she was still determined that she would not be a willing bride.

Yet each day since she had agreed to marry had been pleasant enough, and she had grown accustomed to the thought that she was to be Kit's wife, and to seeing him about the house. Sometimes she recalled the happy times she had spent with him at Drodney and wished them back again, but at others she hardened her heart and was cool to him when he tried to engage her in conversation.

Now that her wedding day had arrived, however, Anne Marie felt an odd sense of calm. Since there was no help for it, she might as well enjoy the day even if she dreaded the night.

Kit had been generous to her, giving her all manner of gifts, including several pretty gowns, shoes of silk and others of leather, gloves, hats and a splendid cloak with a fur lining.

He had also purchased many additions to the silver, glass and pewter for the house. It was fitting that a new bride should have her own things, and most of his purchases were waiting for her in the apartment they would share. This consisted of a large bedchamber, which was well furnished and comfortable, a closet for private functions, and a small parlour where they could retire of an evening should they wish to be apart from the family.

The bed had new hangings and quilts and looked

very well, and Anne Marie knew that by the time they returned from church all her personal belongings would have been taken to the bridal chamber. *But she would not think of that!*

Sarah Hamilton had been up at first light to see that everything was in train for the wedding feast, but Anne Marie had been allowed to sleep on. She was, however, awake when Sarah came to help her dress, and greeted her with a nervous smile.

Her gown of cream silk, embroidered with gold thread and sown with tiny seed pearls, had been bought for her in London by her husband-to-be. It was an extravagant, costly thing that Anne Marie was almost afraid to wear.

'You will wear it again when you go to court,' Sarah had told her when she had protested at its magnificence. 'Perhaps it is a little too rich for a country wedding, but it will not seem so at court, my love. Besides, Kit has enough wealth to buy you twenty such gowns should you wish for them.'

Dressed in her wedding gown, her hair hanging from beneath a cap of gold, falling almost to the small of her back, Anne Marie looked truly beautiful, if a little anxious. Sarah blinked as tears came to her eyes and she kissed the girl's cheek.

'You are very lovely,' she said. 'I have despaired of my son ever finding a bride, for I believe he had a disappointment in his youth, though he never spoke of it to me. But in you he has found a woman I know to be honest of heart and a friend to me and to my family. I wish you happiness, Anne Marie. I know you are fearful of the future, but I see no need for it. I believe Kit cares for you in his way, though he may not always show his feelings—and I think in your heart you care for him, though you may not yet admit it.'

Anne Marie's throat felt too tight to answer. She was terrified and yet in some strange way elated. If only Sarah was right. If Kit did care for her a little, then they might be happy.

He had been gentle with her of late, no sign of the temper that had so disturbed her, and his gifts had been more than generous, chosen with care to please her. Perhaps he did love her just a little. Perhaps she was foolish to deny her own feelings for him.

Anne Marie's thoughts were confused as the wedding party left for the church. Kit had stayed with Sir Nicholas overnight, but their kind neighbour would be waiting at the church to escort Anne Marie down the aisle. Kit had asked one of his seafaring friends to stand up with him in church, and Sir Nicholas would give the bride to her groom.

A pale sun shone on them as they arrived to cheers from the village folk and Anne Marie felt her spirits lift. She had made up her mind that she would face whatever came with courage and her tears were long dried. She was smiling as she walked to meet her fate, outwardly the perfect picture of a happy bride.

She smiled nervously at Sir Nicholas as he greeted her at the door. If things had been different it should have been her father walking down the aisle with her. Yet he would never have permitted this wedding at all. She was sad that it should be so, but she knew that her father had never truly cared for her. At least she had the support of a true friend. She gripped Sir Nicholas's arm as they walked down the aisle, trembling inside but reassured by her escort's warm smile.

It was very cold in the church, but Anne Marie's hand did not shake as the ring was slipped over her knuckle, though she kept her eyes downcast and would not look at the man to whom she had just been given in marriage. She was very conscious of his powerful figure beside her and did not dare to look into his eyes for fear of what she might see there.

At last the ceremony was over, the blessing complete and the register signed. To the sound of pealing bells, the newly married couple walked side by side from the church.

Anne Marie gave a squeal of laughter as they were showered with the petals of dried roses. Then several children were pushed forward by their grinning parents to present the bride with tokens of good luck. They paused while Kit distributed the usual wedding coin, tossing it into the air for the children to catch, and then they were in their coach and being taken back to the house.

'So, my lady,' Kit said, the glimmer of a smile upon his lips. 'We are married after all.'

'Yes, sir, I believe we are.' Anne Marie would not look at him, playing instead with a token one of the children had given her. Kit reached across to pull it from her hands.

'You know what this is I suppose?'

'I thought it a token of good luck.'

'It is a fertility doll,' Kit said with a wicked gleam in his eyes. 'If you place it beneath your pillow it will ensure that you conceive a child.'

'Then you may be certain that I shall not do so!' He had her attention now, and she gave him a glaring look for daring to tease her. Did it amuse him to know that he had his own way despite her—and would he keep to the condition she had imposed?

'Are you still determined to resist your duties as a wife, Anne Marie?'

'You knew my condition when I agreed to the marriage.'

'But I did not accept it.' He tossed the crude doll to one side. 'I think we have no need of that, my love. You are young and comely, and I believe I have a man's true appetites and will acquit my own duties right lustily. I have no reason to doubt that we shall make many children together—and enjoy the getting of them, Anne Marie.'

Her cheeks were on fire as he mocked her, but she averted her eyes from his and would not let him provoke her. He was making it clear that his intentions were to bed her as soon as they were alone, and she was equally determined that he should not find her an easy conquest.

However, she would behave decently, even if he did not, and it would not do to allow him to provoke her into a quarrel on their wedding day.

'We shall discuss these matters later, sir. I believe that this is not the proper time.'

'Proper, Anne Marie? How can it be improper for a groom to talk of loving his bride?' His brows arched at her. 'Perhaps you are right, yet I think I shall taste the delights to come.' He moved across the carriage in one lithe, catlike spring and seized her in his arms, kissing her with a hungry, slightly angry passion that set her heart racing.

'Please do not,' she protested. 'The horses are slowing, and we are nearly home. In a moment we must get out and greet our guests as they come back from church.'

'They will not mind that you have a little colour in your cheeks. A bride is supposed to look happy, Anne Marie. Pray try not to look as if you are about to face a martyr's death. You will find the marriage bed less hard than a cot in a prison cell, I'll warrant.'

'If they were not about to let down the steps I would hit you!' she hissed, and ground her teeth in frustration as she saw his teasing smile. 'I shall not be so circumspect when we are alone, sir, I promise you.'

'I am relieved to hear it.' Kit's eyes danced with wicked delight at her discomfiture. 'That is very much better, my love. You have some life about you now. Fear not, Anne Marie. I dare say you may find marriage more to your taste than you imagine. I promise that I shall not hurt you. I want only to make you happy, to teach you the pleasure that comes from loving.'

'I do not wish to learn that from you!'

The flash of anger in his eyes from her careless

words was lost on Anne Marie, because the groom was opening the door and waiting respectfully to help her down.

She allowed him to do so and walked on ahead of Kit to the house, her head lifted proudly as she fought to control the temper rising inside her. He had made her so angry!

Kit caught up with her at the door, taking her arm firmly and forcing her to pause as they were greeted by the servants lined up to welcome them home.

The smiling faces of Kit's household and the warmth of their congratulations could not be ignored. They were not to blame for her unhappiness. Anne Marie remembered her manners and responded as she ought, thanking them all for their hard work and accepting their good wishes with a shy smile.

'God bless you, Lady Hamilton,' one of the serving wenches cried. 'May you both live long and happy lives.'

Anne Marie thanked her and, laying her hand upon Kit's arm, she went with him into the long gallery, where tables had been set up and they were to receive their guests for the wedding feast.

A footman at once offered them a tray bearing two large cups of wine. Anne Marie hesitated, but Kit took both and pressed one into her hand.

'We shall toast the future, my lady. Drink it all, Anne Marie. 'Tis but a sweet honey wine and will make you feel better, more able to face all the congratulations of our friends. I fear that some of their jests may make you blush, but you must accept them with a good heart, even though you may think some crude.'

'Lady Hamilton warned me what to expect.'

'You are Lady Hamilton now,' Kit reminded her. 'My mother asks that she be known as Lady Sarah in future, for it would make her feel old to be called a dowager.'

'I had not forgotten.' Anne Marie's head went up, her eyes meeting his with pride. She finished her wine defiantly. It had a sweet, pleasant taste and she did not think it at all strong, not like some of the bitter wines that gentlemen seemed to enjoy. 'You have made your position more than clear, sir.'

'I would argue that point,' Kit murmured mischievously. He was smiling at the way she had finished what was a potent wine so happily. If she continued to drink the wine he had ordered be supplied to her she would lose her nerves by the time they were alone. 'But I hear Lady Sarah's voice in the hall and I believe they are upon us.'

Lady Sarah came into the gallery even as he spoke, her younger sons following with their tutor. Behind them were Sir Nicholas and Lady Grantly, and then almost at once came twenty others, filling the room with their laughter and chatter.

Anne Marie was kept busy greeting and thanking their guests. They had all brought gifts of linen, silver or glass, and she was overwhelmed by the generosity of people, most of whom she had met no more than once or twice and some who were unknown to her. All of them were Kit's friends and relatives, for she had none of her own—or none that would have been acceptable wedding guests. Beth and Thomas would have been welcome, of course, but were unable to leave Drodney at this time, though they had sent their good wishes and written of their hope to see the happy pair at some future date.

'You look beautiful, my dear,' Lady Grantly told her and kissed her cheek. 'I am so pleased that you have married Sir Christopher, for I know that you will be happy. We shall be neighbours and friends, and it will all be exceedingly pleasant.'

'Yes,' Anne Marie said. 'It will be pleasant to have such kind friends.'

She realised as she spoke that her life would be very different from what she had known at Drodney. Now that she was married she could be of no further use to Lord Fraser and was therefore surely safe from the fear of abduction. She would be able to come and go much more freely than before.

'A cup of wine, my love.'

Anne Marie accepted the wine from Kit's hand and sipped it. She was beginning to feel so much better. She was smiling as she finished her wine and then took her place of honour at the head of the table. Another cup of wine was placed to her right hand and she lifted it to her lips as Kit saluted her with his.

How pleasant this all was. She did not know why she had thought it would be an ordeal. Even the rather bawdy jests and suggestive leers from some of the gentlemen, who were beginning to be a little free with their tongues, did not much upset her, though as Kit had warned, some of the suggestions she overheard brought a fiery flush to her cheeks. However, although she ate but a few morsels and sipped now and then at her wine, she discovered that much of the fear and apprehension that had haunted her earlier was slipping away.

The feast itself consisted of course after course of rich dishes. Besides the baked carp there was crab and shrimp caught from local seaports, followed by a huge baron of beef, suckling pig with delicious crackling, onions in red wine and cabbage with almonds and sweet plums; this was followed by capons, goose, a comfit of duck and apples, and then all manner of syllabubs, creams, junkets and rich honey cakes.

Lady Sarah had surpassed herself, though many of the delicacies had been sent down from London at Kit's behest. The guests proved themselves good trenchermen, demolishing the intricate confections of sugar and cream with a hearty will, though Anne Marie noticed that Kit ate sparingly, as she did.

Once their eyes met and something in his made her heart jump, though whether it was from fright or some other strange emotion she could not be certain.

After most of the food had at last been consumed, those who were able to move from the table repaired into the next parlour, where the floor had been cleared to allow for dancing.

The minstrels had begun to play on their instruments of woodwind and viol as Anne Marie and Kit began the dancing with a stately pavane. This particular piece was of Spanish origin, a ceremonial, processional dance usually performed by a column of couples and a little old-fashioned these days. As this was a wedding, for a while the bridal couple danced alone, and then as the music changed to the more lively chords of the galliard they were joined by others. The two dances usually went in pairs, the galliard following because it was so much more athletic and heated the faces of those who took part.

In this dance the gentleman threw the lady into the air and caught her about the waist as she came down. It was popular with the gentlemen and had not started to die out as the pavane had because it allowed for intimate contact, which might otherwise be frowned upon in company.

Anne Marie was certainly aware that it heated her blood, as Kit held her above him, laughing up at her. His eyes glowed with what she could not doubt was desire, and there was a look of the hunter about him as he performed the dance, his manner seeming to challenge her, as if daring her to deny the feeling that was building between them. Her nerves tingled and she felt a strange sensation in her stomach, a fluttering and trembling that made her breathless—though fortunately as the music died she was able to blame that on the dancing.

'I fear I must rest for a moment,' she said, fanning her heated cheeks. 'It is very warm in here, do you not think so?'

'Shall I take you out to the terrace for a breath of air, my lady?' Kit asked, and the look in his eyes scared her to death.

'No, no, I thank you,' she said. 'I shall be better in a moment. Pray excuse me, sir. I think I should mingle with our guests a little.'

Kit laughed and let her go, well aware of the effect the dance had had on them both. He watched her circulate among the smiling happy guests, well content now to wait for the time when they would at last be alone and he could claim his prize.

The celebrations had gone on until late into the evening, and Anne Marie had danced with several gentlemen before dancing once more with her husband. Although she had taken part in both the country-dances, and the galliard with others, it was only with Kit that she became so heated, something she knew he was aware of and which caused his eyes to gleam.

He smiled at her, a half tender, half mocking look in his eyes, as their fourth dance of the evening ended.

'So, my love, I think we begin,' he murmured softly against her ear as he released her. 'The hour is late. I believe your guests will forgive you if you retire now.'

Anne Marie inclined her head in assent, not speaking. She could not find the breath to speak because her heart was beating like a drum. She left his side and made her way to Lady Sarah, who smiled her understanding.

'You want to leave now?'

'I—I believe it is time.' Anne Marie ran the tip of

her pink tongue over her lips. 'May we slip away quietly?'

'I fear that may not be possible, but we shall try.'

However, once it was seen that the bride was about to leave, those gentlemen who had imbibed a little too freely of their host's good wine gave a great cheer. Several of them followed her and Lady Sarah from the room, singing and jesting as everyone trooped up the stairs to the upper landing. At the door of the bridal chamber, Lady Sarah turned and stopped them with a shake of her head and bid them good-night.

'You will respect my daughter-in-law's modesty, good sirs,' she said firmly. 'She thanks you for your kind wishes and she wishes you good night.'

There were a few protests, for the custom of seeing the bride bedded had been a popular one and some would have liked to see it continue. However, in these enlightened days there were many who believed it belonged to the past and Lady Sarah had her way, and with some grumbling the guests went back to their feasting, though still singing and calling out in a bawdy fashion.

'There, that was not so very bad,' Sarah said, smiling at her new daughter as the door closed behind them. 'You must forgive them their manners, Anne Marie. I dare say a few will have sore heads in the morning, and some of them will have their ears severely boxed by their good wives if I am not mistaken.'

Anne Marie laughed, her embarrassment gone as she listened to her mother-in-law's good sense.

'They have drunk too much,' she said. 'I think I may have drunk a little too much at dinner, though I have not touched a drop of wine since.'

'Then have a little of this,' Sarah brought her a cup of the sweet honey wine she had enjoyed earlier. 'It will relax you, my love—and now I shall help you to undress myself.'

Anne Marie stood still while her laces were unfastened, sipping her wine as she was helped out of petticoats and the embroidered overskirt, which a maid took away to sponge and press before storing it in a chest with lavender sprigs to keep it sweet.

When Anne Marie was dressed in a soft nightgown, her hair hanging loose down her back, Lady Sarah kissed her cheek and bid her goodnight, taking the maids away with her.

Anne Marie's head was spinning a little as she walked to the bed, which had been turned down ready for her, and used the steps to climb up on the high box mattress. That wine must have been stronger than she had thought earlier, she reflected as she relaxed against the pile of goose feather pillows, and her eyelids felt a little heavy. If she were not careful she would fall asleep.

She must not do that! Remembering belatedly that this was her wedding night and that she had intended to deny her husband his rights with all her strength, she forced herself to stay awake, her back ramrod straight as she fixed her eyes on the door and waited for Kit to come to her.

She did not have long to wait. The door opened almost at once and Kit came into the room. For a moment she heard sounds of revelry still going on within the house, but none close to—which meant that he had somehow avoided his friends to come to her in private.

He stood just inside the threshold, gazing at her, and she felt her throat tighten, her heart beginning to race in the same way as it had when they danced the galliard. Why must he look at her so? He was sapping her will, robbing her of the determination to resist at all costs.

'You look beautiful,' he said as he came towards her. He had taken off his splendid wedding doublet and was clad only in trunk hose and a shirt of soft linen, which was opened to the waist, revealing his smooth, hard chest. His skin had a golden sheen that seemed to suggest that he had often gone without even a shirt when at sea, and he retained a little of his once deep tan. Beneath that tan, strong muscles rippled, threatening her with his power and strength. 'Do not be afraid, Anne Marie. I know that I have teased you unmercifully but you did make me so angry. However, all that is at an end now that you are my wife, and I want us to understand one another.'

Anne Marie swallowed hard as he came to the bed and stood gazing down at her. Her mind denied him as fiercely as ever, but her body was strangely compliant. She felt a kind of lassitude, a languor that seemed to hold her limbs, making her incapable of resistance. She was tired but in a pleasant way, luxuriously relaxed like a cat in the sun, too content to spring up and walk away.

'I do not want…' she began, but he was sitting beside her, his eyes seeming to caress her as his hand reached out to touch her hair, lifting it and letting the strands fall through his fingers. His caress was so pleasant, so compelling, making her feel so relaxed. He leaned closer, touching his lips to her forehead, and as she closed her eyes, trying to still the trembling that had suddenly seized her, she felt his lips briefly on her lids. 'You must not…'

'What must I not do?' he asked, his lips touching at the little hollow at the base of her throat and making her gasp with some strange wild excitement. 'This or this perhaps…' He pulled her nightgown swiftly away, ripping the fine material and discarding the shreds on the floor beside him to feast his eyes on the beauty of her naked body. 'Or this…' He bent his head, lapping at the rosy peaks of her nipples as they stiffened at his touch, then taking them into his mouth to suck and nibble gently with his teeth, but not in such a way that it hurt her. 'Perhaps you would rather that I did not do this?' He trailed his tongue down over her taut navel, flicking at her and tasting her, and then he parted her legs with his hand and began to kiss the soft flesh of her inner thighs.

'No, no, you must not,' Anne Marie protested. She was aware that he was dominating her, bending her to his will, and yet it felt so pleasant to lie here like this and let him do what he would that she could not raise the necessary energy to defy him. She had planned to fight him, to strike him with her fists and claw him with her nails rather than give in, but she could only whimper and moan with delight as he began to pay attention to the secret feminine centre of her being. 'Please, please…' But in her heart she knew that she did not want him to stop this exquisite torture. She wanted him to touch and caress her, to continue to pleasure her. Her words might seem to say him nay but in truth she knew she was entirely his to do with as he pleased.

'Then perhaps I should do this?' Kit asked, lowering his body to lie close to hers. She felt the burn of his flesh and wondered when he had disrobed. She had not noticed. Was she dreaming? Nothing seemed real, and she was hardly aware of what he was doing as he kissed her lips once more and she felt her body arch into his. And then he was parting her legs wide, his body covering hers as she felt the sudden thrust and heat of him and he was inside her. At first she was so startled that she tried to protest, but his mouth covered hers, kissing and comforting her, and his next thrust was less of a shock than the first; he was moving gently with a rhythm that seemed to take her with him. 'Forgive me if I hurt you a little, my love, but 'tis always so the first time. You will find more pleasure the next time I promise you.'

'Never…' Anne Marie protested, but was forced to stifle a moan of pleasure as his body moved in a strangely pleasant dance that drew her to follow it,

though her mind tried to resist him. She could not
understand why this had happened, why she had been
unable to fight. What was wrong with her? Why could
she not think properly? Her mind was elsewhere, her
body floating as if on air, her limbs refusing to obey
her. She wanted to defy him but she could not, oh,
she could not! Her mind might protest but her body
welcomed him. 'I shall…'

She had meant to say that she would never surrender but she was beyond conscious thought, hardly
aware when the weight of his body came full upon
her and he lay gasping, groaning with the pleasure of
his release.

'Oh, my sweet love,' Kit murmured with his head
against her breast. 'I knew you would be wonderful
but I never dreamed that…' He raised his head to
look at her as she gave a gentle sigh and he realised
that she had fallen asleep at the very moment he
meant to declare himself and tell her of his love. For
a moment he was torn between anger and exasperation as he realised that she must have drunk even
more of the special wine than he had intended. He
had wanted to ease her nerves and make her less
frightened, but it seemed that she must have been intoxicated from the start. 'Oh, Anne Marie,' he said
with a sigh, as he moved away from her. 'Will you
even remember in the morning?'

It was his own fault for plying her with too much
wine, he reflected ruefully, not knowing that his
mother had given Anne Marie a much stronger cup

to make sure that she was not too nervous to receive her husband.

'Forgive me,' he murmured. 'I wanted you warm and willing but I would not have taken advantage of you had I realised. You will think me a careless husband taking thought only for his own pleasure.'

He was angry with himself for not realising that her strangely compliant manner had been brought about by too much wine, and knew that he would rather she had fought him tooth and nail than that he had taken her unknowing. Yet she had seemed to welcome him, and he had been too eager for his bride to suspect that quiet manner.

He had hoped that the differences between them might be at an end now, but he was very much afraid that when she realised what had happened in the morning, Anne Marie was going to be very, very angry—and in his heart he could not blame her.

Anne Marie saw the serving wenches giggling over the blood-stained sheets and felt her temper rising. Those foolish, simpering women, looking at each other in satisfaction because their master had clearly bedded his wife in the proper fashion and proved himself a true man. Their amusement pricked her with shame and disgust at her own compliance.

How dared Kit take such wicked advantage of her? How had it happened at all? She could recall nothing of what had occurred after she climbed into the bed and then the door opened. She thought that he had come to her, gazing down at her and saying that she was lovely, but after that…there were only vague pictures in her mind: pictures that made her hot with shame.

Had he really done all those things that seemed dreamlike? Had she really moaned and pressed her body closer to his as he did things that were surely shameful? No, no, she could not believe that she had been so wanton.

What had been in the cup of wine her mother-in-law had given her to make her lose control the way she had? There must have been something, for the wine she had drunk earlier, while relaxing her and making her feel happy, had not made her lose her senses. Or perhaps she had simply taken too much wine?

She was shamed to think that she had been intoxicated on her wedding night. And she had meant to fight Kit, to show him that she would not be his willing bride. Instead, she feared she had been all too willing to receive him.

She was truly Kit's wife in every way, and must accept that it was so—and yet he had taken her with no thought for her wishes. Mayhap he had asked his mother to give her something so that she could not resist him.

The thought made her angry, and determined that it should not happen again. Next time he came to her he should learn what she thought of his base actions!

Kit saw the flash of anger in her eyes when he entered their private parlour later that morning to ask why she had not yet come downstairs.

'My mother had a tray sent up to you this morning in case you were tired,' he said, his eyes moving over her face intently. 'You look a little tired, Anne Marie. Would you prefer to rest? It was my intention to ask if you would ride?'

'I thank you, and I shall ride,' she replied, giving him a proud cold look. 'I believe Lady Sarah ensured that I slept well, though I would have preferred that she had dealt fairly with me.'

'My mother gave you something?' Kit frowned as he saw the anger in her face.

'A cup of the wine we had earlier that I liked, but stronger somehow. It had a strange effect on me, as you know well, sir.'

'Damn her!' Kit swore. 'I had not intended it, Anne Marie. I swear that I wanted you to drink enough to lose your fear but not that you should lose your senses.'

'Yet you took full advantage of my languor,' she replied with a haughty stare. He must not look at her so! It made her want to throw herself into his arms and confess her true feelings for him. 'I shall not easily forgive that, sir.'

'I did not realise until later,' Kit said, and saw that she did not believe him. 'You must know that I care deeply for you.'

'Your actions have not been that of a man who loves,' she snapped angrily. 'You told me you would have me whether I was willing or not—and you seduced me while I was incapable of resisting.'

'I swear that was not by my desire,' he said, silently cursing his mother for her well-intentioned interference. Anne Marie was justified in her complaint, and he was aware of both guilt and disappointment within his own mind. 'I would not have had it happen had I known.'

'I believe you said you were ready to go riding?' Anne Marie's eyes flashed with annoyance. Did he hope to sway her with a few impassioned words? If so he was sorely mistaken. It would take more than that to make her forgive him!

She stormed into the bedchamber ahead of him, ordering a startled servant to bring her a hat and gloves and her riding whip. Kit leaned against the doorway and watched her, a rueful smile on his lips. How well she had concealed her temper when they first met! He had little suspected her fiery nature then, and yet he had caught glimpses of it.

There was passion in her. Even though she had scarcely known what was going on when he made love to her the previous night, she had responded to him with both passion and what he believed was love.

If she loved him why would she not admit it?

Perhaps she needed further proof of his own love for her? He must find some way to turn her from this raging termagant into the love goddess of the previous night—but next time she would not be drugged by some damnable concoction of his mother's.

Anne Marie kicked the flanks of her horse, surging ahead of both Kit and the groom. She suddenly felt free, the fresh air having lifted the dull headache that had plagued her that morning.

At least her marriage had brought her this! She could ride when she pleased and as often as she pleased, and she was soon to be taken to Queen Elizabeth's court. From what she had been told, she believed that she would see many splendours there. Not least for Anne Marie the work of Hans Holbein the younger, who had sadly died of a fever at the age of six and forty years. Sir Nicholas Grantly had told her that in some respects the work of the great miniaturist Nicholas Hilliard was even better than that of the master he had admired.

And there would be shops! Anne Marie had never been shopping in her life, buying only a few trinkets from the travelling pedlars that had come her way. She had been told that she was to have an allowance for her clothes and other things, and that meant that she would be able to choose what she wanted for the first time in her life—and she owed it to her husband.

The anger that had overtaken her when she saw the blood staining her wedding sheets had been made worse by the satisfied looks of the serving wenches. It had abated a little now, though she was determined that she would teach her husband a lesson when he came to her that night! She was a woman with a mind of her own, not merely a wife.

Perhaps they would have a true marriage in time, but not until she had made him suffer a little for what he had done. His behaviour had been base indeed. If they had been evenly matched, if she had known what was happening to her—perhaps she might in the end have surrendered.

Being an essentially honest girl, Anne Marie knew that it was more than likely she would have done after some resistance. A part of her admitted that she loved him, but her pride would not let her smile when he smiled at her. She was grateful to him for the things that he had given her, and the touch of his hand as he lifted her down from her horse made her heart race, but she could not forgive so easily.

Anne Marie had said nothing to her mother-in-law about the wine she had been given the previous night. She had no doubt that the act had been well-intentioned, but she would think twice before accepting such a drink from her hands again.

Had she but known it, Lady Sarah was thoroughly chastened having been told harshly by her son that she had had no right to give his wife such a concoction.

'It was merely to help her, Kit,' she replied uncomfortably. 'I knew that she was very nervous and I wanted to make her first time easy for her. I am sorry if it did not suit her.'

Kit's eyes flashed with annoyance. 'You will never do such a thing again. Do you hear me? It was wrong and deceitful, and I am very angry.'

Sarah had bowed her head in shame. She knew that what she had done had been a mistake.

Pride helped Anne Marie to sail through the day, taking a smiling farewell of those guests who had stayed overnight, and ignoring their sly looks. No doubt every servant in the house knew that the master had done his duty by his wife!

Oh, but she was not finished, Anne Marie thought as she smarted with indignation. She would have her revenge yet! There would be no staining of any kind on her sheets this next morning.

Anne Marie could not wait for night to fall. Soon after supper she began to yawn, kissed her mother-in-law's cheek and whispered into her ear that she forgave her, and then took her leave of them all.

After the servants had helped to disrobe her, she dismissed them and sat in the window embrasure to brush her hair. She was still sitting there when the door opened rather tentatively and Kit came in. She rose and turned to face him.

'I hope you do not expect a repeat of what happened last night?'

Kit looked at her cold, proud face and sighed inwardly. He had hoped that when she retired early she was as eager as he, but it seemed that he had been mistaken.

'I am sorry for what happened last night,' he said. 'I would undo it if I could but it is beyond my power.'

'It is not beyond your power to leave now and promise that you will never come to me in that way again,' she challenged with a flash of her eyes.

'I cannot do that, Anne Marie. You are my wife. I care for you. To live as you suggest would be agony for me—for us both, I believe.' He moved slowly towards her, his voice soft and persuasive. 'Will you not forgive me for what was merely a mistake? My mother did not mean to rob you of your senses, only to relax you—and I would have held back if I had realised.'

'Surely you must have known? When I had told you that I would resist?'

'You did a little at first. When you gave way I thought that you had discovered you were enjoying my kisses—that you wanted me to love you.'

'I—I was not aware of what was happening,' Anne Marie said, though it had come back to her a little during the day and she seemed to recall that she had enjoyed at least some of what he had been doing.

'Then I am truly sorry, for you were so warm and sweet, and you made me very happy, my love.' He stood before her, lifting his hand to touch her hair, which had the fresh scent of flowers and hung about her face like a silken curtain. 'You always smell so sweet…'

Anne Marie jerked her head away as if stung, unwilling to be caught by the soft persuasion of his voice. He said that he cared for her but she did not believe him; he wanted only to bend her to his will— and then he would desert her. Had she not been told that it was what men did when they had married against their will?

'Do not think to seduce me so easily a second time, sir. I shall fight you if you try to bed me this night.'

'It was not my intention to do so,' he said, surprising her. 'I would have you love me, as a wife should, Anne Marie. For the pleasures of the marriage bed mean little without mutual warmth. I can find a dozen women to please me an I wish it.'

'I am well aware of that!' She glared at him. 'I heard the serving wenches laughing this morning as they changed the bed sheets. They seemed to find it funny that you had clearly proved your mettle!'

'I fear that is something we can neither of us control,' he replied with a wry look. 'Please forgive me, Anne Marie. I do truly care for you. I would be happy if you could love me just a little.' He leaned towards her, brushed his lips briefly over hers and then turned and left her to stare after him in bewilderment.

Chapter Eight

It had been impossible to sleep. All night Anne Marie had lain wakeful, tossing this way and that as she tried to unravel the confusion of her thoughts. She ought to be pleased that she had defied her husband and won. Yet what had she won? Certainly not satisfaction, for he had seemed to win in showing such consideration for her wellbeing.

Drat the man! Her chagrin was all the more for knowing that she enjoyed his company, when she allowed herself to do so, and that she could be happy as his wife if her pride would let her. She was dressed for riding when she went downstairs, to discover that Kit had gone out earlier without her.

Annoyed that he had not asked her to ride with him, she sent one of the servants to the stables to inform the grooms that she would need a horse and a groom to accompany her. The horse was brought for her within a short time, and Anne Marie found her irritation melting away as she saw it was her own beloved mare Starlight. Kit must have had the horse brought down from Drodney for her.

'Oh, you lovely, lovely thing,' Anne Marie said, and laid her face against the softness of the mare's silken mane as she patted and caressed it. 'I am so glad to see you again.'

The mare whinnied as if agreeing, and Anne Marie laughed. She felt very happy as the groom came to help her use the mounting block, and sat easily in the saddle. There were other horses in Kit's stable that she could ride, but none that suited her so well as her own mare—which Kit had chosen and bought for her. And now he had arranged for the mare to be brought here.

His thoughtfulness was more than she could ever have expected, particularly after the way she had behaved to him these past weeks, and Anne Marie was chastened. She had begun to realise that she was being unreasonable, her actions those of a petulant child rather than a grown woman, and it was a wonder that Kit had not lost patience with her before this.

She had to admit that his behaviour had been that of a gentleman throughout, except for what had happened on their wedding night—and perhaps he was not so very much to blame for that. She *had* drunk all the wine Lady Sarah had given her because she was nervous, and if Kit had been as eager to love her as he said...but why had he been eager? Was it the natural feeling of any man taking a new bride, or did it go deeper?

Anne Marie puzzled over these thoughts as she enjoyed her ride. Everywhere was white with frost and the air had a clean fresh taste. Once again she relished the fact of her freedom, and found that she was happy despite the problems her marriage presented. Yet if Kit truly cared for her, there was no problem and she was indeed fortunate.

He was waiting for her when she returned from her ride, her cheeks pink from the cold air, and he smiled as she went towards him quickly, her eyes alight with excitement and pleasure.

'You had Starlight brought here for me,' she cried. 'I had no idea. It was a wonderful surprise, Kit, and I must thank you for your kindness.'

'I am glad that you are pleased,' he said. 'We shall not take her with us to London, for she needs a rest after her long journey, but she will be waiting here for you when we return.' He reached for her hand and lifted it to his lips, kissing the palm and sending a little tingle of pleasure through her. 'I had all your things brought down from Drodney, and I believe you will find your mother's cross among them, also your book of drawings. As you know, Beth was keeping them safe for you. Your things have been taken to your room, and I think there is also a letter from Beth to you.'

'How kind you are,' Anne Marie exclaimed and then blushed as his eyebrows lifted. 'No, please do not look at me so, Kit. I—I know I have been foolish and harsh to you, and—and I shall try to do better.'

A soft laugh escaped him, but he merely inclined his head before offering his arm. 'Perhaps we can both do better? It has not been a good beginning but I do not despair of the future.'

'Perhaps…' She looked at him uncertainly.

'Shall we go in, my lady? I think we should break our fast together, and then perhaps we might attend to estate business. I have been told that some of our people want to wish us well, and I have arranged for gifts to celebrate our wedding to be distributed to those in need. It would look well if you would stand with me and smile as they are given out.'

Anne Marie agreed to this willingly. Again she was struck by his thoughtfulness, for he had made nothing of her apology when he might have crowed over her in triumph. She realised that he had once more become the man she had fallen in love with at Drodney, his frowns and glowering looks gone—at least for the moment.

She did not know why he had been so angry with her on his return from London, but he seemed to have put it behind him now. Taking the arm he offered her, she decided that there was no sense in fighting a lost cause. She was his wife in every way, though she had not confessed her love and would continue to hold that at least back from him, but there was no reason why they should not be happy together for a while.

If in time he tired of her and decided to leave her in the country while he went off somewhere…but she would not think about that. For the moment it seemed that he could not do enough to please her, and she must look no further.

* * *

Kit heard his wife's gentle breathing and knew that she slept. Lifting the covers carefully, he rose and stood looking down at her in the light of a flickering candle. She was so lovely, so sweet and innocent in repose, and she had responded to his lovemaking earlier, though not with the passionate abandon of their wedding night. Even though she had accepted his kisses, clinging to him as he played on her body and brought her to a shuddering climax, he had felt that she held something back from him.

There was an ache inside him as he realised that she did not love him in the way he had hoped. She was no longer resisting him, no longer defiant, and she was all he had hoped for in a wife—but she was not wholly his. She had told him that she did not wish to wed him, using all manner of excuses to deny him, but he had not listened. He had been sure that he could win her to him, certain that once she knew herself loved she would respond with all her heart. It seemed that he had been mistaken.

His disappointment was bitter, though he blamed himself, not her. He had gone to the Queen and asked for Anne Marie in marriage, but she had never been given a choice. Was there perhaps someone else she would have liked to marry?

He was sure that she had met no one at Drodney. The tutor then? They had spent many hours together and had seemed to be very comfortable in each other's company. Indeed, Kit knew that Master Mountjoy had had hopes of her until he had told him that she was to be his wife, for the young man had found it hard to hide his disappointment.

The only other man she had met to his knowledge was Sir Robert Herriot, and their acquaintance had been so brief that he hardly thought it likely.

He knew that he had won Anne Marie's acquiescence to their marriage. She had realised that there was no going back, and had accepted that she must make the best of the situation—but she did not love him as he loved her.

Too restless to sleep, Kit left their chamber and went out, needing some physical exercise to ease the ache that might otherwise become anger. He knew that he would lose her again if he allowed his temper to get the best of him, and that he too must learn to accept what he had and to make the best of it. Perhaps in time she would learn to trust him, and with that trust might come the kind of love he so desired.

Anne Marie woke soon after first light to find the bed empty beside her. It felt cold, and she realised that Kit must have left her long ago; it hurt her that he had not slept beside her. Where did he sleep when he left her bed? Did he return to his old room? Was that to be the pattern of their nights? He would come to her when it pleased him and then leave her, because that was the nature of their marriage.

Lady Sarah had explained to her that many marriages were like that, a matter of convenience. Hurtful as it was to her, she must accept that their marriage had been just that. Kit wanted sons to inherit his wealth, and he had found her comely enough. It was clearly sufficient for him. Besides, she must never forget that their marriage had been by order of the Queen.

Remembering the exquisite pleasure his loving had given her the previous night, Anne Marie knew that she had been close to confessing her love, but thankfully she had not said the words—though he must have guessed it from her response. Her face flushed and she was covered in shame as she recalled the way she had cried out and clung to him. He must have known how she felt!

Of course it was not the same for men. Men often took mistresses and some of them tumbled the serving wenches in the hay, but they did not love them. Kit had married her because he was bidden to it, and she could never forget that, no matter how sweet were his kisses.

She was thoughtful as one of the serving wenches laid out a travelling gown of heavy green silk for her. She had almost forgotten that they were due to begin their journey to London today, and she felt a mixture of excitement and apprehension.

The Queen had commanded she be brought to court once she was Kit's wife. What would she be like and what would she have to say to the daughter of a traitor?

The journey to London seemed long and frustrating, despite the care Kit took to make it as comfortable as possible for Anne Marie. Because the roads were so bad at this time of the year, the cumbersome travelling coach was left behind as well as most of their baggage.

'My house in London has all we need,' Kit told her, 'and I have ordered some new gowns for you to be delivered there ready for our arrival.'

It was an age when most people of consequence preferred to travel with a large train of servants and many of their possessions, but Kit had learned the habit of economy on board ship. For himself he took only a few changes of linen, though the packhorses carried more personal items for Anne Marie's comfort.

Three trusted grooms accompanied them, and Kit was armed to guard against attack. By travelling only during the daylight hours in easy stages, they managed to avoid being accosted by vagrants or robbers. However, they were several days upon the road and Anne Marie was heartily sick of staying at inns by the time London was reached. The accommodation was often poor and she suspected that the beds harboured fleas.

She was itching by the end of the journey, and since her long-handled bone back scratcher had been left at home, she asked Kit to perform that office for her. He was amused when she demanded that he examine her head for the offending flea.

'As soon as we are home you may bathe and wash your hair, Anne Marie. Truly I think the flea is present only in your mind.'

'I swear I have been bitten at least thrice,' she said

and scowled as he laughed. 'It will serve you right if you take them from me!'

'If that is a ploy to keep me from your bed, my love, it will not work,' Kit teased, giving her a wicked look. 'I swear it would take an army of fleas to drive me from your arms.'

Anne Marie blushed, but merely shook her head at him. They had shared a bed every night of their journey and he had not failed to take full advantage of that, his lovemaking bringing her both pleasure and grief. For she could only give so much of herself for fear of revealing her growing dependence on him.

Their arrival in London brought an end to the intimacy they had shared on the road. Here their apartment consisted of two bedrooms and a small parlour, and when Anne Marie discovered that her monthly flow had come, Kit left her to sleep alone for several nights.

She discovered that she missed the warmth of his body beside her, but was too proud to tell him so. His behaviour seemed to indicate that his feelings for her were of a physical nature and she found that a little hurtful. However, she gave no indication that she would welcome a return of his attentions.

Had he already begun to tire of her? The nagging doubt at the back of Anne Marie's mind made her even more determined not to confess her love, and she sometimes held back when she longed to cling to him.

When they had been in London for six days they received an invitation to a court masque. Anne Marie was nervous as she dressed that evening in one of the new gowns Kit had bought for her. It was finer than anything she had ever worn before, except for her wedding gown, of course.

The overskirt was a deep rich blue, heavily embroidered with silver and pearls, and the petticoat was a pale rose. The sleeves were shaped to high, rounded shoulders, tapering to fit tightly at her wrists. She had a cap of silver threads to wear over her hair, which was braided and coiled high on her head, and her pearls were looped twice about her neck.

'You look beautiful,' Kit told her when he saw her dressed. 'I shall be the envy of every man at court this night.'

There was a flicker of some emotion in his eyes as he spoke, which seemed to indicate that he might be angry or jealous. But why should he be jealous? There was no reason, and Anne Marie dismissed the notion as foolish.

Kit wanted her and she believed that he was fond of her in his way. She knew that his need of an heir was most likely the reason he had accepted Her Majesty's decision that they should wed so readily.

She had nothing to complain of in his treatment of her. He was a more than satisfactory lover and very generous. His manner was usually kind and considerate, though at times he could seem cold and distant. However, these moods did not often last long, and he had not lost his temper with her since she had apologised for her own harshness towards him.

Had anyone asked if she was happy, Anne Marie

could not have answered them. She was for the most part content with her life and she had come to believe that she could expect no more.

'You flatter me, sir,' she replied as the gleam in Kit's eyes did not abate. 'I am certain there will be many other ladies more beautiful than I this evening.'

'You have not been to court. Allow me to be the judge,' he said, his voice harsher than she had heard it of late. 'Are you ready?'

'Yes.' Her heart jerked nervously. 'What will the Queen say to me?'

'She may not even speak to you,' Kit replied. 'Her Majesty does not always deign to notice newcomers. Just be natural and modest should she address you. Otherwise, stay close by me. You may be asked to dance and you may accept—but only with gentlemen I approve. There are those at court I would not have you trust, Anne Marie.'

'I prefer to dance only with you, Kit.'

'Do you?' He gazed down at her anxious face and his frown lifted. 'I have friends who will treat you with respect, my love. You have my permission to dance with them—Drake and Frobisher, should they be at court, Hawkins and others—but be careful even with them. You are too innocent and do not know the ways of the world.'

Anne Marie felt slightly chastened and a little annoyed. Did he think her so naïve that she would allow some drunken fool to molest her?

His attitude made her even more nervous than she already was, but she need not have worried. Kit's friends were glad to see him at court that night, and though she did not meet Sir Francis Drake or any other of the famous sea captains, there were several young men Kit was pleased to call his friends. In particular one Tobias Frenshaw, who kissed her hand gallantly and congratulated Kit on being a sly dog at securing such a lovely bride. He flirted with Anne Marie gently, dancing with her and fetching her cool drinks, but his manner was always respectful and gave neither her nor Kit cause for alarm.

Kit had been right to suggest that Her Majesty might not even notice them. Elizabeth swept by with her most favoured courtiers in train, her eyes moving over Anne Marie with apparent indifference.

Anne Marie felt only relief. She did not wish to be singled out for notice by the Queen. Had she been free to choose, she would have come to court as seldom as possible.

Kit, however, was pleased with her when they returned home that evening. 'You behaved perfectly, my love,' he said, when the serving wenches had helped her to disrobe and left them. 'You were friendly but modest with the gentlemen who danced with you, and I know you were much admired.'

'I am happy that you were satisfied, sir.' She smiled a little wryly. 'But Her Majesty ignored me. As you warned, she did not even notice me.'

'You were noticed,' Kit replied, and laughed. 'Elizabeth will give her approval only when she is ready.'

'If I have your approval I am content.'

'You must know that I am well contented with my bride.'

Anne Marie's heart caught as he reached out for her, pulling her hard against him so that she could feel the burn of his arousal through his night-shirt. His mouth fastened on hers in a hungry, eager kiss, and then he was sweeping her up in his arms, carrying her to their bed.

She did not resist him as he began to kiss and caress her body, knowing that she had missed this intimacy between them. His tongue lavished her nipples so that she moaned for sheer pleasure. In another moment he was riding her, his loving passionate and swift as it sometimes was. At other times he took more thought for her pleasure, but this night it was as if he wanted to mark her as his own. She guessed that he had been both pleased and angered to see her enjoy herself in the company of other men.

He wanted to assert his ownership, to show that she belonged to him alone, and a part of her responded to that.

She gave a cry as her body arched and shook with little spasms, and then she clung to him as she reached hitherto unknown heights of pleasure. In her joy she almost cried out her love of him, but recalled the words just in time.

'Kit, I...'

He smiled down at her, feeling some part of her respond in a way she had not previously, and instead of rolling away from her as he often did, he held her to him. As his hands caressed her back, Anne Marie found that she was crying, her tears wetting his shoulder.

Kit drew back to look into her face.

'Did I hurt you, my love?'

'No. I—I am crying because I am happy.'

He smiled and touched his lips to her forehead. Perhaps she loved him a little despite herself.

He knew that at the end she had given more of her inner self than ever before, and he felt that he was winning her. Little by little, she was becoming his. One day he would have all of her.

'Sleep now, my sweet,' he murmured against her hair.

'Will you stay with me?'

'Would you like that?'

'Yes please. I do not like to wake and find you gone too soon.'

It was the closest she could bring herself to confessing her love. Kit sensed that she had surrendered a part of herself to him that night. He did not yet have the whole, but he could wait.

'I shall stay until dawn,' he whispered. 'Sleep you content, for I am here.'

The Queen sent for Kit and Anne Marie the next afternoon. She smiled at them graciously as they made their obeisance to her.

'So, Lady Hamilton,' Elizabeth said. 'I trust you enjoyed your first visit to court?'

'Yes, Your Grace.'

Elizabeth nodded, her eyes bright and a little hard.

She did not like the ladies of the court to be too beautiful.

'We shall expect you again this evening. There is to be a play performed and dancing afterwards. I have observed that you like to dance, Lady Hamilton.'

'I believe we all take our love of dancing from you, Your Grace,' Kit interceded, seeing that his wife was at a loss for an answer.

'Dancing was once my chief pleasure,' the Queen replied, a far away look in her eyes. 'But We have other things to concern us now,' She waved her hand imperiously to end the subject. 'I would have private words with you, sir. Your lady may wait elsewhere. One of my ladies will show her whatever she wishes to see.' She clapped her hands and a Lady in Waiting appeared. 'Amuse Lady Hamilton for a while, Hester.'

'Yes, ma'am.'

The Lady in Waiting curtseyed respectfully and backed from the chamber, Anne Marie following her example.

Her brief interview was at an end. She felt a little deflated. Was this why she had been summoned all the way from Devon? Yet in a moment relief followed swiftly on the heels of chagrin. She had been approved and could forget the shadow of disgrace that had hung over her for the time being at least.

'Last night was your first visit to court,' Hester Stanton said as they walked down a lengthy corridor together. It was cold and draughty and Anne Marie was reminded of the castle at Drodney. She was becoming soft after so much luxury at Kit's houses! 'You have not been here before I think?'

'No, never,' Anne Marie replied. 'This is my first visit to London.'

'And what do you think of it?' Hester laughed as she hesitated. 'You may speak truthfully without fear of offence. I thought it noisy and dirty when I first came.'

'It does smell a little at times.'

'In summer it stinks,' the other girl said. 'But we are fortunate that we can move out to other palaces and houses to avoid the worst of it. Much of the winter is spent here at Whitehall, but the Queen prefers Hampton Court or one of her other palaces.'

'Yes, I should not like to be in London in high summer,' Anne Marie agreed.

Her first sight of London had been exciting, but the press of traffic in the streets had amazed her, and she had discovered that most people used the river to get where they wanted to go because it was easier. In some areas the houses had been built so close together that the overhanging upper stories seemed almost to touch in places, making the streets dark, and the gutters were filled with filth thrown down from above.

However, Kit's house was in a better area, with larger houses that had gardens stretching down to the river at the back, and it was often not necessary to venture out into the noisy streets unless one wished to go shopping.

Kit had already taken her to various silk merchants, and they had visited the Royal Exchange, where all kinds of merchandise was offered for sale. However, it was the habit of wealthy men to have merchants call at their house to offer their wares, and they had been importuned almost from the moment of their arrival with sellers of all manner of trifles.

Anne Marie had purchased a pretty fan for herself from her allowance, but in most things she had been guided by her husband, who seemed to have fixed ideas about what he wanted his wife to wear.

She could not complain; the gowns were all rich and costly—but she had noticed that they were more modest than many of the ladies at court wore. Perhaps Kit had deliberately chosen them so to protect his wife's modesty?

'What would you most like to see?' Hester Stanton asked, recalling Anne Marie's thoughts to the present. 'Some people like to see the gardens, others the State rooms.'

'I have been told that there are some fine paintings here by Master Holbein and others,' Anne Marie said looking at her eagerly. 'Could I possibly spend a little time looking at them?'

'Why certainly.' Hester smiled at her in a friendly way. 'Are you interested in painting, Lady Hamilton?'

'I paint a little,' Anne Marie said shyly. 'I am not as clever as the gentlemen who have painted Her Majesty, of course—but it is something I enjoy.'

'I wish I could do something like that,' the other girl said. 'I can play the harp and dance but I fear I have few other talents.'

'Oh, I am sure you have many,' Anne Marie said, warming to her. 'Perhaps one day you might like to sit for me to take your likeness?'

'Would you?' Hester's sweet but rather plain face lit up. 'I have never had my likeness draughted.'

Anne Marie replied that she would be happy to do it, and asked if Hester would like to visit their house for luncheon one day, and in this way they reached the gallery where several pictures of the family belonging to the House of Tudor were hanging together.

'That was done by Master Holbein,' Hester said, pointing to a splendid portrait of King Henry the VIII. 'And that is by Hans Holbein the Younger—it is a fresco of Henry VII, Elizabeth of York, Henry VIII and Jane Seymour, and was painted especially for the Palace of Whitehall.'

Anne Marie stood lost in wonder at the magnificence of the paintings, seeing for herself that her friends had flattered her poor efforts. She knew at once that she had much to learn and would never equal the skill of such artists.

'There are many others along here,' Hester said as Anne Marie continued to linger. She looked and sounded extremely bored, and Anne Marie realised that she had no interest in the paintings.

'May I stay here alone for a while? I think I can find my own way back to the public gallery where I shall meet Sir Christopher.'

'Very well, I shall leave you,' Hester said. 'But if you should get lost you have only to ask someone.'

'Oh, I am sure I shall do well enough,' Anne Marie said.

She stood for some time admiring the work of Master Holbein and that of some lesser artists she discovered in another small chamber near by, and then, thinking that Kit might be looking for her, began to make her way back to where she had promised they would meet later.

It was some minutes before she realised that she was lost and in a part of the old palace that she had never seen before. There was a chill about these rooms that seemed to indicate that they were seldom used, and she was unable to discover anyone of whom she might inquire the way.

Indeed, she spent a very long time wandering and then found herself once more in the picture gallery. She was debating where she ought to try next when Kit strode in at the far entrance, looking angry and impatient.

'Pray where have you been, Anne Marie?'

'I—I was lost,' she explained. 'I came to find you and turned the wrong way. I am sorry if I kept you waiting.'

His eyes narrowed suspiciously as if he had thought something different, and he took hold of her arm, hurrying her with him impatiently, his fingers digging into her flesh, bruising her so that she almost cried out.

'Why did you send Mistress Stanton off like that?'

'She seemed as if she was bored with looking at pictures, and I wanted to look at them in detail. They are so beautiful, and so well executed. You were wrong to say that I might be a court painter if I were a man, Kit. I have not one tenth of their skill.'

'I wished only to please you—and your drawings are well done whatever you might think, Anne Marie. Catherine Grantly was delighted with the painting you did of her children. She said it was better than the one Sir Nicholas had commissioned for her from a much-admired artist.'

'I have a small talent perhaps, but also much to learn, and it was to study the skill of a master that I lingered here today, Kit.'

'Yes, I see that now. I was merely anxious when I could not find you, that is all.' He did not tell her that for a while he was afraid she had either run away or been abducted, for it seemed foolish now that she had explained.

Anne Marie noted that his anger seemed to have abated and he was thoughtful as they left the palace together and took a chair for her to his house while he walked beside. She heard church bells ringing from all parts of the city but did not ask her husband what it meant. It was not until much later, when they had eaten a light meal together, that he told her what was on his mind.

'I fear I have news that will distress you, Anne Marie.'

'Is it my father?' she asked anxiously, her pulses racing.

'No—as far as I know he has not been taken. But it concerns him in a way, for I have been told that

Mary of Scots has been beheaded at Fotheringay Castle.'

'Oh no!' Anne Marie's hand flew to her mouth in shock. She stared at him in silence for a moment before she could find words to express her feelings. 'Is that why the bells were ringing earlier? I suppose the people had heard the news and felt it right and proper, for she was a condemned traitor. For myself, I am deeply sorry that it should have happened. I had hoped that Her Majesty might spare her, though I know Mary was found guilty of treason and that others have called for her death.'

'It is others who have brought this about,' Kit replied. 'Her Majesty was persuaded to sign the warrant but she swears that she never meant Mary to die. Others took the warrant and put the execution into train without her knowledge or permission and she was furious when she discovered what had happened. Indeed, I believe she is still very angry, though also worried. The news of Mary's death will not yet have reached Elizabeth's enemies, but when it does...'

'It will provoke a wave of anger,' Anne Marie finished for him, not needing to be told the consequences of this tragedy. 'I know that my father will be devastated by this news, as must all those who were loyal to Mary of Scots.' She lifted her head as Kit's eyes narrowed suspiciously. 'I do not take sides in this, sir. I only say what I know will be so.'

'Her Majesty is of the same opinion. She fears a backlash from Spain and believes that we must prepare for war.'

Anne Marie felt a cold shiver down her spine as she guessed what was coming next. 'That is why she wished to have private words with you, was it not?'

'Yes.' Kit was silent for a moment. 'If I confide in you I must have your word that it goes no further, Anne Marie.'

'I swear it on all that I hold dear. I would not betray you—or your Queen, for I know that would hurt you, my husband.'

Kit nodded, moved by her pale face. 'Then I must tell you that we are to return home at the end of the week. I shall stay a day or so with you and then join Drake's fleet. Our mission is to harry the Spanish and cause them as much nuisance as we can so that any fleet they try to bring against us is weakened and where possible destroyed.'

'You are to join Sir Francis Drake?' Anne Marie felt a thrill of fear as she looked into his face and saw the mixture of emotions he was fighting. That he was sorry to bring her first visit to London to an untimely end she did not doubt, but there was also excitement. He was looking forward to this mission that the Queen had asked of him and others. 'Yes, I see that it is so. Shall you be long away, sir?'

'It may be some weeks or months, I cannot tell,' he replied. 'I am sorry to leave you so soon after we were wed, Anne Marie, and that I must leave you in the country. But I think you would not be happy at court alone?'

'I should dislike it of all things,' Anne Marie said. Her heart was aching and she felt that she had been dealt a mortal blow, but she was determined not to show it. He cared for her but his excitement was plain, and she knew that she must not weep and beg him to stay. He was prepared, nay eager, to do his duty, and she had no real claim on him. 'I shall be much better at home with Lady Sarah and your family.'

'Yes, I was sure of it,' Kit replied, mistaking the shadows in her eyes. 'I know that you expected to be in London at least another three weeks but you shall come again as soon the threat of invasion is over—and before we go we shall visit as many shops as you wish and order whatever fripperies you please.'

'You have already been more than generous, sir,' Anne Marie replied, blinking back her tears. What did she care for silken gowns that she would seldom wear? It was the loss of him that was breaking her heart, but of course she could not tell him so. She had withheld the final surrender and to declare her love now would ring a false peal. She could not beg him not to leave her, but she could at least wish him well and a safe return. 'I shall miss you, Kit. I pray it will not be too long before you are safely home again.'

'I shall make sure that you are provided for should I not return,' Kit replied, and seeing the flicker of fright in her eyes, he smiled. 'But I swear that you shall not be so easily rid of me, my sweet. I shall come back to plague you again one day.'

'We do not return home until the end of the week?' she asked and he nodded. Her heart lifted, she had a few more days at least. 'Then we must make the most of our time together, sir. I hear there is to be a performance of the Queen's Men this evening. Mayhap Master Richard Tarleton will take part. I heard that Her Majesty once said of him that he made her sides ache with laughing.' She smiled up at him, apparently without a care in the world. 'Pray tell me, what gown should I wear this evening to court?'

Chapter Nine

All over the country there were those who celebrated the death of Mary of Scots, for it was thought that she had been the main threat to Elizabeth's throne. Yet Walsingham's network of spies in Spain, France and Flanders had warned of the reaction abroad, and even in England there were many who reacted angrily and chanted the song that was repeated in inns and meeting places the length and breadth of the land.

> The noble famous Queen
> Who lost her head of late
> Doth show that Kings as well as clowns
> Are bound to fortune's fate,
> And that no earthly Prince
> Can so secure his crown
> But Fortune with her whirling wheel
> Hath power to pull them down.

Anne Marie, however, could think only of the parting that must come too soon.

The return journey took nearly as long as the trip to London, but Anne Marie did not find it tedious this time, for she knew that once they were home Kit would leave her. As the time drew nearer she dreaded the moment of their parting, and often at night when he held her in his arms, loving her with such sweetness and tenderness, she was close to confessing the depth of her love. Yet still pride held her back, pride and a fear of giving that small part of herself she had held back.

Lady Sarah confessed that she had been surprised to receive Kit's letter telling her that they were to return so soon, but she welcomed Anne Marie warmly, embracing her and saying that she had missed her.

'Yet I would not have had you return for my sake,' she told Anne Marie. 'I am sorry that you are to lose your husband so soon to the sea, my dear. I had hoped that once he was married he would give up his adventuring and take up his rightful position here.'

'While England is in danger, my rightful place is with Drake and the others who would defend country and Queen,' Kit replied. 'Anne Marie understands that I must go.'

'Yes, of course,' she said, raising her head proudly. 'It is your duty, sir. But I hope you will not go until the morrow?'

'No, I shall stay one more night with you,' Kit promised, his eyes warm as they caressed her face. 'I do not leave you easily, my love, believe me.'

He came to her that night in their chamber, loving

her passionately and then slowly with tenderness, bringing her body tinglingly alive so that she cried out with pleasure and clung to him as the spasms shook her. Afterwards, he held her in his arms, stroking her hair.

'You will take care?' she said, her face buried against the moist, hard flesh of his shoulder. 'I fear that you will be in danger and I—I do not wish to lose you, Kit.'

'Do you not?' he asked and smiled in the darkness, his lips moving against her hair. 'I wonder why. Is it perhaps that you would miss me?'

'You know I would,' she said in a strangled voice. 'You know I care for you. You must know it!'

Kit held her closer but did not answer. He sensed that it was the closest she would come to confessing her love, and he felt the satisfaction of it warm him.

'I know that I care for my wife,' he murmured. 'Hold that thought, Anne Marie, and believe that it will bring me back to you.'

Hearing her breathing become deeper, he laughed softly. He was not sure whether she had heard him or not, but he would take away the memory of her words with him, and God willing they would meet again before too many months had passed.

He held her close until the light began to strengthen, and then slipped carefully from the bed so as not to wake her. With one regretful look at her sleeping in their bed, he went out and closed the door softly behind him. Much as he loved his wife, he had his duty, and there was a part of him that was eager for what was to come. He knew that the sea would always call to him, even when the time came for him to stay at home, and there was something exciting about seeking out the enemy and fighting a glorious battle.

He also knew that the battles they must seek would need to be glorious if England were to beat off an enemy more powerful and much richer than herself. And at this moment England needed her sea captains more than at any time in her history.

Anne Marie opened her eyes as the door closed behind Kit. She had woken as soon as he left her, but she had not cried out, for she knew that if she had she would have wept and begged him not to go. Now that she was alone the tears began to slide gently down her cheeks, for she already felt the ache of loneliness that their parting must bring, and the fear that he would not return to her.

'I wanted to see you before I left,' Kit said to Sir Nicholas as they met later that morning. 'I wanted to confide in you, to tell you a little of my wife's history and beg you to have a care for her while I am away.'

'You know that I shall do all in my power to assist your family, Kit.'

'It is more than that,' Kit said and frowned. 'When I spoke with Walsingham last he mentioned your name—I believe you once warned him to beware of a certain Bevis Frampton?'

'Frampton?' Sir Nicholas frowned. 'Yes, I once suspected that the man might be involved in some plot against Her Majesty, but Walsingham thought I was mistaken.'

'He may not think so now,' Kit said and went on to tell him of his own suspicions. 'I think Frampton may have had a hand in abducting Anne Marie from Drodney. The Makepeaces believe there was no way down to the cove from the cliffs but I cannot be sure. Anne Marie was rendered unconscious and taken somehow—either through a secret way or through the castle yard. If she went that way someone either bribed the guards or...' he broke off and shook his head as if in disbelief.

Sir Nicholas nodded as he paused. 'You suspect some black art may have been used in this, do you not?'

'It seems ridiculous but I fear it.'

'I also believe that the man you have named may have some dealing in the black arts, Kit. Catherine was once a victim of something similar to what you have described, and I suspected it was because I was getting too close to Frampton. Either Catherine had some information unbeknown to herself, or I was the danger and he worked through her to warn me. I have never been certain. I do know that her life was threatened, and I took steps to rectify the matter. We have been left in peace since I ceased to go often to court— or to meddle in Frampton's business.'

'Then I am right to be anxious for Anne Marie?'

'Catherine had a friend who married a certain Master Morton, and he once told me that he believes Frampton is a disciple of the Devil. Morton says that

Frampton speaks of *his master* but that he has no earthly master. I believe that Frampton is evil and that he has worked ceaselessly against Elizabeth and the Protestant faith, but rest easy in your mind, Kit. Anne Marie is no longer of use to her father or to Frampton. Indeed, with Mary of Scots dead, I think any plots against Elizabeth must be forgotten for the moment. Frampton and others of his kind have been dealt a huge blow and it will take them a long time to recover. For now I believe the main threat comes from Spain, not from within.'

'Then I may go with an easy mind,' Kit said. 'I am glad I decided to confide in you, Nick, for I was mightily concerned.'

'Trust me to do what I can to help your family, and think only of your duty, Kit. England needs you and men like you, and until the threat of invasion is at an end we must all forget self.'

Kit nodded, and the two men shook hands and parted, Kit to join his ship and Sir Nicholas to help raise the militia that would keep a watchful eye on England's shores. The coming months would be uneasy ones, for Spain was a powerful enemy and the whole fabric of English life was now at risk.

Glancing out of the parlour window, Anne Marie saw that there were primroses and other spring flowers poking their heads through the earth. It seemed that after all the bitter winds and frosts of the past weeks, spring had at last come, and she felt the need to go walking. She had taken short walks about the garden most days, but now the sun was shining and she knew an urge to go for a really long walk, something she had not done in what seemed like an age.

'You will not mind if I go for a walk this morning, Sarah?' she asked of her mother-in-law as she came into the parlour. 'I know that we had planned to make an inventory of the linen cupboard today, but it is such a lovely one and I would not waste it.'

'Certainly you must go,' Sarah said and smiled at her. 'We can put the linen off until another day—but be sure to wear your cloak, my dear. It seems warm but there may be a chill wind out. I would not have you become ill while Kit is away.'

'Yes, of course,' Anne Marie said. 'You would not care to come with me?'

'You must excuse me, Anne Marie. I do not care for long walks and I have much to do here. But perhaps one of the boys would like to go with you? Poor Master Mountjoy is still laid upon his bed with the chill he took last week, and the boys have been moping about the house all morning for lack of something to do.'

'Then I shall certainly ask them,' Anne Marie said. She had become quite fond of her husband's brothers, more particularly Jack. Edward was a little reserved with her at times, though at others he would join his brother in teasing her. She sometimes wondered if it was because he had been punished on the day she had first come to Hamilton House for being rude to her. 'But I am not sure they will come—they may prefer to be off on some mad escapade of their own.'

Having fetched her cloak, Anne Marie found Edward and Jack Hamilton in the kitchen, plaguing Cook for some of her freshly baked honey cakes. When she asked if they would like to come for a walk with her, Jack immediately agreed, but Edward shook his head.

'Oh, come on Edward,' Jack said. 'It will be better than staying here.'

'I have other things to do—you go if you want.'

'I shall then,' his brother said defiantly, and stole a cake from the cooling tray before running after Anne Marie. 'Edward is in a fit of the sullens,' he said as he skipped happily at her side, and then called to one of the dogs that were always about the yard to follow them. 'I do not know why he would not come with us.'

'Perhaps Edward has lessons to do for Master Mountjoy,' Anne Marie said, knowing that the tutor had set them both lessons despite his illness. 'If you are scolded for playing truant you must blame me, Jack.'

'Oh, Mountjoy won't care what I do,' Jack replied with a careless shrug. 'It's Edward he beats if he does his sums wrong, not me. I am not sure why. I think it is because Edward stares at him arrogantly and he resents it.'

'Does Master Mountjoy often beat Edward?' Anne Marie asked with a frown. She knew that the boys had deserved the occasional caning when the tutor first came, but she had thought them well behaved these days.

'I think he hits him most days,' Jack said. 'But I've only been beaten twice. It isn't fair, Anne Marie. I'm the one who gets into most of the scrapes, and poor Edward gets punished for it.'

'No, that certainly is not fair,' she agreed, making a mental note to speak to the tutor about his treatment of Edward. It was right that he should be beaten if he did something that deserved it, but not without reason. She did not think that Kit would sanction that if he was here. 'I shall see what can be done to help Edward. I am glad you told me, Jack.'

'I like you,' Jack told her with a grin. 'I'm glad you came to live with us.'

'So am I—very glad,' she replied and placed a hand unconsciously on her stomach, which had a small bump that did not yet show, though she was certain that Sarah had guessed her secret. She had hoped that Kit might return from sea for a visit, and was keeping her silence for the moment so that she might tell him first. Several weeks had passed since his departure and as yet they had heard nothing.

It was pleasant walking in the April sunshine, and Anne Marie watched indulgently as the boy ran ahead of her full of energy and life as he played with his dog. Once she thought she heard a slight noise behind her and turned to glance over her shoulder, but when she looked she could see nothing. A second time she caught a glimpse of a shadow, and smiled to herself, as she suspected that Edward was following them.

She did not call out to him, thinking that if he wished to join them he would do so in his own good time. Now that Jack had confided to her that his brother was being beaten too often, Anne Marie thought that she understood his moods. She made up her mind to speak with Master Mountjoy as soon as the opportunity arose.

Anne Marie and Jack spent almost two hours walking and Edward did not attempt to join them. After a while she thought that he had given up his game, and was not surprised to see him outside the house when they returned, though she was unsettled when he told Jack that he had been riding. If Edward had not been following them, who had? She was certain that someone had for a while, and a shiver of apprehension went down her spine.

However, her thoughts soon took another turn when she discovered they had a visitor. Sir Nicholas had ridden over to see them and bring them news.

'Oh, it is wonderful,' Lady Sarah cried as she walked in. 'Sir Nicholas has news of a victory—but I shall let him tell you himself, my dear, for I can scarcely believe it.'

'You speak of Sir Francis Drake's ships?' Anne Marie asked, her heart beginning to pound madly. 'Pray tell me what has happened, sir?'

'It was on the nineteenth of this month,' he replied with a smile. 'Drake and others of his fleet entered the harbour of Cadiz, where thirty-three Spanish ships were destroyed.'

'That is good news indeed,' Anne Marie said. 'But what of our ships?'

'From what I heard, Drake's squadron escaped unscathed. The Spanish were caught napping, and they are saying that Drake hath singed the King of Spain's beard.'

'Will the ships come home now?' Anne Marie asked eagerly.

'I do not believe so,' Sir Nicholas replied. 'I understand their mission is to continue to harry the Spanish fleet wherever they can. They will return to England when they think the threat of invasion is near—and for the moment the Spanish Armada has been badly wounded.'

'It is indeed good news, sir,' Anne Marie said, but her heart sank as she realised that it was unlikely she would see Kit for some months. 'It was kind of you to come and tell us.'

'In Kit's absence I shall always be there if you need me,' he said. 'Besides, I had another purpose in coming today—Catherine asks if you will pay her a visit soon. She would like both you and Lady Sarah to spend a day with her.'

'I am sure we should both look forward to it,' the older woman replied. 'Now that the weather is so much better we shall all be able to get out more often. Anne Marie has been for a long walk today. Did you enjoy it, my dear?'

'Yes, very much,' she replied and wondered whether she ought to mention that she thought they had been followed. Yet she had not seen anyone and it might have been Edward playing a prank. She had only his word for it that he had been riding. 'I shall walk more often now that the weather is so much nicer.'

After Sir Nicholas had taken his leave of them, Lady Sarah looked at her a little doubtfully. 'I should not like to interfere or to curtail your pleasure, Anne Marie,' she said. 'A little exercise is I am sure good for you—but you will not overtire yourself, my dear?'

Anne Marie gave her a rueful smile. 'You know, don't you? I was hoping that Kit might return so that I could tell him first—but I fear he will not be back for some time.'

'It has always been so once he was at sea,' Sarah replied and shook her head. 'My son has an adventurous side to his nature, my dear, and he will not give up the chance to take a prize if he can—a treasure ship or a rich merchant. It is the reason this family has prospered, so I suppose we must not complain, but I hope he will be at home for the birth of his son.'

Anne Marie laughed. 'I may have a daughter.'

'So you may,' Sarah agreed. 'And I shall be just as pleased with a girl as a boy, for I never had a daughter that lived. All that matters is that you should keep well and the child be safely delivered.'

Anne Marie could not disagree, and she promised that she would not do more than she safely could without exhausting herself. She put her disappointment to one side, feeling the joy of knowing she was having a child assert itself. Now that she had shared her secret with Sarah they would have many happy hours planning for her confinement and the future.

She had decided to say nothing of being followed, believing that it probably had been Edward after all. She had made up her mind to speak to Master Mountjoy as soon as possible, though she would say nothing to Sarah for fear of distressing her. The tutor must understand that although she deferred to her husband's mother in many things to do with the house out of respect for her superior knowledge, Anne Marie was the mistress when Kit was from home. And she would not have Edward beaten for no good reason!

'Who told you this, Lady Hamilton?' Master Mountjoy's gaze narrowed in annoyance as he listened to what she had to say. 'If it was Edward he was lying. He has been beaten no more than twice or thrice at most, and that for misdemeanours that deserved such punishment.'

'I am not sure that is the truth, sir,' Anne Marie said, meeting his angry look fearlessly. 'In future I would like you to consult me before Edward is beaten. I shall decide whether or not what he has done deserves such a harsh penalty.'

'That is ridiculous! How do you expect me to keep order? If the boy misbehaves he must be shown immediately the error of his ways. I should be running to you a dozen times a week!'

'But you told me he had been beaten no more than thrice the whole time you have been here.' She saw his guilty flush and knew that he had been lying to her. Jack had told her the truth in the way of children, without realising what he was doing. 'In my husband's absence I am responsible for his family's well being. If I am not satisfied I believe he would agree that I should make any changes I feel necessary.'

The look in Mountjoy's eyes sent a shiver of ice down her spine, and she saw a side of him that she had not suspected before. His mouth hardened to a thin line and he inclined his head, understanding that she did not speak idly.

'Very well, Lady Hamilton,' he said coldly. 'It shall be as you wish, but I warn you that I may seek employment elsewhere—and I do not imagine that Sir Christopher would be pleased to find his brothers left without a tutor.'

'I believe I know my husband's mind, and I dare say I am capable of finding another tutor should it become necessary, sir—though I hope you will decide to stay with us.'

He inclined his head, excused himself and walked swiftly away. It was as she was leaving the schoolroom, where the interview had taken place, that she heard a stifled giggle and turned to see Jack peeping at her from behind a curtain.

'You were hiding there when I spoke to Master Mountjoy?'

'I heard you give him a right wigging,' Jack replied. 'Wait till I tell Edward this!'

'You must not tell him,' Anne Marie said with a little frown. 'That interview was supposed to be private—and do not suppose that it means you will get away with mayhem, Master Jack! I may not tolerate unnecessary beatings, but I shall not hesitate to give you one myself if need be.'

'But if I've been wicked I deserve it,' Jack said, and gave her his angelic smile. 'Edward gets beaten even if he hasn't, and that's not right or just, is it?'

'No, it isn't,' Anne Marie agreed. 'But I want you to promise me that you will not tell Edward what I've done—will you promise?'

Jack agreed, making a dramatic sign across his breast.

'Shall we go for a walk today, Anne Marie?'

'Not today, Jack. Your mother and I are promised to Lady Catherine for the day, but we shall go to-morrow if it is fine.'

'I'll see if Edward wants to go riding,' Jack said. 'But I won't tell on you, I promise.'

'Make sure you do your lessons,' Anne Marie called after him, but she did not think that he was listening.

'We do not see you often enough,' Lady Grantly said as her guests took leave of her later that day. 'We must visit each other more often now that the fine weather has come.'

'You must come to us next week,' Lady Sarah said. 'I think we have both enjoyed ourselves, have we not, Anne Marie?'

'Very much.' Anne Marie smiled at their hostess. 'I think the frame you commissioned for my portrait of your children very fine, Catherine—though I am not sure it was deserved.'

'Oh, but you have captured them beautifully, the mischief of one and the thoughtfulness of another. One day I should like you to paint a miniature of Sir Nicholas and me as a surprise gift for him.'

'I should enjoy that,' Anne Marie said. 'I have several sketches and can work from memory so that he does not suspect.'

They left their hostess and travelled home in the coach that Anne Marie found cumbersome, but which Lady Sarah preferred to riding on horseback. It had been a holiday for both of them and they were laughing as the groom came to help them down, but a moment later Jack came hurtling towards them, his face stained with tears.

'He beat him,' he cried, pulling frantically at Anne Marie's arm. 'It was worse than all the other times. Edward is crying on his bed because he hurts so bad.'

'What is this?' Lady Sarah asked of her son, but Anne Marie was already striding into the house ahead of her. 'What are you saying, Jack? Why has Edward been beaten?'

'Because Anne Marie told him he wasn't to do it without asking her in future. I heard him say it when he was hitting Edward, over and over again. He said it would teach him not to tell tales, but it wasn't Edward—it was me. I told Anne Marie what a brute Master Mountjoy is to Edward.'

'I must go to Edward,' Lady Sarah said. 'I must

see for myself…' She hurried into the house after her daughter-in-law, Jack following behind more slowly.

Giving no thought to anything but the deliberate flaunting of her orders, Anne Marie threw open the door of the tutor's private chamber, which adjoined the schoolroom. She found him at his desk, apparently studying some work one of the children had done. He glanced up as she entered, getting to his feet. The colour washed from his face as he realised that she was very angry.

'He deserved every stroke of it,' he faltered. 'He had been slacking over his work, which is what Sir Christopher was most particular about. He desires that his brothers shall learn…'

'Edward's work is not in question here,' Anne Marie said, her tone cold and imperious. 'You have overstepped your authority, sir. You were given a free hand because Sir Christopher expected justice—but what you have done today was not justice. It was revenge and sheer brutality.'

'But see for yourself how disgracefully he has done this essay.' He pushed the book at her. 'It is badly written and full of mistakes. Edward is lazy and must be made to work.'

'You were given your instructions earlier this morning. You knew that you were not to administer a beating without coming to me first.'

'But you were not here.' His tone was condescending as if she were incapable of understanding. 'As a woman you naturally have a tender heart but I…'

'You are dismissed, sir,' Anne Marie said, allowing

him no time to finish his wheedling argument. 'You will be given a month's wages and you will leave in the morning. In the meantime you will have no contact with either of my husband's brothers.'

'But you cannot do that,' he blustered, his face red with indignation. 'I shall take my dismissal from no one but Sir Christopher.'

'You will leave this house immediately,' Anne Marie replied. 'I had intended to give you a reference as to the nature of your work, though not a personal one—but now I shall give you nothing but the wages due to you.'

'You cannot…'

'Lady Hamilton may do whatever she pleases,' said a voice behind her. 'She and I are custodians of Sir Christopher's estate—and the boys are my sons and therefore I have control of them while the head of the house is away. My son engaged your services on my behalf, sir, and I no longer require them. You are a savage brute and I have been cruelly deceived in you.'

Anne Marie gave her mother-in-law a grateful look, then turned her eyes on Master Mountjoy once more. She drew her shoulders back, every inch the imperious lady of the manor. 'If you do not leave at once, sir, my servants will escort you from the premises.'

'I shall go,' he muttered furiously. He glared at Lady Sarah. 'And gladly. Your sons are ignorant louts, madam, and my talents have been wasted on them these many months.'

'Your talents are perhaps more suited to other professions,' Anne Marie replied before Lady Sarah could master her temper enough to speak. 'I shall not name them, but I hope with all my heart that you never find such a position as this again. You have an hour to pack your possessions before my servants throw you off our land.'

With that, she took Lady Sarah's arm and propelled her from the room, walking swiftly, her cheeks heated, and not stopping until they were alone in the parlour downstairs.

'If I had stayed there another moment I should have hit him,' she declared to her mother-in-law. 'But he is not worth another breath—pray tell me, how is Edward?'

'In some pain,' Sarah replied. 'He refuses to let me look at his injuries, but I have sent his nurse to him, and he may let her help him. Sally was always good with him when he had the earache as a baby, and she will tend his hurts with her salves.'

'He is not badly injured? I feared when Jack came to us in a panic like that, that it might be worse.'

'I think Edward finds it difficult to move at the moment,' Lady Sarah replied. 'That man is a savage brute and there is no telling what he might have done to my poor son in time. It is a wonder that his spirit has not been broken.'

'Edward is like Kit,' Anne Marie said with a fond smile. 'He would simply grit his teeth and bear it— but once I knew what was happening I was determined to end it. Unfortunately, I fear that the warning I gave Master Mountjoy may have been the reason behind this latest beating. I gave him another chance, and that was foolish. I should have dismissed him as soon as Jack told me.'

'How could you know what he would do as soon as your back was turned? I was completely taken in by his charm, Anne Marie. I knew that he beat the boys occasionally, but in the past I have had to chastise them myself and I was relieved that he was keeping them in order. I had no idea he was capable of this!'

'We are well rid of him and I am confident that we shall find another tutor,' Anne Marie said. 'The boys must not be allowed to become little rogues again, but we shall choose our man carefully, and make sure that he does not use the rod too freely.'

'I will send a note to Sir Nicholas,' Sarah said. 'He may hear of someone suitable for our needs.'

'I think that an excellent idea,' Anne Marie said. 'Why do you not make a soothing tisane for Edward? Perhaps if he is able to sleep it may heal his pain.'

'Yes, I was about to do so,' Sarah agreed. 'But when Jack told me of your warning to Master Mountjoy I guessed what you would be about and I came to lend my support.'

'It was timely and very welcome.'

Sarah smiled. 'I believe you would have managed well enough, my love. I did not know you had such a temper—I swear my own knees trembled and I almost pitied Master Mountjoy.'

Anne Marie blushed and shook her head. 'You waste your pity on such a man, Sarah. He deserves only our disgust, for to ill-treat innocent children is the worst of crimes.'

'Edward is not innocent, my dear—as we shall discover once he is feeling himself again.'

'Oh, I know that he is not perfect,' Anne Marie said as she too smiled. 'But I am very fond of him—of all your family, Sarah.'

'And you miss Kit?' Sarah nodded sympathetically as she did not answer. 'Of course it must be the case—but perhaps he will return soon. We can only pray that it will be so.'

'I pray for his safe return every night,' Anne Marie said. 'I know that he must be in danger and I do not know what I should do if he did not return to us.'

'You must try not to be too anxious, for the sake of your child,' Sarah said, and put her arms about her to give her comfort. 'We love you, Anne Marie, and no matter what the future may bring, you belong with us—with this family.'

Although confined to his bed for several days by the doctor whom his anxious mother had called when he could not rise the next morning, Edward had suffered no lasting injuries and within a week he was back to normal. He and Jack had begun to neglect their duties again without the firm hand of their tutor, and Anne Marie knew that this situation could not continue.

However, by the end of the second week Sir Nicholas rode over to say that he had discovered a man he thought suitable as a replacement, and to ask if the ladies would like him to interview the candidate for them.

'We shall be grateful for your advice and presence, but we would like to talk to him ourselves,' Anne Marie said and saw a flicker of appreciation in their neighbour's eyes.

The next day she took a part in questioning the applicant, who was a man in his middle years. He seemed less knowledgeable on matters of the world than Master Mountjoy, but was capable of teaching the boys all they needed to know and came with excellent references.

'Master Harris,' Anne Marie said after he had been telling them of his various posts in schools and the households of gentlemen. 'What is your policy on beating an unruly boy?'

'I do not consider it worthy of myself or the boy,' he replied seriously. 'If I cannot gain a pupil's respect without beating him then I have failed. I believe in the withdrawal of privileges and extra work, Lady Hamilton. A thousand lines of very boring Latin to write out in best copperplate will make most lads think twice about repeating a misdemeanour.'

Seeing the twinkle in his eyes, Anne Marie smiled and nodded her agreement. 'I believe you are right, sir. The withdrawal of a privilege was something I have always found hard to bear. If you are willing to come on a month's trial I think we can settle this immediately.'

'I shall hope to satisfy your requirements, Lady

Hamilton—Lady Sarah.' He inclined his head respectfully to them both.

'I shall hope that you will find your pupils respond to your methods, sir,' Lady Sarah said a little doubtfully. Later she remarked to Anne Marie that she thought Master Harris might be a little too soft with the boys, but found that her daughter-in-law did not agree.

'I believe that he knows what he is about,' she said. 'And I like the temper of the man. We must hope that he will gain the boys' respect.'

It became clear from the first few days of Master Harris's regime that he had a way of handling them. Within two weeks they had ceased to roam aimlessly about the house, and appeared to work diligently, going out for their rides and exercise only when permitted. It was obvious that Jack adored the new tutor and would hang about him even when he was free to do as he wished, but Edward's thoughts were not quite as easy to read.

Outwardly, he appeared to respect the new man, and he worked when told to work, but there was a reserve in him, and Anne Marie thought that he was marking time, waiting to see what happened before passing judgement.

She suspected that he blamed her for the savage beating Master Mountjoy had administered before he left, though both his mother and Jack had told him that Anne Marie had stood up to the bully and sent him packing. She regretted that there should be a distance between them, and made several attempts to engage his interest.

His behaviour to her was always polite, but she felt a barrier between them which was not there with Jack, and felt sad for it. However, life at the manor was now peaceful, and she found that her thoughts began to turn more and more to the child growing within her as the weeks passed.

Where was Kit? She longed for his return but there was no word from him, and sometimes she feared that he might be killed and she would never see him again.

Kit frowned as his ship closed on the Spanish vessel. She was a merchantman, heavy with cargo and a sitting duck for the lighter ship. Her armaments were woefully inadequate and a warning shot across her bows was enough to bring the white flag from her captain.

'Shall we board her, cap'n?' one of his men asked. 'Seems she surrendered a mite fast, don't it?'

'Keep a careful eye out,' Kit ordered. 'I shall go aboard myself and speak to the captain.'

'We'll watch your back,' the sailor promised.

'Do that.' Kit looked grim. 'Her crew are Spaniards and I'd as soon trust a ravening wolf as any Spaniard, but mayhap her captain has a good reason for not wanting a fight.'

He swung himself up on the ship's rails, clambering over the side to the Spanish vessel, closely followed by four of his most trusted men, all armed to the teeth and suspicious.

'Consider yourself our prisoners,' Kit informed the captain at once. 'Surrender quietly and you need not fear for your lives.'

There was defiance in the captain's eyes, but he glanced at a gentleman standing close by as if for reassurance. Kit followed the direction of his anxious gaze, realising that the man dressed so finely in black and silver was not a seaman by trade.

'What is your business aboard, sir?' he asked. 'You are not the captain of this ship yet you have some authority...' Before he could finish, someone came rushing towards them and Kit's hand went to his sword as if expecting an attack. 'Good God!' He exclaimed in astonishment, for the newcomer was a woman, and a pretty one at that from what he could see.

'What are you doing to my father, sir?' she cried in creditable English. 'Do not dare to harm him or it will be the worse for you!'

One of his men moved to catch her around the waist, causing a murmur of protest amongst the Spanish crew. Before a mutiny could be sparked, Kit ordered her release.

'Watch her, cap'n. She might have a weapon.'

'I think myself capable of matching her if she tries to murder me,' Kit replied. Something about the girl reminded him of his wife and he was prepared to treat her leniently because of it. 'Stay your hand, Señorita. Your father is safe enough and so are you if you behave yourself.'

'You are a lying English dog!'

'Isabella!' her father warned, his face pale. 'You were told to stay below and wait until I came for you.'

'How could I wait when we were being boarded by these...murderers?'

Kit's smile faded as he heard himself so accused.

'My men do not murder the innocent,' he said. 'It is not we who plunder the natives of the New World and steal their silver and gold. We merely relieve your countrymen of their spoils. Rest easy, lady, you will not be harmed, nor by my pledge will your father and the crew of this ship. You will render up your gold, jewels, and other valuables and be allowed to go on your way in peace.'

'You will pay for this in hell!'

Kit smiled at the fury in her flashing eyes. He took a step towards her, towering over her, making her step back and tremble before him.

'You may think yourself fortunate that I spare you for the sake of the woman I love,' he said. 'Given their head, my men would take you for their sport, kill every man aboard and commandeer the ship. Speak softly from now on, Isabella, or I may change my mind and let them do as they will.'

It was not Kit's policy to behave so brutally on ships that surrendered, for he preferred to show mercy when possible, but she could not know that and turned pale. His smile was inward and hidden this time, for he could not afford an unpleasant incident. His crew were obedient to his word, but they hated the Spanish to a man and if something untoward happened he would not be able to hold them.

'You will come here to me, Isabella,' her father said, and then looked at Kit. 'I thank you for your forbearance towards my unruly daughter, sir. Take what you will and allow us to be on our way.'

His words to Kit were in English, but he had harsher ones for the girl in her own language. She subsided into shamed silence, the fight going out of her at her father's reprimand.

Kit breathed a sigh of relief as he summoned his men to begin the task of stripping the vessel of its rich cargo. It had been touch and go for a while, and he would not have the blood of innocents on his hands.

He swung back on board his own ship, watching as his men worked. For the moment what he did was as a privateer but very soon now there would be a bloody war between England and Spain.

It might be many months before he was able to see his wife again. He wondered how she was and if she was missing him. Or had she found consolation in the arms of another?

Summer had turned into autumn, and the months seemed long and lonely as Anne Marie waited for the birth of her child. By late summer her ankles had begun to swell and she had almost constant backache.

Lady Sarah sympathised with her, giving her something to rub in for the pain and telling her to rest with her feet up on a stool and cushion to ease her ankles, but there was little more she could do.

'It was just the same for me when I was carrying

Edward,' she told Anne Marie. 'I am almost certain that you are carrying a male child, my dear. I vow they are always more trouble than girls.'

During the days of inactivity Anne Marie thought more and more often of Kit and wished that he would return. Hopes that he would do so after the victory at Cadiz had faded and she realised that he would not be there for the birth of his child.

'Oh, Kit,' she whispered as tears trickled down her cheeks. 'Why did you not love me enough to stay with me?'

Yet in her heart she knew that she was unfair to think too harshly of him. He had his duty and must do it regardless of his personal hopes and fears. Besides, she had given no sign that she wanted him to stay, nor had she confessed her love.

And so the days wore on, days in which she learned much about the management of a large country house and estate, weeks and months in which she came to love the family who lived there as her own.

Her child was born towards the end of October of the year 1587, a healthy boy who screamed the moment he came into the world and did not cease his crying for many hours. Anne Marie's milk would not satisfy him and they had to call in a wet nurse from the village to supplement his feed, for he was a huge lusty lad and had caused his mother much pain and grief in the getting of him.

'We shall call him Christopher,' Anne Marie told Sarah as she cooed over the child and congratulated her after the birth. 'When he is older we shall shorten it to Christy but for the moment he shall bear his father's name.'

'Would that Kit were here to see him,' Lady Sarah said and felt anger with her son for his neglect of his young wife. Surely he might have returned before this if only for a visit? 'It is too bad of him to send no word, for I am sure some of the ships must have returned to England before this.'

'I dare say he is busy,' Anne Marie replied, and yawned as the exhaustion crept over her. 'I am sorry but I am so tired. All I seem to do is sleep these days. I seem to have no energy.'

'You will feel better soon,' Lady Sarah promised her. 'You have done your job well, my dear, and deserve to rest as much as you wish. I am sure that when Kit does come home he will be well satisfied with his son.'

When he came home! It seemed to her sometimes that it was a lifetime since she had seen him, and she began to despair and wonder what she would do with the rest of her life, the blackness coming over her in waves some days.

However, within the month Anne Marie was back to normal, her good humour restored and the tiredness gone. She took long walks when the weather permitted and helped with many of the endless tasks of housekeeping, as she had from the beginning. She made a point of spending time with Christopher each day, and she believed that he knew when his mother held him in her arms and sang to him, though they had engaged a nurse to care for his needs.

Anne Marie was conscious that time seemed to drift in a haze of contentment now that she was no longer suffering from the aches and discomforts of childbearing. Christmas came and went, celebrated at the home of their neighbours Sir Nicholas and Lady Grantly, this year, and then the New Year arrived, cold and crisp, covering the land in a blanket of white. For weeks they were confined to the house because the lanes were too icy and treacherous to venture out, and then quite suddenly it was spring again. Birds were singing, the mad March hare began his courtship ritual, and the sun shone. Anne Marie thought that if Kit were to return her happiness would be complete.

Here in this house she had everything she could wish for other than the love of her husband, but he was kind and generous and perhaps they could find happiness together when he returned.

If only that day would come!

Chapter Ten

It was a warm June day in 1588 when Anne Marie
set out on her walk alone, and she could hear the birds
singing all around her as though they too welcomed
the summer. She had been told that there was a place
where wild strawberries grew at the edge of the wood,
and she wanted to pick some for a special preserve
she was making. Wild strawberries tasted very different from those they grew in their kitchen garden, and
she hoped to fill her basket before she returned to the
house.

The wood itself was very dense and stretched on
for miles, and Anne Marie never ventured into it
alone, for she had been told that gypsies and vaga-
bonds sometimes camped there. She knew that there
were deer roaming in the woods, and there had been
reports of wild boar, though Sir Nicholas said that he
believed most had been hunted for food.

She was feeling relaxed and happy, and it was not
until she had picked her strawberries and was about
to return to the house when she suddenly sensed that

she was being followed. She turned round, calling out to whoever was there to show himself.

'Is that you, Jack? Edward—are you hiding from me? Please come out, whoever you are.'

For a moment nothing happened, and then she heard a rustling sound in the trees. A sense of shock ran through her, making her blood turn cold as a man stepped out from the wood to confront her. His clothes were filthy and looked as if he had lived in them for months; his hair and beard were tangled and matted, and yet she knew him instantly. Her heart beat erratically and she glanced around to see if there was anyone nearby to hear her.

'Father?' she cried. 'Is it truly you?'

'Aye, it is me, daughter,' Lord Fraser said and scowled at her. 'Why look so surprised? I have been hunted like a dog since that man you married betrayed me. For months I have not slept in a bed nor eaten a decent meal.'

'It was Kit's duty,' Anne Marie said her throat tight with emotion. 'If you had not tried to spirit me away to France he might never have known…' She caught her breath as he moved towards her, a threatening look in his eyes. 'You broke the bond of good faith you gave when I was taken to live with Thomas and Beth Makepeace. And the plan you hatched to place Mary of Scots on the English throne was foolish and always doomed to failure.'

'Aye, I know well enough that it was my own daughter that betrayed me. I have watched you laughing with the children of the household these many months, and waited for my chance to find you alone. I waited, for I did not want the trouble of your bastard brat, but now I shall have my revenge. You have wronged me, daughter. You have turned your face against your faith and against me. 'Tis sharper than a serpent's tooth to be betrayed by the one who owed me her duty.'

'It was not so, Father,' she protested. 'Had I confided in Kit he might have been able to help you. What you did was wrong, and you must know that in your heart.' She gave a cry of fear as he seized her wrist, his thin fingers clawing at her flesh and hurting her. 'I cannot condone your behaviour, sir. You acted against our lawful Queen and…' she screamed as he struck her across the face. 'You should not have done that, sir.'

'I have the right to do what I will with you. You are my daughter, my property. You betrayed me and I see they have made a whore of you, but you may yet prove useful to me.' His grasp tightened on her wrist and he started to drag her towards the direction of the woods. 'Mayhap the man you married—though in the sight of the Lord it is no marriage—will be willing to pay to get you back. Or I may sell you to any who will have you and your bastard brat.'

'My child is not a bastard,' Anne Marie cried and began to struggle against him. 'Let me go! Let me go! I shall never come with you.' She screamed again and fought him, kicking out and making him shout in pain as her stout, walking boot connected with his shinbone. 'I shall never be your slave to be used, as you will. You have never cared for me. I was merely something you thought to bargain with. Leave me be. You have no power over me.' She broke free of him as he panted for breath, his strength easily spent after so many months of hard living and near starvation.

'More's the pity,' he grunted. 'Had Frampton been here I swear you would have come without a struggle. He told me it would be so the first time, that's why I let him fetch you the day I put you on that ship for France. I dare say you would have defied me then if I had tried to fetch you myself—but you could not resist his powers. I swear he is in league with the Devil himself!'

Anne Marie felt the coldness seep though her as she stared at him. It was as she had always suspected, though she had never been able to remember the truth and could not do so now.

'What foul trick did that man play on me? I have never known how I came to leave that clifftop...' She shivered, feeling revolted by his confession. 'If you had cared for me you would not have let that evil creature have sway over me.'

'Evil? Aye, that he is,' Lord Fraser said and spat on the ground. 'Frampton is a clever devil, for I have never known what goes on in his mind. He speaks of his master, always pretending to be the servant of another, but I am not quite the fool he thought me. He is eaten up with hatred, of the Tudors and his fellow man. A strange man, secretive and sly—but a coward when all is said. Left me like a rat from a sinking ship at the first hint of trouble. I was a fool to listen to him. He is safe in Spain, while Walsingham's men hunt me at every turn.'

'I am sorry for it, Father,' Anne Marie said. 'I would help you if I could—but I shall not go with you. If you try to make me I shall scream and fight you with my last breath. There are people working in the fields near by. You could not hope to get me away without being seen.'

'You have let these people turn your mind, and are no longer my daughter,' Lord Fraser said, his face working with fury at her stubbornness. 'Be damned to you, Anne Marie Fraser. I hope you burn in Hell for your sins!'

Anne Marie's hand flew to her throat as she saw the hatred in his eyes, and for a moment she thought he meant to attack her, and then she heard voices shouting and suddenly Jack and Edward accompanied by one of the dogs came running towards her.

'Anne Marie…' Jack cried. 'We heard you cry out. What is happening? Who is that beggar? Is he bothering you?'

'No, I am safe now,' Anne Marie said her face pale as she looked at her father. 'I think you should go now, sir. You have my answer, and you see that I am protected, surrounded by those I care for. Please do not trouble me again.'

Lord Fraser made no reply, looking at the two lads and the dog, which was bristling and growling low in its throat, clearly thinking him a threat to its young masters. He knew what such dogs were capable of, and that there were probably men working in the fields nearby. Looking at the proud, cold face of the daughter he had neglected all her life, he realised that his cause was lost. Scowling, he turned and slunk off into the trees without another word. Anne Marie watched him in silence, turning only as Jack spoke to her.

'Who was that rogue, Anne Marie? We heard you cry out and thought you were being attacked. We ran as fast as we could to help you.'

'He is someone I used to know and he wanted me to go with him,' she said. 'He tried to make me, but I would not.'

'He should be arrested and hanged,' Jack cried imperiously. 'He is a vagrant and trespassing on our land.'

'They don't hang vagrants,' Edward said. 'They only imprison them or brand them and turn them out of the parish—they hang traitors though.' His eyes narrowed as he looked at Anne Marie, a hint of resentment in his eyes.

'Please do not tell Lady Sarah,' she said. 'He is just a foolish man—and I would not have him harmed. He will not come back again.'

'All right, I shan't tell if you don't want me to,' Jack said, stealing a handful of strawberries from her basket.

Edward did not say anything, but there was something about his expression that warned Anne Marie he had remembered what he had overheard the day she arrived at Hamilton Manor. And she thought that he had guessed the identity of the man Jack had called a vagrant. He knew it was Lord Fraser and not merely a beggar.

'You won't tell, Edward?'

'I shall say nothing to my mother.'

Looking into his eyes, Anne Marie was uneasy. Jack's promise had been easily given, and she knew that he would keep it, but she was not sure about Edward. She had sensed his resentment of her and she knew that he blamed her for some of the beatings he had received in the past.

Would he take this chance to be avenged on her?

Three days had passed when Anne Marie came down the stairs to find Sir Nicholas talking earnestly with her mother-in-law. They both looked at her, the same odd, guilty expression in their faces. She was suspicious at once, sensing a secret they did not wish to share.

'Has something happened?' she asked, her heart jerking. 'Pray tell me that you have not had bad news of Kit, sir!'

'I have heard that his ship may be on its way home,' he replied, and hesitated. 'The *Golden Fleece* was sighted a week ago by one of my own merchant ships, and I believe all is well with your husband.'

'Then what?' Anne Marie looked from one to the other. 'I am sure that something has happened. What is it that you do not wish to tell me, Sarah?'

Sarah sighed and shook her head. 'I fear Sir Nicholas has brought news that you will not like to hear, Anne Marie, and I am truly sorry for it.'

The colour drained from her face as she saw Sarah's expression, and somehow she knew. She knew that what she had feared for so long had come to pass.

'You have news of my father, sir?'

'Lord Fraser has been arrested,' he confirmed. 'I have not all the details yet, but we believe he may have been trying to make contact with you...' He saw her face and frowned. 'Perhaps he had already done so?'

'I spoke to him three days ago and told him that I would not go with him and did not wish him to contact me again,' she said in a hoarse whisper. 'Yet I would not have had him harmed. He is a broken man, a filthy wretch, near starving and hunted—he can surely do no more harm to Her Majesty?'

'He is a traitor,' Sir Nicholas said sternly. 'I am sorry but I cannot defend a man who plots against England and the Queen. It was Lord Fraser's intention to help raise a foreign army to invade this country, and I have no doubt that he will be punished for his misdeeds.'

'No!' Anne Marie's hand flew to her throat. She had lived with this threat too long and now it had become a reality. 'How was he taken, sir?'

'The magistrate was warned that there was a dangerous vagrant in the area, and on his arrest he confessed his identity. Word was sent to me, as it was thought I was the proper person to deal with the situation. I saw him myself and arranged that he should be decently treated while held in prison. He has not been harmed and I believe that he no longer had the will to resist the soldiers when they surrounded him. I was told he did not attempt to fight, but accepted his arrest quietly.'

With her refusal to go with him he had lost all hope. She could not have helped him, and yet felt guilty and distressed that she had thus contributed to his downfall.

'What will happen to him now?'

'Word has been sent to London. I expect that Walsingham will send his own men to take Lord Fraser to the Tower...'

'Where he will be tortured and then beheaded.'

'Anne Marie,' Sarah cried. 'Do not do this to yourself. It is not of your making. Your father was a traitor and this was bound to happen one day.'

Anne Marie knew that she was right, but her mind was reeling from the horror of what would happen to her father. Whatever he had done, she would never have wished such a cruel end for him.

'I know you think he deserves his fate,' she said, the tears very close. 'You all think it and perhaps you are right—but I cannot forget so easily.'

She turned and went hurriedly up the stairs, tears trickling down her cheeks so that she could taste their salt. At the top she saw Jack and Edward talking in whispers. They looked at her as she paused to catch her breath and there was guilt in their faces. In that moment she knew who had betrayed her father.

They had told someone of the vagrant, and Edward

had voiced his suspicions—and that had led directly to Lord Fraser's arrest.

For a moment her eyes met Edward's, then she turned away and went on to her chamber without a word.

They had betrayed her after she had asked for their promise that they would not, and she was hurt beyond measure. She had believed herself a part of this family, and now she felt as if by this action they had cast her out.

Anne Marie's manner had become reserved towards the family she had loved as she withdrew into herself, often leaving her rooms only to go walking and taking many of her meals alone. Her love and attention was all given to her son, and it was her chiefest pleasure to spend time in the nursery, rocking him and crooning a lullaby.

She was bitterly hurt that they all seemed to have turned against her, and now that her tears were shed, she had put into place the shield that had served her at Drodney for so many years.

'You must not think that we blame you for your father's sins,' Sarah had told her one day. 'But try to see it from our point of view, Anne Marie. Lord Fraser plotted against the Queen—and against us, for he would have brought back the Catholic faith by force if necessary. Too many Protestants suffered in Queen Mary's reign to make that something we could easily accept.'

'I am aware of your feelings, ma'am,' Anne Marie

replied quietly, her head held high. 'Pray respect mine by allowing me to mourn in private.'

'Do not turn your face from us,' Sarah said looking at her sadly. 'For if you do you hurt us all, including yourself.'

'I was never given a choice,' Anne Marie reminded her. 'Your son took me from the ship my father had paid to take me to France and married me against my will. Despite that I had come to love you, and now you have betrayed me.'

'How can you say that?' Sarah looked at her in bewilderment. 'We have done nothing to bring about your father's arrest.'

'Perhaps you have not yourself, ma'am,' Anne Marie replied with cool dignity. 'But there is another in this house who played some part in it. And now I beg you would excuse me. I am tired and would rest.'

She refused to explain further, for she would not betray Edward even though he had betrayed her trust. Seeing the hurt in Jack's eyes as they passed on the stairs sometimes, Anne Marie was conscious of sadness, and yet she could do no more than give him a faint smile, for to relent towards one would break down the barrier towards all and then the pain would flood in.

Anne Marie was not sure whether it was distress for her father or the hurt occasioned by Edward's betrayal of her that gave her most pain. She had longed for Kit's return, but now she dreaded it. For in shutting out his family she had somehow shut a door on part of herself and did not want to open it even for him.

Her solace now was found mostly in her painting and in the solitary walks she took, often before the household woke. Her only happiness the thought of the child she had brought into the world through pain and blood.

It was the first week of July. The sun was shining brightly outside her window, calling to Anne Marie. She had almost made up her mind that she would go down to the garden for a while when she heard the sound of heavy footsteps in the hallway. Her heart began to race; then her door was thrust open without ceremony and she saw the man she had longed for during so many lonely months standing there glaring at her. Pain and shock washed over her as she realised that he blamed her for what had happened between her and his family.

'What is this nonsense I hear?' Kit demanded as she stared at him in shock. 'Why have you shut yourself up here in your chamber for the past two weeks?'

'Kit…' Anne Marie's heart jerked painfully, her breath catching in distress. 'When did you return? You sent no word…'

'I was eager to see you,' he said, eyes narrowed, intent. This was not how he had imagined her and the disappointment was strong in him. 'You look pale, unwell. Why are you not sitting in the garden on a day like this?'

'I—I was thinking I might go down,' she replied. 'You do not understand, sir.'

'I understand that you have been sulking,' he replied harshly. 'My mother has told me that you have scarce spoken to her in days. Why do you blame this family? You always knew that Lord Fraser would be taken one day, and the penalty that must follow.'

'I do not deny that,' she said, her eyes downcast. 'But it has distressed me sorely.'

'Why?' he demanded brutally. He had arrived home eager to see her, and what he had learned had aroused his anger, blinding him to her feelings, making him insensitive. 'He did nothing for you, Anne Marie. It was Beth who cared for you and provided for you all your life, and you have received more love from this family than your precious father ever gave you. All Lord Fraser wanted was to use you for his own good. If you are honest you will admit the truth and have done with these sulks.'

In her heart she knew that every word he spoke was the truth, but he did not realise that his words only plunged the dagger deeper into her breast. She had believed herself loved and she had loved in return, which made the betrayal even harder to bear. Whatever Lord Fraser was, no matter what he had done, he was her father. Edward's betrayal had hurt her, as had Sarah's seeming lack of understanding— and now Kit was trying to bully her into submission! It was unkind and unfair, and she would not permit him to use her so!

'You are harsh, sir,' she replied, a flash of temper

in her eyes. 'I had hoped that you might show some understanding of my feelings, though your family has not.'

'My mother apologises if her frank words hurt you, Anne Marie, but she thought it best to be honest. It would be wrong to live with a lie between you. She did not wish your father harm, but she could not have let a traitor escape detention if she had known of his presence—fortunately she did not.'

It was on the tip of her tongue to say that others were not so innocent but she held them back. Even in her distress she would not condemn Edward to his family for what he had done to her.

'Am I not to be allowed a little time for grief, sir?' she demanded proudly. 'Would you not have grieved had it been your father?'

Faced with her cool dignity, Kit realised belatedly that he was perhaps being a little harsh towards her. His mother's tale had enraged him, and he could not in all conscience be sorry that Lord Fraser had been arrested. For as long as he had remained free there was always a possibility that some attempt might be made to abduct Anne Marie—something that had worried him in his absence.

'If it was only grief,' he replied looking at her thoughtfully. 'But my mother says that you have cut yourself off from the family entirely.'

'For the moment I feel the need to be alone,' she said, a faint flush in her cheeks. 'In time things may be almost as they were.'

'But not quite?' Kit's eyes narrowed as he sensed

that she was hiding something. 'Why do you blame this family? What has happened that I do not know? I can see by your manner that something has. You cannot hide it from me, Anne Marie. I know you too well.'

'I have nothing more to say, sir. You must condemn me or absolve me as you will.'

'And you expect me to be satisfied with that?' He strode towards her, taking hold of her arm and jerking her to her feet so that he was looking into her face. 'What of us, Anne Marie? Before I left I thought we had reached an understanding. Your manner suggested that you cared for me at least a little.'

'I am your wife,' she said remaining outwardly calm and emotionless, though inside she was pulsating with emotion. The burn of Kit's fingers imprinting themselves on her flesh had awoken the feelings she had tried to deaden. Yet her words were emotionless, cold. 'A wife must show her husband duty...'

'Damn you!' Kit saw her pale face through a red mist of fury. He might have shaken her or slapped her had she not stared at him with those accusing eyes, as if he were to blame, not she. How could she behave so coldly towards him? Did she care nothing for him after all? Were all his dreams merely that? 'You are a hard-hearted witch and I have done trying to please you. Stay here and rot if you choose. I shall not beg you to love me again!'

With that he turned and strode from the room, leaving Anne Marie to stare after him in dismay. He had gone and she loved him so! But her pride and her hurt had kept her from telling him. Even now she longed to run after him and beg him to forgive her, but her feet seemed as if they were glued to the floor.

The tears were beginning to trickle down her cheeks as she recalled his words. When had he ever begged her to love him? And yet he had been so thoughtful for her comfort, so loving and tender when he came to their bed, giving so much of himself— while she had held back her love.

Self-recrimination filled her with shame as she realised that he had much to complain of in her behaviour, both before and after their marriage, and yet he had seldom criticised her until now. And that only because she had hurt his family.

Oh, but they had hurt her! Surely she had good reason to feel that they had treated her unfairly?

Anne Marie looked into her heart and realised that she had also been unfair. It was true that Edward had betrayed her trust, but she had blamed all the family equally for her hurt. That was not well done of her, and she knew she must try to make amends.

She poured cool water into a pewter basin and bathed her face, then she tidied her hair and, lifting her head, proud but determined to apologise, went downstairs.

She would apologise to Lady Sarah and to Kit, and she would try to repair the breach between them.

'Kit has gone already?' Anne Marie stared at her mother-in-law in dismay. 'But how can he have gone so soon? He has been away for months. I thought he had come home for a while at least.'

Sarah looked at her sadly. She had known when Kit came downstairs that he was in one of his rages. He would not stay, though she had begged him to, but he seemed beyond reason and she had let him go, knowing that it would pass in time. As a boy he had sometimes flown into terrible tempers, but as a rule they did not last long. However, she believed that this time it was more serious, and the expression in his eyes had frightened her.

'When he came home he went first to see his son, and I understood that he intended to stay for a few days before leaving to join Sir Francis Drake once more, but he was very angry after speaking to you, Anne Marie. I asked him where he was going and he said that he had business elsewhere and there was no point in staying here.'

'Oh…' Anne Marie caught back a sob of distress as she realised that Kit was even more angry with her than she had thought. 'It was my fault. I would not listen and I—I was so cold to him.'

'He should not have come to you the way he did. I asked him to let me speak to you first; I tried to tell him that you needed to grieve in your own way and that he must be patient, but he would not listen.'

'No, it was my fault from the beginning,' Anne Marie said. 'He has been more patient with me than you know, and now I have driven him away. I have killed any feeling he had for me.'

'Surely not,' Sarah said and reached out to touch

her pale face with a little smile of understanding. 'Kit is very angry for the moment. He has always been a passionate man. As a child he had tempestuous rages and tantrums that he learned to control as he grew to manhood, but for good or evil, you have aroused those passions, my dear. Kit loves you so much that he is not always able to see things as he ought.'

'Loves me?' Anne Marie stared at her in surprise. 'How can you say so? I know he has been kind and considerate and—and he feels some passion towards me, but he has never spoken of love. Besides, our marriage was an order from the Queen.'

'If you still believe that you are indeed blind to the truth,' Sarah told her with a little laugh. 'Do you not know that Kit asked Her Majesty for you in marriage? He was kept waiting for weeks while Elizabeth decided whether to grant the boon he craved or throw him into the Tower for disobeying his orders.'

'Kit asked…' Anne Marie stared at her. Surely she was mistaken? But no, she seemed confident of her facts. But if she was right—this changed everything! 'But he never spoke of this to me. Why did he not tell me? Why did he not say that he…' She broke off in confusion, her mind in turmoil.

'That he loved you?' Sarah raised her brows. 'Forgive me if I intrude, my dear—but have you ever told Kit that you love him?' She smiled as Anne Marie blushed. 'No, I thought not. I believe I am right in saying that you do love him?'

'Yes,' Anne Marie spoke in a choked whisper that was barely audible. 'I have loved him from the first—

when he took me riding at Drodney and bought the mare for me. No one had ever been so kind to me and I did not want to run away from him. I did not want to be married to my cousin in France and I was glad when Kit came and took me with him. I resisted our marriage for several reasons, but afterwards I was happy.'

'Have you ever said any of this to him?'

'No, I could not,' Anne Marie said, her cheeks hot with shame. 'I was afraid to tell him, because I thought he had been forced to marry me and that he would soon tire of a wife he had not truly wanted.'

'And Kit believes that you were forced to marry him and cannot love him,' Sarah said with a shake of her head. 'What a pretty pair you are!'

'I wish that I might apologise to Kit, ma'am.'

'The chance will come,' Sarah said. 'Do not despair, Anne Marie. He is angry now and I think that necessity may keep him from you for a while, but in time he will return—and then I shall hope there will be no more of this silliness between the two of you.'

'You are very good to forgive me, ma'am,' Anne Marie said. 'I have been harsh to you these past two weeks.'

Sarah was silent for a moment, then, 'You spoke of someone in this house betraying your father. I have questioned both Edward and Jack, and although neither would breathe a word I believe that one of them had some part in it. I am truly sorry if that is the case, Anne Marie. I particularly warned you that first day that it would be my duty to report your father should

I learn of his presence in the area, and hoped that the case would never arise.' She nodded as Anne Marie was silent, reading from her manner what she would not say. 'I cannot blame you for your anger, but I do ask for your forgiveness on behalf of my son.'

'Please say no more about it,' Anne Marie said quickly. 'I was hurt by the fact of my father's arrest, and because I felt that this family had turned against me. Although I must always grieve for Lord Fraser, he never gave me love. It is this family that has done that, ma'am—and I am sorry that I was so foolish as to think that you had turned away from me simply because you were honest enough to speak the truth. This is something upon which we must learn to think differently without letting it tear us apart. I ask you to forgive me for my harshness to you.'

'Then we shall say no more about it.' Sarah reached out to embrace the girl, who hugged her back and then they both shed a few tears before sharing Sarah's kerchief to wipe their faces. 'I have told Edward and Jack that they must respect your privacy, but I know that Jack in particular is very upset. He has asked after you every day and…'

She was interrupted by the arrival of a serving wench, who bobbed nervously and looked uncomfortable as if she did not like to intrude when they were talking.

'Yes, Prudence,' Lady Sarah said. 'Did you want something?'

'It's Master Jack, mistress,' the girl said. 'He was running around in the kitchen and then he made a funny moaning sound and fell down foaming at the mouth and writhing. We all thought it was one of his tricks, you know the way Master Jack carries on sometimes, mistress—but he won't wake up and he's burning up with a fever.'

'Jack is ill?' Anne Marie cried. 'Where is he? In the kitchen?'

'His nurse had him carried up to his bedchamber so that she could look after him,' Prudence said. 'The thing is, mistress, I think Master Edward might be sickening for the same thing. He didn't pass out or nothing, but he looked proper queer when he went upstairs after they carried his brother up.'

'I must go to Jack at once,' Sarah said, clearly distressed. She looked at Anne Marie. 'You must stay away from the boys, my dear. If they have caught some vile fever it might harm Christopher should you take it from them.'

'I have never been prone to fevers,' Anne Marie said. 'If both the boys are ill you will need help to nurse them. I shall leave Christopher to the care of his nurse and do what I can for your sons. I have had some little experience of nursing when I helped Beth to care for the men at the castle and sometimes the poor folk in the village.'

Sarah was too distracted to argue, and hurried off to discover what was happening to her youngest and favourite son. Anne Marie hesitated for a moment, then followed her slowly up the stairs, going to Edward's room. She paused outside, then knocked at the door before entering.

Edward was lying on his bed, his eyes closed. He did not open them as she approached and laid her hand on his brow. He was burning up! She did not doubt that he was suffering from the same complaint as his brother. He opened his eyes as she bent over him, stroking the damp hair back from his forehead.

'I am going to bathe your face, neck and arms to help cool you,' she said. 'And then I am going downstairs to fetch a drink that may make you feel a little better.'

'Why should you help me?' he asked a sullen look in his eyes as he stared at her. She guessed that he was feeling too ill to repulse her physically but was yet defiant. 'It was me that told on him—your father. He was a traitor and deserves to die a traitor's death.'

'Yes, perhaps he does,' Anne Marie said quietly. 'But I would not have wished it for him, because he was my father.'

'Then go away and leave me alone.'

She could see guilt and regret in his eyes and knew that he suffered despite his defiant words.

'I may not do that, Edward,' Anne Marie said gently. 'I am hurt that you betrayed your promise to me, but I still care for you. Your mother is busy tending Jack, and I want to help you—if you will let me? We might try to forgive each other if you like?'

'It was your fault Mountjoy beat me that day. You should not have interfered as you did.'

'I wanted only to help you, Edward.'

'It was still wrong,' he said. 'But I have forgiven you—and I am sorry for what I did.'

'Then we shall be friends,' Anne Marie replied and touched the cloth wrung out in cool water to his forehead, smoothing it over his heated flesh. 'This may ease you a little, and the drink I shall make you will take away some of the pain.'

His lips curved in a wry smile that reminded her so much of Kit that her heart felt as if it would break. Some of the heat seemed to go out of him as she bathed him in the cool water, and he was resting a little more easily as she left him to go downstairs.

Sarah was in the stillroom preparing something of her own for Jack. She looked anxiously at Anne Marie as she entered and began to busy herself about her own task.

'How is Edward?'

'He has a nasty fever but I think we may have caught it in time in his case,' Anne Marie said. 'I have seen something similar to this before at Drodney, and the cure I am preparing has often helped to ease the symptoms. How is poor little Jack?'

'He is in a delirium,' his mother said, a catch in her voice. 'He does not know me.'

'You must not be too fearful,' Anne Marie said. 'Children often react more violently to fevers than adults, and they recover much faster too. At least there are two of us to nurse them, Sarah.'

'Yes, and I thank God for it,' Sarah said. 'I pray that you will not take it from Edward, for I should blame myself if you were to lose your own child.'

'Have no fear for me,' Anne Marie said. 'Beth often said I must have a charmed life, for I never took any of the fevers, even though she did—and then I nursed her.'

Sarah nodded and, having prepared the tisane she had been making for her son, hurried off to give it to him herself.

Anne Marie continued with the mixing of her own preparation, then poured it into a cup and sweetened it with a little honey before going back up to Edward's room. He was getting hot again, but he took the drink from her and seemed to settle afterwards. Satisfied that he was sleeping, she went along the corridor to see Jack.

One glance at the boy tossing feverishly on his bed told her that he was very much the worse of the two, and she went to stand by his side to look down at him.

'I have never seen him this ill,' Sarah said, her voice catching on a sob. 'I fear for him, Anne Marie. I think he is going to…'

'Hush, do not say it,' Anne Marie cried. 'We must not give up hope. He seems very hot, Sarah, should we not bathe him again?'

'He was cold a moment ago,' Sarah said, clearly uncertain what to do for the best. 'Perhaps you are right, Anne Marie.'

'Let me do it. You should go and rest for a few minutes, you look ill yourself.' She laid a hand on Sarah's brow and discovered that she was very hot. 'I think you have taken the fever yourself, Sarah. You must lie down for a while. I will sit with Jack for the time being.'

Sarah got up from her chair intending to bathe Jack herself, then gave a little cry and fell back against the chair as she turned dizzy.

'I do seem a little unwell,' she said. 'Perhaps I should lie down for an hour or so.'

'Attend your mistress,' Anne Marie told the boy's nurse who had been hovering in the background watching. 'Bathe her head and arms in cold water when she is laid down, and I shall bring her a cooling drink in a little while.'

She bent over Jack once more as Sarah was helped from the room by the nurse, stroking the damp hair back from his brow and whispering words of comfort to him.

Jack opened his eyes and seemed to look at her for a moment.

'Anne Marie,' he muttered fretfully. 'I am sorry... sorry for what I did.'

'It's all right, Jack,' she said. 'I have forgiven you. It is all forgotten now. I am here and your mother will come again soon. Try to rest now and we shall take good care of you.'

Jack sighed and closed his eyes, seeming to be at peace for a moment, and then he began to toss and turn restlessly once more.

Anne Marie frowned as she finished bathing his heated body. He was much sicker than his elder brother, and she thought that it must have been he who had first brought the fever home. Both Edward and Sarah had taken it from him, but she had escaped because of her confinement in her own chamber. She thought that she might be safe from the infection, being almost sure that she had encountered it before this, but she would drink some of her own cure just in case.

More than three hours passed before Jack seemed to drift into a peaceful sleep and Anne Marie was able to leave him to his nurse's care. She went from him to Edward, who had become hot once more and cried out fretfully as she bathed his forehead.

'It will ease soon,' she promised him as she soothed his face with her hand. 'I shall bring another drink to you shortly and then you will sleep again.'

She had already sent a message to Christopher's nurse, telling her that she must keep to her own chambers and not mix with the rest of the household. Food would be sent up to her, and they could only pray that neither she nor Christopher took the fever from someone else.

When she knocked at Sarah's door she was told to enter, and found her mother-in-law about to leave her chamber fully dressed.

'You should be resting,' she told her. 'You still look flushed.'

'I am a little better,' Sarah told her. 'Nurse gave me a cooling bath and that helped, and I have taken some of my own medicine. I have a headache but I believe I have taken the fever but lightly and shall be better soon.'

Anne Marie laid the palm of her hand against her

brow and nodded. 'You do feel quite cool. It may be that you have had the fever before and it has not affected you so badly this time. Beth told me it was often so.'

'Yes, I think you may be right. Is Jack any better?'

'No, I do not think so,' Anne Marie said. 'Edward is restless. I am about to take him up a drink that may help him. It seemed to ease him earlier. Shall I prepare something similar for Jack?'

'No, I shall do that myself,' Sarah replied. 'You have enough to do with looking after Edward—and you must rest soon, my dear. Or you will be exhausted.'

'I shall sleep when Edward sleeps,' Anne Marie assured her. 'And you should share the care of Jack with his nurse.'

Edward was still restless when Anne Marie returned with his drink, but after she had helped him to take most of it he settled and was soon sleeping peacefully. She smiled to see the change, knowing from all that Beth had taught her that this kind of virulent fever often waned as swiftly as it came. The boys had probably been sickening for a few days without anyone realising it, and Edward had clearly begun to throw it off just as Sarah had.

Going to her own chamber, Anne Marie lay down. She was tired and her back was aching, but it was natural that she should experience some tiredness. She would feel better for a few hours sleep.

She wondered whether they ought to send to Kit. Would he come home if he knew his youngest brother was desperately ill? She thought that he might, and knew that she longed to see him—to repair the breach between them and confess her love.

She wished that she had sent a message that day, but there had been no time to think of it. However, she would do so in the morning.

Anne Marie rose and dressed soon after dawn, going at once to Edward's room. She was pleased to discover that he was sleeping peacefully and that the fever seemed to have left him. A feeling of relief came over her and she believed that he would begin to recover now.

It was not the same case when she went along to Jack's room. Sarah was sitting asleep in a chair by her son's bedside, but she woke as Anne Marie entered and rose to bend over the boy. She gave Anne Marie a worried look as she felt the heat of him.

'He is no better?'

'No, I think he may be worse,' Sarah said. 'I was awake all night with him until I fell asleep.'

'How do you feel yourself?'

'Weak and a little dizzy,' Sarah confessed. 'If you will excuse me I should like to go and lie down for a while, Anne Marie.'

'Yes, of course you must, and I shall sit with Jack, but first I shall make a drink for him. It is one that Beth taught me to make, Sarah, and I think it may ease him.'

'My own seems to have done him no good,' Sarah

said. 'Nurse Sally shall sit with him while you make it, for that may ease him.'

Anne Marie hurried downstairs and prepared a jug of the healing mixture. She carried it up to the nursery and poured some into a cup, which she handed to Nurse Sally.

'Take this to Lady Sarah if you please. I think it may help her sleep—and then go and rest yourself, for you look exhausted. I shall stay here for a few hours.'

She then held some to Jack's lips. He could not swallow much at a time and moaned as if in pain as she soothed his brow.

'My poor, poor Jack,' she whispered and kissed him as he whimpered. 'I blame myself. If I had not kept apart from you I might have noticed that you were unwell.'

Her grief tore at her as she stroked his forehead, blaming herself for her neglect of the boy. She had come to love him as a younger brother and she would hardly forgive herself if he were to die. Pray God he would not!

It was her fault he was so ill, she thought, racked by distress. Had the fever been treated sooner the dread sickness might not have gained such a hold. Remembering his sweet smile, and his naughty ways, her heart broke and broke again. She had been so unkind to him in the last precious days of his life, and she felt the guilt strike into her as she watched his struggle and knew that nothing seemed to ease him.

'Oh Jack, dearest Jack,' she whispered, tears trickling down her cheeks. 'I beg you not to die. Forgive me if I hurt you by neglect. It was not your fault. You did not know what would happen.'

The mixture she had prepared had eased Edward, and when Sarah came to take her place at the bedside she told her that it had helped her to sleep.

'I feel much better now,' she told Anne Marie. 'Which is just as well, since Nurse Sally has taken the fever and is laid on her bed—and three of the serving wenches have gone down with it.'

'It is a virulent one that I believe I have seen often before,' Anne Marie said. 'In some it is merely a matter of feeling unwell for a few hours and in others...' She broke off and was unwilling to say the words, but she knew that Sarah understood.

'In others it kills,' Sarah finished for her. 'I know, for I have seen it in the village, Anne Marie. As you say, some take it more than once and seem to survive while others die of it.' She blinked back her tears as she gazed down at her son. 'Jack has it as badly as any I have ever seen.'

Anne Marie's eyes stung with tears that she struggled to hold back, for if she wept how could Sarah bear it?

'Do you think we should let Kit know?'

'I have written to him this morning,' Sarah said and her voice almost broke with emotion. 'I sent the letter to his house in London, for I believe it was there that he intended to go—but I do not know if he will come in time.'

Anne Marie saw tears in her mother-in-law's eyes and felt them start to her own. 'If only I had not been so foolish. I might have noticed that Jack was ill...'

'You were not to blame,' Sarah told her at once. 'I was with the boys every day and I saw nothing untoward. If Jack was feeling ill he did not mention it to me—though he had been a little quiet. I thought he had something on his mind and I believed I knew what was troubling him. It is my belief that he was the one who spoke of seeing your father that day.'

'Jack—but surely it was Edward? He knew that my father was a traitor.' Anne Marie looked at her. 'When he was ill last night he told me it was him and said that he was sorry.'

'Then he was covering up for his brother,' Sarah replied. 'For I think that Jack reported seeing a vagrant to our bailiff and the alert was set.'

'But Jack did not know it was my father—or that my father was wanted for treason...' Anne Marie nodded, realising finally that it had after all been the reaction of an innocent child and not a betrayal. 'He did it because he thought the vagrant had attacked me—but he did not tell you. I asked them both to promise and they kept their promise, but Jack told the bailiff.'

'I think that is what must have happened,' Sarah said. 'Jack was most distressed that he had hurt you, Anne Marie.'

A whimper from the bed made them both look round, and they saw that Jack had his eyes open and was staring at them. Anne Marie was the nearest and she went to take his hand, bending to kiss his cheek.

'Are you feeling better?' she asked. 'Would you like a drink, my dear?'

'Water…' he croaked and sipped at the cup she held to his lips. 'I'm sorry, Anne Marie. I didn't know he was…'

'Hush, my love,' she told him, the tears slipping down her cheeks. 'It does not matter. I love you and you must rest. I have forgotten it. All that matters is that you should get well.'

'I love you, Anne Marie.'

'And I love you, my dearest.'

She kissed him again, then gave her place to his mother, who sat on the bed beside him, stroking the hair from his forehead.

Leaving them together, Anne Marie went downstairs to make more of the healing mixture. Perhaps it would help some of the serving wenches. She would tell those that were still able to work to take it to the less fortunate ones who were laid on their cots.

She had that second finished making a great bowl of the cure when she heard a wailing cry and went to the bottom of the stairs just as one of the serving wenches came running along the landing to call to her.

'Lady Hamilton,' she cried. 'Come quickly. The mistress is out of her mind with grief.'

'Jack…' Anne Marie walked swiftly up the stairs, her heart beating frantically. Oh please God, let it not be Jack! She had thought that he was on the mend but she knew these things could be very sudden, and her heart caught with grief as she paused on the threshold to see Sarah lying on the bed beside Jack, holding his lifeless body close to her. 'No, please... no!'

Sarah looked up at her, her face streaked with tears. 'He was smiling at me as I stroked his forehead. I thought he was better and then he made a little choking sound and he was gone.'

'I was so sure he was getting better,' Anne Marie said. She went to Sarah as she rose and put her arms about her, holding her close. 'I am so very, very sorry. I wish that I could have done something to save him.'

'We both tried,' Sarah said and wiped her face on her apron. 'It was God's will, my dear. I lost two daughters in infancy, and now my son. There was nothing I could do for my daughters and nothing to be done for Jack. It is the way of things, Anne Marie.'

'It should have been me,' Edward's voice said from the doorway. 'Why wasn't it me?'

'You were ill yourself,' his mother told him. 'You are not to blame, Edward.'

'I should have stopped him playing with those gypsy boys,' Edward said and his face was grey with grief. 'He took the fever from them—they said that there was sickness in their camp. It was my fault. I should have stopped him talking to them.'

'Jack had been told a hundred times not to play with the children of wandering beggars and vagrants,' Sarah said. 'You were not to blame if he disobeyed.'

'He would have listened if I had told him,' Edward said. 'I could make him obey if I tried. It was my fault.'

'It was not your fault, Edward,' Anne Marie said. 'You always tried to protect him, but this time you couldn't—none of us could. We all feel our own blame, but we are not to blame, any of us. We must take comfort from the love we all felt for Jack, and give some of that love to each other.'

Edward stared at her for a moment, the tears rolling silently down his cheeks, then he turned and walked from the chamber.

'Let him go,' Sarah said, as Anne Marie would have followed him. 'He will come to terms with his grief in the end. He is very like Kit.'

'Yes, I have seen it more and more of late,' Anne Marie agreed. 'He is proud and he hath a fiery temper—but his heart is good.'

'I see that you begin to understand us,' Sarah said and smiled sadly. 'I must prepare my son for his last resting place, my dear. Forgive me, but I would be alone with him.'

'Yes, of course. I understand,' Anne Marie said. 'But you know that I am here when you need me.'

She walked from the chamber and went downstairs. There were others who needed help, and though her grief for Jack ran deep, there was work to do. After she had finished her task here, she would write to Kit and tell him of his brother's death.

It would be one of the hardest things she had ever

had to do, for it must hurt Kit terribly. And he was so angry with her. She was not sure that he would ever forgive her.

Anne Marie's letter was indeed difficult to write, for she did not believe that she should confess her own feelings for Kit at the same time as telling him of Jack's illness. She told him that they had all tried their best to save the young boy but that it had been a virulent fever and had defeated them. She also told him that she was reconciled with Lady Sarah, and asked him to forgive her for any harsh words she might have spoken when they last met. She hoped that he would return soon and that they might make up their quarrel.

In return she received a brief note from Kit's steward in London, telling her that he was returning both her and Lady Sarah's letters as Sir Christopher had not been to the house in many months.

'He told me that he was going to London,' Lady Sarah said looking bewildered. 'I had thought it was his intention to seek an audience with either Walsingham or the Queen. Where can he have gone?'

'Perhaps he has rejoined his ship?'

'Yes, perhaps decided that he should rejoin Drake's fleet at once,' Lady Sarah said and sighed. 'I shall send my letter on there and he may get it when he returns to port. It is a pity that we could not reach him, for I know he would have wanted to be present at the service for his brother. As it is we must do the best we can, my dear.' She reached out and took Anne Marie's hand as it was offered. 'I can only thank God that you are here, for I do not know how I should have borne this alone.'

'It is very hard to bear,' Anne Marie said, and wished with all her heart that Kit had returned to them in time for the service for his brother if not the burial, which had had to take place quickly because of the hot weather. 'We shall be a comfort to each other.'

Alone in her chamber later, she stared out at the brilliant sunshine. Where was Kit? She thought of him all the time, the tragedy of Jack's death making her fearful for her husband. If there should be an invasion it was possible that he too might die.

No, no, she could not bear it! There was already too much grief in the family to be borne and she could not contemplate a future that did not hold Kit in it. If she never saw him again…but she would not let herself think of such things.

There was much talk of invasion now. Huge piles of wood and brush had been built at strategic points throughout the land, ready to become beacons at the first sign of the enemy fleet.

Sir Nicholas had told them that a watch was being kept at all times, and that as soon as the Spanish fleet was sighted the beacons would be lit across the land, warning of attack. An army had been gathered and preparations were going on at all levels to defend England.

Sir Nicholas also brought the news Anne Marie had dreaded to hear. He broke it to her solemnly, and she knew that it had not been easy for him to be the bearer of such news.

'I am very sorry to tell you, Anne Marie,' he said gently. 'There was nothing anyone could have done after Lord Fraser was convicted of treason. He confessed his crime, and I believe because of that was spared any further examination. But his fate was sealed. Any plea for mercy would have been dismissed without a hearing—especially at this time when the threat of invasion looms so closely.'

'I know that you are right, and that it gives you no pleasure to bring me this news,' Anne Marie said, blinking her eyes to hold back the tears that threatened. 'It grieves me to know that my father died a traitor's death, but I have come to accept it. He plotted against the Queen and England, and he has been punished. God rest his soul.' She crossed herself and whispered a prayer for her foolish, unhappy father.

'Amen to that,' Sir Nicholas said. 'I know Sir Christopher wrote to Walsingham asking for clemency but I warned him it would be to no avail.'

'You have seen my husband—recently?'

'He came to see me before he rejoined his ship,' Sir Nicholas told her gently. 'He asked me to have a care for you and his family should he not return.'

Anne Marie gave a little gasp, her heart contracting with pain.

'I see. Thank you for telling me, sir. I was not sure…we had expected him to go to London first.'

'He decided against it and requested that I should forward his letter. To London.'

'There was nothing for me?'

'Nothing. I am sorry.'

'I understand.'

'I believe Kit was upset about something, but he did not choose to confide in me and I do not ask questions. I say only that he was concerned that both you and his family should be cared for in the event of his death.'

'We—we had quarrelled.'

Sir Nicholas nodded, his expression grave. 'It is not unusual for husband and wife to quarrel. Lady Catherine and I have done so often enough, but we have always found that things right themselves in time. Catherine is hopeful of seeing you soon, but Lisa was unwell for a time and she dare not leave her or she would have come before this.'

'It is as well she did not,' Anne Marie replied. 'The fever is waning in this house now, sir, but she was right to be careful. I would not have your family suffer as ours has.'

'I am more sorry for your loss than I can ever say,' Sir Nicholas replied. 'We know the grief of losing a child, though not to fever. I pray that you will be luckier with your own babe, Lady Hamilton, for it is in new life that healing begins.'

Anne Marie had thanked him for his good wishes, but her thoughts had been with Kit. After the news their kind neighbour had brought them she could no longer be in any doubt as to Kit's whereabouts. He was with his ship, and when the fighting began he would be in the thick of it!

Chapter Eleven

Kit woke with a thundering headache. The sunlight was streaming in through the small window that seemed to have no shutters, and he cursed as he opened his eyes. Where the hell was he, and what had he been drinking to make his head feel like this?

'My lord is awake?'

Kit turned his head at the sound of the woman's voice, his nostrils wrinkling in disgust as he caught the unclean smell of her body wafting up from beneath the bedcovers. Now he knew that he was caught in some dread nightmare. Never would he knowingly have taken a woman like that to bed!

'Who the hell are you?' he demanded and then threw back the stained coverlet. 'Where am I?'

'You are in the best bedchamber of the Cock and Feathers,' she said, scratching herself lazily. He saw that her arm was pitted with red sores and blotches, some of which were filled with a yellow pus. 'You bespoke it last even' when you brought me here.'

If this was the best he dared not think what the

other chambers were like! Kit felt his skin start to irritate. He had caught the whore's fleas. Pray God that she had given him nothing worse. He wished he could remember what had happened the previous night. Had he actually bedded that? He felt a surge of disgust as he got out of bed.

'What happened here last night?'

'What would my lord wish for?'

'I am not your lord,' he growled. 'Get out of that bed and tell me what happened, damn you!'

The woman crawled out reluctantly. She was wearing a stained shift, and an equally filthy gown lay on the floor beside the bed. She bent down to pick it up, eyeing him warily. He had a temper, and such men were in her experience unpredictable, especially if she told him the truth about the previous night.

'You have not paid me yet, sir.'

Kit felt inside his doublet and produced two silver coins, which he tossed to her contemptuously. 'Take this and be gone!' She caught the coins but scowled as she looked at them.

'You promised me a gold piece.'

''Tis all I have left. No doubt you or your friends have already robbed me. Get out of here before I have you arrested for theft.'

She gave a squeak of alarm and darted to the door, clutching her gown to her sagging breasts, then she turned to look back at him, a flash of spite in her thin face.

'You were too drunk to do anything,' she flung at him. 'Your sapling hath no juice, my lord.'

'Get out!' Kit flung one of the frowsy bolsters at

her but it hit the door as she slammed it behind her. He laughed as he felt the release of his tension. Her taunt had relieved him mightily. 'Thank God I was incapable.'

Yet it would have been no more than he deserved had he caught the pox from her. He was a damned fool and it was a wonder he had not come to a worse end. He had been drinking heavily night after night and was lucky not to have been robbed and murdered in a dark alley.

His rage when he left his home had been so great that he had not been able to clear his mind of the red mist that filled it. He hardly remembered what he had said to Sir Nicholas, and after leaving his house had ridden without ceasing until his horse was exhausted and then at last, forced to rest the animal, he had begun to drink.

Most of the possessions he carried on his person were gone, but there were still two gold pieces hidden in a secret slit within his doublet. Enough to get him to Plymouth and his ship in time to join Drake and prepare to meet the invading forces.

As for his wife…Kit blocked the memory of her coldness from his mind. He had been eager to see her again, and the letter from his steward awaiting him in port, which had told him that he had a son, had filled him with joy and hope as he rode home that day. His mother's greeting when he arrived had shocked him, wiping out the joy and anticipation of his homecoming, and he had simply lost his temper. That damnable temper of his! He believed he had learned to control it, but Anne Marie's coldness had ignited the torch and frustration had done the rest.

It was little wonder that Anne Marie could not love him, he reflected ruefully as he doused his head with cold water he had found in an earthenware pitcher. He had forced her to marry him, left her alone for months on end to bear her child alone, and then lost his temper with her the moment he got home.

He could not excuse his behaviour by telling himself that it was because his love for her had overwhelmed him. Nor that he had been driven to desperation by the months apart. Both these things were true, but they did not excuse him. Anne Marie must hate him for his treatment of her.

His marriage was a failure. He had had months at sea, time to reflect and realise that he had expected too much of her. Too much time, for he had begun to brood and discover that his old lust for adventure was waning. He knew that his love for Anne Marie was stronger than he had ever imagined, drawing him home despite his duty. He had gained his heart's desire when he married, but she had been given no choice and that was unfair. How could he expect her to love him, as he loved her?

He could not continue to demand her obedience to him. Since she was so very unhappy and felt herself betrayed by his family, he must find a way to set her free. Divorce was one device for ending a marriage that had failed, and there were those who would not hesitate to use it. After all, King Henry VIII had led by his example, and others had followed. Kit found the idea distasteful in the extreme. Besides, it would be unfair to Anne Marie, for as a woman she would naturally be the one to suffer most from the disgrace.

He did not wish for a divorce, yet they could not live happily together. There must be a third way. Many wives remained in the country while their husbands went to court. Kit had his heir. He could take a mistress if he chose. Anne Marie would probably be relieved that he no longer bothered her in that way.

He shut out the memories of the time they had spent in London before he left to join Sir Francis Drake in harrying the Spanish. They had had such a short time together, and the memory had warmed him, sustaining him through the months apart. Those months had seemed long and lonely to Kit and he had missed his lovely wife. Yet he knew that he could have done no other than answer the call of duty. Because of the efforts of the combined fleet, the Armada had been hampered and prevented from sailing the previous year, but Kit knew another great fleet had been amassed by the Spanish King and was probably already on its way.

Nothing would stop the invasion now, unless there was a sufficient force to meet it and drive it back before one foreign soldier could land on England's shores. And he had been wasting his time in drinking himself into a stupor!

Kit's face was grim as he went downstairs to summon the landlord and pay his bill. He must be on his way.

'Philip has sent the Duke of Medina Sidonia against us,' Sir Francis Drake told Kit, his eyes raking him as they shared a glass of wine in his cabin. 'You may know that Santa Cruz died in February?'

'I had heard and I think it a stroke of good fortune. Sidonia hath no stomach for the fight or he would not have delayed so long.'

The two men had not met in some months, having gone their separate ways after the attack on Cadiz. Both had been fortunate in capturing a rich prize. Drake had taken a rich Portuguese galleon loaded with a cargo from the East Indies that had brought him a small fortune. Kit had found a Spanish vessel limping home after a storm and had all but destroyed its rigging and relieved the captain of the silver in its holds. The crew had been released to one of the islands off the coast of Spain, the ship sent to a watery grave at the bottom of the ocean. One less ship to aid the invasion of England!

'I would have destroyed the Spanish fleet before it could leave the coast of Spain,' Drake went on, toying with the stem of his drinking glass. 'But the Queen's advisers spoke against it. An army has been raised and waits at Tilbury to protect London should the worst happen—but I believe England's safety depends on the fleet. Were Parma to land…'

He left his sentence unfinished but Kit nodded his understanding. On land the Spanish were formidable fighters and would probably outnumber and overwhelm the English forces.

'I believe you are right, sir. The Duke of Parma must never be allowed to set foot on English soil.'

'I am glad that you are with us, Sir Christopher. We need all our best captains if we are to beat the

Armada Spain sends against us. The fleet is divided this way…' He pointed to a chart set out on the table before him. 'Lord Thomas Seymour is watching the eastern end of the Channel and we are here at Plymouth. Hawkins, Frobisher and Lord Howard of Effingham are with us as well as many others. I have every confidence that we shall defeat the enemy.'

'Pray God that you are right, sir,' Kit said and lifted his glass to toast his companion. 'Now we must wait for the signal.'

It was on the 19th of July that the Armada was first sighted off the Lizard and the beacon lit in warning. The wind was against the English ships, holding them in the harbour, and they had to be towed out to clear water. Had Medina Sidonia launched his attack at Plymouth he might have caught the fleet before it could mobilise and landed a heavy blow. However, his orders were to sail up the Channel and he did not dare to disobey them.

Under cover of darkness the English ships crept up like thieves in the night behind the unwieldy Spanish galleons to attack them from the windward. The Armada was greater in size than the English fleet but the ships were top-heavy, rather like great ailing castles, and had been designed more to transport troops than as fighting machines. Had they been able to grapple the English ships they might still have had the advantage, but Drake and his captains had worked out a cunning strategy. Their vessels were faster and easier to manoeuvre and they carried guns that could engage from a greater distance. It meant that they could sail in, fire and then retreat before the Spanish could manoeuvre to retaliate.

The first skirmish was off the port of Plymouth. Standing on the deck of his ship, Kit directed his men and scored a direct hit on one of the ships that formed the vanguard of Medina Sidonia's squadron. He smiled as his men cheered their success when the main mast came tumbling, ensuring that at least one Spanish ship would fight no more that day.

Away in the distance he saw two Spanish ships collide, and another seemed to have been slightly damaged. The Armada was, however, only wounded and continued to sail up the Channel with the English attacking at every chance. There were battles off Portland and the Isle of Wight, but in neither case was there a decisive victor.

'It seems that we cannot stop them,' Kit remarked to his trusted lieutenant Tobias Frenshaw. 'Unless we do they will reach Calais and take Parma's men on board. If they land in England there will be a blood-bath.'

For a week the two sides had fought constantly but the Spanish had lost only two ships. It looked as if the advantage was with them, and that England stood in grave danger.

'What news?' Anne Marie asked anxiously of Sir Nicholas as he came into the parlour where they were sitting on the afternoon of the 27th of July. 'Have you heard aught of what is happening?'

Everyone knew that a running battle had been taking place for the past week, but no one knew who was winning it. All kinds of rumours were flying about and many expected the invasion at any moment. Up and down the country goodwives were frightening their children with tales of Spanish monsters who would eat them for their supper, and men sharpened their rusty swords and had kept them near by, determined to fight to their last breath.

'The Queen is at Tilbury,' Sir Nicholas replied. 'A friend of mine—Sir Oliver Woodville—was there with his son when she rode among the men and talked to them. Oliver is now the High Sheriff of Leicester and an important man, and his son has raised a small troop to fight at Tilbury. He thought it was a fine sight and has written to me something of what she said to the people.'

'Pray do tell us,' Lady Sarah said. 'I would hear Her Majesty's words if you can repeat them.'

'This is Oliver's letter,' Sir Nicholas said and took it from inside his doublet. 'I shall read you what he has written if I may?'

'I am sure we should love to hear it.' She looked at Anne Marie, who smiled and agreed.

'And then Her Majesty began to speak and a hush fell as everyone strained to listen,' Sir Nicholas paused. 'This is what she said: ''I have always so behaved myself that under God, I have placed my chiefest strength and Goodwill in the loyal hearts of my subjects...'''

Sir Nicholas paused once again and looked at them. 'Oliver goes on to say that some of her words were lost to him as the people cheered, but he heard this last part, and I quote: ''I know I am a woman; but I have the heart and stomach of a King and a King of England, too, and I think foul scorn that Parma or Spain or any Prince of Europe should dare to invade the borders of my realm."'

'How stirring it must have been to be there,' Lady Sarah cried as Sir Nicholas folded his letter. 'It is no wonder that the people adore her and call her their Gloriana. I wish that I might have heard her.'

'Indeed, we all feel as you do, ma'am,' Sir Nicholas agreed. 'Had I not been called upon to raise the local militia to guard against invasion here, I would have gone as Oliver and his son did to join the army at Tilbury. It is every man's duty to fight if need be.'

'I pray that it will not come to that,' Anne Marie said, feeling pity for all those that must die if war came to England. 'But what of the fleet? Does anyone know what is happening?'

'At the moment all is rumour and conjecture. Some say that the Spanish have reached Calais and Parma's forces will be upon us at any moment, others that half their ships are sunk. In truth no one knows for certain as yet.'

He would not tell her the terrible rumour that half the English fleet were damaged or sunk, but such rumours had been flying from mouth to mouth all week, so conflicting that no one could be sure of anything.

'I pray that Kit is safe,' Anne Marie said. She prayed every night that he would return to her and that she would have the chance to tell him how sorry she was for all their quarrels. 'You will tell us if you hear anything definite, sir?'

'I shall come at once myself,' he promised. 'And now I must go. Catherine has scarcely seen me for a week. But I knew you would be anxious for news and came at the first opportunity.'

The ladies smiled as he took his farewell, but looked anxiously at each other after he had gone.

'You must try not to worry too much,' Lady Sarah said. 'Kit has always returned safely before. We must simply wait and pray.'

'We can do nothing else,' Anne Marie said. The mood of the household had lightened a little since the heavy grief they had all felt for Jack, but sorrow still hung in the air. Yet death was such a constant thing in all their lives, the loss of a child something that most families had to bear, that they all knew they must begin to look toward the future. 'Now that the threat of fever is over, I must go and visit my son. He is weaned from his wetnurse at last and I believe he has a tooth. He was crying all last night with it and I have a salve that nurse may rub in to ease his pain.'

'Yes, you should go to him,' Lady Sarah agreed, and gave her daughter-in-law a sad smile. 'It soothes poor Christopher when you nurse him yourself.'

She watched as Anne Marie left the room. She was very young to be a widow and had known so little of the happiness of being a wife. If Kit survived the terrible battles he was encountering, he would hear from his mother. It was time that he came home and attended to his responsibilities! Perhaps then there would be laughter in the house again, and they were in sore need of it.

* * *

'Calais is too exposed for Medina Sidonia's ships,' Kit said to Tobias Frenshaw as he received the signal from Drake late that afternoon. 'We are going to attack him during the night.'

'As we did at Cadiz?'

'Yes.' Kit smiled wolfishly, his eyes gleaming with excitement. 'You would have thought the Spanish might have learned their lesson there, but fortunately for us it seems they are either too foolish or too arrogant.'

The fire-ships were old vessels and filled with pitch and tar. Volunteer crews towed them in as close to the Spaniards as they could and then cut them free to drift in among the galleons. The Spanish ought to have seen them coming and sent out their own volunteers to tow them out of harm's way, but for some reason they lost their heads. In a panic and fear of their lives, they cut the ropes that held their anchors and fled to the open sea.

It was of course what Drake had been hoping might happen, and the English ships immediately attacked. The Spanish commander and some of his ships fought bravely, but without their anchors most were driven by the wind towards dangerous sandbanks and were too busy trying to save their own skins to support him.

All was confusion and chaos. Medina's ships were badly damaged as the night wore on, but as daylight came the English were in little better case themselves, having used their supplies of shot and powder. They could not continue the attack, which might have finished their enemy. Besides, it looked as if many of the Spanish vessels were drifting to grief on the shoals off the Belgian coast. Had the wind not changed suddenly it would probably have been the end for most that very night.

The winds were ferocious, buffeting both fleets. Many of the Spanish ships were driven out into the North Sea. Kit and a few of the other English ships pursued them for some time, but two weeks after the Armada had been first sighted off the Lizard, Howard turned back and Kit turned with him. The Spanish ships were left to limp home as best they could, their ships carrying wounded, sick and disheartened men, their stores of food and water depleted or gone.

The gales off Ireland caught some, others foundered on the rocks off the west coast of Scotland. Some of the ships that had not panicked but fought to the last with Medina Sidonia were luckier and survived to gradually make their way home.

'We've won,' Tobias Frenshaw said triumphantly to Kit as they headed for port. 'By God, we beat them!'

'I believe it was a combination of luck and the foul weather that did most damage,' Kit replied with a grin. 'But had Santa Cruz not died at such a crucial moment, it might have been otherwise. Medina Sidonia made too many mistakes. In the end he proved a brave man but he did not understand how to fight us.'

'It matters only that England is safe,' Tobias replied and laughed. 'England is saved and there will be celebrations aplenty. I'm bound for London and the court—what of you, Kit?'

Kit was silent for a moment. A part of him wanted to return to his home to claim Anne Marie as his own, but his pride gave him pause. What use to return to a wife who did not love him?

'I shall come with you,' he said at last, almost reluctantly. 'This seems a great victory indeed, but I am not certain that we are free of the threat of invasion just yet. I would speak with Sir Francis and hear what he has to say on this matter.'

'They say that London has gone wild with delight now that it is believed the Spanish are defeated,' Lady Sarah said to her daughter-in-law, as she laid aside her letter and picked up her needlework. 'At first no one seemed quite sure if the Armada had truly been destroyed, but now Her Majesty has returned to London and everyone is celebrating.'

'Yes, I know. I have had a letter from Lady Grantly,' Anne Marie replied and smothered a sigh. 'Sir Nicholas took her to London, and—and she writes that she saw Kit at court.'

Sarah's gaze narrowed as she looked at Anne Marie and saw the unhappiness she was trying to hide. Ten days had passed since news came of the victory and there had been no word from Kit, apart from a brief note to his mother to tell them he was safe in London. Lady Sarah had written to him once again of his brother's death, but he had made no mention of Jack and she thought that his message might have been sent before he received hers. She had thought the news might bring him home, but as the days passed it seemed he would not come.

'You should write to him and ask him to come home,' she said to Anne Marie. 'I do not understand what keeps him.'

'I dare say he has business of his own.'

Anne Marie changed the subject, which was too painful to discuss, returning to the celebrations, which were taking place all over the country as well as in London. There were feasts and fêtes as the common folk danced round the maypoles and life became less anxious in villages and towns. The threat of invasion was over for the moment and England was safe.

Lady Sarah was angry that amid all the joy and celebration Anne Marie was forced to continue her lonely life, caring for her child and taking part in the everyday affairs of the manor without complaint. It was unfair. She was lovely and good, and she deserved better than this. Kit should think shame to treat her so!

Sarah had put off writing her letter, but she would certainly do so that very day. Kit must be brought to his senses and she would tell him what she thought of his behaviour. But she would say nothing to Anne Marie, for she did not want to arouse hopes that might be dashed if Kit ignored her letter.

'I think we should soon begin to make the puddings for Christmas,' she said. 'Or at least to make provision. I shall send to London for supplies of dried fruit and almonds. If you will excuse me, my dear, I shall make out my list now while it is in my mind.'

Anne Marie smiled and set another stitch in the tapestry she was making. It seemed early to think about such things, for it was only August, but if it

pleased Sarah it was not for her to question. She had
begun to make new covers for the cushions in the
parlour and her theme was the defeat of the Spanish
Armada. This one depicted Kit's ship in battle and
had been meant as a special gift for him.

But it seemed that he did not intend to return home
for a while. Lady Grantly's letter had said that he was
much in favour with Her Majesty, who had fêted all
her captains at court. Kit was apparently very popular
with everyone and appeared to be enjoying himself a
great deal, according to Catherine Grantly.

Why should he come home to a wife who had
treated him so coldly on his last visit? Anne Marie
could not find it in her heart to blame him.

Perhaps if she wrote and asked him to come, if she
told him that she loved and missed him he might return? But if it were only for a brief visit that would
make her loneliness even harder to bear after he left
her.

She decided that she would not write. He did not
love her and Lady Sarah was mistaken if she thought
otherwise.

Kit read his mother's letter as he was dressing for
a masque at court. He frowned over it, annoyed to be
told that he was neglecting both his wife and the estate.

He had grieved when he heard of the death of his
brother, for Jack had always been a favourite with
him, but he had hardened his heart, shutting out his
grief. To let any emotion in would destroy him. Only

by shutting out all feeling and love could he survive the pain.

But he would not be told where his duty lay, nor be tied to any woman's apron strings! His wife and mother were comfortable enough and he preferred not to think of them or his home.

He had placed money at the disposal of his family, and Sir Nicholas had told him that all was well with the estate—what more did his mother expect of him? Anne Marie had not written. It was clear that she was content with the situation. She was probably glad that he had chosen not to return too soon.

Kit was finding life at court amusing. His success during the recent fighting was known and admired, and he discovered that his company was sought eagerly by men and women alike. It seemed that everyone wanted to hear about his part in the defeat of the Spanish fleet, and his words were hung on as if they were precious pearls of wisdom.

He was not a particularly vain man, nor had he been in the habit of sleeping with every pretty woman who came his way, but there was no doubt that so many offers were tempting. He could if he chose take his pick from several beautiful ladies of the court, and the fact that he had not done so thus far was due to his feeling for his wife.

He still cared for Anne Marie. She had wounded his pride and he would not beg for her favours. Nor did he wish to impose himself on her in their marriage bed. She had made it clear that she preferred to live alone, and he knew that if he were to see her he would lose his temper. If driven too far he might even force her to accept him as her husband again, and that would be unfair to both of them.

Better to remain at court and take a mistress. Lady Carmichael had made it very plain that she would welcome him to her bed, and there was Jane Frenshaw. She was married to a cousin of Toby's who was many years her senior, and her smiles were enticing.

If only he could forget that shy, sweet, uncertain smile that had first captured his heart at Drodney. Anne Marie had seemed so gentle and vulnerable then, and he had longed to protect her, to take care of her and make her happy. But it seemed that all he had done was bring her grief.

Damn her! She had bewitched him. He was in thrall to her while she cared not a jot for him. He would take Jane Frenshaw to bed that night and forget the cold-hearted woman he had married!

But first he would reply to his mother's letter. It was time she learned that Kit was his own master.

Lady Sarah frowned over her son's letter. It was clear that she had pricked his conscience with her own, though he was stubbornly refusing to do as she had asked and come home.

What a stubborn fool he was! She was certain that it was his pride that was keeping him from his wife. He was in love with Anne Marie, but a series of quarrels and misunderstandings had driven them apart, and they were both either too foolish or too proud to take the first step towards reconciliation.

The situation could not be allowed to continue as it was—but what could she do about it?

If Kit would not come home, why should Anne Marie not go to London? She was even lovelier than when Kit had first married her. Dressed in the right clothes, she would rival any of the ladies at court. And Lady Grantly had also written to Kit's mother, her letter leaving no doubt in Sarah's mind that her son was in danger of falling into bad ways. It was clearly her duty to save him from himself.

She would not write and tell Kit they were coming, for she needed no permission to go to court. Indeed, she had the perfect excuse—that of needing a husband. Her period of mourning was at an end, and though she had no intention of ever marrying again, it would serve her purpose.

The more she thought about it, the more Sarah saw that it might serve in two ways. Kit would not like to think of another man in his father's place, especially if she suggested that her new husband could help to run the estate, and it might make him consider that perhaps his time would be better served at home.

She was smiling as she went in search of Anne Marie. It was an excellent idea; the only difficulty would be in persuading her daughter-in-law that she should accompany her to London.

'Go to London with you?' Anne Marie had been nursing her son when Lady Sarah found her. 'No, I do not think so. It would be too much trouble, for I could not leave Christopher behind.'

'We shall take several of the servants with us. Nurse Mary will take care of Christopher.'

'But what of Edward? He would be so lonely left here with his tutor.'

'There is no reason why Edward and his tutor should not accompany us. I dare say they would enjoy it. We can ask Edward. Besides, I have made up my mind to go, and you will surely not refuse me your company?'

Anne Marie stared at her in silence. She was torn between a desire to see Kit and the fear that he would be angry with them.

'But where shall we stay?'

'Kit's house is large enough for us all.'

'Has he invited us?' She knew a moment's hope but it was soon dashed.'

'I do not need my son's permission to visit the house in London.'

'No, no, I do not think we ought to go,' Anne Marie said decisively. 'He might not wish us to intrude on his life there.'

'I have been thinking of marrying again,' Lady Sarah lied. 'You would surely not deny me the chance of finding a husband with whom I could share my declining years?'

'Marry again?' Anne Marie was shocked, as well she might be, for Sarah had never mentioned such a thing before. 'No, of course I would not deny you that chance—but you could go alone.'

'I could—but I would prefer it if you came with me to lend me courage, Anne Marie. It is many years since I have been to court, and I should feel too awkward alone. Please, my dear, grant me this one small favour.'

'We must ask Edward how he feels.'

How could she deny such a request? Anne Marie was beginning to weaken, and hoped that Edward would refuse.

However, when he was asked, Edward was excited at the prospect of going to London. He had missed his brother Jack more than he would ever say and felt in need of company. It was in his mind to ask Kit if he could go to college to study, for as good as Master Harris was to him he felt the need for advanced tuition.

When Anne Marie learned something of his thoughts, she realised that it would be selfish of her to hold out. They had all missed Jack terribly, of course, and the house often seemed empty without the sound of his voice calling out to his brother, but Edward had missed him most of all. It had changed him. He was growing up into a serious, thoughtful youth and it was right that something should be done about his future.

It must of course be for Kit to decide that, and if he would not come to them they must all go to him.

Anne Marie's feelings were mixed, for although she longed to see her husband she thought that he would be almost a stranger to her. They had had such a short time together before he left to join Drake and the others, and she was not sure how she would react when she saw him.

The packing had seemed endless, for Lady Sarah would not leave without taking all her favourite possessions with her.

'We must take our own bedlinen,' she told Anne
Marie. 'And a feather mattress. The bedclothes may
be damp and the beds crawl with vermin at these
inns.'

Anne Marie remembered her first journey to
London and could not help agreeing with her. Kit had
travelled with as few possessions as possible, but she
thought it would be far more comfortable to travel as
Lady Sarah intended.

Sir Nicholas returned from London a day or so before they were due to leave. He came to visit and
promised he would keep an eye on the estate while
they were gone.

'It will do you both good to have a change,' he
said approvingly. 'Catherine had not been to court for
years and she would not go until she had a whole
wardrobe of new gowns. I am sure she would be delighted to give you the name of the seamstress she
used in London, for the woman was most excellent
in her work.'

'That is exactly what we wish for,' Lady Sarah
exclaimed. 'Please ask one of your grooms to ride
over with it, for both Anne Marie and I must have
new gowns.'

'It will be my pleasure to come myself,' he assured
them. 'Then you may give me any last-minute instructions before you leave. And I shall furnish you
with the names of the best inns on the road. Indeed,
I shall send my best groom to accompany you and
show your own men how to go on.'

'You are so good to us,' Anne Marie said. 'We are
fortunate to have your friendship, sir.'

'I dare say you would do as much for us if it were in your power.'

'One would almost think Sir Nicholas was encouraging us to go,' Lady Sarah remarked thoughtfully after he had gone.

Anne Marie did not seem to notice her remark, for she made no reply, but that was perhaps because she was thoughtful herself. Lady Grantly's letter had been vague when mention was made of Kit, but Anne Marie had wondered if she were gently hinting that he was taking too much of an interest in the ladies of the court.

What could Anne Marie do about it if he had a mistress? The thought had nagged at her over the months they had spent apart, but she had tried to dismiss it as unworthy. It was wrong of her to suspect her husband of such a thing!

Yet what should keep him at court? He had seen his son only for a few minutes in Nurse Mary's arms before coming to her on the day of their last quarrel, and he had not slept in Anne Marie's bed for more than eighteen months. She could not believe that the man she had married, who was a powerful, sensuous lover, could remain celibate for all that time.

The pain of his betrayal flooded through her. How could he do that to her? Yet almost at once she knew that she was to blame for Kit's desertion. Her coldness had driven him away, and it was inevitable that he would turn to a woman who welcomed him more warmly than his scold of a wife.

What was she to do? Anne Marie looked into her heart. How would she feel if she arrived in London to discover that he had taken a beautiful mistress?

Would she want him back even though he had betrayed her?

Yes, oh, yes, her heart, mind and body answered as one. She missed him so terribly, loved him so very much.

But what could she do if he no longer loved her?

He had wanted her once. She could never forget the sweetness and tenderness of his loving, the way he had brought her body tremblingly alive and taught her the meaning of being a woman. There must be a way to bring him back to her.

Pray God there was, for if she had lost him entirely it would break her heart.

Chapter Twelve

The journey in Lady Sarah's cumbersome coach was long and tedious, but the roads were much better than in winter. The two ladies were bumped and shaken, but there were no mishaps and they had an uneventful journey.

'We must thank Sir Nicholas for his excellent advice, which has been of such advantage to us,' Lady Sarah said. 'All the inns he recommended have been clean and decent and we did not suffer a damp mattress once.'

Anne Marie forbore to remind her that their servants had changed the bed at every stop according to her instructions. She knew that Lady Sarah meant well, and she was relying on her to support her when they reached London, for she was not certain of their reception once they arrived.

She had grown more nervous with every league they travelled, but her resolve had hardened. She was Kit's wife and she had made up her mind that she would fight for him if need be. Even if as she suspected he had taken a mistress, she was determined to win him back somehow.

It was not until they approached the outskirts of the city that she confessed what was in her mind to her companion. Lady Sarah was silent for a moment, and then she nodded her approval.

'I must tell you that I have wondered if it is a woman that keeps him away from home,' she said. 'I would not have said as much, for I did not wish to hurt you, but I am glad that you have the will to fight for your husband, Anne Marie.'

'I want him to come home,' Anne Marie said. 'And I am prepared to do whatever I must to win him back—but I am not sure how that may be achieved. If he loves someone else it may be too late.'

'I do not think it a case of love, but Kit is both proud and stubborn. His father was the same. If he has taken a mistress it is because he feels that you have rejected him, not because he loves her.'

Anne Marie's cheeks were bright pink. 'What can I do to make him see that I would welcome him to my bed?'

'I do not think you should beg,' Lady Sarah replied after a moment of thought. 'Kit must be the hunter not the hunted. I think it better if he is made aware of his own feelings for you.'

'But how shall I do that?'

'Oh, my dear,' Lady Sarah laughed. 'You cannot be so innocent. Make Kit jealous. You are a beautiful, desirable woman and other men will admire you. I think my son will very soon respond to a little competition.'

Anne Marie was thoughtful, then: 'Kit was very protective when he took me to court the first time. He said that I must dance only with gentlemen he approved, and indeed I met very few other than his own friends.'

'Then there is your answer. Place your trust in me, Anne Marie. I shall tell you who you may safely flirt with and who must be kept at bay.'

'Do you really think that I should try to arouse Kit's jealousy?'

'I am convinced of it,' Lady Sarah said firmly. 'We shall commission some new gowns for you—and not the modest style you are accustomed to wearing at home. You must be dressed as befits a young woman of your station, but in a way that subtly reveals your charms. If other men find you irresistible, then Kit must surely do the same?'

'Kit would be furious.'

'Is that not what we intend? My son has always had too much of his own way, Anne Marie. I think that he should learn to consider his wife more and to appreciate his home.'

Anne Marie was a little doubtful, yet her mother-in-law's ideas seemed sound. If she could arouse Kit's interest by whatever means were open to her, she would not lightly let it slip away again.

The months of loneliness had taught her how empty her life must be without Kit. She had her son and Kit's family to sustain her, but without his love she had nothing. Her refusal to confess her love in the early days of their marriage seemed a distant memory, and how bitterly she regretted their last quarrel. For the sake of a man who had never cared for her as a father should, she had lost the love of the man she adored. She would give anything if she could but turn back the hours and have him come to her again in love.

Lady Sarah's plan had shocked her by its boldness, yet she knew that she must find the courage to carry it through if she was ever to be happy again.

'I believe that Spain will think twice before trying to invade us again,' Walsingham said to Kit when they met that day in secret. 'And for the moment England and England's Queen are safe.' His eyes were dark, almost unfathomable, as he seemed to stare into the distance, as though he was seeing another time and place. 'I believe that when the next trial comes I shall not be here to see it. I can only pray that another will stay the hand of darkness from this land in my place.'

Kit felt coldness at the base of his spine. There was something strange about Walsingham at that moment, as if he looked into the future and foretold his own death.

'Pray do not speak so, sir. You have been Her Majesty's staunchest friend and counsellor these many years. She needs you still, and you will support her to the end.'

'To the end of my life,' Walsingham said and his

gaze shortened, his thoughts recalled to the present as his eyes centred on Kit. 'Forgive me if I wandered. These days I have moments when I despair. I have waged a long battle against...' A wry smile touched his lips. 'He haunts me, that man of darkness, that tool of Satan...yet I know him not. Mayhap he goes by the name of Frampton, mayhap another. We have fought our battles these many years, and I believe for the moment he is vanquished and the might of Spain with him.'

'I know little if anything of your man of darkness,' Kit said, 'though I believe he may have had a hand in spiriting my wife from the castle at Drodney, but I do know that we have hurt Spain. Every day reports of more damaged Spanish ships reach us, and those that do manage to limp home will be many months in harbour before they dare venture out again.'

'And when they do?' Walsingham's eyes narrowed as he looked at him. 'Shall you be there to harry them as before, sir?'

'I have not yet decided where my future lies.'

'You have given much in England's cause,' Walsingham said, and his voice was heavy with thought and perhaps doubt. 'My advice would be to think carefully, sir. You are young and should look to your own happiness and prosperity.'

Kit was thoughtful as he walked home after that interview. He had spent much of his time of late talking to men of influence at the court, and had discovered that he did not particularly care for the scheming and back-biting that went on apace.

He was fast discovering that life at court was not to his taste. The Earl of Leicester had been a great influence for many years, but his health was failing and he had left London a few days earlier. Kit wondered if Walsingham was feeling ill. There must surely be some reason to account for the strange mood that was upon him. He had always been a man of strong convictions, a powerful force that stood behind the Queen and guarded her from all the evils that had been directed at her over the years. Had it not been for his stout support, one of the many plots to depose her and place another in her stead might have succeeded.

Perhaps Walsingham also felt the wind of change at court? There were new favourites to take the place of the old, and the undercurrent of jealousy and spite ran deep. Kit was not sure that he trusted Robert, Earl of Essex, who seemed a vain young man, more interested in his own glory than any good he might do for others.

He had also met and liked Sir Walter Raleigh, who was a man more after his own heart. They had spent some hours discussing Sir Walter's interest in the New World and the settlers who were trying to carve a living from the wilderness there.

Perhaps it was time to consider a new venture? It was an age when men were pushing out the boundaries of the Old World and seeking new horizons, new markets and new trading partners. Elizabeth's reign had been a golden age for its people; peace and prosperity bringing new opportunities for men with the courage to take advantage. Kit could continue as a privateer—or strike out as a merchant adventurer and trade with the West Indies or the lands to the east. If a western route to Asia could be found, ah then, what fortunes a man might make in trade; but though men of learning like John Dee had once believed it possible, most had now given up and looked to the east once more. Somehow a trading route to the riches of the Spice Islands, and to China, which was not jealously guarded by the Portuguese, must be found.

Kit knew that he would not be the one to find the route that so many sought, though as yet in vain, for his days of adventure on the high seas were numbered. However, he might invest with other men of like minds in a venture to find the shorter route to China and the treasures of the Orient.

As he strode into his house he noticed an unusual bustle, and seeing that his steward was too busy or distracted to note his master's arrival, hurrying on his way without a glance in Kit's direction, he asked a serving wench what was going on.

She bobbed a nervous curtsey, never having been addressed by her master before. 'Why, sir, 'tis Lady Sarah and Lady Hamilton. They have but this minute arrived and nothing ready for them!'

'My wife and mother here?' Kit was startled into an oath, which made the wench stare. 'Why was I not told they were expected?'

'Master Hendry swears he had not Lady Sarah's instructions—but here he is, sir.' She made a hasty retreat as the steward waved her imperiously away.

'I beg your pardon, Sir Christopher. The wench shall be punished for bothering you.'

'Nay, for I asked her what was going on. I understand my wife and mother have arrived—is that so?'

'Yes, sir. Lady Sarah says she sent word some days ago but I have had no communication from her.'

'Have you not?' Kit's eyebrows rose. His mind worked quickly as he sought a reason for this unexpected visit. 'I believe Lady Sarah may have written to me but it must have slipped my mind. Please do what you can to make them comfortable.'

Kit lied easily as he nodded to his servant and proceeded leisurely up the stairs. Underneath he was seething with impatience and a burgeoning anger with his mother for arriving without notice, but it would not do for the household to be aware that this was as much a shock to him as it was for them.

Why had his mother not written of her intention? It was very odd, but perhaps her letter had gone astray. Yet she would surely have sent it with someone she trusted, and Sir Nicholas had been at court until recently with his wife.

Had Anne Marie and Kit's mother come to see something of the celebrations? They had missed the grand review, which the Queen had commanded take place in the tiltyard at Whitehall, and which she had watched with Leicester at her side. However, there were still masques and feasts taking place most evenings at court.

He paused on the landing, wondering whether to see his mother or Anne Marie first, and then decided that he would speak to his wife. Since this meeting was of her own making, she would scarcely accuse him of forcing his company upon her.

The chamber was full of servants when he entered. Anne Marie was directing the stowing of various items and he watched her for a moment, her back towards him.

'Yes, that is right, Mary. Take all Christopher's things with you to the nursery.'

For a moment he thought that she meant that *his* things were to be moved, and then he recalled that he had a son named after him. He had deliberately blocked that thought from his mind until now, because it would have been too powerful a draw and might have caused him to regret his decision not to go home. Now he knew an urgent longing to see the boy and spoke without forethought.

'May I be allowed to see Christopher?'

Anne Marie seemed to start at the sound of his voice. For a moment she remained with her back towards him, and then turned slowly to face him. Kit was struck anew by her beauty. His mind carried an image of her as a young girl but she was no longer a girl. In the months they had spent apart she had become a woman and a very sensual, desirable woman.

'Kit…' She seemed hesitant, almost nervous, and then she smiled in welcome. His heart caught and it took all his strength not to go to her. God, how he wanted her! He felt the urgent need burning deep in his loins and knew that he must be careful. If he let down his guard he would take her in his arms and carry her to the bed, and then he would be lost, for he could not have controlled his need for her. 'Did you ask to see Christopher?'

'Yes, if I may?' His tone was carefully controlled, polite but toneless.

'Of course. He is your son. You were free to see him at any time you pleased.'

She spoke without malice and yet her words cut him to the quick. Did it mean so little to her that he had been away, his life at risk, that he had stayed away for her sake? He felt his temper surge and yet knew he must control it. To quarrel with her would only bring him more pain.

'Business hath kept me at court,' he said coldly, though he knew it to be a lame excuse. 'You are well, I trust? And my mother? There is no urgent reason for your journey?'

'We are all well. I believe Edward has a request to make of you, which I hope you will see fit to grant. And Lady Sarah hath business of her own, I believe.' Her eyes darkened with emotion. 'Your mother and I both wrote to you after Jack died of the fever, but our letters were returned. Sarah wrote again after we had the news of the victory over the Armada. I trust you received her letter?'

Kit's eyes were intent on her face. 'I received that letter and another from my mother—but none from you.'

'I thought what I had to say would be better said

face to face. I destroyed the first, for it seemed that you had not cared to receive it.'

'I did not know it had been sent. Of course I would have read it.'

'It does not matter. What I have to say may be said to your face.'

'And what have you to say?'

The servants had melted away, as if sensing the friction between them, and they were alone. The atmosphere was tense, and for a moment Anne Marie was tempted to tell him of her loneliness and need of him, but she remembered Lady Sarah's warning. If he had taken a mistress she must win him back by arousing his interest. To declare her love too soon might seem false.

'There is plenty of time,' she said. 'Would you like to meet your son, Kit?'

Kit would have liked to settle this now, but he was not certain he could control his emotions. Better to wait a day or so and discover her reason for coming to London.

'Yes, that is my chief concern,' he said sounding harsher than he knew. 'Do not trouble yourself to come with me. I know how to find my way to the nursery, madam.'

With that, he turned and walked from the room, leaving Anne Marie to stare after him in dismay. Her eyes pricked with the tears she refused to let fall. She ought not to have come. He was still angry with her.

'Nonsense!' Lady Sarah told her later when they were alone. 'Of course you should have come. If Kit was unpleasant to you he shall hear what I think of his manners soon enough!'

'No, please do not say anything,' Anne Marie begged. 'He was not unpleasant. I think he was annoyed because I had come without his permission.'

'You came to support me in my search for a husband, and so I shall tell him,' Lady Sarah said. 'Now I intend that we shall go to court tomorrow—so let us see what we can find in your closet that may do until we can buy new clothes.'

'I have several gowns that Kit bought me when we were here last year that I have scarcely worn.'

Lady Sarah was looking at the shelves where the court gowns had been stored with lavender and sweet herbs to keep away the moths. She took one down and shook out the folds of white silk embroidered with gold thread and pearls, and then nodded her head as if pleased.

'I think this will do. It needs a small alteration, but I shall get my sewing woman to do that and it will be ready for you to wear by tomorrow evening.'

'I never did wear that one,' Anne Marie said, glancing at it without real interest. Her plan to arouse Kit's interest seemed empty and foolish after his coldness towards her earlier. 'It arrived the day before we were due to come home, and I left it here because I thought it would be too extravagant for country wear.'

'Then that is all the better,' Sarah replied with a naughty smile. 'Tomorrow morning we shall visit Lady Grantly's dressmaker and see what we can arrange, but I think this will do very well for your first visit to court under my care, Anne Marie.'

Anne Marie smiled, but made no argument as she took the gown away with her. Her courage had revived in Sarah's company, and she was as eager as her mother-in-law to go to court and see what was going on. She wanted to discover what kind of a woman had stolen Kit's love from her, for she was more than ever sure that someone had.

Why else had he been so cold to her?

Kit tossed restlessly in his bed that night and thought of his wife in the bedchamber next door. Why should he not go to her? Why not tell her that he expected her to show duty to her husband, and make her his own once more?

He had the right, and his need was great—and yet something held him back. She was beautiful, but she was not the girl he had rescued from the ship taking her to France. She had changed, grown up, become almost a stranger to him, and he realised that he must seem the same to her. To force her to submit to him so abruptly might cause a rift that could never be breached.

He had tried to put her from his mind, to forget her and think of another woman's charms, but it had all come to nothing when he saw her again, and he knew it was Anne Marie he wanted. Yet he must not make the same mistake again.

He must be patient. He must woo her, coax her into giving herself to him. She had borne him a son, for whom he did not doubt she had great love. Was it too much to hope that she might come to love him as she did the child?

Perhaps if he were patient she might turn to him with affection if not with love.

He had almost made up his mind to return home, but he could not deny Anne Marie the chance to enjoy herself a little. Their visit to London had been cut short the last time, and he must not demand that she return at once when she had but this moment arrived.

He must be patient, considerate and gentlemanly, and then at last she might be truly his.

How dare she come to court wearing that? Kit felt the rage begin to build inside him as he saw what Anne Marie was wearing. It was shameless, immodest—indecent! The neckline was cut so low that it was almost possible to catch a glimpse of her nipples when she laughed. And she was laughing a great deal.

He scowled as he saw that she was dancing with Sir Robert Herriot. He had not forgotten that gentleman, nor that it was *his* chance remark that had caused the quarrel with Anne Marie before their wedding. He had never liked the man, and he certainly did not care for the way he was looking at her now! The fellow was clearly a scoundrel and a rogue, and she ought to know better than to dance with him for a second time.

'Why do you scowl so?' Kit turned as he felt the touch of a soft hand on his arm and found himself looking into the smiling face of Jane Frenshaw. 'Are you angry because Lady Hamilton is so much admired? She is very beautiful, and everyone is talking about her, wondering why you have hidden her away all this time.'

Kit swallowed hard before making his answer. To show his anger too openly at court would provoke laughter behind his back, for he would be thought a jealous husband who feared to be cuckolded by his beautiful young wife.

'No, my lady,' he said and forced a smile. 'My thoughts were elsewhere. I had not seen you and believed you were not at court this evening, but now I see you I shall smile.'

Jane looked at him for a moment. She was not certain whether to believe him, for she had given him every encouragement. And though she had thought one evening that he might be about to ask her to become his mistress, the moment had passed. They had had an intimate encounter in the gardens, when his kisses had thrilled her and she had been ready to surrender to his passion. Unfortunately they had been interrupted, and he had apologised for his impetuous behaviour. After that he had seemed to cool towards her, and she had wondered if he had sent for his wife to come to Court.

'Then you shall dance with me, sir,' she said and smiled flirtatiously at him. 'I shall see if I cannot bring laughter to your eyes, for they have seemed bleak this evening.'

'I should like that more than anything,' Kit said

and bowed over her hand. 'You do me great honour, my lady.'

The dance about to begin was a galliard, and he threw himself into the performance with spirit, appearing to take much pleasure from dancing it with the lovely lady he had chosen as his partner.

Watching Kit as her own partner left her at the end of the dance they had shared, Anne Marie felt a pang of jealousy. Within a few minutes of her arrival at court someone had hinted to her that Lady Jane Frenshaw was Kit's mistress. That Lady Carmichael's remark had been intended to distress her, Anne Marie had no doubt. She was also sure that the lady had an interest in Kit herself, but that did not stop the remark hurting her—and that hurt intensified as she saw how Jane Frenshaw looked at him so intimately.

'You look beautiful this evening, Lady Hamilton,' a voice murmured at her ear and she turned to see Tobias Frenshaw standing there. 'If you have no partner for the moment, will you give me the honour of this dance?'

'Why yes, thank you,' Anne Marie said gratefully. She would rather take part than watch her husband dance with another woman. 'I am pleased to see you again, sir.'

'I am delighted to see you,' he replied, giving her a hot glance, his eyes seeming to dwell for a moment on the lovely swell of her breasts where the revealing gown fell away so dramatically. 'You have grown more beautiful than ever, Anne Marie. I hardly knew you.'

That was not surprising, for at her last visit she had been a shy, insecure young woman who had scarcely left her husband's side, whereas this evening she glowed with incandescent beauty.

She felt the heat of his touch through her gown and shivered as she saw the predatory expression in his eyes. At their first meeting he had been all that was respectful and gentlemanly, but his manner towards her was very different this evening.

It was the gown, of course. She had been shocked when Lady Sarah's maid brought it for her to wear, and had almost chosen another in its place. However, her courage had returned and she had been pleased with herself when she saw how well it became her.

'You look what you are,' Lady Sarah had told her when she was asked if she did not think it a little too daring. 'You are a lovely, shapely woman and your charms deserve to be seen. Do not imagine you will be the only woman at court to wear such a gown, my dear. I assure you that others will be just as daring.'

It was true that other women were dressed as daringly as she, and that their behaviour was often enticing and even a little lewd in Anne Marie's opinion. She found the stares directed at her by men she did not even know embarrassing, and had made up her mind that her new gowns would not be quite as daring as this one.

But when she saw Kit kiss Jane Frenshaw at the end of the dance, her mood suddenly became reckless and she laughed wickedly at Tobias Frenshaw when he whispered something naughty in her ear.

'You should be ashamed of yourself, sir,' she said and tapped him on the arm with her fan. 'Do you forget that I am Kit's wife?'

'How could I forget it?' Tobias asked, pulling a wry face. 'It was unfair of him to marry you before he brought you to court, for none of us had a chance to win you—but see how he amuses himself with my cousin's wife. Why should we not enjoy ourselves a little?' He ran his fingers down her cheek, giving her a look she could not mistake. 'If you would meet me in the courtyard I dare swear we might find some pleasure to amuse us.'

'You are a wicked flirt, sir,' Anne Marie said and shook her head at him. 'I am not so easily to be won, for which you may be thankful. Sir Christopher might not take kindly to being cuckolded by you.'

'He does as much for my cousin,' Tobias replied. 'But I shall not press you—though should you find yourself in the courtyard beyond the fountain in about half an hour I should be happy to risk your husband's temper. I think the prize would be well worth a little trouble, my lady.'

She smiled and turned away, intending to find Kit and ask him if he would dance with her, but before she could do so another gentleman met her, grabbed her hand and hurried her into the dance, which was a carefree country affair, without so much as a by your leave.

Anne Marie would have refused him if he had asked, for she had noticed the lustful glances he had sent her way earlier that evening and had felt that he was definitely one of the gentlemen Lady Sarah had warned her to avoid at all costs. However, to have pulled away would have caused a fuss and she did not care to make a show of herself. It was unfortunate that the dance called for the gentleman to catch the lady about the waist and whirl her about the floor for several turns.

'You are a tempting wench,' the man whispered in her ear lustfully. 'And I would give a ruby ring to bed you this night. Let me take you to the gardens, my sweet lady, and it shall be yours.'

Anne Marie broke away from him, her cheeks hot. 'Forgive me, sir. I think you forget yourself. I am not to be bought by you or any man.'

She walked away from him, feeling angry and dismayed. She needed to be alone with her thoughts, for the evening was not turning out at all as she had hoped. Kit met her as she would have left the chamber in search of some air.

'And where do you imagine you are going, madam?'

'I am over-warm, sir,' she replied, flushing as she looked into his eyes and saw both anger and scorn reflected there. 'I was about to seek some air.'

'And to meet that swine who just molested you, I dare say?'

'Do not be ridiculous,' Anne Marie snapped. 'I was compelled to dance with him and broke away as soon as I could. Believe me, I am not such a fool as to agree to meet a man like that anywhere.'

'Then he did ask you?' Kit's eyes glowed like hot

coals. 'I suppose you prefer to meet Herriot—or Toby?'

'I prefer to meet no one,' Anne Marie said and sighed. This was not at all what she had planned. Kit was angry but that would not make him love her. He was fascinated by Jane Frenshaw and merely annoyed that his wife was receiving some attention from other men. 'You are like a dog with a bone, sir. You do not want me for yourself, but you do not wish others to play with your possessions.'

'A dog with a bone, am I?' Kit stared at her, torn between his desire to beat her and another, even stronger, to make love to her. For a moment he felt his temper threaten to spill over, and then the amusing side of the encounter struck him and he began to laugh. 'Yes, by God, you are right! Your description is very apt, madam.'

Anne Marie stared at him uncertainly. Why was he laughing at her? It was clear that she meant nothing to him. He had been angry for a moment, but now he clearly thought her attempt to arouse his jealousy a joke.

'Excuse me, I think I shall find Lady Sarah and ask her if we may go home.'

'No need to ask for my mother's escort while I am here,' Kit said, his mood suddenly much improved. 'I was about to suggest that we should return home, madam.'

'And pray do not call me *madam*!' Anne Marie said, glaring at him. 'Others call me by my name or *my lady*. I would have you do the same.'

'Indeed?' Kit's frown was back in place as he took her arm and steered her towards the door. He had signalled to a pageboy, who came running, giving orders that her cloak should be fetched and a chair ordered for her. He glanced at her gown and smiled oddly. 'We must not forget your cloak, my lady. I should not want you to catch cold in that gown.'

Anne Marie flushed as his eyes dwelt on the daring neckline, and knew that she had asked for the implied insult in his manner.

When the pageboy brought her cloak, Kit took it from him and placed it over her shoulders, his hand brushing against her bare flesh and making her tremble.

'Ah, here is my mother,' Kit said as Lady Sarah came up to them. His eyes glittered as he smiled at her. 'Do not trouble yourself to leave too early unless it pleases you, Mother. I would not wish to hinder you in your search for a suitable husband. I trust the search goes well? I saw you talking to Lord Hadden. I believe he might be a good choice, for his fortune is even bigger than his girth.'

'Your jest does not amuse me, Kit,' she replied frostily, sensing that he had seen through her ruse. 'I think I shall come with you if you do not mind. I am unused to standing so long and my shoes are hurting my feet.'

'We must all suffer for our pleasures, Mother,' Kit replied with a wicked smile. 'As Lady Hamilton is about to discover.' He nodded to them as the chairs for both ladies arrived and their servants hurried to attend them. 'I shall walk beside you to see that no harm befalls you,' he assured Anne Marie as he saw the look of alarm in her face. 'There is no need to fear, my love. We are well escorted. I promise you, we shall not be accosted by beggars or rogues.'

Anne Marie made no answer, but her heart was beating very fast as she settled into her chair. Just what had he meant by that last remark?

We must all suffer for our pleasures!

What did he intend to do when they got home?

Chapter Thirteen

Anne Marie walked ahead of her husband as she went up the stairs. She was conscious of him following her and her heart jerked with fright. Did he mean to continue their quarrel in private? His words had seemed to indicate that a reckoning was due between them, and yet she had sensed that he was amused about something.

She knew that he was angry with her for wearing a gown that revealed so much of her charms, and in her heart she could not blame him. Her instincts had told her that such a daring gown was wrong for her, but she had been determined that Kit should notice her.

Well, he had certainly noticed, and now she must suffer the consequence!

Heart pounding, she dismissed the serving wench who had waited to help her undress, telling her that she would send for her if she needed her. Then she turned to meet Kit, her hands folded modestly in front

of her, as he closed the door and locked it behind him.

Anne Marie trembled inwardly as she saw what he
had done and his grim expression. What did he mean
by locking the door? Was it to prevent anyone entering—or her escaping? Was it his intention to beat
her? It was his right of course, and she must accept
it if he chose to chastise her for her wayward behaviour that evening.

Yet why should she? Her head went up proudly.
She had done nothing wrong! He was the one who
had stayed away and forced her to chase after him.
Besides, if he had not wanted her to dance with other
men he should have danced with her himself.

'I am glad you have dismissed your woman. I believe it is fitting that we have some time alone, Anne
Marie. I have much to discuss with you. Will you not
sit down? I am sure you must be tired after your ex-
ertions this evening.'

Was he angry or did he mean to mock her? Anne
Marie was not certain. She looked at him uneasily,
aware of a certain gleam in his eyes. Her heart was
beating very fast but she struggled to appear calm as
she answered.

'I think I prefer to stand, sir. I am not at all tired.'

'I am glad to hear it, my love.' The gleam intensified. He was mocking her! 'I must say that I admire
your gown, though it is not what I would have chosen
for you. It is rather something I might give to a mistress—or a woman I desired as my mistress.'

'Have you bought such a gown for Jane

Frenshaw?' The words were out of Anne Marie's mouth before she could stop them. 'Lady Carmichael told me that Jane is your mistress.'

'Indeed?' Kit's tension eased slightly as he saw what he believed to be a flash of jealousy in her eyes. He was, to his discredit, beginning to relish her discomfort. 'I fear that Lady Carmichael hath a spiteful tongue. Mayhap she was disappointed that I did not choose to make her my mistress, though I believe I might have had I been so inclined. I should tell you that when very young I asked her to marry me, but she preferred Lord Carmichael at that time—now she seems to think she may have made a mistake and would be pleased to indulge in an affair with a man she once despised.'

'I believe you may be right, sir.' Anne Marie blinked hard lest she should weep. He had not denied that Jane Frenshaw was his mistress. 'However, Lady Carmichael's spite was unnecessary, for I saw you dancing with Lady Frenshaw and Toby told me that she was...'

Kit took two strides towards her, the purposeful glint in his eyes making her gasp. 'What others may say is merely gossip. I have no mistress, Anne Marie. I will confess that I have thought of it but no more than that. Have done with this nonsense. Jane is a pretty woman with whom I have enjoyed a mild flirtation. She means nothing to me and I have not bedded her.'

'Oh...' the word came out as a whisper, as she found it hard to breathe. He was towering above her,

so large and powerful and compelling—and yet so
attractive that her body trembled and burned for his
touch. 'I am glad that it is not so.'

'Are you?' Kit's eyes seemed to bore into her,
making her feel weak and fluttery inside. 'Tell me
why, Anne Marie? I had thought it might please you
if I took a mistress?'

'Indeed it would not!' she exclaimed and then
blushed as he gave a triumphant shout, his eyes
gleaming. 'Why should you imagine that it might?'

'I should not have needed to bother you, my lady.
You might have slept alone each night and been safe
from my attentions had I a mistress to answer my
needs.'

'I do not wish to sleep alone.'

There, it was out, she had said it and her heart was
racing so madly that she thought she would burst
from the tumult inside her. She could never go back
now, and she did not want to. She loved and she was
suddenly eager to declare her love, to admit that he
was all she had ever desired and more.

'Do you not?' Kit looked at her intently and she
saw a little pulse beating at his temple, as if he were
under some strain himself. 'I think you must explain
yourself, Anne Marie, for I am somewhat confused.
Is it your husband you wish for in your bed or another?'

'My husband, of course,' Anne Marie said finding
the courage to meet his eyes boldly now. What she
saw there made her feel weak inside, for his look was
so hungry and so eager that it near devoured her. 'The

husband I have longed for and missed these many months.'

'Have you missed me?' He moved closer to her so that their bodies were almost touching, gazing down into her eyes so that she felt close to swooning with the heat that suffused her from within, and it was all she could do to hold back from throwing herself into his arms. Kit's eyes were suddenly serious, seeming now almost to beg her rather than command. 'When last we met you were so cold that I believed you hated me, that I could never win your heart.'

'I beg you to forgive me for what I said to you that day. I have bitterly regretted it and would have taken back the words as soon as they were spoken. I came looking for you to apologise and try to explain, but you had gone.'

'In a fearful rage that carried me until my horse was exhausted,' Kit confessed. 'For some nights I drank to forget the pain of your rejection, Anne Marie. I had hoped until that moment that you might have come to love me, but your coldness made me feel that all hope was lost.'

'But I have always loved you, Kit,' she said softly, her eyes large and soft as she gazed up at him, a sheen of tears making them more brilliant than ever. 'I loved you almost from the moment that you came to me on the clifftop that day and admired my drawings. Each day that passed I looked for you and fell more deeply in love. And then you went away and I felt that my heart would break…'

'And when I was coming back to claim you and

declare my love for you, you had gone,' Kit said taking up her story. 'When I found you on that ship, having apparently gone of your own free will, I was so hurt and so angry that I lost my temper with you. Instead of telling you that I intended to ask the Queen for your hand in marriage, as I ought, I was unkind enough to threaten you with imprisonment. After weeks of delay in London I was finally able to come to you and then I saw you with Master Mountjoy and once again I lost my temper. You seemed so at ease with him, so uneasy with me.'

'I was easy with him for he meant nothing to me, whereas you meant too much. Your frowns made me unhappy, and I believed you were angry because the Queen had forced you to take me as your wife. I was afraid to confess my own love lest you found it irksome.'

Anne Marie smiled as she reached out to touch him, trailing her fingers down the side of his beloved face, her heart too full for words. He took her hand, and turned it up to kiss the palm with a hunger that made her weak with longing.

'So we have been at cross purposes and it seems that it was mostly my fault.' Kit gave her a rueful smile. 'I have a damnable temper, my love, and I fear that it may cause many arguments between us, for I cannot bear to see you looking at another man.'

'I too have a temper, though for years I learned to control it,' she said. 'You must try to curb yours, my dearest husband, for I would have us live happily together.'

'If I know I have your love...' he began, and caught his breath as she smiled and took his hand, beginning to lead him towards the bed. 'Anne Marie, be careful, for you know not what you do. It has been too long since I held you and I am like a ravening wolf. I fear to devour you, for I have an endless aching need inside me.'

'Do you not think that I am also hungry?' she asked softly, her lips moist and enticing as she gazed up at him. 'You lit a fire in me, my love, and then you left me. Do you think it has been easy for me to lie alone every night—especially when I believed someone else had taken my place with you?'

'There has never been another who could take your place,' he vowed huskily. 'I meant to take a mistress, Anne Marie. It was my avowed intention when I thought you did not love me, but the memory of you, of your sweetness, your inner loveliness, kept me from it.'

'Then waste no more time in regret,' she whispered, beginning to unfasten the ties at her waist. 'I fear you must help me undress, Kit, for the servants will have retired for the night, and I am laced so tightly into this gown that I cannot get out of it without help.'

She laughed as he caught at the loosened strings of her overskirt and it fell to the ground in a heap at their feet, to be kicked impatiently away as he pushed at her bodice, revealing the plump mounds of her sweet breasts. He bent his head to feast on them, licking at the nipples with the tip of his tongue and sucking gently until her head went back and she moaned with desire.

Then in a fervour of passion mixed strongly with humour as they fumbled at each other's clothes in their urgency to be rid of them, they tumbled on to the bed still partially dressed, too eager to care what happened to the costly finery they discarded.

Anne Marie lay back, drawing her lover to her, smiling at him with no reserve. Kit's kisses thrilled and aroused her in a way that she had never known before, and she sensed his need, his love. What a fool she had been to ever doubt him! This was meant to be, for they were as one, joined in love and desire, perfectly matched. She arched and cried out in ecstasy as he kissed and caressed her with his tongue and mouth, stroking her and bringing her tinglingly, beautifully, to a climax that sent her spiralling into paradise.

It was a long, long time before she came back to find herself curled into his body, her face buried against his shoulder, the warmth of him surrounding her, holding her so close that she felt as if they had become one, indivisible ever again.

'I have dreamt of you like that for so long,' Kit murmured huskily. 'Longed for you to give yourself to me so completely.'

'I held back because I was afraid you would tire of me, that you resented having been ordered to marry me and could never truly love me.'

He drew back to look at her, mockery in his eyes. 'You could not have thought that I might tire of you?

How foolish you were, my little love. Did you not know from the start that you held me in the palm of your hand? I would have done anything for you.'

'Would you do anything for me now?' she asked and reached up to smooth a lock of damp hair from his brow, then smoothed her thumb over his bottom lip.

'Anything except let you leave me,' he said, suddenly fierce, his fingers gripping her arms as if he were afraid that she might disappear from them. 'You know that I shall never let you go now, don't you?'

'I do not want to leave you ever,' she murmured and nibbled at his ear. 'I want you to come home, Kit. Oh, not immediately. We must enjoy our visit to London, for both Lady Sarah and Edward have looked forward to it—but afterwards. Will you not give up your life of adventuring and be content to look after your estate and raise our children?'

'I have been thinking of what I might do,' Kit said, and ran his hand down the length of her back, pressing her close to him so that she could feel he was already beginning to be aroused again. 'I do not wish to stay at court. The life does not appeal to me, and I believe that I have had my share of luck as a privateer. It was in my mind that I might build a fleet of merchant ships and trade with countries to the east. There are other men I know of like mind, and great riches are there for those with the courage to pluck them from beneath the noses of the Portuguese, who have had the monopoly too long.'

'Would that mean you had to go away for long periods?' She looked at him anxiously.

'I do not mean to sail in the ships myself,' Kit said and began to stroke the sensitive skin at the nape of her neck. 'It would mean visits to Portsmouth or Bristol to speak to my captains and to sell the cargoes they bring back, but I see no reason why you should not accompany me there. We might even build ourselves a fine house in Bristol, Anne Marie. We could divide our time between our homes, and it would seem wise to acquire more property if we are to have several sons.'

'I like the sound of that,' Anne Marie said, and gurgled with laughter as he pushed her over on to her back and began to kiss her body once more. 'If you go on in this way, husband, I dare say we may soon need more houses to accommodate our family.'

Kit laughed and then moved to cover her with his body, thrusting into her so that she gasped with the shock of his sudden entry. Their loving was swift and urgent, pleasing the mood of both, and afterwards they fell into a deep sleep that carried them through until after cockcrow, when Anne Marie awoke to find Kit lying beside her, supported on his elbow and gazing at her face.

'What is it?' she asked. 'Is something wrong?'

'I wanted to watch you wake,' he said. 'It feels so good just to lie here next to you and know that you are not simply a dream and will not disappear as soon as I open my eyes.'

She laughed and reached up to kiss him. 'Nevertheless, I must disappear for a moment, my love. Christopher is weaned, but it is my habit to go to him first thing in the morning. He expects it, and may cry if I am not there to give him his early morning cuddle.'

'So I am to lose you to my son?'

'Why not come with me?' she invited. She smiled as he got out of bed, unashamedly naked, his manly beauty revealed, as powerful and glorious as any Italian marble statue of the pagan gods in Sir Nicholas's garden. 'I suggest you find something suitable to wear or the serving wenches will do no work the rest of the day. Hurry, my love, and I shall wait for you. It is time that our son learned to associate you and me as a pair, for he has had too many months without his father.'

'It shall not be so with my next son,' Kit said, and gathered up the remnants of his clothes, disappearing into the chamber next door to dress in suitable morning attire.

Anne Marie stretched, smiling happily as she left her bed and pulled on a wrapping gown to cover her own nakedness. She did not bother to hide the evidence of what had happened the previous night, for she no longer cared that the servants might laugh to discover that their master had spent the night in her bed.

She turned as Kit came back to her dressed in similar apparel to that she wore herself, holding out her hand to him.

'Come, my love,' she said. 'Let us go to our son…'

* * *

They spent some five days longer in London, for Lady Sarah wanted to do a great deal of shopping, and it would need a score of wagons to carry it all home. Anne Marie had decided to buy several new gowns, though none of them would be quite like the one she had worn at court that had made Kit so angry. That had served its purpose, and she preferred something a little more modest.

Edward was making the most of the visit, his tutor taking him down the river to Runnymede near Windsor, where King John signed the Magna Carta. They went also to the Royal Exchange, to the bear pit at Southwark, to a college that Kit thought might suit his brother, for it had a medical school, and Edward had told him that he wanted to learn about medicine, and to various other places of interest. They all visited the theatre together one evening.

A playwright by the name of Christopher Marlowe was being talked of much these days, for he was said to be very clever and his work was anticipated with eagerness.

'It is his first play and it is called *Tamburlaine the Great*,' Kit told Anne Marie when they first heard there was to be a performance. 'Someone once told me that he would be a great playwright one day. This is a masterly tragedy, I understand.'

'Yes, I have heard about it,' Anne Marie said with a smile. 'Lady Grantly told me that she intends to come up to town for the performance. She met Kit

Marlowe when he was but a child and he told her then that he intended to write wonderful plays one day.'

'Then I shall arrange a party and we shall all go together,' Kit said. 'We must support the man, Anne Marie, for after all, he and I bear the same name, though his may go down in history and mine will be long forgot.'

'You and the men who fought for England's freedom shall never be forgot,' Anne Marie said and kissed him. 'The defeat of the Armada will be remembered as long as Englishmen live and breathe.'

Kit smiled and kissed her. Life was good, and he cared but little if his name should be remembered in times to come. It was enough that he had good friends, a family he cared for, and his beloved wife.

It was a merry party that set out for the theatre the night Kit Marlowe's play was performed for the first time. Afterwards everyone agreed that the new playwright had great talent, though Lady Sarah did not particularly care for the play, which she thought too violent.

'I prefer a comedy,' she confessed. 'Something the Queen's own players might perform, for Her Majesty too is a lover of comedy. I think she believes as I do that there is too much sadness in life as it is.'

Anne Marie agreed with her, though for herself she had much enjoyed the play, but more than anything else she was looking forward to going home with Kit.

'We shall go to court once more before we leave,' Kit said. 'I am proud of my wife, and I want to show them all how much I adore you.'

'In that case, I shall be pleased to go,' she told him. 'For I want everyone to see that I love you.'

The news stunned everyone at court that evening. Some had heard it earlier in the day, but for Anne Marie and her family it came as a bolt from the blue. The Earl of Leicester, who had been on his way to take the waters at Buxton, had died, and Her Majesty had locked herself in her chamber and would not come out for anyone.

'He was my *Eyes*,' she wept as her ladies tried to comfort her. 'I have his last letter and now I shall see him no more. Leave me, for I would be alone with my thoughts.'

'But you must not lock yourself away,' her ladies said. 'There are others who love you, Your Grace.'

'None hath ever loved me like my sweet Robin,' Elizabeth replied. 'Go away and leave me, for my life is over and I wish that I might be where he is now.'

Elizabeth had given herself to duty for most of her life, but now at this saddest of occasions she was allowing herself the time for private grief and would not be moved. Around her the people for whom she had given so much continued to celebrate the defeat of the Armada, but for Elizabeth the pain was too great to be borne. Robert Dudley was her youth, the symbol of her aspirations and hopes, of life when it was good and sweet that now tasted only of ashes.

The year of 1588 had been predicted as a year of disaster, but for England it had been one of glory.

Now for Elizabeth perhaps the prediction seemed all too true.

Anne Marie asked Kit to take her home as soon as she heard the news. 'For we cannot celebrate when the Queen is suffering so,' she told him. 'I know how she must feel, for it is how I should have felt if you had not returned from fighting the Armada.'

'It is sad that at such a time, when all England rejoices for the great victory, that Elizabeth should lose the friend she has loved for so long,' Lady Sarah said agreeing with her. 'She must be devastated, beside herself with grief. Who knows what more he was to her or what she would have wished him to be had things gone otherwise?'

'Had his wife not died so tragically...' Kit said and shook his head. He had known what it was like to feel that all hope had gone. 'Had Robert Dudley never contracted that foolish marriage in the first place, what might have been his destiny?'

'Do you think that she would have married him?' Anne Marie asked. 'I do not know Her Majesty so I cannot tell—and yet I believe that there was too much against her. Her counsellors wanted a marriage with a foreign prince, and she was said to favour the Duke of Alençon but the people did not like the idea of a Catholic King at her side on England's throne. She could not marry the man she loved, nor would it have been wise to marry any of the other princes who offered for her.'

'Perhaps that is why she never married,' Kit said, looking thoughtful. 'Perhaps she was wiser than her counsellors and knew that if she were to rule as the people wanted she must do so alone.'

'I am so sad for her,' Anne Marie said. 'She must feel so alone tonight.'

Kit put his arm about his wife. 'I know this of her—if Elizabeth has anything, she has courage, my darling. She will come through this and she will go on, for it is her way and her duty.'

'Home at last,' Kit said, and came to put his arms about Anne Marie as she stood at the window looking out. 'What are you thinking, my love? You looked pensive, almost sad.'

'I was thinking about the Queen,' Anne Marie said. 'She has given so much for England—do you think she feels it is worth while?'

'Who can say?' Kit kissed the back of her neck. 'It is strange to hear you speak so of her. I thought you did not particularly care for Elizabeth?'

'I hardly knew her,' Anne Marie said, and turned to look at him, her face soft with love for him. 'My father hated her and all his life he hoped that Mary of Scots would one day be Queen of England. He was a staunch Catholic and he was angry that Elizabeth had brought the Protestant religion back, for he truly thought it an abomination—and I was taught that my mother was a Catholic and told it was my duty to worship as she did. But it seems to me that too much suffering comes because people are so divided. Why cannot we all worship as one and be content to live in harmony with each other?'

Kit laughed, his smile warm as she gazed earnestly up at him.

'You would have the lion lie down with the lamb, my love,' he said. 'I agree that it would make things much easier if we could all agree, but it is human nature to quarrel and find things to disagree about. We are restless, troublesome creatures and were cast out of Paradise because we grew bored with perfection. Human life is about struggle and achievement, and true happiness comes from knowing that we have fought for what we have.'

'Yes, I suppose so,' she agreed and laughed at herself. 'But I have decided that I shall adopt the religion of your family, Kit. It will be much easier so, and I find I am as comfortable with one doctrine as another, for there is but one God, is there not?'

'You are a remarkable woman,' Kit said, looking at her intently. 'If you do this to please me there is no need, for I would not mind if you continued your mother's way of worship in private.'

'I know that,' she said. 'But I have reached my own decision, and I believe I prefer the simple way of your family. Our children shall be brought up as you would want, and that is best for all of us.'

Kit gazed down into her face and saw that her beauty ran deeper than he could have imagined, for she was as good as she was lovely, and he knew himself blessed.

'You give me so much,' he said and touched her face with his fingertips. 'Every day you bless my life with your smile and your love, Anne Marie. Tell me what I can do for you to repay some of what you give me?'

'You give me all that you have just described as my gift to you,' she said and smiled. 'What more should I want other than to live my live in freedom and peace with you? I want no more than to look up and see you there every day of my life, to bear your children and know that I am loved.'

'Then we have everything that any man or woman could want,' he said. 'And yet, I think that I may have something you might like.' He went over to his coffer and took out a small package wrapped in silk, which he brought back to her. 'I had this done for you. It was my intention to send it for your birthday, but I would like you to have it now.'

Opening the package she saw an exquisite miniature of Kit, done by the hand of a master. On ivory and set in gold surrounded by an oval of pearls, it was a treasure beyond price to her.

'It is lovely,' she said. 'Thank you so much, Kit. I shall keep it with me always.'

'It was done by Nicholas Hilliard,' he said. 'I meant it to be a reminder and intended to send it in the hope that it might make you think of me sometimes.'

'You were always in my thoughts,' she whispered, and leaned into his body, offering her lips for his kiss. 'And evermore shall be…'

Turn the page for a preview of
THE BLACK SHEEP'S BRIDE
from
Paula Marshall

In the chilling winter of Elizabeth's reign...

*Ambitious nobles threaten the ageing
Queen, as an ill-sorted arranged
marriage turns into a wild adventure.*

Available June 2004
from Mills & Boon

Chapter One

Early Autumn, 1600

'Sing it again, maister, sing it again!'

Martin Chancellor, buccaneer, merchant and poet, was roistering in a tavern in Deptford known as the Bull, not far from the lodging-house where Christopher Marlowe had so mysteriously died. He had not shaved for days and was wearing the well-worn clothes of an ordinary seaman. The only valuable thing about him was the lute which he had been playing to entertain the grimy and crowded room.

He was lying back in the room's one armchair, his booted feet on a stool. He had a tankard of ale in one hand, and the other was busily waving acknowledgements to his audience. When at last it fell silent, he said, 'I usually make it a habit, gentleman, never to repeat myself, so, in a moment or two, after I have wet my whistle, I will favour you with another song, this time one of my own invention.'

His hearers particularly liked being addressed as gentleman, seeing that they were so patently nothing of the sort, and allowed themselves to fall silent on being promised further amusement. For the moment Martin occupied himself by drinking his ale and examining the faces of the crowd. On his way to the Bull he had had an uneasy feeling that he was being shadowed, or watched, but every time he had turned round to try to find out who it might be, if anyone, he had seen nothing.

Which did not, in his world, mean that there was nothing to see. However, he was not going to allow his enjoyment to be spoilt by such whim-whams. His ale finished, he hammered on the table, lifted his lute from where it rested beside him, and made ready to play and sing. He possessed a good, baritone voice, with which he had enlivened more than one dull moment on the different ships in which he had sailed.

'As promised, gentlemen,' he announced, 'my offering to my own truly fair,' and began, without further preamble to sing:

'A sonnet to my mistress' eyes
Avoids the parts I really prize.
So I will celebrate instead
Those that we enjoy in bed...'

The entire room sent up a howl of mirth on hearing this. Tankards were banged on tables, cheers rose to the dirty rafters, and most of the rest of the ditty was lost in the uproar. Several complaints were made by many furthest away from him, that the later verses of the song had been lost in the applause created by the first, but to no avail: called on to repeat it, Martin refused with a grin.

'It's too late,' he told them, rising, 'and I'm too tired. I'll be off to my bed now.' He offered his audience a highly suggestive wink, while slinging his lute round one shoulder and making discreetly sure that the poniard he always carried was ready for him to use if aught went amiss on his journey home. Before leaving he flung some coins to the landlord, to treat those who were nearest to the bar and had made the most noise.

Once outside, he took a deep breath and made for the nearest steps down to the Thames, where, despite the lateness of the hour, a wherry might be waiting to row him back to his temporary home, a small house in one of the City of London's back streets.

Before he reached the riverside he heard running steps behind him. He turned rapidly just in time to see a burly man, wielding an upraised knife, ready to attack him. The lifted knife was a mistake, although it might have put paid to most of the would-be thief's victims, for Martin, skilled in dirty fighting, chose instead to use the poniard which he had rapidly drawn, not to stab the fellow but to strike him hard in the face with its heavy hilt.

He had chosen the fellow's nose to aim at: streaming blood, the thief blindly staggered away, dropping his knife. Martin caught him by his left hand, twisted his arm behind his back and, reversing his poniard, now drew it gently across his prisoner's throat, saying, 'Can you offer me any reason why I should not slit your throat on the instant?'

'Aye, master, for it was only your purse I meant to cut, not your throat,' he managed to gasp.

'Now, why do I not believe you?' Martin told him, negligently sliding his poniard once again across the thief's neck, so that it drew a little blood. 'For you were busy watching me in the tavern, and before that I thought that I saw you in the street on the way to it. Were you hired to kill me? Speak up before I decide to finish you off at once, and then I might spare you.'

'Your word on it,' gasped the thief.

'For what it's worth, yes. Now talk, before I change my mind.'

'To tell truth, master, I know not who the man was. He was a little fellow, richly dressed and gave me a couple of groats if I would kill you after such a fashion that it looked like a robbery on a drunken man. As God is my witness that's the truth on't.'

It might be, and it might not. Martin had no wish to kill the clumsy fool, even if he might be doing the state some service by ridding it of such a clodpole, so he privately decided on mercy, but also decided to let his attacker stew for a few moments before he released him.

'And that's it? Someone unknown points you in my direction and for a few trifling pennies, and the small sum in my purse, you will cheerfully dispose of me? You sold yourself uncommon cheap!'

'Aye, maister, so I did. I'm but a poor man. Now will you let me go?'

'Only when you hand over the groats your unknown master gave to you.'

'You said yourself they was only trifling…'

'You,' said Martin, tightening his grip on his would-be murderer, 'are trifling with me. Hand over the groats and think yourself lucky that I did not call the watch.'

Now this was an empty threat because, for a variety of reasons, Martin did not wish to involve the law in his business, but the thief was not to know that.

'Aye, if that will save me.'

Martin released his grip a little so that his assailant could pull the groats out of his purse and hand them over, moaning under his breath while he did so.

'Now, your name, and where you may be found,' asked Martin, resuming his iron grip on the fellow.

'You may find me at the Bull, they know me there. I'm hight Wattie Harrison, an it please you.'

'Oh, it doesn't please me at all, but life being what it is, I might need your incompetent services one day. Life is full of such surprises, as you are finding out. One word of warning before I let you go. Try this trick, or any other, on me again and I shall not spare you a second time.'

'Aye, aye, maister.'

'And don't take your knife with you.' This last instruction came as Wattie bent to pick it up. 'I've a mind not to be attacked after being merciful—I shouldn't like to have to kill you after all.'

'By Satan and all the devils you're a hard man, maister,' offered Wattie admiringly.

'Never mind that. Be off with you—and if your paymaster complains because you didn't kill me, tell him that.'

Wattie pulled a grudging forelock. 'Aye, so I will,' and ran lightly down the path, away from the river.

Martin bent down to pick up the knife. He looked at it and gave a wry smile. 'Now was I a complete fool to let him go? But I do hate to kill a man for nothing—even though I might regret it later.'

He was still pondering on this when, after his journey in the wherry, he reached his small home in an alley just off Forge Street. As he expected when he let himself in by the back door, Rafe, his lieutenant and his best friend, who had sailed with him many times, was waiting for him in the kitchen.

'You are back earlier than I expected, master.'

Martin put his lute carefully down on a shabby settle before he answered with, 'I grew bored with low company, I must be getting old. I am ready for bed and the night is still young.'

'Never say so, but you cannot retire yet. Two hours ago a high-nosed sort of clerk—or lawyer—arrived, demanding to see you if you were one Martin Chancellor. I told him to come again tomorrow at a more Christian time, but he said that his master had bade him not return until he had met you, since the matter was urgent. He would not tell me what it was so I put him in the parlour to await your arrival.'

Martin gave a great yawn. 'I suppose I ought to see him, if only to find out who the devil he can be and why he is here. You told him nothing of me, I trust. He thinks this is my one home? And that I have but the one name?'

Rafe put a finger by his nose. 'Take me not for a fool, master. He thinks me one—which is all to the good. He asked me about you, but I wittered to him some nonsense which had you working down at the docks and having gone to the Bull in Deptford for the odd dram after a hard day of it—which seemed to surprise him a little.'

'Excellent. He may be friend, or he may be enemy, but a confused man waiting for me can only be to my advantage.'

'So, I thought, master. May I go to bed now?'

'Certainly, if only to stop hearing you call me master. I am Martin to you, Rafe, ever and always.'

Rafe laughed softly at that. 'D'you know, Martin, I have the strangest feeling that we may be sailing into waters where the old rules which guided us no longer apply.'

'Dear God, I hope not,' Martin riposted.

And now to find out who the devil it was who needed to speak to him with such urgency that he was willing to wait so long to meet him.

The parlour which he entered was a small but clean room, furnished with the minimum of cheap possessions, except for a rather splendid clock on the shelf above a primitive hearth. A well-dressed young man with a clerkly air was seated in the one armchair before the fire. He had been reading a book which he had obviously brought with him and which he put down on the small table beside him. A leather satchel stood by this chair.

He rose as Martin entered and stared at him. At his rough clothes, at his heavily bearded face, his unruly black hair, and his blue eyes, startlingly bright against what could be seen of his brown skin. His lip involuntarily curled a little.

He made no effort to speak and it was Martin who finally broke the silence by asking, 'Who are you? And what business brings you here, sir, that you were willing to wait so long for me to come home?'

The young man picked up the satchel, saying, 'My name is Thomas Webster, and you, I hope, are Martin Chancellor?'

'And if I am?'

'Then I also hope that you can prove to me that you are the man of that name for whom I have been looking.'

'But why have you been looking for me? That is, if I am Martin Chancellor.'

'More strictly, it is m'lord the Viscount Bretford who is Martin Chancellor's father and who has the most urgent need to speak to his son.'

'Has he, indeed! You surprise me greatly, since I could scarcely describe such an act as sending for me after fourteen years' absence as an urgent one.'

Martin had often wondered whether he would ever

see his father again. He might once have thought that
he might seek him out, but never that the first overture
would come from his father.

'So, you need proof that I am the rightful Martin
Chancellor!' He gave a short laugh before saying,
'Oh, I can prove that—if I need to—the marks of the
flogging he ordered for me two days before I left
home are still on my back—as well as the brand on
my shoulder marking me as thief and rapist. Will that
do for you and m'lord? Would you have me strip
here? And if I told you to take yourself back to him
with the message that I have no desire ever to meet
him again, what then?'

'That he is old, lonely, like to die soon, and wishes
to see you, and yes, the message is urgent.'

'Yet you may not tell me of it.'

'No, he wishes to speak to you himself.'

'You say that he is lonely. He has my brother John.
Is he not enough for him?'

Webster's face grew shuttered. 'M'lord has said
little to me of his reasons for wishing to speak to you,
but of your mercy, I would beg you to do as he asks.'

'He showed me little enough when I lived with him
as his son, so why should I trouble with him now?'

'I know nothing of the past, but I would ask you
to reconsider. We are all sinners who need mercy,
either from God or our fellows, you, I, and m'lord.'

Martin turned his back on him and stared into the
fire as though he could read the future in its flames.
To go, or not to go? What had he to gain or to lose?
No talk of mercy moved him, and as for God, he was

one with Sir Walter Raleigh, since they neither of them believed in such nonsense. If he gave way and agreed to accompany Webster to Bretford House at this unwonted hour, it would be out of curiosity, simply to find out why in the world his father wanted to see him so urgently.

'Very well,' he said abruptly. 'I will return with you—and I will bring my friend, Rafe Dudgeon, with me.'

'Oh, I am sure that m'lord will agree to that. May I say how pleased I am that you have made this decision.'

'No, you may not. It is no affair of yours, and I do not yet know whether it is any affair of mine that my father should, after so many years, seek me out. I go to find out what bee is buzzing in his bonnet and for no other reason. Now, sit down for a moment while I speak with Rafe and make ready to accompany you. Have you been offered any refreshment during your long vigil?'

'A little—but a pint of ale would be welcome before we set out.'

'That you shall have—and at once. I will see to it myself.'

With that Martin took his leave.

Some instinct told him that neither he nor Rafe would return to Forge Street that night, so after he had fed Webster, they both packed small satchels with a change of linen before accompanying him to Bretford House, that magnificent palace on the

Strand, so different from the small cottage where Webster had tracked him down.

Late though it was, there were footmen on duty. It was apparent that they had orders to admit him to m'lord at once. This they did, after staring at Martin's appearance—as the butler later said to the staff, 'It was hard to tell which was master and which was man.'

Despite Martin's protests, Rafe was detached from him, to accompany the butler to the kitchen where, Martin later discovered, he was wined and dined. Once he had gone, a footman led Webster and Martin up the great staircase to m'lord's bedroom and not, as Martin had expected, to the downstairs withdrawing room, the latest word for a place where a gentleman might be private, far away from the chambers of state.

His father, propped up by many pillows, was seated in his great bed, with its Viscount's coronet mounted at the top of the green and gold curtains. Martin scarcely recognized him. He remembered his father as a large man of great presence, ruddy of face, hale and hearty, with a voice which could, as his retainers were fond of saying, be heard half a county away.

Now he was shrunken and withered, his face was as grey as his hair and his hands were ceaselessly plucking at the sheets. His voice was still cold and severe when he spoke at last, after his faded blue eyes had ceased to roam over Martin's face and figure. It was, however, low and hoarse, quite unlike the commanding bellow of old.

Martin offered him no bow, no filial deference, merely stood there waiting to be spoken to.

'Martin?' his father said, and the word was a question not a statement.

'Unfortunately so, m'lord.' He would not call the man before him *Father*.

'I've had you sought by my agents for the last six months. I was beginning to think that Martin Chancellor had disappeared from the face of the earth.'

'Did you indeed?' Martin was quite determined not to initiate any subject of conversation with his father. He would not tell him that his existence as Martin Chancellor had ended on the day he had fled from his home, until he had revived it in mockery of what he had once been.

'Yes, and the matter which I need to raise with you has become more and more urgent.' The man on the bed fell silent as though speaking over-much tired him.

Still Martin said nothing. What he found surprising was the raging anger which was beginning to overcome him. At first when he had run away, hatred of his father had ruined his days and nights, but gradually, as time passed, he had left it behind. It was of no consequence: he had created a life for himself far from the one which he might have led before that fatal night.

Perforce his father spoke again. 'I have only sent for you out of necessity. Nigh on six months ago your brother, John, died of the great pox—something which only my physician and I knew he had contracted. His death left you, my remaining son, as the one person who could get an heir to ensure that the Chancellor estates do not revert to the Crown— with all the ills that such an act might entail.

'Some months before John's death Lord Clifton and I had arranged that he should marry Lady Kate Wyville, his ward. She was his dead sister's daughter and the heiress of the late Earl of Wyville's estates and fortune. John fell ill shortly afterwards and the marriage was postponed pending his recovery. After his death I asked Lord Clifton if he would agree to my other son, Martin, who would become the new Baron Hadleigh, replacing him as Lady Kate's future husband—if you could be found, that was.

'Lord Clifton, who has been my friend for many years, was most agreeable, provided only that you were found before six months were up. That period of time ends in ten days. In short, you have become my heir and the future husband of one of the richest heiresses in England.'

Martin began to laugh. He laughed so hard that he started to stagger, and only saved himself from falling by seating himself on a bench before one of the windows. His father and Webster, who had been standing near to the door, stared at him in astonishment.

Lord Bretford said, frostily, 'I fail to see why what I have just told you should have caused you so much amusement.'

'You do?' Martin stopped laughing, rose and

advanced to the foot of his father's bed. 'Your brain must have become addled since you have grown old if you do not find it a subject for comedy that your good son should have died of the pox and that the bad one should then be desperately searched for in order to save the family fortunes by marrying the so-called good son's leavings.'

His father's grey face turned even greyer. Martin heard Webster behind him give an involuntary gasp after he had finished.

'You have not changed,' his father finally achieved. 'You come here looking like a piece of scum from the gutter and when I make you a grand offer—which you do not deserve—you choose to insult me.'

'A grand offer? I have a life of my own. So why should I choose to live the one you have so belatedly offered me?'

'A life of your own! And pray what might that be? I understand from Webster that you are living in a hovel in a dirty back street and you come here looking like a beggar. Yet I still stand by my offer. Accept it—and I am ready to forget the past.'

'*You* are ready to forget the past! I, however, am not. I shall not remain here this night, but will leave immediately. I would bid you goodnight, but that I do not wish to bid you a good anything.'

He moved towards the door, to walk past Webster, except that the man followed him out and shutting the door behind him took him by the arm.

'A moment,' he said abruptly, 'I would speak with you.'

Martin felt a deathly tiredness overcome him. 'Whatever can you have to say to me?'

'This: you are throwing away a fortune, a rich and clever wife, and the chance to allow the old fool in there to die happily. Now, I must inform you that I have also discovered your many secrets. I know that you do not need his fortune, that you have another name and that it is a good one and an honoured one, even if you occasionally amuse yourself by enjoying yourself as you did when you first went to sea. Moreover, what have you to lose by obliging your father?

'Those whom m'lord employs, the estate itself and all its dependants will lose everything. I do not name myself as one of their company, since I shall still have my good name to sell—but they will have nothing. Why are you doing this? To satisfy your need for revenge? M'lord thinks that you are a penniless ne'er-do-well and I have not disabused him of that false belief. Can you not see that your best revenge would be to accept his offer? And, saying nothing of your own truth, laugh at him while you deceive him, and at the same time save those unfortunates who cannot help themselves?'

'You know the truth of me—and have not told him?'

'Why should I? His judgement is poor: he worshipped his so-called good son, and he believes that he is doing you a favour by forgiving you, the so-called bad one. Do yourself a favour—go back and tell him that you have changed your mind—with one condition only.'

Martin was fascinated. The previously anonymous man before him had changed colour like that odd animal the chameleon—or like himself, for that matter!

'And that condition is?'

'That you will be allowed to employ me to assist you in your new life. After all, he believes that you will not be accustomed to such grandeur.'

To Martin's amusement, the wily fellow had the audacity to offer him a wink when he had ended his sentence. 'I had not believed you to be a rogue,' he said at last.

'No? As you must well know, we are all rogues when it comes to acting on our own behalf.'

Should he do as Webster had suggested? Did he really want a wife to be chosen for him by two old men? On the other hand, as Rafe had so often told him, he ought to marry, and in the class from which he had sprung most marriages were arranged ones. And since he no longer believed in love, he might as well marry without it.

Was the fellow trying to blackmail him? Almost as though he had read his mind, Webster leaned forward and said confidentially, 'Have no fear that I shall use my knowledge of your true self to gain a hold over you. After all, it would be a strange sort of power to use against a man—that you knew that he was a success when everyone else thought he was a failure!'

'True enough.'

The more Martin thought about it the more attractive Webster's advice become. To pretend that he was virtually a beggar by allowing his father to believe that, in accepting him as his son again, he was doing him the greatest favour, was indeed a joke. Life had grown dull lately, which was why he was masquerading as Martin Chancellor, a poor seaman, to try to enjoy himself as he had done when he had been a poverty-stricken lad trying to make his way in the world.

'Very well,' he said at last. 'I will do as you suggest, but if I should choose to tell him the truth at any time, I shall do so.'

'Oh, that is your choice, and if the lady does not please you—then that is your choice, too.'

'Amen to that.' Many women had pleased Martin Chancellor since he had fled the family home, and he doubted that this one would be any different.

He walked back into the bedroom to tell the old man that he had changed his mind. 'I will agree to become your son again,' he said, 'on one condition—that you allow Webster to be part of my household in order to help me to behave as Lord Hadleigh should.'

To which Lord Bretford said, smiling a little, 'At last, the prodigal has returned. Of course you may have Webster to serve you; I can think of no better task for him.'

Webster, still in the background, had a hard time of it trying not to laugh aloud. Martin's face remained impassive.

'First of all,' said his father, his face alive with interest for the first time since his son had arrived, 'you must consent to live here for a time, ready to meet your future bride when I have informed her guardian of your return.'

Martin shook his head. He might have guessed that his father's attempt to control him would begin immediately and he intended to have none of that. 'Not so. I have a home of my own, and duties connected with it to which I must attend. I will visit you whenever it is convenient to do so.'

He was lying, of course, for the home to which he was referring was not that in Forge Street. It struck him that he and the truth had rarely been friends since he had ceased to become Lord Bretford's son, and being restored to that position had certainly not changed matters. If anything it had made them worse!

His father's hands began to pluck at the bedclothes again. 'It is a bad omen, Hadleigh, that you have begun your new life by defying me, but if you must, you must. I am prepared to allow such a course of behaviour, but for a short time only.'

'Most gracious of you, sir. And now you must allow me to retire. I am tired, so I must believe that you, being bedridden and old, must be even more so. We will discuss matters further in the morning.'

By using the word 'discuss,' he was telling his still tyrannical father that he would not blindly obey every whim and fancy which the old man might care to wish of him.

'Very well,' said m'lord, 'in the morning, then.

Webster, see Lord Hadleigh and his servant to the rooms which have been prepared for their use.'

Martin bowed, not a low bow, but it was the first act of courtesy which he had offered his father since he had met him again. Despite himself he was shocked by the old man's frailty—and what it told him of his own mortality. Again, on the other hand, the past fourteen years could not be ignored as though they had never been.

'I agreed, uncle, to be betrothed to the late Lord Hadleigh to oblige you and not myself. It was wrong of me I know, and quite un-Christian, to be pleased that his death relieved me of that marriage. You know perfectly well, for I have often told you so, that I have no wish to marry. Yet, knowing that, and behind my back, without any form of consultation, you have arranged yet another marriage for me. This time with the new Lord Hadleigh, whom I have never even met because he ran away from home fourteen years ago and no one has seen or heard from him since then. You must cancel this proposed marriage at once, for I will have none of it.'

Lady Kate Wyville was speaking to her uncle and guardian, the Earl of Clifton, who had just informed her of his and Lord Bretford's decision—that she should exchange the dead Lord Hadleigh with the live one. As always, even when she was angry, she was speaking in a quiet and measured voice, totally in control of herself and all her emotions.

'Now, now, my sweet child,' murmured Lord

Clifton in an attempt to placate her, 'you know as well as I do that you must marry. You are a woman, and women need a husband to protect them and their lands. Yours and Bretford's run side by side, so to marry his heir is a most sensible arrangement. Fortunate it is that the missing young man has been found so that he, too, may do his duty to his present name and his future title.'

If Kate had been a different sort of young woman she would have said, 'To the devil with *his* future title—it is my present one that I wish to keep!'

Instead, maintaining her iron self-control which was at such odds with the cool and classic beauty of her face, where only her bright green eyes told of the passion which lived somewhere inside her, but which she never revealed for the world to stare at, she said, 'Uncle, if our Queen could remain unmarried and rule this kingdom with such success without marrying, then I can see no reason why I should not follow her example.'

'But you are not the Queen, my dear, and look how she is ending her life. She is an old woman with no chick nor child to comfort her and all the friends of her youth are dead and gone, including those whom she might have married. Her beauty has gone, too, and such upstarts as Essex seek to defy and demean her, since she has nothing to control them with any more. Oh, she may punish and disgrace Essex for his incompetence and his various follies, but that leaves her even more alone, a creature to pity.'

Kate could not deny the truth of this, yet she still

clung to her wish to be independent, to rule her own lands as the Queen had ruled hers, and hope that the end of her life might be different from that of her monarch's.

She shook her head, saying, 'Even so, but at least she had the right to choose. You have not given me that. I would take the chance of suffering a lonely old age if I could but once do something as remarkable as the Queen's behaviour when she defied Philip of Spain and his Armada.'

'You may say that now—but what might you say or think when you have reached that old age? Is it possible that you might look back and wail, "Had I but known, I would have done thus and so, rather than what I actually did."'

Kate rose and began to pace the room. 'None of us can guess what the future might bring, but in the present in which we live I would wish to be my own mistress, as a man is his own master, rather than have another make my decisions and rule my life.'

Her uncle sighed. He thought that she had never looked more beautiful, more fit to make some fortunate man's life happy, but the questioning intellect which ruled her was preventing her from choosing to follow the path which most women were wise enough to take.

'My dear,' he said, still gentle, so gentle that Kate wanted to rage against him for sounding so reasonable, 'I fear that you have no choice in the matter. Like it or not, you signed a binding contract of *verbis de praesenti* to marry one Lord Hadleigh, and it is Lord Hadleigh who has told the lawyers that he is willing to fulfil that contract and marry you.'

'But he is not the Lord Hadleigh that I was willing to marry. He is Martin, the younger son, not John the elder.'

'As the contract was drawn up on his side, merely in the name of Lord Hadleigh, then that argument cannot hold water.'

'Oh!' Kate sat down, frustrated, fearing that her hard-won composure was in danger of flying away altogether. 'I don't know him, and since he returned there the servants at Bretford House have told ours that he is a savage, totally unlike his elder brother. How could the contract have been worded so loosely? Could it not be broken?'

Lord Clifton, who knew the truth behind John Chancellor's sudden death and was of the private opinion that Lord Bretford had cunningly allowed it to be drawn up after a fashion that would enable the next heir to take the marriage over, muttered, 'Very difficult, my dear. No, the die is cast, as they say—and the result will work to your benefit. It is likely that after the marriage, given the increased size of the Bretford estates, Her Grace will elevate the Viscountcy of Bretford to an Earldom and you will become a Countess.'

For some reason this last piece of information was, so far as Kate was concerned, the very last straw. Her green eyes flashing fire, she whirled on her uncle with such force that he started back.

'Oh,' she exclaimed fiercely, 'I have not the

slightest desire to be a Countess, and I wish most heartily that you would stop calling me *my dear* in an attempt to wheedle me into doing what I would rather not—particularly since it seems that I have no choice at all in the matter because of some clerk's stupid mistake. If I must go to what I regard as my execution then I must, but do not expect me to like it—or him. More than ever I wish that I had been born a man.'

Suddenly appalled by her own behaviour, she sat down and tried not to burst into tears, tears which would merely serve to reinforce her uncle's opinion that every weak woman needed a man to protect her.

'Now, now, my dear,' said her uncle tenderly, 'I am sure that all will be well. You will look back on this day and agree that you were right to do your duty, marry Lord Hadleigh and live the life for which you and all women were born. Forget the Queen; you are not royalty and her example is not a good one for you to follow, as you will agree yourself when you are older and wiser.'

'And resigned to my fate,' muttered Kate, tears banished. 'I suppose that I am to meet my future husband before we actually stand at the altar.'

'Of course, my dear, we are not barbarians. We are to visit Bretford House when Lord Bretford sends for us—at the moment he is unwell.'

My dear again! It was the sort of phrase with which one handed a child a sweetmeat. Well, from the gossip, Lord Hadleigh was far from being a sweetmeat. He had run away from home at the age of sixteen after some unspecified piece of misbehaviour and nobody had heard any more of him until the other day, when it had become common knowledge that his father had tracked him down.

And what did that tell you about him?

Nothing good for sure.

But she, God help her, was to be his wife.

Unless, of course, he found her undesirable and indicated that he did not wish to fulfil the contract— and she, equally of course, would be only too willing to oblige him.

Her smile broadened. Lord Bretford and his new-found son would be unwise to count their chickens before they were hatched...

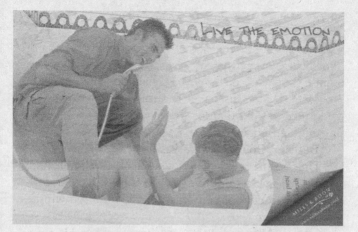

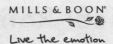

MILLS & BOON®

Live the emotion

PENNINGTON

Catherine George
PENNINGTON
Evidence of Sin

MILLS & BOON

BOOK TWELVE

Available from 4th June 2004

Available at most branches of WHSmith, Tesco, Martins, Borders,
Eason, Sainsbury's and most good paperback bookshops.

PENN/RTL/12

MILLS & BOON

Summer

Temptations

Lori Foster
Kristine Rolofson

On sale 4th June 2004

Available at most branches of WHSmith, Tesco, Martins, Borders,
Eason, Sainsbury's and all good paperback bookshops.